BURN

NEVADA BARR

St. Martin's Paperbacks

This is a work of fiction. All of the characters, organizations, and events portrayed in this novel are either products of the author's imagination or are used fictitiously.

BURN

Copyright © 2010 by Nevada Barr.

For information address St. Martin's Press, 175 Fifth Avenue, New York, NY 10010.

Library of Congress Catalog Card Number: 2010021411

ISBN: 978-0-312-38180-6

Printed in the United States of America

St. Martin's Press hardcover edition / August 2010
St. Martin's Paperbacks edition / June 2011

St. Martin's Paperbacks are published by St. Martin's Press, 175 Fifth Avenue, New York, NY 10010.

10 9 8 7 6 5 4 3 2

"Abundant suspense."   —*The Oklahoman*

"*Burn* will smolder in your heart long after you're done."
                    —*Madison County Herald*

"Barr's strong, evocative writing explores the scenery as well as the characters."   —*South Florida Sun-Sentinel*

"From the fabric of fiction Barr creates real worlds, sometimes beautiful, sometimes terrifying, but always convincing."   —*San Diego Union-Tribune*

"Solid and suspenseful plotting. A definite winner."
                    —*Booklist*

"Barr has written another hit [that] her fans will devour."
                    —*Library Journal*

"A rare treat . . . Told with all Barr's usual verve and eye for detail and with a solid, tight plot."
                    —*The Globe and Mail* (Toronto)

Also by Nevada Barr

FICTION
Anna Pigeon Books
The Rope
Burn
Borderline
Winter Study
Hard Truth
High Country
Flashback
Hunting Season
Blood Lure
Deep South
Liberty Falling
Blind Descent
Endangered Species
Firestorm
Ill Wind (a.k.a. *Mountain of Bones*)
A Superior Death
Track of the Cat
Nevada Barr Collection

OTHER NOVELS
Bittersweet
13½

NONFICTION
Seeking Enlightenment—Hat by Hat

*For my dearest
Deb and Ed, whom I have loved
since we were all young and
magnificently foolish*

ONE

S hit, Blackie, this one's dead, too. What're we gonna do?" The speaker, scarcely more than a boy—the lines cruelty would carve deep into his face not yet showing more than petulance—looked with disgust into an aluminum cargo box half the size of a semitrailer. His nose, high bridged and straight, the only feature of his face that suggested an ancestry not devoted to the baser things, wrinkled at the stink, a stink not from the bodies, or from the way they had died, but from the way they had lived for nineteen days.

"A jewel?"

"Maybe more'n one."

"We get rid of 'em."

Drops of water on the younger man's thick black hair glittered in the harbor lights like a cheap sequined hairnet. As his head pushed into the shadow of the shipping box, Blackie, fifty last birthday and made of hard muscles and hard times, turned away. For a second it had looked as if the head vanished and left the body standing stooped over by itself.

Blackie didn't like magic. Didn't like things that vanished or shifted or weren't what they seemed to be; things that couldn't be relied upon.

"Dougie, get your goddam head out of the box," he snapped. "What're you doing? Sniffing 'em? Jesus."

Unoffended, Dougie did as he was told. "What're we going to do?" he asked again, sounding plaintive.

Absurd burbling notes of "Baa Baa Black Sheep" swam through the moisture-laden air. Blackie tensed, his eyes seeking and sharp with the keenness of the hunter—or the hunted. He wished the night were darker. Seattle's interminable drizzle caught the light from the quay and the street above the docks, giving everything a shadowless glow, robbing the place of depth, reality.

"It's your cell phone," Dougie said helpfully.

"Fuck." Blackie fumbled the phone out of his jacket pocket and pawed it open, his blunt fingers clumsy as hooves on the tiny plastic cover. "Yeah? Oh, hi, sweetie pie." A vicious glare, at odds with the sugary voice, abraded the smirk from Dougie's face. "No, Laura, Daddy didn't forget. I thought you got to stay up later's all. Okay. Ready? Nighty night, sleep tight, and don't let the bedbugs bite." As he closed the phone, Dougie began his lament.

"What're we gonna—"

It was cut off by another few bars of the children's nursery song. Blackie's daughter liked to program the ring on his cell phone.

He flipped it open again. "Sweetie . . ." he began, then trailed off. His flesh tightened over wide cheek and brow bones, drawing the rigid lines of a man in pain—or in thrall to someone who enjoyed the dark arts.

"Yeah," he said. And "Yeah." And "Clear." Putting the phone back in his pocket, he jerked his chin toward the freight container. "Throw 'em in the back of the van. We got another job."

Dougie padded happily into the reeking darkness of the metal coffin. He knew Blackie's look, the freaky frozen look. The other job would be better. It was way more fun when they weren't already dead.

TWO

Old Man River. What a crock, Anna thought as she sat on a bench on the levee, the April sun already powerful enough to warm the faux wood slats beneath her back and thighs. The Mississippi was so unquestionably female, the great mother, a blowsy, fecund, fertile juggernaut that nurtured and destroyed with the same sublime indifference.

Rivers were paltry things where Anna had grown up, fierce only when they flash-flooded. Compared to the Mississippi their occasional rampages seemed merely the peevish snits of adolescence.

Half blind from the hypnotic sparkle of sun on ruffled water, she squinted at her watch. Geneva was about to go to work. Grunting mildly because there was no one close enough to hear, Anna shoved herself up from the bench and started back toward the New Orleans Jazz National Historical Park on North Peters, a block from Café Du Monde and Jackson Square.

Young persons of the sort she seldom ran across in

the parks had laid claim to a swath of the river walk. Six males, three females, four dogs, one puppy, and nine bicycles created a barrier that could either be detoured around or run as a gauntlet. Hostile glares from thirteen pairs of eyes—the puppy looked friendly enough—suggested Anna choose the detour.

Sheer orneriness suggested she take the puppy up on his tail-wagging invitation and plow through the pack. The alpha male, tall with hair pulled into a tail of natural dreadlocks, the kind created by aggressively bad hygiene and not kinky hair or salon manipulations, and a beard Charlie Manson might have sported before prison barbers took over his personal grooming, could have been close to thirty. The youngest was the girl holding the puppy. Anna put her at no more than thirteen or fourteen.

Age was hard to guess. Male and female alike wore only blacks and browns. Not a speck of color alleviated the drab of their thrift store clothing. Decorations were a study in sartorial nihilism: slashes, iron pins, rag-over-rag T-shirts with swastikas inked on. Piercing and cutting and tattooing moved seamlessly from fabric to flesh. Nothing was symmetrical, soft, or suggestive of kindness. Dirt, soot, sweat, and various effluvia dulled cloth, hair, and skin. Something more immutable dulled the eyes.

If life were to be found in T. S. Eliot's wasteland, Anna believed it would be in the discovery of roving bands like this one; parentless, homeless, hopeless children, more like the child-soldiers of Rwanda—or little girls pressed into sexual slavery in World War II Japanese prison camps—than children from middle- and upper-class American families who chose to reject the plenty for the ride.

Geneva—Anna was staying in the apartment behind her house on Ursulines in the Quarter—called them "gutter punks." They were purported to call themselves "travelers" because they jumped trains, living the nomadic life once followed by hobos.

Just how dangerous they were, Anna hadn't a clue, but it was clear they wanted to inspire fear in civilians. Even without the stink and the rags and the self-mutilation, that alone would have earned them a wide berth as far as she was concerned. These kids were not her brand of criminal. She wasn't well versed in their migration patterns, did not know their natural habitat, what they preyed upon or what preyed upon them—but people who valued fear and enjoyed pain were scary. Healthy animals, bunnies and foxes and cougars and grizzlies, ran from what frightened them and avoided pain at all costs. When they stopped behaving this way it was because they were sick, rabid.

Anna felt it was the same for people, except one wasn't allowed to put them out of their misery.

Avoiding eye contact, she cut across the grass in the direction of the flood wall and the Jazz National Historical Park. As she reached the tracks between the levee and the city where the Julia Street trolley ran, she heard a piercing whistle, the kind that can only be produced by sticking one's fingers in one's mouth, the kind that leaves grooves in the gray matter of anyone in a hundred-foot radius.

Stopping, she shaded her eyes and looked up the grassy slope she'd just descended. A gutter punk, a man in his late twenties with a double-pierced eyebrow and a crown of thorns tattooed across his forehead, was yelling and waving his arms at a small black dog racing down the levee after a flashily dressed white man who looked more Bronx chic than New Orleans cool.

Anna recognized the black terrier as one of the pack milling around on the river walk. The punk whistled again, and the mutt, as shaggy as his owner, hesitated and looked back. His feathery tail waved once; then he sat down no more than a yard from Anna, made a perfect O of his lips, pointed his chin at the sky, and howled a tiny wolf-puppy howl so perfect and unscary that Anna laughed.

Communication completed—at least as far as the dog was concerned—the little guy upended and ran off after the man he'd been following.

The punk on the levee howled then, and the hairs on the back of Anna's neck stirred in the heat. The punk's howl was all wolf, old and crying-sad as if the fuzzy-rumped pooch disappearing through the gate in the flood wall was absconding with all the love and light in the world.

Punk or not, Anna couldn't stand the anguish. She ran to catch an undoubtedly filthy and probably flea-ridden mutt. The flood wall opened into a wide alley paved in brick and peopled by three-quarter life-sized bronze sculptures: a butcher, a woman sitting on a park bench—citizens from a previous century sentenced to eternity in the town that had passed them by.

Anna skirted a fountain squirting three pathetically weak streams of water into the air and stopped in front of the Dutch Alley art gallery. The doors were open and could have swallowed a man and dog before she'd arrived. Shops in New Orleans seldom closed their doors, leaving them wide summer and winter in hopes the increase in tourist traffic would offset the energy bills. Man and dog could have stepped into any one of these invitations. New Orleans was dog friendly; animals in stores and bars were commonplace.

"Hah!" Anna said as she caught the last few inches of a tail disappearing into an archway farther down the alley. "Gotcha." She trotted after the dog.

From behind she could hear the clatter of heavy boots on brick. The punk was rounding the fountain. He wasn't as tall as he'd looked standing atop the levee and was thin to the point of starvation. Though the distance from where his clan usurped the public walkway to where Anna stood was less than a hundred yards, he was breathing heavily and had one hand pressed hard into his side.

"This way," Anna called and ran into the shade of the arch. To one side was another art gallery, to the other the public toilets.

The flashy dresser might have ducked into the john, but Anna had no intention of checking the men's room.

Seeing men urinating against trees, though a perfectly natural transaction, was bad enough. She had no desire to witness the phenomenon as an indoor sport. She ran through to North Peters Street.

A flash of greasy lemon caught her eye. The dog whisperer's sport coat and, faithful as a shadow, the little feather-tailed dog had crossed North Peters and were halfway down Dumaine. The punk gasped up beside her in a gust reeking of old cigarettes and older urine as yellow jacket and pup turned into a slit between two brick buildings. The light had turned and traffic was flowing, but Anna figured she could make it across the four lanes without getting squashed. Stepping off the curb, she heard the punk yell, "Wait!" but she was already committed.

A horse-drawn carriage slowed cars coming from the French Market. Anna darted between two frustrated SUVs and jumped onto the sidewalk, where, if they did hit her, they'd be poaching. None of the drivers even bothered to flip her off. The Big Easy might have the highest per capita murder rate in the country, but the citizens were nice folks for all of that.

Sprinting through lackadaisical tourists like Drew Brees through linebackers, Anna zigged down Dumaine and into the narrow alley where the punk's dog had gone.

Alleys in New Orleans were unlike alleys in other American cities. Rather than being skinny runs given over to garbage cans and used condoms, many were transformed into impossibly slender gardens, with plant hangers drilled into the brick walks, ivy and creeping fig cloaking age and decay, and bright scraps of found art alleviating the gloom.

"Stop!" somebody yelled, but she paid no attention. She had spotted the dog. Partway down the verdant little urban canyon, tail up, it trotted on the heels of the stranger.

"Excuse me!" she called.

The man turned back and stared at her for a second longer than seemed necessary. "You talkin' to me?"

Robert De Niro, *Taxi Driver*. The guy was dead on, and Anna laughed. He squinted and looked suddenly dangerous. He hadn't been mimicking De Niro intentionally, Anna guessed. That or he believed he *was* De Niro.

"That your dog?" Anna asked.

The man looked down at the black terrier, noticing it for the first time. "He following me?"

"Since the levee," Anna told him.

"Get the fuck away from me," the guy shouted and kicked the little animal so viciously Anna screamed in pain along with it. Fury swept over her till the fern-feathered walls, the brick path, and even the whimpering dog disappeared. All that remained at the end of her tunnel vision was the oily man in the yellow sport coat and the need to rip him into teensy-weensy pieces.

Without thought, she started for him. What she would have done had she reached him, she never found out. Into her truncated view flashed silver, a knife, an edged weapon. The glint of hard steel kindly brought Anna back to her right mind. Stopping abruptly, she knelt and picked up the dog, pretending that had been her goal all along.

"Your filthy cur follows me again, I kill it. You got that?"

"I got it," Anna said and, the dog cradled in her arms, took a step back, then another.

The knife wielder didn't take his eyes off her, but she had the oddest sensation she was vanishing. The moment she ceased to be a threat, she ceased to exist for him. The old "Dog's Philosophy of Life" seemed to apply to this creature: If he couldn't screw it, eat it, or piss on it, the hell with it.

Whistling under his breath—"Some Enchanted Evening," it sounded like—he folded the knife closed and continued down the alley. Hugging the dog, Anna watched until he turned a corner and was gone from sight.

Labored breathing dragged her attention back toward the Dumaine Street entrance. The punk, still clutching his side and moving with a slight dragging of the left foot as if he'd been born clubfooted and it had never been corrected, half fell in from the street and leaned heavily against the wall.

Anna turned on her heroine's smile and waited for the accolades. She deserved at least that for facing down an armed man to save a gutter punk's dog.

"Where is he?" the punk screamed as he lurched toward her between the mossy walls. "You bitch, you goddamn bitch." Spittle flew from his mouth as he turned on

Anna and cursed her. The crown of thorns was tight across his brow, and his eyes were wild, whites showing around the irises, pupils dilated and bottomless. Above his lip a pencil-thin mustache contorted into Etch A Sketch angles, and the thumb-sized tuft of beard beneath his lower lip jutted out like the spine of a horned lizard.

"Stop, goddammit! Wait, goddammit," he screamed, but the yellow jacket was long gone. Arms outstretched like a B-movie zombie's, he lunged. Anna flattened herself and the dog against the brick and aimed a swift kick at his knee. He went down like a puppet whose strings had been cut and began to cry, wailing like a child.

Various courses of action skittered through Anna's mind. She could kneel and try to comfort this tortured soul. She could pull out her cell phone and call 911. Yell for help. Try to find the knife man. In the end all she did was set the dog down by its master and walk away. Since she was on administrative leave for mental instability—or something very like—the dog would have as good a shot at doing the right thing as she would. Probably better.

Leaving the alley, she hazarded a backward glance. The punk had managed to pull himself into a sitting position. He was hugging the dog. The dog was licking his face. For a moment Anna watched them. There was something about the dog that was off, niggling at the edges of her mind.

Breathing in the cooking smells on the street, the

whiff of exhaust, the hints of horse manure, it came to her. The little terrier was a mess—it looked as if its hair had been chewed off in a dogfight rather than clipped by a sane groomer—but it was silky soft, shampooed, brushed, and smelled faintly of lilacs.

THREE

Clare was not a big fan of the wee hours. The phrase "dead of night" was too apt. Time was hollow between 2:00 and 4:00 A.M. She felt it in the pit of her stomach, in the back of her brain; a toxic emptiness like the ghost of a hangover or the memory of a one-night stand.

Slipping in from darkness made manifest by drizzle so fine it hadn't the initiative to fall but must be harvested by passers through, she turned, closed the front door, and threw the bolt.

David's trench coat, snatched up because it was convenient and because when he'd rushed out that evening he'd forgotten and left his wallet and cell phone in the pocket, was half off before she sensed more than just the nauseous touch of disenfranchised sleep. Years of training and practicing the art of Method acting had sensitized her to any emotion, any feeling, that might one day be useful. Or so she insisted when she grew tired of thinking of herself as high-strung, high-maintenance, or just downright neurotic.

Something was wrong with the house.

She shrugged back into the coat, the collar rain-wet and cold against the nape of her neck. Unaware she did so, she backed up against the solid oak of the door.

Darkness was never absolute in the city, even a city as befogged and cloudy as Seattle. The unsettling orange of sodium arc lamps starred the water drops on the panes of the bay window in the living room and cast lurid dripping shadows on the far wall.

A panic attack.

Lord knew Clare had sufficient experience to know what those felt like. Her Xanax were in the upstairs bathroom, on the highest shelf of the medicine cabinet where the girls could not reach, not unless the little monkeys climbed into the sink basin, which was not beyond the realm of possibility.

Though her scalp was tightening, her fingers tingling, and her nose going numb, she made no move to get the medication.

Trust your paranoia.

An actress, older, wiser, and two divorces more cynical, had once whispered that in her ear.

Yes, she was having a panic attack.

And, yes, something was wrong with the house.

Eyes wide, trying to see into shadows, through walls, she fumbled for the belt of the coat to pull it more tightly over her nightgown, armor against what-

ever was coming. The whisk and slither of fabric sliding over itself shrieked in the quiet of the room. She
let go of the belt. Shoving her hand in her pocket, she
clutched the children's cough syrup she'd just bought at
the all-night pharmacy. Pulling the bottle out, she looked
at it as if it might return her to a state of normalcy. It
didn't.

*Vee's breath scraping in her throat, gathering to-
gether into a cough so violent it folded her tiny body
nearly in two.*

"Mommy?"

"Hi, sweetie."

*Sitting on the edge of her younger daughter's bed,
laying a hand on her forehead.*

"My chest hurts."

*Dana's sleepy voice from beyond the elephant night
table.* "My chest hurts, too, Mommy."

Cough syrup.

The wrong was in the silence. Vee's coughing, the
painful broken sound that had clawed Clare out of her
sleep and into sneakers and a raincoat, was gone. No
coughing child. No click of Mackie's claws on the hardwood as he left the girls' room to see who'd opened the
front door so stealthily. Silence swallowed the life of
the house. Even the grandfather clock that guarded the
foot of the stairs had ceased ticking.

"What?" Clare whispered as if seeking answers
from the ether. Yell for David? David had gone. Switch
on the lights? Wake the kids, the dog, and the au pair?
Jalila was with David. Craziness.

Breathing in. Breathing out. Nothing to fear but fear. This too shall pass. I'm okay. Inhaling and exhaling on a mishmash of mantras picked up from a mishmash of philosophies and psychologists, Clare walked her body to the stairs, had it lift one foot, then the other. Checked to make sure it put its hand on the railing for safety.

Never once in the thirty-five years before Dana was born had it occurred to Clare that she could love children. When she'd gotten pregnant she'd wanted an abortion. David called her a murderess and threatened lawsuits. Hers was the rare shotgun wedding where the groom was holding the shotgun.

Three years later, when she was pregnant with Victoria, abortion was no longer an option; the baby might be another Dana. Vee was different from her sister. Where Dana was graceful, Vee was sturdy. Where Dana was quiet, Vee shouted. Where Dana walked, Vee ran.

Another facet of Clare's heart made manifest.

Usually these thoughts embarrassed her. Too mawkish. Too clichéd. Not now, not in the gaping dark of the stairwell. Focusing on her girls, she felt the out-of-body experience began to wane; her soul dripped back into her body.

The kids' room was across the landing from the one she shared with David. Four steps, sneakers soundless on the hardwood, and Clare stood in the doorway. Two neat four-poster beds, bought new in 1899 when their great-great-grandmother and her twin sister turned twelve, sat to either side of an incongruity the kids adored, a glass-topped table held up by an elephant.

The night-light, shining up through the glass, cast elongated ear shadows on the ceiling.

No dog trotted over to greet her.

Clare clicked on the overhead light. The covers were rumpled as if little girls had just climbed out of them; the old blanket where Mackie slept was across the foot of Vee's bed, yet Clare felt an emptiness that spoke of a thousand years of genocide, a crumbling of ancient walls. Not a whisper of her children remained.

"Vee! Dana!" she began screaming and couldn't stop. "Mackie! Victoria! Damn you!"

As she cried out the names she ran down the hall, the rubber soles of her shoes squeaking against the polished wood. The bathroom was empty. The playroom. When the girls were scared and their father was gone, they'd get in her bed. Clare darted past the head of the stairs, slipped, fell, scrambled up. Catching herself on the door frame of the master bedroom, she slid her palm down the wall just inside the door, turning the light on.

No little girls. No dog.

Nightmare closed around her. She could not move, could not see; her screaming produced no sound. With the dislocated tunnel vision of the dreamer, she pushed through the paralysis settling in her legs and flung herself in the direction of the master bath.

Empty.

A sound, a vibration maybe, like the slamming of a door downstairs, penetrated Clare's narrowing world.

The girls had gone to Jalila's room. The au pair slept on the first floor in the maid's room behind the old pantry.

Stairs, living room, dining room, kitchen, passed in a blur, in a shout of the children's names honed razor sharp by terror. Jalila's room. Lights on. The bed was unmade, as she'd left it when she'd rushed out with Clare's husband just before midnight. No little girls, no bright dark eyes, no shaggy dog, just a preternatural chill undisturbed by living heartbeats.

Dropping the cough medicine, her one link with a warping reality, Clare pulled David's cell phone from the trench coat pocket and pushed 911 as she ran. Babbling her emergency, she slammed on lights, yanked open closet doors, peered under and behind furniture till she reached the half-sized Harry Potter closet under the stairs to the attic and wrenched open the door. This being the last place the girls might have secreted themselves, finally she stopped. Breath coming in cries and gasps, it took a moment to hear the tiny voice from the phone held at her thigh.

The 911 operator was saying something, had been saying something for a while. Clare held the phone indifferently to her ear and heard what was being repeated with such urgency.

"Get out of the house. Get out of the house."

"No." Clare would never leave.

"Maybe something happened and the sitter took the children to a neighbor's."

Relief flooded Clare's being. Hope acted on her like

cocaine had during her flirtation with the wild side in college. Maybe the operator said more; Clare wouldn't have known. Phone at her side, she ran into the front yard and across Laggert Street. The children could have gone to the Donovans'. If they'd woken and found themselves alone, they would have run over to Crimson Rose and Coltie's like she'd taught them to.

Frenzied pounding brought the reassuring sound of feet on hardwood stairs; then Robert Donovan, looking tousled and concerned, opened the door. Just past thirty, tall and thin as a rail with the most beautiful brown eyes Clare had ever seen except on a dog, Robert was the father of four children. The middle two, Colt and Crimson, were Victoria and Dana's best friends. Sleepovers were a weekly event. In a few years all this would become problematic. For now they enjoyed innocence.

Dana and Vee were not there.

Clare heard Robert say the words, and walls of night folded in. As if the racing fury of the past minutes had burned all her reserves in an adrenaline flash fire, she no longer possessed the strength to remain upright. As she swayed and began to crumple, she was bizarrely aware of the high drama. Like a director watching a ham actor, she noted how her knees folded and one hand stretched ineffectually toward the door frame, how, still vaguely elegant even in T-shirt and sweatpants, Robert stepped forward to catch her. How the essence of romantic melodrama went awry when he hadn't the strength to hold five feet nine, one hundred and twenty-four pounds of out-of-balance female flesh and they both toppled off the steps into the shrubbery. Robert, who neither swore nor smoked and only drank sparingly, yelled, "Whoa!"

Clare began to laugh. *Tears and snot and convulsive yucks.* Hysteria. She knew it, but could not stop. Robert extricated them from the bushes. The look of genuine fear for her on his face ought to have had a sobering effect, but it only brought on more laughter.

Not merriment, the acting coach in Clare's head noted. There was no relief, joy, or amusement, just emotion so violent it would come out willy-nilly on any vehicle it could find. Psychic diarrhea, spiritual projectile vomiting.

"Robert?"

Tracy, Robert's wife of twelve years, stood in the doorway, her long frizzy hair backlit by the hallway light, her small body childlike in a long white cotton nightgown. In her arms was the littlest Donovan, just a year old.

It was the sight of the baby that brought an abrupt end to Clare's hysteria. To wake the baby, to make him cry, would be too much to bear.

Sirens did the evil in her stead. Not a long wail for blocks and blocks but a sharp stab of sound and a brief flash of blue light as a patrol car announced its arrival at the curb.

Robert left Clare for his wife as the police came up the walk. Both cops were middle-aged, not the officers central casting would have sent. The driver was a small woman, a little thick around the middle but strong-looking, with graying hair cut short. The officer riding shotgun was probably close to retirement age and had eaten too many doughnuts over the years. Both wore glasses. Both looked like they'd seen it all and didn't believe over half of it. The female officer looked as if she still cared. The man just looked tired.

Clare addressed the female officer. "I'm her. It's me. I called." For the briefest of moments Clare believed she was going to be a rational adult, but in saying the words the desperate fear that had sent her racing from room to room screaming claimed her again, and the story of her missing children poured out in a semicoherent flood.

The officer nodded. "I'm Officer Shopert. This is Officer Dunn. We'll check your house out as soon as another unit arrives."

Clare had thought she'd reached the maximum overdrive of panic, that place where vision becomes unreliable and speech breaks into pieces chasing fractured thoughts, but when the lady cop mentioned delay it worsened. A force rose in her throat, a power that would come out high-pitched and shrieking. A sound that would get her slammed into the loony bin.

Officer Shopert sensed it—or heard the indrawn breath—because she said quickly, "One minute, three at the most. A hundred and eighty seconds. They're right behind us."

Clare clamped lips and jaws together and nodded.

"So you went to check on your children and they were missing?" Shopert said.

Clare nodded. She could feel the jarring as her brain slid forward and back inside her skull.

"And you ran through the house looking, then out the front door and here?"

Again she nodded. *Slide. Stop. Slide, stop.* Vision shook.

"Just when was it you stopped to put on lace-up running shoes and a coat?" Officer Dunn interjected. Suddenly he didn't look the least bit tired.

Clare blinked; once, twice. She could not make sense of why he asked about her clothes, could scarcely remember the meaningless details of life before the empty little beds.

A second patrol car arrived, pulling up behind the first and saving her from having to string together words that would waste more precious seconds.

Two more officers, both men this time and both fairly young, sprang energetically from their vehicle and trotted up the walk. From the orange glare of the streetlight and the kinder spill of light from the Donovans' hallway, Clare could see their faces. Strong manly concern was writ large.

All the world was a stage, and the men and women on it mostly bad actors. These guys were not just cops; they were also *playing* cops, and tonight was turning into a good show. Her 911 call probably saved them from a tedious graveyard shift with nothing but coffee-induced heartburn for dramatic tension.

The four officers met midyard and held a hasty con-
ference. Clare hovered, listening so hard her ears rang,
but didn't step toward them. A horror had gripped her
that time was running away with her children, that each
tick of some hideous clock pushed them farther from
her. She didn't want to do anything that might delay the
police.

Straying out from the murmurs like loose hairs
from a topknot came bits of the conversation. "Around
back . . . give me about a ten count . . . you and Jim . . .
bad knee . . . no, I'll go. You'll strain . . ."

They broke up half a moment before Clare's head
was going to explode. Officer Dunn got on the radio.
The two younger men and the female officer trotted
across Laggert toward Clare's house. Mist and wet
pavement caught the light from the street lamps, and
they moved as if through an orange fog that shattered
and then re-formed as they passed.

Hysteria morphed to hyperawareness and tightened
Clare's brain. She noted each step the officers took, the
way their shoes left fleeting tracks in the moisture on
the pavement, the way the off-worldly light played along
the barrels of their drawn weapons. Two of them, a man
and Officer Shopert, split off and ran around toward
the back of the house.

The back door was locked, and Clare thought to call
out to them, but surely they, as policemen, would have
thought of that, and she didn't want to offend them or
appear foolish. As part of her marked this disturbingly
ordinary response to an extraordinary situation, they

passed from sight behind the lilacs at the side of the house. The lone policeman stood to one side of the front door, his back against the siding, pistol held in stiff arms and pointed toward the ground between his feet.

Just like on TV.

"Just like on TV," Clare said aloud, trying to dispel the creeping surreality clotting in her throat.

"That's right, Miss . . ."

"Sullivan," Clare answered automatically. It was the older officer, the heavy one. She reached for, but couldn't remember, his name.

"Dunn," he said as if he'd read her mind, pointing to the name tag above the breast pocket of his uniform shirt. "Sullivan, huh? The 911 operator's got a Daoud Suliman listed at this address."

The way he pronounced the Arabic name reminded Clare why David had changed it after the attacks on the Pentagon and the World Trade Center.

"Yes. My husband changed it to David Sullivan for business reasons."

"Yeah," the cop said.

The sneer in his voice served to help Clare focus. Briefly, she took her eyes from the house across the street.

"This Daoud Suliman, he a U.S. citizen?"

Clare knew she must have said she didn't know by the cynical echo she got in return, but her eyes and mind were again across the street, going into the house with the picture-perfect policeman. Blocking executed faultlessly, he crouched, entered the front door quickly, then stepped to the side lest he provide a tempting backlit target. Because her mind's eye was less short-sighted than those in her face, Clare no longer saw Officer Dunn, though she felt him scratching at the edges of her attention. She saw the stairs, the banister, the upstairs hall.

Then she was on her butt seeing nothing but fire.

FOUR

The entire adventure, from punk to nuts, had taken less than a quarter of an hour. Geneva was just going on when Anna arrived back at the National Park Service center. Slipping in quietly, she settled in the last of eight rows of folding chairs more than half filled with tourists, shopping bags and purses cluttering the floor between their feet. At the opposite end of this humble auditorium a small raised stage jutted out from the wall. A pianist hunched over an electronic keyboard, a guitar player perched one buttock on a folding chair identical to those used by the audience, and a vocalist—Geneva Akers—swayed gently behind a floor mike.

The musicians wore green and gray, cordovan belts and shoes, and tidy brass nameplates over their left breast pockets. They were park rangers; their job was to protect and preserve the musical heritage of the historic city of New Orleans. Anna loved it. In the name of political pork, the Park Service preserved so many worthless bits of history that some said the NPS was where white elephants went to die. Then there were places like this, where the sacred torch of a time long past was carried, still burning, into the present.

Anna slid down as far as the anti-ergonomics of the chair allowed and opened herself to the experience as Geneva began to sing "Swing low, sweet chariot" a cappella. On "comin' for to carry me," the keyboard crept in. Tendrils of the first guitar notes wrapped around the word "home" till the sound was like that of distant hearts catching up a single thread of emotion.

Geneva reminded Anna of a woman she'd known—seen, rather—when she lived in New York City with her first husband, Zach. She was a street singer, a big woman, tall and heavy, with long hair in so many tiny braids that where she tied it at the middle of her back the ponytail was easily six inches in diameter, who worked the north entrance to Saks on Fifth Avenue. White was her signature color: white headdress, caftan, flowing trousers, sandals in the summer, white boots in the fall, and a long white cane with a red tip on the end as an exclamation point to the black-and-white canvas. The Blind Blues Singer, as traditional as the music she sang.

Once, on the 7 train, Anna had seen her, cane folded away in her bag, drugstore reading glasses perched on her nose, perusing *Newsweek*. Sighted or not, she put on a good show, and the only revenge Anna took was winking at her when she dropped a bill in her box on Fifth.

Geneva genuinely was a blind blues singer. Behind

the black Ray-Bans she always wore, her eyes were slashed and burned from an accident on her dad's farm in Illinois when she was four. Like the New York street singer, she was of regal size and royal bearing, but she wore her hair cropped so close to her skull it dusted the skin like the first snow in the high desert. In the 1980s she had trained at Juilliard, but, because of her seemingly boundless talent, she never sounded "professional." She sounded real, a blind eyewitness to the sorrow and love and joys of the world.

Proud as Anna was to have a talent like Geneva's in the green and gray, the uniform jarred with the music, and she closed her eyes hoping the rich imagery of the old gospel song, colored in the many hues of Geneva's voice, would cancel out images of punks frothing at the mouth and belting out the B-word every other sentence and pimped-out white boys with dead eyes and sharp objects.

Unquestionably, Anna was less crazy than she had been when, in the wake of the incidents on Isle Royale, Rocky Mountain National Park's superintendent had recommended a leave of absence. Coming off winter study on ISRO, Anna had been so crazy she had no idea how crazy she was. The intervening weeks had moved her a long way toward sanity. Now the black hole that had threatened to swallow her was a mere speck on her mental horizon.

Paul worried that the net of evil that caught them up during their belated honeymoon in Big Bend would set her back, but the events in the Chihuahuan Desert were not comparable to what she had gone through on Isle Royale. For one thing, it was warm in Big Bend. The sun shone. Mostly, though, it was because she'd found strength and courage, kindness and honor, in her comrades. And they had found it in her.

Maybe this wasn't enough to heal the deep wounds, but it was sufficient; with that and the love of Paul Davidson, she could sustain life. Whether or not she could sustain life as a law enforcement ranger with the National Park Service remained to be seen.

Had she Geneva's musical abilities, she could sing for her supper rather than hunt and kill and drag it home. Unfortunately Anna's singing voice was better suited to clearing large numbers of people out of places in record time. She knew for a fact it didn't soothe savage beasts.

Despite the gift of gospel, her thoughts wandered, the gutter punks reinfiltrating her inner landscape. As a tribe they exhibited the familiar one-size-fits-all hostility of any urban gang. The oldest, the Charlie Manson of the group, carried himself with angry arrogance, the chip on his shoulder clearly one of his most prized possessions. The others, the drab, the dim, the nondescript ashes of his followers, had a piece of his mettle, enough of an edge to hold the ambient kindness of strangers at bay.

The terrier punk had cursed her and tried to attack her; still, he felt a little different against her psychic skin than the rest. Two of these differences came to her clearly as she drifted on Geneva's music and New Orleans's dark waters: The terrier punk was dying, and he still cared desperately about something. Maybe the dog, or maybe the dog was only a manifestation of it.

The man's frailty was obvious; he was as thin and brittle as spring ice, he was malnourished, exhausted, and very possibly the victim of AIDS or tuberculosis or drug addiction, but that wasn't the kind of dying Anna saw when she pictured him. Demons were killing that punk. She could almost see their claw marks at the backs of his eyes, sense them jerking at his limbs when he tried to strangle her. In a moment of revelation she realized the dog was all that kept the satanic hordes from dragging him down into the fires of hell. Anna felt a sudden and powerful kinship with him.

"Jesus H. Christ," she whispered and opened her eyes. After all these great healing weeks with her husband, sun, orange juice, and cats on her lap, her mind still wasn't anyplace she needed to be playing by herself.

Punks were an urban blip; her run-in with the dead-eyed knife man and the dog lover had no more lasting importance than an aborted mugging or a snatched wallet. If blood was not spilled nor bones broken, one counted her lucky stars and didn't dwell on it.

The set was finished. The musicians turned back into plain old rangers; the tourists gathered up their loot and headed back out into the sun for more. Anna stayed in her chair watching Geneva strike the floor mike, then help the pianist dismantle his keyboard and pack it in its carrying case. The guitar player, speaking to no one, had left the stage while the last note of the last song was still reverberating to let himself out through a door on the inside wall.

"Is that you I hear breathing out there, Anna?" Geneva asked as the piano player latched his case.

"I breathe silently," Anna said. "You're just guessing." She rose from the chair and walked toward the front of the room. "I think you were a bit sharp there on that last note. You know, just a hair pointy."

Geneva laughed. "You've been to too many firearms trainings without earplugs. I bet you can tell the difference between a .22 shot fired and a .38, but you've never been able to tell the difference between E-flat and middle C."

"Early childhood trauma," Anna said. "I could never pick out 'Twinkle, Twinkle, Little Star' on the piano."

"Shoot, anybody can pick out 'Twinkle, Twinkle, Little Star.' You must not have been trying."

"Where's Sammy?" Anna changed the subject. Geneva was right about her musical disability. She'd been the only sophomore Sister Mary Judette told to just mouth the words in choir, the only waitress excused from singing "Happy Birthday" to customers.

"He's around." Geneva whistled "Dixie" softly, and a tall champagne-colored standard poodle unfolded itself from behind the raised stage, stretched long and lean as a cat, and yawned hugely. "Sammy likes World War II songs," Geneva said as she dug Sammy's leash from a patchwork shoulder bag big enough to carry a small child.

Sammy sat still with his back to her while she latched the leash onto his harness.

" 'Boogie Woogie Bugle Boy' and all that. A pretty little blonde number comes in with her hair done up and a forties' dress and heels and does Andrews Sisters stuff. Sammy laps it up. But then Sammy laps up cat shit."

"A seeing-eye poodle," Anna said as they fell into step in the bricked alley outside the auditorium. "Who'd've thunk?"

"A poodle!" Geneva exclaimed. "Here all these years I thought that kinky hair just meant he was an African American Lab."

Anna laughed, and Geneva took her arm companionably. She didn't need the guidance; she had Sammy and years of walking the same route to and from work for that. Geneva was just a warm, touchy sort of woman. Anna wasn't, but she didn't want to seem ungracious, so she quelled the urge to squirm free. The afternoon sun had been obscured by dark clouds, and a salt-and-swamp breeze kicked up the litter of yellow blossoms that dusted the walkway.

"When's this man of yours coming down?" Geneva asked as Sammy stopped them to wait for the light to change on North Peters. "When I'd heard you'd gotten married, and to a Mississippi preacher to boot, I didn't believe it. I mean I did *not* believe it. I made a major fool of myself arguing with the messenger. This guy must be a man of God to want a prickly old thing like you lying next to him at night."

"He's the sheriff of Adams County up on the Trace," Anna said.

"Ah, at home with criminals and firearms. That makes the union more explicable," Geneva said. "So you're honeymooning in my back apartment?"

Anna'd called Geneva to see if she could stay with her for a week but hadn't told her much more than that. Gossip in the Park Service spread with the speed of the Internet, and she guessed Geneva knew about her administrative leave and the investigation into the deaths on Isle Royale. After her and Paul's adventure in Big Bend, Anna, her dog, Taco, and her two cats had reunited at his home in Port Gibson. The leave was of an unspecified length—five weeks being the best guess—and Anna didn't want to sit around all alone in Rocky Mountain National Park thinking herself into a pit.

"Not so much a honeymoon," Anna said. "A getaway is more like it. He'll be down in a few days."

"Newlyweds. I bet you can't wait."

Anna could wait. She loved her husband and would be missing him before long, but she'd been by herself most of her adult life. She liked it. She was good at it. She needed it. Since they'd left for Big Bend in March, she and Paul had scarcely been more than arm's length from one another. Paul loved it. If he had his way, Anna and her menagerie would have lived in his shirt pocket. Anna needed a bit of breathing room to process the beginnings of sanity, the joys of matrimony, and possibly the end of a career.

Geneva's house was an easy walk from the Jazz

Historical Park. Moving at a southern saunter, Anna enjoyed the narrow streets, the two- and three-story buildings, wrought-iron balconies heavy with ferns and flowers. Age, and two hundred years of crooked politicians taking more from the city than they gave back, overlaid everything with a sleepy decadence that was more seductive than alarming.

Katrina might have brought much of New Orleans to its knees, but it had done wonders for the French Quarter. Anna had never seen it so clean and painted and primped. The seediness was still there. The undercurrent of lasciviousness and overindulgence that had been luring Christian leadership conventions to the area for a hundred years remained. But it smelled a lot better.

In the Quarter, Uptown, the Garden District, in many of the neighborhoods in New Orleans, it was easy to forget the underlying menace of a city with a people who had declared war upon themselves.

Dumaine, the street they walked down, was the home of many of New Orleans's voodoo shops, windows filled with charms and books and spells and all things pertaining to the African magic as filtered through an American—and commercial—perspective. Anna's favorite was Vieux Dieux. It always had weird displays set on a table outside the door. Today it was a tiny graveyard complete with miniature crypts.

When they reached Geneva's door, Sammy woofed once politely. Two nine-foot-tall French windows fronted the narrow house, but both were blinded with heavy shutters peeling mauve paint. The entrance Geneva used was through an iron gate beside the house that let into an alley barely wider than Anna's outstretched arms. Beneath their feet a pathway, two bricks wide and grouted with moss, snaked between what had once been raised beds but were now low mounded hillocks of greenery spilling onto the walk.

The peach-colored stucco of the house was to the left. To the right was a wooden fence that rose twelve feet, then was overtaken by vines, which climbed another five or ten feet, their tendrils bridging from the top of the fence to the house next door. Peeking through this dense curtain of greenery were beasts and faces, flowers, and patterns made by bits of ironwork collected over fifty years and nailed onto the fence.

On her aunt's death Geneva had inherited not a single house but a ramshackle complex with three rental apartments and a two-car garage—unheard of in this part of town—with three brick, cavelike rooms behind it that local historians said were where the house slaves had lived. Hearing the bare-bones facts of Geneva's real estate, it would be easy to assume she was rolling in money, and she probably could have sold the buildings for close to a million dollars, but Geneva had no intention of selling.

Probably, Anna thought, because moving would be an impossible task. Geneva's mother had been a pack rat, and the property was a maze of saved wrought iron, old tools, wooden shutters, memorabilia from the music world, and Lord knew what else. So Geneva held the property, and the property held Geneva hostage with a constant need for money to keep the roofs from leaking and the toilets flushing.

The walkway ended in a courtyard no more than twenty feet square. It, too, was paved in brick and overgrown, vines hiding the fences to either side and mounting an assault on what had once been a carriage house but at some juncture had been made into a guest cottage. The cottage was one room wide and three tall, each of the upper rooms fronted by a tiny balcony and the walk-through sash windows common to the Old South. No lines were straight, no angle true to another. All that was rigid had cracked. That which was not rigid had warped as the house threw off the constraints of the rectangle. Vines and age blurring the edges, it looked as if the structure were melting into the garden. To accentuate the illusion a pond, the basin of brick, the fountain stilled, lay at its foot, and the wind, its coquetry hinting at a storm to come, stiffened the bleeding heart and voracious wisteria until they moved and snapped audibly.

The only jarring note in this romantic decrepitude was the gutter punk. Smoking a cigarette, his gaunt frame hunched into a wary question mark, he sat on the low fountain wall with his dog at his feet, as if they waited for Anna.

FIVE

A freakish hail of burning wood and glass fell from the sky. Pieces striking the street burst like comets hitting earth, fire breeding fire. By Seattle's dripping grace, nothing else was ignited.

This horrible glory unfolded in near silence for Clare. The blast that knocked her down had momentarily deafened her.

Silence, and the peculiar stop-frame way the explosion cracked through seconds of the night, ended simultaneously.

Tracy's baby cried. People ran toward the flaming house. A crowd appeared, born of the conflagration as maggots are born of dead meat. Neighbors. More police. Cars. Gawkers drawn by the noise, the light. A news van. The sound of sirens. The petty star pecks of camera flashes fighting the sun of the burning house.

Clare got to her feet. By the effortlessness of her rise she guessed she was unhurt. The information was of no interest to her. Like others, she was pulled toward the fire till a sensation, so different from those that had been racking body and brain it startled her, brought her to a standstill. Relief. She was suddenly desperately grateful her children had been taken.

Otherwise they would have been inside the house.

"Hallelujah," she whispered.

"What the hell . . ."

The officer with the bad knee—Dunn—was standing a few feet away, his fleshy face dyed demonic red by the flames. His eyes, black cuts enlivened by reflected sparks, slewed toward her.

"Jesus Christ!" he muttered as if he'd just had a revelation from the Man himself. Then a voice cut through the murmur of the growing crowd and the fierce chewing sound the flames made as they devoured the house. The radio clipped to Dunn's belt said, "Jim. Behind the house. Call the medics."

No preamble. No formal radio protocol.

Clare's thoughts, centered on her children, widened slightly to encompass others' lives, others' pain. The handsome young officer who'd gone theatrically in the front door; he was dead now. Had to be.

The voice on the radio was male, and Clare guessed Shopert, the woman cop she'd liked, was the one hurt. Dunn's eyes left her. Thumbing the mike clipped to his epaulet, he made calls as he ran, his gate lopsided and slow.

Bad knee.

More sirens. Or the same ones closer. Fire trucks arrived.

Feeling detached and outside of time, Clare drifted across the street.

Fire painted the world garish red, much as Clare imagined dawn would on Mars. Each bush, tree, each burnt-black shadow, stood out in high relief. The crippling numbness of shock broke, releasing her. Time was exploding in a rain of fire, and no one was looking for Dana, for Vee. Ignoring the shouts of newly arriving authority figures to stay back, she ran toward the darkness behind the house crying out her children's names.

Shoes slipping on the wet grass, she rounded the corner to the unfenced backyard. Officer Shopert lay on the pebbled walk. Dunn knelt over her. There must have been a good deal of blood—there was a shard of glass the size of Clare's palm protruding from the policewoman's neck and another embedded in her cheek, but in the saturated light color deceived.

Clare didn't slow down. There was no garage, but David had built a carport for one car—his, a Lexus SUV. The bloated station wagon was in its customary place. David had come back. Or had never really left. The SUV's doors were unlocked. No kids. Her 1997 Honda was unlocked. Four or five times she checked the backseats of both vehicles, under the chassis and around back of the carport, certain, if she looked one more time, Dana and Vee would be there.

Had to be there.

The act of searching fed her frenzy until she found herself prying desperately into places where not even a cat could hide. Before her mind snapped and sent her to the ground howling like a deranged wolf, she forced herself to stop, to breathe. Then, with careful steps, she followed the north side of the house toward Laggert Street. There were things she should do. Things to tell the police. More places to look. People she needed to call. Her mind would not complete these thoughts, and they crashed into each other till only a jumble of words remained of what was once sense.

Night glittered, glared, ran black and orange, as the water on leaves, grass, and street mimicked flames. Steam rose as it dried in sudden heat. A brighter flash, a green diamond in the shadow of the lilac hedge, penetrated the shattered structures of Clare's mind. Like a child or a monkey she reached for it. The blast had thrown it twenty yards, then, with the peculiar idiosyncrasy of explosions, left it resting on a leaf as neatly as the dew might leave a single drop of water.

It was an eyeball. Clare let it roll into the palm of her hand. The white shone orange; the green was flecked with fire. The glass orb was no bigger than the tip of her little finger, the eye of a doll. Jalila made dolls, beautiful things of porcelain and paint. Vee and Dana had each been given one. Clare only let them play with them on special occasions. They were too precious for everyday.

"Every day is precious," she whispered. The glass bauble felt heavy and hot in her hand. It hurt her heart. Still she couldn't bring herself to throw it away.

Behind her car doors were slamming. Authoritative voices warning people back. If art truly mirrored life—or vice versa—the police would be putting up yellow tape to cordon off the scene.

From the deep shade of the lilacs and an enormous elm, Clare watched the fire devour her home. Windows were blown out in the living room and, on the opposite side of the front door, the parlor David used as a study. The second story was only just beginning to burn: shingles smoking or steaming, fire in the window of the girls' bathroom at the head of the stairs.

Like the tail plumes of a great bird, arcs of water from the fire trucks appeared. The noise of firefighters, police, and gawkers began overtaking that of the fire itself. An ambulance arrived. To her right, behind the house, Clare could see the white of a sheeted gurney and the black plastic body bag being strapped to it. Officer Shopert. The nice cop. She had not survived. Clare's mind skidded off that hard surface.

A whine crept from the darkness of the shadows behind her. Her heart flopped like a fish trying to breathe air. Vee, Dana, hurt, alive.

"Here," she said. Then louder, "Here!" as she turned from the glare and felt her way into the nearly liquid darkness beneath the elm to the wall of lilac bushes separating her yard from that of her neighbor's.

"Here. I'm here." She was on her hands and knees reaching, pushing under the leafy spread of branches. Bizarre inchoate visions of the children, like the doll's eye, blown safely into the cushiony arms of the hedge were followed by the broken knowledge that the children were not in the house. Then she saw them running from the explosion, frightened, cowering under the elm, waiting for her to come to them. "Talk to me. Please. It's Mommy."

Something wet and warm touched her fingers.

Blood. She thought first of blood.

Then fur. Then the entire dog was in her arms, shivering in her lap, whining, licking her face. His fur stank of smoke. His usual black-and-white coat was nearly all black with soot. Clare held him tight because she loved him and cried because he wasn't a little girl.

"Where are they, Mackie?" she asked over and over as she rocked the Lhasa apso.

The conflagration died down. The police relaxed their vigilance. People crept closer, standing on the edges of Clare's darkness as if they feared the shadow beneath the tree or sensed the bleaker shadows in her mind. Because her eyes had burned out with the fire and she had nowhere else to look for her daughters, the force of half a lifetime's habit took over. Clare studied the bystanders, noting nuance of voice, peculiarity of stance, language of movement—the tools of an actor's trade. Nearest her was a man in hiking boots wearing a sport coat over his pajamas. Clare recognized him from around the neighborhood. Two teenagers, African American, fully dressed in the rodeo-clown pants that had a stranglehold on boys' fashion, were clearly not from the neighborhood. Probably they'd been out looking for fun and found fire. A man a bit taller than Clare, broad of shoulder, arms looking muscular under a thin khaki jacket, held the hand of a little girl. Even as Clare's heart demanded it her eyes knew it wasn't one of her daughters. This child was younger, maybe three, and darker, her black hair straight and shining to the middle of her tiny bird-boned back.

With the exception of the birdy girl, all were on cell phones. The overloud one-sided conversations fell with the same meaningless urgency as the final cracks and pops of the ebbing fire.

"Yo, dude, you should check it out."

"The Southerlands' place—Sullivan? The Mideastern guy."

"Crusin' and blowie! Thought we'd . . ."

"White wife."

"Tell the Magician the problem has disappeared." This, in an American regional accent, stood out in Clare's ears.

"Probably did it himself to make Americans . . ."

"Yeah. The whole suit give or take ringers and salvage." Clare had studied accents for years, yet she could not place this one.

"I know it's three A.M., jackass, I'm telling you . . ."

"Okay, sure. Bourbon Street Nursery . . ."

"Half these guys are terrorists . . ."

The roof crashed through the second floor, driving the cellular addicts a few yards farther back. Soon lights from the street lamps and emergency vehicles were brighter than that of the dying conflagration. Sated with flame and telephone calls, people began to wander off,

no doubt hoping to find better entertainments. The first
to go were the man and the little girl. The child turned
back for some reason and looked into the shadows as if
her keen young eyes could cut through darkness where
adults' could not. The doll's porcelain face was smudged
with the soot that drifted from the fire, its green glass
eyes bright under black painted lashes.

"Come on, brat," the man said and gave the child's
arm a jerk.

"Aisha," came a tiny whisper.

"Aisha?" Clare echoed. The word reverberated fa-
miliarly against her tongue, but she had no idea why.
Maybe a child's name that was in fashion at the moment. The two of them walked out of earshot, heading
toward the darkness of the tree-shaded sidewalk along
Laggert Street.

"Holy shinola!"

The shouted idiocy startled Clare. Still holding
Mackie, she struggled to her feet. Her legs were numb
from the damp and being still so long, and she teetered,
trying to keep her balance. Officer Dunn stood at the
front of the house. Clare was behind him, not far, maybe
a dozen feet. She could see his wide rear end, the bulge
of his waist where it oozed out over the butt of the gun
on his hip. Two firemen walked into her line of sight.
Clad in protective clothing and breathing apparatus,
they looked as if they carried hazardous materials in a
medical drama, but what they were carrying was charred
bodies. Little charred bodies. The bodies of children
burned to death.

"Jesus, Mary, and Joseph," Dunn murmured as he walked toward the burdened firemen. "Where were they?"

"In the bedroom. Still in their beds. Smoke probably got them. They were gone before the fire ever reached them."

"Small frigging blessings," Dunn growled.

They were not in the house! Dana and Vee were nowhere in the house!

Hot and blistering as molten lava, her voice made its way up her throat. "No," she screamed. And screamed. And screamed. Police, firemen with their monster masks and gaping empty eyes, the teenage boys in their clownish clothes, turned toward her. Nearly to the sidewalk, the man with the girl stopped. From his jacket pocket he removed a cell phone and held it up in front of his face. He was taking pictures of her, pictures of the burned bodies.

Then Mackie was on the ground, and Clare was running toward the smoking remains of her heart, of her life, of her sanity. Maybe she was screaming, maybe she wasn't. Maybe her feet pounded the sod, maybe they struck only air. There was no way to tell.

Hell was a place of eternal disconnect.

SIX

There was a time of nothing but a red-black spin of pain: smells that made a charnel house of her heart, sights that could not be expunged by the clawing out of her eyes, which, but for the strong arms of an EMT, Clare would have tried. Then came quiet, a place away. Bustle and beings, sound and light, coiled in around the charred bits on the lawn.

Clare was left alone on the tail end of an ambulance, a soft fleece blanket wrapped around her shoulders. Mackie, ever faithful, shivered on the ground near where her feet dangled. Across Laggert Street the dark man, the tiny girl towed behind, had vanished into the shadows of the elms lining the sidewalk. The boys in the baggy pants were gone as well. Much of the crowd, leaving before the bodies were carried out, had returned. Like flies on carrion, they'd lifted in a black cloud and now, new meat arriving, resettled.

"They weren't there, the girls weren't there," Clare shrieked again and again, but only in her mind. Her mouth didn't open. Her lips wouldn't move. She tried to swallow but couldn't. Her throat was too dry.

The pathetic little bodies in front of the house had been covered by dun-colored sheeting from somewhere. Maybe the fire trucks. It didn't matter. Clare could still see them. She would always see them.

Another body was carried from the burning house over a fireman's back. This one wasn't so badly burned; David, or somebody wearing David's silk pajama bottoms, striped in silver and gray. Being in the clothing business, Clare's husband dressed well for pennies on the dollar. She had liked that at first, back when she'd liked him.

Riding lightly on the back of her silent and unending scream, it came to her that the pajamas were as wrong as the house had been wrong. David had gone out. Now he was in. Now he was wearing pajamas. Now he was dead.

I've gone mad, Clare thought and experienced the briefest breath of relief. If she were mad surely she'd forget soon.

"The dad was in the master bedroom," a fireman said before Officer Dunn asked.

"Jesus." Dunn thumbed the button on his shoulder mike, and for a bizarre instant Clare thought he was radioing Christ.

"Yeah, Sergeant Pate? I think we got the doer." He described Clare down to the wet sneakers without socks. "You can make book on it," he finished. "When the blast

hit she looks at the flames and says, 'Hallelujah.' Yeah.
I kid you not. A Susan Smith is my guess.

"Nobody touches anything," he said to the firemen,
then jogged toward the Donovans'.

For a minute Clare continued to sit, legs dangling,
mind dangling. The policeman thought she had killed
Vee and Dana. The incomprehensible insanity of such
an act rendered his opinion void. There were those who
believed the world was flat, that aliens walked among
us, that God made the world in seven days. These people
didn't matter to Clare. She worked in fictional realms
but lived in the real world. Actors had a better grasp of
reality than other people. Perhaps because they spent so
much of their time trying to re-create it onstage.

The little bodies were removed. The big body was
covered up. Clare didn't need to be here anymore. She
didn't need to be anywhere anymore. Like all children,
Vee and Dana had secret passages. Like all mothers,
Clare knew about them. Picking up Mackie, she drifted
into the darkness of the trees behind the ambulance
and moved along the dense hedge running between her
house and that of the neighbor to the north. A few
yards down she and the dog pushed into the leaves and
were gone.

An intruder light, hooked to a motion sensor on the
side of the garage next door, flared on, and the ivory of
David's coat lit up. Not wishing to be in a world where
people killed their own children, Clare let the coat drop
from her shoulders. Beneath it she wore only a pink

satin nightgown that fell to midthigh. Not subtle. Not invisible. Feeling schizophrenic, a ghost and a corpus, she watched her hands turn the coat inside out, hiding the light color and replacing it with brown-and-burgundy plaid.

As she pulled the coat back on she had a respite so short it felt like a spark in a windstorm: For half an instant she was a spy, a lunatic, a character in a matinee of *Drood*.

Anything, anything, was better than being Clare Sullivan.

"Someone will find you," she whispered apologetically as she tied Mackie to the neighbor's glider with the cloth belt from the raincoat. "Stay." In the heartbreakingly trustful way of his kind, Mack stayed and did not bark as she walked away.

Because of the vagaries of sound, suddenly Clare heard a single sentence loud and clear from the other side of the hedge, "I'm glad Washington has the death penalty."

Too bad they seldom used it. There would probably be no help there; no kind needle to take her from this place before the true and crushing weight of what had happened hit. Before she went crazy: memories cutting when recalled, cutting sharper when forgotten, sleeping in nightmare, waking to worse. For the length of an indrawn breath she saw herself in a straitjacket crouched in front of an old-style radiator covered in layers of paint. Above it was a window, opaque with years of grime and further darkened by heavy black wire mesh. Nothing sharp, nothing pointed, nothing edged. No way out of life. Clare staggered and nearly fell as she moved out of the yard. Where her children had once been was a terrible hole, a black hole in inner space. Should she fall into it she would be taken to that room with the radiator, and, once there, she'd be kept alive.

For years.

And years.

Turning from the streetlight into the greater dark of the alleyway, she forced her thoughts to her husband, David. Daoud. He was dead; she was a widow. The thought left her strangely unmoved. She stopped. A stream of water trickling down the alley dammed up behind her heels to run over the back of her shoes. The cold and the wet went unnoticed.

Hyperaware of feelings, Clare was unaccustomed to having none. She hadn't hated David, nor had she loved him, not for a long time. David controlled, had to control: her, the girls, everything. He never hit her, never lifted a hand to the girls. There was nothing that would be called verbal abuse in modern courts. He'd not interfered with her work at Seattle Repertory so long as it did not interfere with his comfort.

David controlled with money and ice.

Leaving was not an option. David would never give her the girls. He'd told her that, and she'd believed him. If she'd ever dared look like she might try to take them he swore he would spirit them off to the Middle East to be raised by his mother and sisters. He could and would do it, Clare knew, no matter what legal pressures she might try to bring to bear.

David manufactured clothing. Most of his workers were women from Pakistan, India, and Nepal. They appeared and disappeared from his factory near Puget Sound with unremarked rapidity. Many were illegal, Clare suspected, but she never would have reported David, even if her welfare hadn't been wedded to his by a justice of the peace. Though the wages his factory paid were low, the women were probably better off than they had been in their home countries. Why else come to the Promised Land?

Clare knew she'd been complicit in her easy imprisonment. David made good money. It allowed her and the girls to live well, and since Jalila had come over from Saudi Arabia a year before, there hadn't even been the unpleasantness of sex. David and Jalila were lovers. Clare'd suspected from the first week the au pair had arrived—and she hadn't cared. Jalila was not David's first, just the first he'd brought home.

Clare's strongest emotion concerning the affair was a vague sense of pity for the mistress. She would even have been glad Jalila's body was not among those carried from the house had she been capable of gladness.

The water in her shoes finally penetrated the cloud of thought, and she woke to the alley, the stink of smoke, the remembering. She began to move. Suicide was not a new thought. At one point in her life—not a point so much as a plane, it had lasted seven years—death had been her fail-safe plan. Over time Death had become her comforter, the friend she turned to when life became untenable. Then Dana was born and Death lost a devotee. It was incomprehensible that she leave that child, and, if an absolute could be doubled, twice as incomprehensible once Vee came into the world.

Now Death was the only place she could look without seeing corpses. The only place where even the smallest spark of hope resided. The gods, if gods there were, must love irony.

Shock or post-traumatic stress or God or something very like took her mind for a while. Clare walked and did not run. She stepped up curbs and turned corners without any sense of where she went. Occasionally she was peripherally aware of blue strobing lights, the faint wail of sirens, of rain or no rain.

In time she came back into herself; eyes began to see, ears to hear. Whatever had driven her, ridden her, had brought her full circle. She was standing in front of the all-night pharmacy where she'd gone for Vee's cough medicine so many thousands of years before. For a brief and glorious moment she believed the clock had miraculously been turned back, that she'd left home only minutes ago, and, if she turned and ran, she would be able to find the girls, get them out of the house before it exploded.

Except they hadn't been in the house.

And then they had.

Clare opened the door and went inside. In the old dark days when Death was her bodyguard, ready to snatch her from fates worse than He, she'd had the luxury of time to prepare for their meeting: to buy a gun, pills, a rope, a car with emissions problems.

Tonight all she could think of was fire. From the starkly lit shelves she pulled out accelerants: rubbing alcohol, fingernail polish remover, and hair spray. Not for her the questionable dignity of a red gasoline can in the middle of Tiananmen Square. She'd go up like an American girl, reeking of perfume and paint.

At the checkout counter a sleepy middle-aged woman, made as garish and bleak as the shelves by late-night fluorescent lights, rang up her purchases.

"May I have some matches?" Clare asked and was stunned at how normal she sounded. At least to her own ears.

The woman behind the counter wasn't as sluggish as the hour and the lighting suggested. Her pale blue eyes darkened as she glanced at the inflammables on the counter.

"And a pack of cigarettes," Clare added. Vigilance relaxed.

"What kind?"

Clare hadn't smoked in twenty years. She pointed.

"Camel nonfilters?"

Clare nodded.

"You must have a death wish."

Clare returned to the alley behind the houses. It was important to be as close to where her daughters had been as possible, close enough her ashes could blow into theirs.

As she rounded the neighbor's garage, a sharp bark welcomed her. Mackie. She'd forgotten him. He was still tethered to the glider with the belt of her dead husband's raincoat. At the sight of his fuzzy face with its lopsided grin, the tongue ill-fitted to his mouth and peeking out one side, an upwelling of joy hit her so hard it nearly doubled her over. Happiness was betrayal. Proof she'd never deserved Vee and Dana, that some karmic how, some karmic where, she'd killed them. Falling to her knees, she tried to retch. Even this homage was denied her.

Inside out, the coat's pockets were next to her bare skin. On her hands and knees, the tops of the bottles touched her thighs above the lip of fabric. The faint pressure of cold plastic against her naked flesh brought back the life of the body: a cool breeze, the scent of lilacs. A memory came from the jangled mess of her mind: a little girl being bundled into her dad's bathrobe—a disreputable plaid flannel from Sears Roebuck. There in the dirt, Mackie whining in her ear, she remembered how safe she felt folded in the worn softness, in the smell of Lava and Aqua Velva.

David's robes were of silk; too fine to spill cocoa on, throw up in, or wet the bed in. Vee and Dana had never been bundled up in Daddy's robe. They never would be. A second recollection battened onto the first, the reason she had been in such need of comfort, and the warmth of the remembered flannel turned to flame. A sense memory of a burning log rolling from the fireplace onto her bare foot exploded in her skull: smell of cooking flesh, searing overwhelming pain. The vomit Clare had been denied came then, thin and sour.

She was afraid to die the way her children had died, and she hated herself for a coward.

SEVEN

Anna automatically stepped in front of Geneva to absorb any blows coming as punishment for her earlier good deed. If Sammy hadn't had such excellent reflexes, Geneva would have plowed into her.

"Can I help you?" Anna asked the punk, ranger-speak for "What in the hell are you doing here?"

The scruffy black dog danced over and greeted Sammy like an old friend.

"That you, Jordan?" Geneva called.

The singer had squatted on the brick, and the punk's dog wriggled gleefully under her hands.

"No. That's my dog," the man said and stood.

"I thought he smelled better," Geneva joked. "Anna, this is Jordan. Jordan rents the apartment on the other side of mine. Jordan, this is Anna Pigeon, a *fed-ee-ral law en-force-ment agent*." She drew out the words the way she always did, and Anna suspected it indicated equal parts rebellion and respect.

It meant something altogether different to Punk Jordan. He lost the ability or the desire to look Anna in the eye, focusing instead on the ground to the far right so his face could only be seen in partial profile. Shoulders, already stooped from the lash of his personal demons, rounded down further as if they were a cape he could use to hide himself.

As Anna watched the metamorphosis, she decided he looked guilty as hell. Maybe it was only that he'd made a feeble attempt to assault her earlier, but she doubted that was the whole of it. An educated guess was that Jordan was on the run from more than just demons.

Mumbling something that started with "I gotta" and trailed off unintelligibly, he slouched toward the side of the house where his apartment was, his dog at his heels. He'd said nothing about having met Anna before. For reasons she wasn't clear on, Anna decided not to say anything either.

"What do you know about Jordan?" she asked Geneva. Her voice was sharper than she'd intended, and Geneva, rooting through her bag for her house keys, stopped and shot a sardonic look over her shoulder. Why Ray-Bans and lack of vision did not inhibit her ability to do this, Anna wasn't sure.

It wasn't any of Anna's business who Geneva had as tenants, but, should her friend end up murdered, chopped into bits, and simmered on a stove top, as had happened to a woman mere blocks from where they stood, Anna wanted to at least be able to say, "I told you so." She pressed on.

"Did you get references? Do a security check on the guy?"

Geneva turned her attention back to the key search. "The rent is always paid on time and in cash. The little dog is sweet, and she's quiet. As a landlord it doesn't get much better. On occasion she smells a bit ripe, but the apartment didn't stink the couple of times I had to go in. That's all I need to know."

Geneva had gotten her back up. Anna would get no more out of her.

"She. The dog is quiet?"

"Only barks when this one old cat comes over the wall to kill my birds."

"She. The dog smells ripe?" Anna asked, remembering the silky brushed coat smelling of lilac.

"No. He's okay, but she can get a little whiffy."

Anna was still confused. "The dog is male?"

"I guess." Geneva had lost interest in the conversation and Anna couldn't blame her. Anna's questions— those that weren't prying or downright rude—sounded like the musings of a dullard fixed on canine behavior patterns. It wasn't species that had her baffled; it was gender.

A whirl of wind carrying bougainvillea blossoms and a few drops of rain rattled down through the trees into the courtyard. At the far edge of hearing, thunder murmured threats. Geneva threw back her head, face to the sky, arms open wide. "God, but I love thunderstorms," she exclaimed. "They make me feel like I could be lifted on the wind and fly."

Anna laughed. "Probably because where you grew up that was true."

"Tornadoes, I don't like," Geneva said.

"So you live in hurricane country?"

"Hurricanes don't sneak up on you and pounce. They don't single you out the way tornadoes do. Hurricanes aren't personal. I'll tell you one thing for sure," she said as she unlocked the French doors that led from the garden to the part of the house in which she lived. "Sammy and I are not evacuating again. The powers that be all got massive amounts of egg on their faces for screwing up with Katrina. Now every time a butterfly farts off the coast of Africa they issue mandatory evacuation notices."

The doors blew open, and Sammy trotted in, his leash snaking behind him. Once Geneva was home he was officially off duty. The change was as obvious as if he ripped off his tie and threw his suit jacket over the back of the couch.

"Do you want to come in for a drink?" Geneva asked.

"Sure. This sounds weird—"

"Everything you say sounds weird."

"—but do you think Jordan is a woman?"

"Jordan is a woman."

"Nope," Anna said. "He's a man, pathetic excuse for a mustache and all. Didn't you ask?"

"Right. 'By the by, now that you're going to be renting from me, might I inquire as to whether you have a penis or two? Could I see it? Oh, right, I'm blind. I'll need to feel it.' The name Jordan goes both ways; the voice does, too, I guess. Now I'm going to be all convoluted. For your information, I see quite clearly in my brain. I see this woman. Now it's like you snatched her up and presto change-o she's a guy. Thanks a heap."

Sammy got kibble, Anna and Geneva a California sauvignon blanc. They sat side by side on the sofa, their feet on a wide ottoman, and watched the rain, illuminated periodically by flashes of lightning, sluice down into the courtyard. Or, rather, Anna watched. Geneva listened to the pound of the rain and thunder and saw whatever memories of storms her four-year-old brain had treasured up for a rainy day.

An inky black cat, easily sixteen pounds, stretched across Geneva's ample lap, front paws extended so he could knead the edge of Anna's thigh whenever he felt her attention wandering from the admiration of his magnificence. M'Boya was never allowed out of doors. As a consequence, he never killed birds, and thus could he and the musician maintain a loving relationship.

Anna enjoyed a sip of wine and watched the liquid night through the convex lens of her glass. She and alcohol had a long and rich history. In her thirties she had declared herself an alcoholic and eschewed the stuff. After nearly losing her life—and losing a good friend—in the bowels of Lechuguilla Cave in New Mexico, she'd taken it up again, but it had never gotten the hold on her it had in the early days when she grieved for Zach. Now that she had apparently lucked into true love twice in a single lifetime, wine had become simply an old friend she visited from time to time.

"I should go," Anna said finally. The rain had stopped falling from the sky, but there was still the passive drip from trees, eaves, and vines. "I want to call Paul; see if I can catch him between things. He's being all things to all people at the moment. Port Gibson lost a deputy and a deacon. It falls to Paul to do triple duty till there are new hires."

Neither moved nor spoke for a moment, hypnotized by the darkness and the dripping of the rain.

M'Boya reached out a black paw, invisible but for the sheen on his fur from a patio light on the far side of the walled garden, and sank the tips of his claws into Anna's flesh. Spell broken, she pushed up from the sofa. "See you in the morning," she said to her three hosts.

"Anna?" Geneva's voice stopped her as she was stepping through the French doors.

"Yeah?"

"Jordan is really a guy? This is not some cruel hoax perpetrated on the visually handicapped but massively talented?"

"Jordan is a guy," Anna affirmed.

Geneva groaned theatrically. "My reality has crumbled. My self-confidence at an all-time low. I must ask you a personal question."

Anna didn't much like being on the receiving end of personal questions, but she was, after all, a guest.

"Shoot," she said.

"Please be blunt with me. I'm a big girl. I can take it. Tell me, do you have a penis?"

"I do," Anna replied gravely, "but it is not with me at present. More's the pity."

Closing the doors quietly behind her, Anna paused a minute to breathe in New Orleans in spring after rain. In the mountains and deserts of the West there would be the ozone and pine, sage and dust—scents that cleared the head and the vision, made the heart race and the horizon impossibly far away and alluring.

Here spring's perfume was lazy and narcotic, hinting of hidden things, languid hours, and secrets whispered on breath smelling of bourbon and mint. In Rocky Mountain National Park, the clean dry air scoured the skin, polished bone, and honed Anna's senses to a keen edge. Here it caressed, nurturing flesh with moisture, curling wind-sere hair. It coddled and swathed till believing in dreams and magic seemed inevitable.

The Big Easy, Anna thought, letting the darkness carry her past the still fountain and into the guest cottage. Easy living, easy dying, easy come, easy go: It was as much a place of tides as the ocean that waited beyond the levees to reclaim it.

The guesthouse's bedroom was on the third floor. The bath was on the second along with an armoire. A living-room-cum-kitchen took up the ground floor. Three rooms stacked one on top of the other with a zigzag ledge of a stairway that would have intimidated a mountain goat stitching them together. The building dated from the 1800s. Everything else was a hodgepodge of eras, half-finished projects, and passing fads. The bathtub was a relic of the 1970s, big and pink and square, and the kitchen and living room were an uneasy alliance of dark wood veneer paneling and fifties Formica.

The bedroom was the saving grace. None of the bright ideas of owners over the years had made it to the third floor, and, though it was as seedy as the last gasp of a failing octogenarian and the NPS salary of Geneva, her one living heir, would suggest, Anna found it charming: worn hardwood floors, peeling white-painted cornices, yellowing wallpaper, sconce lighting, and two-inch-thick hardwood-and-antique-glass French doors opening onto a balcony twenty-four inches deep and seven feet wide.

The room was as close to a tree house as grown-ups usually got. The place had running water but no electricity. That, too, Anna liked. She'd lit her way up the narrow stairs connecting the vertical home with a kerosene lantern with a chimney and a heavy glass base and set it on the room's only table, a battered TV tray scarred and daubed with so many colors of paint Anna guessed it had served a number of years in somebody's studio before it got recalled for house duty.

A double bed, looking tiny after decades of queens and kings, leaned against the back wall. It had a painted iron head and footboard, the metal twisted into vines and beaten into leaves. The only other furniture in the room was a lawn chair, the kind Anna remembered from picnics as a kid, an aluminum tubing frame with woven plastic strips riveted on for the seat and back.

Having opened the French doors wide, she blew out the lamp and dragged the patio chair to the edge of the balcony. When she'd first arrived she'd hazarded a step out from the doors, but the resulting creaks and groans had undermined any faith she might have had in its structural integrity.

Settling in, the breeze stirring life into the rain-wet leaves of her bower till they twinkled with captured fragments of city lights, she dug her cell phone out of her backpack to call Paul. Her husband's home and work numbers were both on her contact list, but she didn't use it. Numbers important to her she kept sharp in memory because somewhere, sometime, technology always failed and one was left to rely on one's wits.

Before she had punched in the last number, movement in the courtyard below caught her attention. Folding the phone shut, she stood and stepped silently to one side of the French doors. The tail end of the thunderstorms that had racketed around the city for the past few hours tossed tendrils of vines and stirred the leaves of the oak that sheltered several houses under its wide umbrella.

Abandoning a phone call to her lover to watch in silence and darkness was natural to Anna. Fleetingly she wondered if that in itself was unnatural. Did other people habitually still themselves to listen and wait to see what or who walked unknown and uninvited into their camp? Anna's watchfulness wasn't born of fear, or at least it wasn't most of the time. It was because she loved watching creatures—deer, grizzlies, mountain lions, foxes, jackrabbits—in their natural habitat. At ease in their perceived privacy, they would startle and run if she intruded, so she'd learned to be still.

Relaxed, breathing gently, she waited to see if the marauding neighbor cat had come in to hunt. It could even be a raccoon. Absurd as it seemed, raccoons did occasionally find their way into the gardens in the Quarter.

A slim shadow slipped out from the walkway on the far side of the house. Jordan, probably out for a smoke. Anna was about to leave him to it when he looked furtively up at her darkened windows; not a casual glance or a voyeuristic stare but a hunch-shouldered, head-ducking peek that would have landed him the role of Uriah Heep if she were holding auditions for *David Copperfield*.

He didn't see her; that was obvious by the way his eyes, dark smudges in a pale oval face, darted quickly from her balcony. Determining he was unobserved, he hurried across the courtyard with quick catlike steps. Cradled in his left arm was a parcel wrapped in white paper or cloth. As quietly as the feral cat he put her in mind of, he turned down Geneva's side of the house. Another iron door at the end of the alley on his side opened to the sidewalk. Anna had seen it from the street; separate entrances provided a nice bit of privacy for both landlady and tenant. Given he didn't need to cross by both Anna's and Geneva's glass houses to come or go, why creep down Geneva's alley in the dead of night?

Anna drifted back from the windows and padded

quickly down the two flights of stairs to the ground floor. She wasted no time trying to be sneaky; each step had its own complaint. Traversed they sounded like a chorus of very old women levering themselves out of overstuffed chairs.

Reaching the front of the cottage, she stopped. The panes of glass in the door were wavy with age and fogged with grime but clear enough to let her see a grown man less than twenty feet away. The only reason Anna could think of for a nocturnal foray into the landlady's territory was mischief. Halfway down the skinny ribbon of path, another set of French doors let into Geneva's kitchen. She never used them. Her aunt had nailed them shut for reasons she'd taken with her to the crypt. Jordan might not know that. He might see it as a good place to break in.

Stupid, Anna thought. Sammy would bark. The guy had just been informed a federal law enforcement officer had moved in next door. Jordan didn't strike Anna as stupid; massively unbalanced, yes, but smart.

The characteristic *whump* of a hinged plastic lid falling closed on a garbage bin let Anna know it was she who drew the short straw in the cerebral sweepstakes. Jordan reappeared walking normally, no parcel under his arm. Anna had successfully surveilled a young man taking out the trash. She considered going back upstairs, calling Paul, taking a bath, but she didn't move.

Jordan hadn't carried the parcel like it was garbage. One didn't cradle garbage in the crook of an arm as if it were a baby. Jordan didn't move like a man on a domestic errand either. Normal people don't creep like the fog on little cat's feet checking windows to be sure they're unobserved when they dump the wastebasket.

Anna sighed, a sound so like the wind in the foliage she scarcely noticed she'd made it. "Go ahead," she whispered. "Get it over with." Her daypack with the Maglite she carried was upstairs by the folding chair. She retrieved the little flashlight, let herself out of the cottage, and followed Jordan's path with the same stealth he had exhibited.

Treading lightly into the greater darkness of the vine-shrouded walk, it occurred to her that maybe Jordan had been sneaking for the same reason she was. Maybe he was not embarked on evil, but doing something foolish and didn't want to get caught.

Maglite in her mouth, using both hands to raise the hinged lid so it would not bang against the house and rouse Geneva, Anna looked into the collected refuse. A cockroach trundled across a banana peel laid like a yellow brick road over a mound of coffee grounds. In other places Anna had lived, cockroaches had the decency to skitter and run from the light. In the Crescent City, they ambled.

Newspapers, crumpled as if they were going to be used as packing material, were piled up against the far side of the bin. Wishing she'd had the foresight to get a pair of latex gloves out of her first aid kit, Anna gingerly pinched a corner of the paper and moved it over the cockroach's run.

Under this hasty covering was the parcel Jordan had thrown away.

The fabric had been torn in a rough square, from a bedsheet, Anna guessed, and one that was none too clean before its ultimate sacrifice to the ragbag. The corners of the cloth were tied up, making a bundle reminiscent of the sacks cartoon hobos carried on a stick over their shoulder.

Gingerly she closed her hand over the knotted corners of the bundle and hefted it experimentally. Soft dead weight pulled the makeshift hammock into a rubbery curve. Rust-colored spots speckled the side and pooled into a stain where the bundle had rested on something other than the trash; the pooling was on the side of the fabric, not the bottom.

Anna set it on the bricks between her feet. Wind, still warm and heavy with moisture, gusted from all directions, carrying leaves and litter on its feathered back. It was the kind of wind that made Anna's cats rampage around the house; that made her feel wild and dark. It snatched at the cloth, fluttering it with sudden life, and she jerked her hands back. Belief in things unseen was carried on the air in New Orleans, and Anna's hardheaded rejection of superstition momentarily abandoned her.

"I'm going in," she whispered to the spirits on the breeze. "Cover me." Smiling to herself, she teased the knots from the corners and pulled them apart.

It was a pigeon. Dead.

For a cold moment she believed the message was for

her, a pigeon for a Pigeon. The parcel hadn't been delivered to her, however; it had been put in the garbage in such a way that she might never find it. Using the fabric to roll the bird from side to side, Anna looked it over. Its head had been crushed and its right wing twisted as if someone had wrung it the way a washerwoman would wring a mop. What she'd taken for random blood seeps from the outside were crude but intricate drawings done in blood and probably with a fingernail or stick. The figure looked like a cross on an altar with coffins or pineapples to either side. Anna had no idea what, if anything, it was supposed to mean. She turned her attention back to the bird. Despite the scribbling in blood, it was possible Jordan had found the bird dead rather than killed it. Either way a sick mind worked behind it, sick and dangerous.

Gently she rolled the bird onto its back. A wooden skewer, slender and smooth—the kind that could be bought anywhere for backyard shish kebab—had been colored black and green with a Magic Marker, then plunged into the pigeon's breast. Blood blossomed around the puncture.

So much for the found-dead school of thought.

Rocking back on her heels like a Bedouin, Anna retied the corners of the cloth, then stared down the narrow brick path. The murder of an animal, however humble the beast or lowly by society's standards, always hurt her in a deep and personal way. "Bastard," she whispered, then, having gathered up the butchered bird, rose to her feet, staggered, and saved herself from falling by grabbing the trash bin, an action that dragged an ache from the soft tissue below her arm where a bullet had gone through a month before.

Two months prior to the bullet a psychopath had smashed her ankle with a wrench, and, though these wounds had ostensibly healed, her body could no longer be trusted. Periodically the bones and flesh remembered the brutal injustice and collapsed in a welter of self-pity.

Or revenge. If the body and the mind/spirit were not, indeed, one, but separate entities as many religions suggested, her mind had a lot to answer for. Her ankle and underarm weren't the only portions of her anatomy that had been sacrificed to whatever she believed to be the greater good at the time.

Maybe old age was the inevitable revolution of the oppressed before the dictator is ousted from the land. Anna hoped, when the time came, the coup would be quick and not a prolonged uncivil war between flesh and spirit.

Anna put the tortured pigeon, in its tawdry shroud, back into the trash and closed the lid. Harming animals, even those as unappealing as subway rats and city pigeons, saddened her on a level violence to humans did not. There was no point to it, nothing to be gained, no power to usurp, no obstacle removed: It was cruelty for cruelty's sake, the basest instinct made manifest.

As the thought rolled unspoken through her mind, another rose to contradict it. This bird had been tortured and killed, but the colored stick, the markings on

the cloth, suggested voodoo. Voodoo was still practiced in New Orleans, a mishmash of African beliefs
and lore and superstitions that had sprung up in the
South to encompass all kinds of magics—or what dev-
otees believed were magics: spells, curses, rituals, love
potions, pointing the bone—a killing curse, if Anna
remembered—zombies, spirits, gods, snakes.

It was possible her new neighbor Jordan, the tattooed gutter punk with hostility toward women who
saved dogs, was into the dark arts.

EIGHT

Slowly Anna walked back to the cottage. The sensuous embrace of the city and the storm, of ancient trees and vine-covered walls, had changed subtly. Beneath the fecundity and the history, she sensed a core of rot, the feeling that New Orleans's endless party was in the spirit of Nero fiddling while Rome burned or musicians playing on the deck of the *Titanic* as the lifeboats were lowered into the sea.

Men and women singing the blues and blowing jazz while their sons and brothers shot each other down in the streets of Center City.

Closing the door behind her, she leaned against it and let the dark thoughts clear from her head. Over the past winter she had more or less lost her wits. This spring she had found most of them again. Still, she wasn't yet strong enough to walk on the dark side for any length of time. It was too easy to go from a dead bird in a trash can to the sorrow of the world, to see the rust and rot and gangrene rather than the beauty in her surroundings.

"Yea, though I walk through the valley of the shadow of death," Anna whispered. Paul had once suggested the valley of the shadow was simply a way to describe life because in life one was in death, dying from the moment of one's birth. He didn't seem to think it was a somber thought at all, only a perfectly natural journey toward a land where death didn't hold so much sway.

Anna shook off the arguable comfort of Paul's words. They, too, seemed to lead toward a grimness of mind she wasn't interested in.

"Hi, Molly, it's me, Anna," she said into the cell phone. In the dark, windows open onto the balcony, she lay across the double bed in her tree house.

"To what do I owe this honor?" her sister asked with only a hint of sourness. Anna had been actively not calling her for a while. She'd been afraid she was too crazy and Molly would spot it. Now that sanity was just around the corner, she'd felt safe enough to let her sister in.

"Voodoo," she said.

"What? Somebody made a little Anna doll and stuck a telephone in its ear?"

"I'm in New Orleans, and some weirdo voodooed a pigeon and put it in the garbage where I'm staying."

"And because I'm a psychiatrist, you figure I'm very nearly a voodoo practitioner myself?"

Anna laughed because that was precisely what she

thought. "Didn't you have to study that stuff some-where along the line? Drugging people into zombies, behavior modification, repressed memories, multiple personalities, Rorschach tests?"

Molly thought for a moment, the comfortable—comfortable because it was familiar—silence between the sisters strung cross-country by telephone wires or, with the advent of cell phones, without wires at all. The ultimate voodoo.

"Actually we did. It was a long time ago. We're mostly into drug therapy these days, and doggone if it doesn't actually work. Though there are not nearly so many funny stories to tell at cocktail parties as there were in the good old days of analysis."

"Tell me," Anna said and wriggled down more comfortably in the bed. The motion set the springs to singing like a comic chorus in a French farce.

"Are you alone?" Molly asked as if on cue.

"Yes. Old bed. Bed with springs, no less."

"Ah. For a moment I thought you were having more fun than me. From what I remember, voodoo, curses, pins in dolls, spells—all that kind of thing—require belief in the power of magic on the part of the victim and a perpetrator with a powerful personality to be efficacious—the flip side of the placebo effect, a blend of hypnosis, faith, and intimidation. If mind-altering drugs are used, the effect is considerably enhanced. There are quite a few fairly credible accounts of people dying of curses or of being made into what the popular literature would call 'zombies.' If you believe the pigeon in the garbage means you will die, then you're doomed. That is, unless you go to a graveyard, swing a dead cat around your head three times, and say, 'Devil be gone.' "

Anna laughed. "How about Frederick?" she asked. Frederick was Molly's husband. A retired FBI agent, he now made a tidy living renting himself out as a cyber-detective, hunting mostly money but occasionally fugitives, throughout the World Wide Web.

"Freddy? Do you know anything about voodoo?" Molly called, presumably across their spacious Upper West Side apartment. There was a moment of faraway sounds; then Molly returned. "All Frederick knows is 'voodoo science,' the term they gave to the work the two jackass psychologists came up with to justify the torture of prisoners at Guantanamo and other black holes. Is there any more to the story?"

Starting at the levee, Anna took Molly through the many twists and turns till she was squatting on wet brick in a narrow alley fiddling around with a dead bird.

When she'd finished, Molly said, "The guy's possibly on drugs. If not, maybe he should be."

"I think he probably should be. During his myriad examples of bizarreness I never got the sense he was high, but there's something going on. He looks like he has a wasting disease that's burning him at his own personal stake."

"Maybe he was the target of a vodun, a mambo, or a loup-garou—see, I did remember something. A mambo is a witch, and I think a loup-garou is a werewolf. Google it before you embarrass yourself by assuming I'm right," Molly suggested.

Anna'd been so swayed by the pigeon it hadn't occurred to her that Jordan might have gotten crosswise with someone who believed in the practice—or believed the punk did—and was being stalked. It made sense. He had tried to hide the thing, not to use it to affect Anna's behavior, and, after all, that was the point of these things, she supposed.

"I have to think about that," she said. "He's the kind of guy who probably doesn't make friends easily, what with the reeking clothes and penchant for sudden unexplained violence."

"Sounds like half the people you've met in the backcountry," Molly laughed.

Anna was offended. Backcountry people were the nicest people in the world. Since she'd just been stomped and shot by a couple, though, she didn't think it was the best time to argue the point.

They talked a while longer. Then Anna tried Paul again, but he wasn't answering. When she'd married him, she'd chosen not to worry when she couldn't get in touch. Both his job and hers guaranteed there would be times when answering phones was not reasonable. Not yet ready to sleep, she filled the funky tub—set corner to corner in the square of Pepto Bismol–colored plastic—and set the kerosene lamp on one of the solid corners.

The more she thought about it, the more likely it

seemed that Molly's hunch was correct, that Jordan and not Anna was the target of the messenger pigeon. She hadn't been in town long enough to ruffle anyone's feathers so badly they'd resort to complex and messy magic to dispose of her. Jordan would have had to be quick to have gotten it all together between the time he discovered he and Anna were neighbors and the moment of the trash dump. Less than three hours all told; not much time for capture, torture, painting, and wrapping. Not to mention there were surely lengthy spells or incantations with this sort of thing.

Anna had been raised without religion of any sort. Her parents neither attended church nor read the Bible. They had no objection to Anna and Molly trying out churches with their friends, going to church camps if the opportunity knocked, or weaseling into a Christmas pageant when the acting bug was upon them. Neither parent was outspokenly atheist; both bowed to the concept that there was probably something, but never evinced any particular interest in trying to guess what that something was, what form it would take, or what it required of them.

Anna'd grown up with that, and it seemed a particularly sensible way to live. As she'd gotten older her view of believers shifted from disinterest to mild alarm. Faith could move mountains. It could also put Jesus' face on a pancake, destroy statues of Buddha, raze cities, and, in the case of voodoo, entice the powerless to feel powerful by promising that words and weeds and bits of bone could get them what they wanted or destroy what they feared or hated.

From what Anna had seen of the commercial side of voodoo, it was more a craft than a religion. Faith was important, but so were recipes. It was hands-on, much like primitive Catholicism and other fundamentalist belief systems. One of the major tenets was that humans can barter with the gods, offer prayers or actions, sacrifices or money, and, in return, get an intervention here on earth.

Sitting up in the tub, she pulled the plug and stared down at her body. In her own way she had made a number of animal sacrifices for her beliefs; unfortunately, the only animal she seemed willing to skewer was herself. Across her abdomen was the raised white weal of scar tissue left behind when she'd been cut with a fish gaff. The still-healing bullet wound from the through-and-through of the soft tissue under her arm was angry purple and puckered. Given the depredations of the life of a small creature at odds with bigger creatures, she figured she was in decent shape. Scars on the outside simply kept score; it was the scars on the inside one had to watch out for.

Levering herself out of the tub, she toweled off. No electricity, no air-conditioning; the cottage wasn't hot, but the humidity was so high she didn't feel a great deal dryer out of the tub than she had in. Damp and drowsy, she padded naked to her bower and her squeaky bed.

The last of the wind put her to sleep. She dreamed,

as she often did, of those whose lives she had failed to save. That she seldom dreamed of those whose lives she'd taken was a blessing she never forgot to count.

Geneva's set was from noon to one. Anna closed *At Home in Mitford* and looked out from her tree house. It had been a long time since she'd done nothing, and she was rusty at it. Awake at 6:00 A.M., and suffering the need to do something productive since she'd finished her coffee, it had taken a heroic effort not to give in and tidy the bungalow, pull weeds from the garden, *do* something. One of the reasons she'd retired from Port Gibson to Geneva's backyard during Paul's marathon sheriffing and priesting duties was because, at someone else's house, there was nothing to do. At home, even a home as unfamiliar as Paul's neat two-story house in Mississippi, Anna could not resist the need to stay busy. When she'd caught herself, wounded side aching, bum ankle threatening to buckle, scraping paint from a screen door at 7:00 P.M., she'd called Geneva.

Anna loved to work, loved to push her body and her mind, loved to cover distance and to capture stillness, lift heavy objects and glide quiet as an otter through lakes. Working was a good thing. Compulsively keeping busy was a way to hide. What she was hiding from wasn't any mystery: She had a husband in Mississippi, a job in Colorado, and was not, at the moment, one hundred percent committed to either. Paul should have been a shoo-in if it came down to an either/or choice. Anna loved him like she hadn't thought possible after her first husband, Zach, had died. She had sworn to love and honor him till death them did part, and she had no objection to that.

The only thing between her and Paul Davidson was hundreds of miles of American soil. Paul had two more years to serve out his stint as sheriff of Adams County. Though he would do it if their marriage—or her happiness—depended on it, she couldn't ask him to leave early, not when so many people counted on him.

Their love—and their ages—being sufficient, she believed they could survive a long-distance relationship. The question she'd been avoiding with busyness and other neurosis was whether or not she could go on being a ranger. Not just being away from Paul—though that had become increasingly unpleasant as she grew to know him more deeply—but working for the National Park Service.

There were a lot of NPS jobs that didn't require the wilderness, guns, backpacks, compasses, and campfires. Probably a majority of the jobs were city jobs, office jobs. Geneva worked in the French Quarter. Interpretive rangers had roamed the Quarter interpreting the history for tourists until local tour guides protested. Rangers often "homesteaded," stayed at one park for the bulk of their careers, lived in towns, had children, and bought houses just like real people. Anna could get a job like that.

For her, though, national parks—despite the fact she was about to go to one where a row of chairs and musicians made up the biggest part of the draw—were about the wild places.

Throwing aside these thoughts as another form of busyness not suited to a lady of leisure, Anna caught up her daypack and pattered down the stairs and out into the courtyard. She hadn't seen Jordan this morning and wondered if he was back at the river walk playing punk with his tattooed pals.

Geneva's tenant was a study in misconnections. He hung with the gutter punks—or had been with them when Anna'd first noticed him—but wasn't homeless and, according to Geneva, paid his rent on time, so he wasn't without an income. His personal hygiene was such that a person of taste and discernment wouldn't choose to be downwind of him, yet his mutt was shampooed and brushed to scented softness. He'd nearly taken Anna down for trying to keep his dog from running away, viciousness boiling off him till she'd been surprised it hadn't manifested in frothing at the mouth or a heat mirage radiating from his dusky skin, but was charming and gentle with Geneva and Sammy.

The man's peculiarities on her mind, Anna stopped at the trash bin intent on retrieving the sacrificed pigeon. In the dark and drizzle she hadn't studied it properly.

The French Quarter's new garbage czar, a handsome young man who'd managed to make hauling trash a glamorous profession, was too efficient. The bin was empty.

"Rats," Anna muttered and, letting herself out onto Ursulines, tried to remember the disposition of the little avian corpse and, most particularly, the symbols or diagrams that had been sketched in blood on its shroud.

Across Dumaine, a block from New Orleans's Historic Voodoo Museum, was the magic shop Vieux Dieux. The museum might have provided more scholarly observations but, when dealing with the bizarre, Anna's instinct told her to go with the practitioners of the bizarre. She didn't want an intellectual; she wanted a witch.

Vieux Dieux's door was open and, beside it, a strange sculpture of a many-armed creature sitting in what had, at one time, been a birdbath. To the right of the door was a large picture window, sans glass, shutters folded to either side and used as display boards, one for T-shirts printed in a pastiche of skulls and other sinister clichés, the other supporting a black signboard as long and thin as the shutter it leaned against. Hand lettered in white was a menu of the shop's specials: Magiks, Spells, Curses, Psychic Self-Defense, Tarot, Love Potions, and, at the bottom but written with no less respect, Souvenirs.

Anna left the bright sunlit street and entered the dim confines. The shop felt witchy enough—a little kitschy as well, but even practitioners of the occult needed to make a living. It was deserted: no customers, no salespeople, not even a black cat lounging amid the esoterica. Nobody.

At least nobody *visible,* Anna thought with a smile.

The tiny shop was stuffed with the necessities of a well-maintained occult life. The center had been given over to an island covered with tiers of gargoyles, demons, crosses, headstones, tiny tombs and zombies to go with them, sarcophagi and coffins, Barbie-sized skeletons, and rocks—with some arcane powers, Anna presumed. On a wire rack thrusting up from this macabre landscape was the solution to the world's problems just a shake away, vials filled with different colored powders and identified by neat hand-lettered instructions tied around the necks with bits of string. One could sprinkle bad luck or good luck, sprinkle away a bad boss, a sloppy neighbor, an abusive lover, or simply sprinkle general all-purpose Evil Repellent around the house. What the powders were comprised of was not disclosed. They varied in color and texture. To Anna they looked to be filled with Comet, colored sand, dried ground herbs, talcum powder mixed with blue glass beads, and a dozen other creative combinations.

Another rack held "witch bottles," squarish glass bottles about the size of Anna's palm with bits of stone and fabric and other magical ingredients inside. These Anna rather liked. They went one notch higher on the continuum of force. The powders fended off evil. The witch bottles actually caught the wickedness sent by the enemy and boomeranged it right back at him.

In the herbal display was a nod to the classics; eye of newt was represented, as was toe of frog.

The walls were as densely covered as the island. On a floor-to-ceiling shelf near the back of the shop were candles. Some were tall votives in holders that could be "dressed" for any specific event. What that meant, Anna could only imagine. Beneath these were strobe candles to be burned to grant wishes, bring relief, or cast spells—depending on the color of the wax. Anna's mind flashed on banks of votive candles burning before statues of the saints in cathedrals, each small flame representing a desire burning in someone's breast.

Vieux Dieux was crammed with the promise of fulfilling unfulfilled hopes, granting unrealized wishes, curing feelings of helplessness, yearnings for revenge, and unspoken anger. The knot that had sat in her belly like an undigested acorn since she'd seen Jordan's macabre donation to the refuse heap began to loosen.

Maybe the world needed more magic shops. Far better lonely, frightened souls come to this store, redolent with incense that could soothe, lure, avert, abate, and generally make the world a better place, than spend their hard-earned cash on the modern voodoo of psychology. Religion and old magic knew the power of faith and good theater.

Opposite the candles were books: vampires, witchcraft, tarot, vampires, herb cultivation, vampires, spells, histories, vampires. Anna learned voodoo had come with slaves from Africa to the West Indies, and as tribes were mixed in slavery, their religions were shared and reinvented, mingling gods and stories from the Dark Continent. This amalgam of belief systems was imported to New Orleans along with the enslaved believers. There was no single set of rules for the practice any more than there was for Christianity, where one church speaks in tongues, another prescribes penance to clear the soul of sin, and yet another baptizes dead ancestors.

Thumbing through the books on voodoo, she didn't find anything that looked like the symbols on the rag the bird had been wrapped in. She was about to move on to books on witchcraft when a silky voice insinuated itself into her solitude.

"Can I help you?"

Anna turned toward the source.

As befit the circumstances, a pale disembodied face manifested out of the gloom behind a dark drape sequestering the inner sanctum from the eyes of the uninitiated. Form coalesced around the specter, and a woman, not five feet tall and as fine-boned as a child, was standing behind a counter draped like an altar and lit by two votives. The effect was somewhat spoiled by the prosaic intrusion of a cash register and credit card machine.

The proprietress's hair was unremittingly black, parted in the center and grown to the middle of her back. Blunt-cut bangs hung straight and thick just above eyebrows plucked into thin arches that made her eyes seem larger than perhaps they were. A high-necked, long-sleeved, floor-dusting dress the same unrelieved black as her hair left only the white face and long-fingered white hands, devoid of rings or nail polish, exposed.

"I'm Patty," the apparition said.

Leticia, Serena, Cosmos, Guinevere: Anna would have taken in her stride. "Patty" took her off guard. "Surely not," she said, then, to cover her rudeness, added, "Yes, maybe you can help me. I found a dead pigeon that looked like it had been used in some sort of voodoo ritual."

Patty's lips thinned into a hard line, and the face Anna had taken to be in its thirties looked more like late forties. Anna stepped closer and folded her hands on the erstwhile altar. Unsure what she'd said to offend Madam Patty, she soldiered on.

"It had a stake—like a barbecue skewer—through its heart."

Patty turned so abruptly her long ink-stained hair swung out, ruffling across Anna's knuckles in a feathered kiss smelling of patchouli oil. Her back to Anna, the miniature voodooienne busied herself tidying a basket filled with mood rings, or what Anna took to be mood rings. For all she knew they could be zombies' teeth powdered into glittery resin, sure to bring down plague and pestilence or at least a bad case of acne.

"Voodoo is a peaceful religion," Patty said dismissively, her tone at odds with the stone face she'd recently whisked from Anna's view. "Kids will sometimes find a dead bird or rat or cat or something and fiddle with it to freak out their friends. It's nothing to do with magic, just pranks in bad taste."

The Amazing Patty was clearly a believer. She was reacting to the dead bird the way a rabbi might react to the news that hoodlums had carved a Star of David into the Baptists' cross down the block.

"I hope it wasn't child's play," Anna said. "The bird was alive when the stake pierced its heart. Runes were written in blood on the shroud." Anna had no idea whether or not the marks were runes. She didn't even know if the skewer had pierced the bird's heart or torn an artery or collapsed a lung or if the poor thing had died from shock at the pain and fear caused by rough handling. Patty's gravity and portentousness were contagious. Faith—or disinformation (a.k.a. lies)—was also contagious, and Anna had to remind herself that the only magic in the shop was the kind manufactured in the human mind.

The woman's pale hands quit playing across her inventory like spiders tapping out chopsticks. She turned to face Anna across the counter. For a long moment she studied Anna's face. Finding no malice, mockery, or slyness there, she relaxed.

"People want to believe the worst of voodoo the way they do of any religion not their own," Patty said with a trace of defiance. "They do the same with the Wiccan religion," she added, fluttering her fingers. They weren't as long as Anna'd first taken them to be. The nails extended a good inch past the tips of her fingers and appeared to be homegrown rather than acrylic. Maybe Patty really was a witch. Anna's nails split or broke before they were long enough to bother filing.

"Do you know anyone around here who might not be as peaceful as the rank and file?" Anna asked carefully. "Someone mean enough to kill a pigeon to make a point?"

"Modern voduns don't customarily sacrifice animals, and the few that are sacrificed are raised for it,

pampered. It's a gift, you see, and it has to be sacrificed
by the right person, someone who's trained for it. If just
anybody does it they won't see." To make her point she
drew her hands over her eyes, then covered her ears.

The spirit world, it would seem, was deaf and blind
to inappropriate sacrifice.

"It used to be common enough. Even into the thirties and forties. Your dead pigeon might have been killed
by somebody trying to make it look like a voodoo curse
to scare you."

"There are no throwbacks to the bad old days still
hanging around?" Anna asked. "Every religion has a
darker side. For every god, there's got to be a devil or a
demon to make him necessary."

"There is something called voodoo witchcraft,"
Patty admitted. "Just like there are people who practice
black magic. This could even have been a mix—hex and
voodoo—to give a spell added power. Voodoo witchcraft is that darker side. The practitioners of it don't
care who they hurt," she added with a bitterness that
suggested she had been on the receiving end of a dead
pigeon or two in her time.

"Come." Patty wove her way through the crowded
shop to the window that opened onto the sidewalk.
Anna followed. Beside the bookshelves was a narrow
doorway partially obscured by a curtain that she hadn't
noticed. Inside the protected alcove was a tiny round
table covered with symbols. A candle sat in the center.
A handwritten sign above the table read: KNOW THE
FUTURE $45.00.

Seers' clientele seemed ever unperturbed by the fact that the fortune-tellers hadn't made a killing at the racetracks or on the stock market. They simply believed and, in believing, didn't question. Faith and blind faith were not different things. What a comfort faith would be, Anna thought wistfully. Then, ushered into a chair between a scaly, fanged gargoyle and a bag of herbs guaranteed to deflect killing curses, she remembered faith and paranoia were two sides of the same coin.

Flanked by two straight-backed chairs, the table at which Patty seated her was in front of the window opening onto Dumaine. A nice marketing choice on Patty's part; a bit of theater to draw in customers.

When they were settled, Patty laid her hands, palms down, on the table, her fingers spread as if she expected the spirit world to knock or make the table dance. "Tell me," she said.

Anna described the dead pigeon in detail, including the symbols on the cloth as best she remembered them.

After she'd finished, Patty thought for a moment then said, "It's a psychic attack. Wait." She sprang to her feet, then flitted through the curtain into the alcove where the future waited to be unveiled for forty-five dollars.

"Shall I follow you?" Anna asked, starting to rise.

"No. I'm coming out." She reemerged in a whirl of black fabric, a battered trade paperback in her hands.

"*The Witches' Formulaic*," she said as she plopped it down on the table between them. "Spells and curses handed down the way cooks hand down recipes that work. It's out of print, but I can probably get you one."

Patty gracefully slid into her chair and flipped through the pages. "Here," she said, pointing to a page titled "Black Blood and Feathers." "This is a slash-and-run curse. There's a belief that it causes magical harm to the victim, but it's a public curse, meant for the neighbors to see."

"Intimidation?" Anna asked.

"Among other things." Patty leaned over the book and traced the words with one long fingernail as she read with undisguised relish: " 'Get a trussed black chicken,' *trussed,* what a wonderful sound. What is a *trussed* chicken, do you suppose?"

"Tied up," Anna said. "Usually by the feet."

"Trussed. I love learning new things." Patty went back to the book. " 'A *trussed* black chicken and a black candle. Hang the chicken up and burn the candle down to a nub beside the chicken, but not touching the chicken. Carry the nub and the chicken to the door of the house to be cursed. Hang the trussed fowl over the door. Drop the candle end some distance away, but not too far away. Slash the chicken's throat and run. Do not get any of the chicken's blood on your body or your clothes.' "

Color had come to Patty's cheeks, and she was gesturing and making faces as she mapped out the magical means to an end. For a witch who professed to be white, the owner of Vieux Dieux seemed at home and happy with birds and blood.

"Do you know anyone in the Quarter who might do a slash-and-run curse?" Anna asked.

Patty's lips pressed together as if she were blotting her lipstick, and her eyes slewed to the left, looking out of the window. She was about to get down and dirty with the gossip in the occult world, Anna thought. Witches weren't the only ones who could read signs.

"I had something like it happen to me." Her voice was barely above a whisper, and Anna had to lean in to catch all the words. "The shop on the next block, part-way down on the other side of the street, Authentic Voodoo—" Patty's long nails etched quotation marks around the word "authentic," and she rolled her eyes to underline her scorn. "This woman moves in like six months ago and opens the shop. She does this all-white thing: long blonde hair, white dress—too stupid for words. If you ask me, she looks more like Alice in Wonderland than a voodooienne—and she's got a mini-me! Her little girl gets the same exact dresses all in white. Her hair is the same long Disney thing with the white headband. They must go through a lot of authentic bleach—"

Patty stopped talking, and her eyes narrowed as she stared at Anna. "You know who left the pigeon," she said shrewdly.

"No," Anna started.

"You always know. You know." Patty was all business now, annoyed that Anna was trying to play her. "Let me see the symbols."

A long explanation wasn't going to rectify things, so

Anna did as she was told and sketched the symbols on the back of a Walmart receipt with a government pen she'd stolen at one time or another.

Patty looked at them for a few seconds, then shook her head. "I don't know what they mean. Maybe nothing," she said coolly.

Anna couldn't tell whether Patty didn't know or just wouldn't say. "The pigeon wasn't given to me," Anna said. "So I really don't know who might have done it. I honestly don't."

Patty softened marginally. "Who was it for?"

"A neighbor. A guy named Jordan. He lives up Ursulines."

Patty's eyebrows drew down till they formed a knot of flesh between them. "That creepy guy with the dog and the wispy chin hair? Stinks and hangs with the gutter punks?"

It always came as a surprise to Anna that cities weren't vast sprawls of humans unknown one to the other, but clusters of incestuous social groups no different than those in small towns or isolated parks. "That's him," she said.

Patty stood abruptly. "He probably did it himself for attention, or one of his greaseball friends did it as a joke." The interview most decidedly at an end, Patty left Anna seated at the table and headed back to the recesses of the shop.

"Thanks," Anna called after her.

Safe behind Vieux Dieux's altar to capitalism, one

hand resting on the credit card machine, the other on the cash register, Patty gave Anna a long level look. Anna wondered if she was trying to cast a spell on her.

In a low voice Patty said distinctly, "Life is not random. What appears evil might be necessity." In a more normal tone, she added, "Don't mess with this guy. He's not—" She seemed at a loss as to what Jordan wasn't.

Anna waited politely, but Patty turned her back, waggled white fingers in farewell, and vanished through the curtain behind the counter where she'd been when Anna first entered the shop.

NINE

Clare collapsed against the side of the glider. The wooden corner jabbed between her shoulders. She didn't mind the pain. Because dogs sense the emotions of their humans—or because he was cold—Mackie crawled into her lap. After a time of stillness, the intruding intruder light went out, leaving them in darkness made incomplete by orange streetlights burning the underside of the sky.

Lurid. The streetlights made things look lurid. Ever aware of language, the actor in Clare noted this but ascribed no meaning to it. Digging beneath the damp dog, she fumbled the Camels from the pocket of David's inside-out raincoat. Pack opened, she put one between her lips and lit it. She noticed without interest that, though she had stopped smoking years ago, her hands had never forgotten how to hold and strike, how to protect the nascent flame.

The first drag was like she'd never quit. She drew smoke and tar and carcinogens deep into her lungs. It was the least she could do. Closing her eyes, she let the smoke trickle from nose and mouth. The end of the world smelled of smoke, not the smoke of Turkish tobacco but the wet reeking smoke of lives ruined, goods destroyed by fire, futures incinerated. Tears ran from the corners of her eyes.

She didn't cry for Dana and Vee, for their pain, their fear. She didn't even cry for the pain she would bear over a lifetime of their loss. These things were too great for tears. Screaming and pounding one's face on the stones of the seashore, rending one's garments, raking the flesh from one's bones with broken fingernails as other cultures, other times, had recognized the need for, might have given some relief, but Clare wasn't them. Americans had no way of expressing the big emotions. Americans weren't even supposed to have them.

She cried because she cried. Then she slept because she was tired.

Childish whispers entered her dreams.

"She's on fire, like the house."

"No. Look. There's a cigarette in her hand."

"Smoking's bad for you."

"Doesn't matter. She's dead."

"Stop it. She's not. She's sleeping."

"No sir. Mackie's dead, too. Look at his tongue."

"His tongue's always like that."

"Wake her up. I'm cold."

Clare smiled. A little girl's voice. Vee. Dana. Something pushed into her eyelid; then light, piercing and painful, spiked into her brain. To escape it, she flailed.

The dog was dislodged. The ghosts scattered in a flutter of white cotton.

"See. Not dead."

"She smells dead."

The ghosts reconvened around the flashlight that Philip, at eleven the eldest Donovan child, shined into Clare's face.

"What are you kids doing out at this time of night?" Clare whispered because they had, because it seemed right. *Why did she still sound like a mom when she had no children?*

"Nobody would tell us anything," Philip said.

"So we came to see." This from eight-year-old Colt, who, if born a cat, would have been long dead from curiosity.

Crimson Rose, youngest but for the baby, was not yet six. She'd come because where her brothers went she went, and they were too besotted with their fairy-like sister with her waist-length hair and angel face to deny her much of anything. Standing close enough to Philip to keep one hand clamped on the folds of his bathrobe, she nodded gravely over the threadbare brown head of a stuffed dog.

Vee's stuffed dog; Sleepy Dog. A toy she'd gotten when she was three months old from Clare's sister, Gretchen. It had a bell in its tail and perennially shut eyes, the felt lashes worn nearly off from being loved so long by Vee. Vee never went to bed without it, carried the ragged toy with her from room to room when she was sick, made up stories and acted them out with

Sleepy Dog. It took a control Clare didn't know she still had not to snatch the stuffed animal from Crimson Rose and shriek at the child for profaning it. Lest this gossamer thread of discipline snap, Clare pushed herself to her feet. Her legs had gone to sleep, and she had to hold on to the glider to keep from falling.

"Are you sick?" Crimson Rose asked.

"Are you drunk?" Colt said at the same time.

"Let's get you guys back home," Clare said as she stomped life back into her limbs.

"There's policemen waiting for you," Philip told her as she gathered them in front of her to shoo them through the secret passage in the lilac hedge. "Can we wait and listen to them asking you stuff?"

Police. Of course there would be police. Clare had murdered her children. Somebody said that. The officer with the bum knee. As soon as they saw her they would lock her up. She shrugged, a spastic twitch of the shoulders. Since cowardice dictated she live, it didn't much matter where. Prison was as good a place as any.

The boys disappeared into the lilac branches. Crimson Rose, waiting patiently for Mackie to follow them, turned to Clare. She held out Vee's beloved Sleepy Dog and said, "I found this by Mr. David's big car. Will you give it to Vee? She won't sleep good if you don't."

Crimson Rose held up the dilapidated stuffed dog. Clare watched as, too quickly, her greedy hands pushed forward to grasp it. Then, with the speed of thought, which puts the speed of light to shame, jagged pictures clattered onto her brain pan: the house exploding—not burning, exploding—someone had dynamited it.

Did anyone but Wile E. Coyote use dynamite anymore? Wasn't it done with plastic or something? She shook the question off. It didn't matter. It didn't matter that bombers didn't target middle-aged clothing manufacturers and certainly didn't target character actors in small repertory companies. The house had been blown up because somebody wanted her dead, the girls dead, all of the Sullivans dead.

David—Daoud—was Saudi Arabian. A hate crime, maybe; there were skinheads in Seattle, mostly boys and men who had to hate somebody a little more than they hated themselves just to prove they weren't at the very bottom of the barrel.

David could have done it.

Clare startled herself with the thought. David had never been violent. The abuse that had sucked what love there might have been from the marriage was comprised of indifferent neglect and an iron-willed assumption of superiority. Not an assumption—it was stronger than that—an unassailable truth, a mandate from David's god. When things were done David's way, life was easy. When they were not, she and the girls froze in the northward of his opinion. When he was displeased, the three of them simply ceased to exist for him.

As did the money for them. Checkbooks became unavailable. Credit cards and ATM cards failed to work. Clare's salary from Seattle Rep wasn't enough to fund the enormous home and fuel-guzzling automobiles and private schools David felt necessary to his dignity and to theirs as members of his household.

Frustrating and embarrassing as that was, what always brought Clare to heel wasn't the money but Dana and Vee. They adored their handsome daddy—and he was handsome, almost faintingly so, a fact Clare seldom remembered till she saw other women looking at him. When David shut out his daughters, he broke their tender loving little hearts. Clare could bear anything but that.

Her mind raced on: Sleepy Dog by David's SUV, Mackie out of doors.

Why would Vee's favorite toy be outside the house? A freak of the explosion? Why was Mackie outside? A freak of the explosion might leave a stuffed dog intact, but it would surely kill a flesh-and-blood dog. Somebody had let him out. David, Jalila—somebody—had let the dog out. They had let Sleepy Dog out, too, out in Vee's arms. It was the only way the stuffed creature ever traveled.

Another girl, tiny, hair black as an obsidian knife, her hand held by a man with an odd accent, a man who'd jerked her arm, flashed behind Clare's eyes.

"Aisha," she'd said. Suddenly, blindingly, Clare knew why the word had sounded so familiar. Over the years with David, she had picked up a good deal of Arabic. Both girls were fluent in it. They and David and, this past year, Jalila chattered away in Arabic for hours together. Sometimes, Clare knew, they were shutting her out intentionally. So she'd learned.

Aisha, in Arabic, meant "alive."

Her children were alive.

The lion's share of her brain knew she was kidding herself, building her bright and shining castles upon the shifting sands; still, hope was life, and she couldn't let go of it. She held to the thought, and it took root. As she realigned her world to this new and wondrous possibility, it occurred to her that she had gone mad.

The bodies. The little burned bodies of children.

That was a precipice she could not afford to fall over. She would think about the bodies later, when she was stronger. *I'll think about it tomorrow, at Tara. After all, tomorrow is another day.* Her brain rattled out the lines from a *Gone With the Wind* monologue she hadn't thought of in fifteen years, and again the possibility of madness threw its shadow over her mind. The shadow was not as dark as the hard night of reality, and without conscious thought Clare chose to embrace it.

The police were waiting. They'd seen the bodies. They'd know soon, if they didn't already, that she and David weren't Ozzie and Harriet; that David was cheating on her under her own roof with a woman who looked after her children. They—the all-powerful and faceless They—would never believe that she didn't mind.

Arrest, questions, scrutiny, and arraignment: All this would take time. With a surety she'd seldom experienced even when contemplating the sun's rising in the morning or death or taxes, Clare knew Time was her enemy. Time was running off with her daughter, maybe both her daughters.

"You run, Crimson, honey, you run and catch your brothers and tell them not to tell the police you guys saw me. Okay? Can you do that? It's a game we're going to play. I'm hiding and the police are seeking. Can you do that?"

The perfect oval face turned up to her, the sick orange of the sodium vapor lamps unable to transform it from its celestial lines. "It's not a game," Crimson Rose said. "They think you did something bad. Did you?"

Clare fell to her knees. "No, honey, no, I didn't. I've lost my girls, and I have to find them. Nobody but me knows they're waiting for me." She put her arms around Crimson the way she had a hundred times over the years the Donovan children and hers had been playing together. This time it was harder to let go, to relinquish that special softness and warmth that is a child. Time refused her the luxury of prolonging it. "Run! Catch your brothers. Tell them."

Crimson Rose ran, a flash of white swallowed by the black of the lilac's glossy leaves. Whether she ran to tell the police there was a murderess in the bushes or to stop Philip and Colt from doing so, Clare had no way of knowing. She turned and ran as quickly in the opposite direction. Mackie, torn between the two options, dithered but a heartbeat, then ran at her heels.

TEN

As they headed out of Seattle, Blackie watched the road beyond the windshield wipers. Dawn was leaching the mystery from the liquid light running psychedelic on rain-dark streets, and he felt the same relief he always experienced with the coming of the day. Night was a time when things he didn't want to think about were around. Things like him, like Dougie.

Worse, he thought, then smiled to himself. There wasn't much even long dead that was worse than Dougie was, or would be when he grew into his vices. The smile was short-lived, as were all Blackie's joys. He knew too much of the world to allow something so fragile to show for longer than a moment. It was bad juju to dwell on certain things, bad juju to mock them. Abruptly, he stabbed the ON button on the radio.

A talk program, that was good, took more thought.

He glanced at his companion. The kid wasn't watching the road like any normal person; hot-eyed, lips loose and damp, jaw slack, he was staring into the back of the van. Blackie knew the look; he'd seen it on the faces of Rick B's clients. It was the look men get when they want something real bad and are dreaming they've already got it.

"Fucking watch the road," Blackie snarled.

"It don't hurt 'em none. They ain't moving. 'Cept the little darkie. You're moving, ain't you? Bet you move and wriggle and—"

Blackie took his hand from the wheel and slammed the back of it across Dougie's face. He didn't worry the kid would hit back. His kind never did, at least not when you were looking. "Watch the fucking road," Blackie said but with less venom this time. Dougie was just a tool. No sense blunting your tools as long as they worked.

Dougie dutifully turned his eyes to the front, apparently taking no umbrage from the fact he'd just been backhanded. Blackie had been to college; he read the papers, listened to National Public Radio. The legends and lore of modern psychology had not passed him by. Dougie was a perfect example of what happens to a boy when he's abused as a child and grows up finding comfort and familiarity in violence as well as a need to create it by tormenting other helpless beings. Except none of that had ever happened to little Douglas Dewitt. His folks didn't live more than two miles from Blackie's family. Nice people, nice house, nice kids. Except for Dougie. He'd been a bastard since he'd been old enough to kill the family gerbil.

"Bad seed," Blackie muttered and turned up the radio. For a blessed few miles Dougie didn't say anything. The radio did the talking, that, and the sound of wheels on wet pavement, almost drowning out the faint whimpers from the little girl sitting in back with the two lumps under the blankets. Blackie slowed the van to sixty-nine miles per hour and switched on cruise control. With this load, getting stopped by even a stupid cop would be bad trouble. The road unrolled between the knuckles of his hands on the wheel; the white line came at him in a blur; the talk radio droned.

"Do you think Mr. B might give me a freebie?" Dougie's thin voice squirted into the emptiness Blackie was nurturing so assiduously in his mind. "You know, a pass, like a reward? A finder's fee." Dougie laughed as if "finder's fee" were a clever witticism. Blackie failed to see the joke and didn't try too hard. He'd long ago given up trying to figure out what went on inside the boy's head. The closest he could get to picturing the inside of Dougie's skull was a kind of reddish sandstorm.

He tried to go back to that place where there was only the radio and the road.

"He did once, you know, when one of the jewels got broken. He gave me the pieces. Piece." Dougie laughed again. This time Blackie got the joke but didn't find it funny. He never found Dougie funny. Nobody needed to. Dougie always laughed at his own jokes. Blackie wished the kid had a screeching bray or a weird cackle, instead of the rich warm burble that seemed full of Christmas and candy and evenings around the dinner table. It creeped him out to put that laugh with what Dougie laughed at.

"You're like a dog," Blackie said. "Feed it once and it keeps coming around begging. Fuck." He was disappointed in himself for getting drawn into conversation.

"Stray dogs used to come around our place. I'd sneak table scraps out so they'd come back." Again the beautiful laugh; the laugh that would lure toddlers onto a man's knee. Blackie didn't want to think about why Dougie fed the strays.

"Watch the fucking road."

"I ain't driving," Dougie complained, but he watched the road.

A few miles passed in relative peace. Even the trickling whimper from the back of the van had dried up. Blackie knew it was too good to last and was almost relieved when Dougie broke into the murmur of the voice on the radio.

"Uh-oh," he said in a childlike singsong. "Man, you're gonna be pissed!"

Blackie didn't doubt that. He waited to be informed on just why.

"Really, really pissed," Dougie said.

"Cut the crap."

"I forgot something."

"Jesus fucking Christ. What?"

"Remember me taking my coat off so I wouldn't get stuff on it? I think I left it on the couch there."

Blackie laughed. "Good. That thing was a pimp's advertisement."

"It cost two hundred dollars," Dougie said, affronted.

"You got ripped off. Somebody saw you coming."

"No sir."

Blackie shook his head. "Christ on a crutch," he muttered.

"You know what else?"

Blackie could hardly wait.

"I think my wallet is in the pocket."

ELEVEN

Running shut out thought. The burn of cold air in her lungs and the rasping squeak of her sneakers on the wet pavement filled voids where she might have lost herself; places where logic killed her children all over again and the future housed nothing but an antique radiator and windows black with wire mesh.

A block, two, and she realized she had to find another way to shout down the monsters in her mind. Running would call attention to her more surely than a man's inside-out raincoat on a lone woman in the dark of early morning. She needed to get out of sight, get to a place she could stop and decide just how long the rest of her life would be and how she might best spend it.

Jalila was the key.

Jalila and David had left the house together. Only David was carried from the fire.

If it was David.

For a dizzying moment Clare realized she hadn't recognized her husband's body, only his bathrobe.

"Jalila," she whispered to focus her mind. The au pair would know why the two of them had run out in the middle of the night, why David had returned.

Clare slowed her steps; her heart ceased its hammering; her mind cleared to a degree. David had warehouses and two factories down near the docks. For the past several years, maybe more—Clare was not kept apprised of David's business dealings—he'd kept a small apartment nearby to rest in when he worked late, change clothes, shower.

And entertain, Clare didn't doubt. She'd never been invited there, nor had she had any desire to barge in. A time or two she'd seen the outside of the building when she'd been called on to pick David up for a social function of one kind or another. He kept a tuxedo there as well as a couple of suits.

Beneath a street lamp, she came to a stop. Standing in the pooling yellow light on a deserted corner, she suddenly saw herself from above: *Harvey.* The movie, not the play. Seven years ago Clare played the psychiatric nurse. Now she watched herself slipping into the skin of Elwood P. Dowd.

Jimmy Stewart, patting his pockets. Looking for what? Channeling the tall actor in stance and posture, she frisked herself. As it often did onstage, action informed motivation: She was looking for tools, if any, that were hers to work with.

In the breast pocket of the coat—once on the inside,

now on the out—was David's cell phone. It took up less space than the foreshortened pack of unfiltered cigarettes she'd bought. Dare she use it? On television and in the movies the police could find a person from a cell phone call; they could blow up a pinhead-sized picture to perfect clarity, break passwords in seconds, and hack into anything in minutes. What worked in the real world? The Seattle police couldn't know she wore her husband's coat, carried his wallet, and had his cell phone. Could they?

She'd dialed 911 from his cell, and with modern magic they'd come up with his name and address. Or had she given it to the operator? She couldn't remember. The EMTs and cops at the fire, they'd seen the coat. Not the phone, though, not the wallet, and Clare was tall, nearly as tall as David. There was no way they could know it wasn't her coat. One Burberry trench coat is much like another. The cell phone question wasn't pressing. Who would she call? Her sister, Gretchen, was in Japan teaching English for the next seven months. Friends she trusted, she wouldn't endanger by asking them to harbor a fugitive. Those she didn't might believe she was a child-murderer. A lifetime of not killing and eating the neighborhood children would do her no good. Everyone knew it was always the quiet ones.

There'd been so much madness in the night, for a gaping instant she wondered if she *had* killed her children and her husband and fired the house. People went crazy all the time. The devil or the family dog told them to do unspeakable things and they did them. Had she murdered Vee and Dana?

A cry grated from her lips, and she fell against the rough brick. Mackie put his paws on her thigh and howled like a dust mop deluding itself that it's a wolf. He didn't do it often. It was too dear to waste on everyday performances. The effort was not in vain; Clare rose to the surface of the poisonous thoughts drifting over her soul.

"Stop it!" she ordered herself. Believing she spoke to him, Mack was shocked back onto four paws.

Clare knew she could not have hurt the girls. David, maybe. The girls, never. "That way madness lies," she murmured and shook herself, a palsy that ran from her heels to her head. One thing at a time. *One day at a time. Like an alcoholic. One minute at a time.* She'd get through one minute at a time doing only what that minute demanded.

This minute demanded she assess her resources.

David's wallet was more a purse than the sleek leather envelope one might expect from a well-dressed man. Clare had never looked inside. Her husband wasn't the sort to leave it lying about. As far as she could remember, tonight was the first time he'd ever forgotten it. When she'd gone out for Vee's cough medicine, she had not taken it simply because it happened to be in the pocket of the raincoat, she'd taken it because he and Jalila had run off in such a peculiar and insulting manner. Spending his money wasn't much of a revenge, but spending it from his sacrosanct secret wallet was.

There was cash, four or five hundred dollars at least, the bills fanned out from a brass clip in the middle. The expected credit cards were in place, as well as three she hadn't known they—he—had. A key she recognized as a spare to the back door of the Laggert Street house was beneath a flap. On the other side of the wallet, tucked behind his ATM card, was another key, one she hadn't seen before, and the security cards he used to let himself into the warehouses and factories where the clothing was assembled.

She lifted the strange key from the wallet and slipped it into her pocket. She dearly hoped it was to his apartment by the docks. There was a good chance Jalila would be there, and she was the one person who might know why the children weren't in the house and David wasn't and then they were, dead, but Vee's Sleepy Dog and Mackie the real dog were safe and sound outside.

Clare rubbed her face hard. *One minute at a time: the apartment, then Jalila.*

Two more hours' walking brought her to the waterfront just before daybreak. Streetlights were still on, but, with the coming of day, the sky was changing from sodium-arc-orange to pewter. Standing outside the run-down building she'd watched her husband emerge from several times over the years, Clare realized that even if the key in the wallet was for the door, she didn't know how to locate that door. She had no idea which apartment was his.

Holding horror at bay, supporting an insupportable

hope, going without sleep, and walking for miles on concrete had exhausted her till her insides felt as if they, too, had burned and all that remained was cold wet ash. Mackie was so tired she'd carried him for the past half hour. Vision swam. Dead children pulled at her from an abyss where she could do nothing right, where her judgment was twisted and her ears stopped up with the words of crazy people.

Cinderella.

Because of her height and build she'd been cast as Prince Charming. Like the slipper on the ladies of the kingdom, she'd try the key in every door. Maybe one would open. Maybe it wouldn't. That was trouble for another minute, and she'd promised herself to deal only with this one.

Not for the first time, Clare was glad to be a woman nearing a Certain Age. Middle-aged females were considered the safest, most innocuous of Americans, often invisible, sometimes tedious, but never alarming. Had she been a young black man, she'd have thought twice about going up stairs and down halls trying all the doors.

The process was mercifully short. The building had but three apartments on each of the four floors. David's key turned easily in the lock of the fifth she tried. The door swung inward at a touch, hinges silent and smooth. The lock itself was shiny, state-of-the-art. David might choose a slum, but he wasn't precisely slumming.

The inside of the hideaway had also been given a face-lift. The windows were the same gritty hue as those she had noted from the outside—dirt kept intact as camouflage—but the walls were painted David's favorite winter white, as was the woodwork. The furniture was modern and spotlessly clean, the floor covered in white carpet. No pictures broke the planes of the walls; no pillows cluttered the divan and chair; there were no bookcases or clocks, just a wide-screen television set with the remote left on top and a coffee table with two opened bottles of water on it. One had fallen over, pooling water on the glass and darkening a couple of inches of carpet where it had spilled. Lipstick, a dark, nearly purple shade, ringed the bottleneck. Jalila's. It looked good with her olive and raven coloring. On anyone else it would have been ghoulish.

The only other scrap of color was a canary yellow leather sport coat. It wasn't David's; David had more taste and conceit than to be seen in the sartorial equivalent of a pink Cadillac.

"Jalila?" Clare called softly. Could the au pair have been having an affair with somebody other than David? Maybe the guy with the peculiar accent who'd been on the cell phone? Was that why the house had been burned? Was Jalila's other lover murdered by David in a fit of, if not jealousy, then outraged owner's rage, then dressed in David's pajamas and burned? After a night of hideous surprises, Clare was unmoved by the fact that she didn't think an act of such cold malice beyond the man she'd slept next to for so many years. "Jalila?" she called again, louder this time.

The faint creaks of an old building thinking about waking up for the day were her only answer.

Mackie, tired—or intimidated by the expanse of white canvas—chose to flop on the floor rather than jump on the couch as he would have done at home. If he'd still had a home.

Too anxious to sit and too worn and stupid to move, Clare stood in the middle of the room, unsure what she should do next. Fleetingly, she wondered if the police had already thought of this place. The scene, a staple in a million cop shows, flickered behind her brow bone: black-and-whites surrounding the building; grim-faced policemen, guns drawn, crouching behind open car doors. *What was that about? The car door thing? Wouldn't bullets punch right through a car door?*

Surely if the police had known of David's pied-à-terre, they'd have arrived long before her and Mack. For once she had cause to be grateful for her husband's secretive nature. As his wife, she'd never seen any record of this place. He never spoke of it in front of family or friends. Without being told to, she'd never mentioned it either. She'd thought this was because of the women, but maybe it was just the way David was. Secrets were power.

"We have some time," she said to the dog. Mackie didn't intrude with "Time to do what? Time to go where?" Dogs were good about that sort of thing.

A liquor cabinet, also white, also topped and fronted with sparkling glass, came into her awareness. David didn't drink. He was a Muslim and took his religion seriously. Clare drank, but never in front of him and never much. As she opened the cabinet door she considered breaking the second of those rules. A bottle of red wine was closest. She grabbed it and unscrewed the cap. Screw caps were the new snobbery. David wouldn't have had a bad—or at least a cheap—vintage. It wouldn't have looked good to whoever the hell it was he wanted to look good for in this white box.

Not women, Clare thought. David liked to seduce women, to wow them with his good looks and charm, but he'd never thought well enough of the gender to bother impressing any member of it further than that.

Clare tossed the cap onto the pristine carpet, trying not to wince at her effrontery, and gripped the bottle by the neck. Because she had to believe at least one of her children was still alive—and to swig from the bottle was not something a good mother would do—she picked up a glass and poured as she wandered toward the bedroom. She would drink only enough to take the edge off, sleep a few hours, then think of what came next.

Her mind shifted into neutral as she watched the liquid curling down the side of the crystal.

The wine never reached the bottom. Bottle and glass fell from nerveless fingers, spreading wine in a sudden stain on the carpet.

The first watery gleam of day and the spill of electric light from the living room caught the edges of the almost perfect black of Jalila's hair. Unbound, it fanned out through the blood as if trying to escape the jagged wound in the back of her skull. Bits of white and gray, bone and brain, clung to the edges of the ruin, prosaic reminders that mortals were mere constructions of disposable matter.

As red of wine ran into red of blood, Clare sank to her knees. She uttered not a sound. A soft pad-pad announced Mackie's arrival. For a moment he sat beside his mistress, seemingly as stunned as she, but for all his civilized demeanor, he was a dog at heart. He trotted to the corpse and began to lick at the wound as he might with any newly dead thing.

Clare added the contents of her stomach to the wreck of the carpet.

TWELVE

B reathing a sigh of relief, Anna escaped Patty's emporium of the arcane. Until the last few moments, the potions, candles, and spells (three for ten dollars) had struck her as charming and silly but basically harmless. The warning Patty had tossed like a hand grenade before pulling her vanishing act changed that.

The stoniness of her voice and the deadness in her eyes spoke of indifference to life, to Jordan's life. Or Anna's, should she align herself with him. That iciness had not manifested when speaking of her archenemy at the rival shop, the woman in white. Relating her transgressions had enlivened the little witch in the way delicious gossip can.

The Walmart receipt, on which Anna had sketched the symbols from the ill-fated pigeon's winding cloth, was still clutched in her hand. Beside her the many-armed creature sat in its derelict birdbath. Up close the poor old monster looked foolish and tired. It had been carved of some kind of plastic that had grown pitted from too many days in the sun. At one time it had been painted, apparently by the simultaneous application of orange and purple Day-Glo spray paint. Except for the shaded areas in the many armpits, the colors had faded.

Standing beside this sorry representative of the nether-world, Anna felt her quest was pretty silly as well. Jordan had gotten crosswise of Patty and probably a few other residents of the Quarter. Anna had stuck her nose into the middle of a local squabble.

Shrugging it off, she shoved the crumpled receipt into the pocket of her shorts and turned left toward the NPS. Half a block and she was under the sign for the rival shop: Authentic Voodoo. Her intention was to stride purposefully by it, righteously minding her own business. Instead, she allowed the cool air emanating from the open door to lure her inside.

What the hell? Another few minutes of surreality wouldn't kill her.

The woman in white's store was as different from Vieux Dieux as a garden from a cave. Windows let light into a spare, well-organized space resembling a library-cum-herbarium. The shelves were well stocked but not jammed; herbs, bits of bone, and other necessities were as neatly labeled and displayed as the spices at Whole Foods. The back left corner of the shop, farthest from the windows, was set off by a four-foot-square carpet, green with pink roses. A little girl, dressed in white, with fine, stick-straight blonde hair falling to her waist, sat barefoot, marching a plastic horse with a one-armed

Handsome Prince through the gates of Sleeping Beauty's Castle, the Disney logo displayed proudly as the castle's coat of arms.

"Welcome to Authentic Voodoo. What troubles you today?"

Anna turned toward the cool ripple of sound. The child's mother—the resemblance was not only obvious but uncanny, heightened by the similar clothes and hair—stood behind a counter opposite the play area. The countertop was clear but for the cash register and credit card machine. Behind its glass front, as bloodlessly displayed as artifacts in a museum, were wax dolls, pins, tiny scarecrows, realistic-looking miniature black mambas, and other presumably useful staples of her trade.

The proprietress, wearing a sleeveless white linen shift with no jewelry, belt, pockets, or frills, her blonde hair parted in the middle and falling straight as a die to either side of a face as round as a coin, was the physical embodiment of Innocence. Had she not been clutching what appeared to be a hank of human hair in one fist and a headless black stuffed animal in the other, the vision would have been flawless.

"I just have a couple of questions," Anna said. Then, realizing she sounded clipped and authoritarian, she threw out some softening conversation. "I'm interested in symbols, kind of a hobby, I guess. I'm not very good at it yet." She smiled disarmingly and wondered why she was bothering to lie to the woman. Maybe because

of the way Patty had shut down when she realized why
Anna was evincing such an interest in magic. "Are there
symbols in voodoo?" she asked disingenuously.

"Lots of them," the woman replied. "Many are veves."
She pronounced it "vay-vays." "They pertain to a particular god or to a set of attributes like fertility, rain, generosity or chance, unfaithfulness, danger. That sort of
thing."

"Do you have a book of . . . veves?" Anna turned
vaguely in the direction of the fourteen-foot-high bookshelves. Geneva was scheduled to sing in a few minutes. If Anna was to leaf through that many books,
she'd best wait till the singer's set was over.

"I don't," the woman said. "I used to order them, but
they weren't moving. I could special order one for you
if you like." As she'd been speaking, she'd slid the headless black dog beneath the level of the counter and secreted it somewhere out of sight. The move struck Anna
as furtive, but it was probably simply an indication of
the woman's compulsive tidiness.

"Do you practice voodoo?" Anna blurted out.

"I am a voodooienne," she replied in the tone one
might use to say, "I'm an Episcopalian."

Precisely what that entailed, Anna wasn't sure.
Judging by the few stories she'd heard of Madam La-
veau, New Orleans's most famous voodooienne in the
old days, a bit of dancing with large snakes and wild
sexual orgies was de rigueur. It was hard to picture the
blonde in the linen shift doing anything much more

alarming than hanging stuffed dice from the mirror of her minivan. In the modern era it was probably all done with virtual snakes and sexting.

Except for those who loved the classics; for them there were pigeons skewered with striped sticks.

Tired of playing cat and mouse when apparently there was no mouse, Anna reached into the pocket of her shorts and pulled out the wadded-up receipt.

"Are these veves?" She smoothed out the wrinkles and pressed the paper flat on the glass countertop. A small pile of business cards she hadn't noticed before caught her eye: AUTHENTIC VOODOO, RACINE GUTREAUX. "Racine?"

"Yes."

The blonde leaned over the scrap, her hair cascading off her shoulder to fall in a curtain hiding both her face and the sketches. She remained like that, face obscured and unmoving for an unusual length of time, so long Anna began to suspect her of using the veil of hair to hide behind while she mastered emotions or got all her lies in a row. Shortly before Anna decided the woman was just fishy as hell, Racine lifted her moon face, a face devoid of lines or freckles, moles or bags beneath the eyes. Checking IDs for much of her life, Anna was fairly good at guessing ages, but Racine defied her experience. She could have been anywhere between seventeen and thirty-seven.

"What's this supposed to be a drawing of?" Racine asked politely enough; still, Anna was stung. She'd thought it rather good, given it had been done from a rain-wet and garbage-soaked memory.

"I saw it somewhere," Anna said. "Or something like that. I drew it afterward and didn't recall the details. I thought it might be a symbol used in the voodoo religion." She used the word "religion" with care, not knowing where religion left off and magic—or insanity—began. The outward show of respect bore fruit.

"Let me get my book from upstairs," Racine said. She didn't move right away but stayed a moment, staring at the child playing in the corner as if debating whether it was safe to leave her alone with Anna. Anna started to offer to keep an eye on the little girl but decided against it. For some reason, maybe the strained look that had formed on the otherwise unmarked face of the voodooienne, she knew it would be more alarming than reassuring.

Racine glanced out the window fronting Dumaine Street, her face moving so suddenly the curtain of hair was set to swinging, and Anna caught a faint scent of something unpleasant, a damp stale odor like that of a little-used basement. Or an unopened grave, Anna thought with a smile that she didn't let reach her lips. She was rather getting into the spirit of this whole ghoulies and ghosties thing.

"Laura?"

The girl looked up from her game. Her face was not as round as her mother's, and her gray eyes held traces of fear that Racine either didn't share or hid magnificently.

"Yes, Mama?"

"Will you be okay down here by yourself for a minute?"

"Yes, Mama."

"Don't go outside."

"I won't, Mama."

Still Racine made no move toward the back of the shop, where Anna presumed the stairs up to their apartment were located. Decision flickered a touch of age into her smooth face, and, leaving the counter, she walked past Anna and closed and locked the door of the shop. "I'll only be a minute," she said to her daughter as she crossed to a door in the rear of the shop. There she stopped again, hand on the knob, eyes on the window.

Anna found herself looking to the street as well, as if demons from hell might be visiting the Quarter this morning. Racine was beginning to give her the creeps in a way the little, long-nailed black witch with the many-legged doorkeeper had not. She was put in mind of when she and Molly used to scare each other when they were kids by pretending to hear or see something in the dark.

Suddenly, Racine pulled open the rear door and, leaving it gaping wide, ran up the narrow stairs behind it. Within seconds, she ran back down, the leather soles of her flat white shoes loud on the old wood. When she burst forth, book in hand, her eyes went first to the windows fronting the shop. Racine's face was one of the more impenetrable Anna had seen, but she was fairly certain there was a flash of relief at seeing the demon hordes had not formed on the sidewalk in the seconds she was away. The coast being clear, she unlocked the door but didn't open it. Having returned to her post behind the counter, she put the book she'd fetched down on the glass, opened it, and turned it so Anna could see it right side up.

"These are the most common veves," she said. "This one is for Damballa. He's one of the most important loa—a sort of god. He's to do with snakes and the color white. He likes offerings mostly of eggs and flour but sometimes other things. If you think of maybe St. Patrick, you get an idea of Damballa." Pointing to the drawing on the opposite page, she went on. "This is Papa Legba's veve. Papa is the liaison between the loa and us, people. Kind of like St. Peter guarding the pearly gates. If you want to talk with any particular loa, you need to go through Papa Legba. He likes dogs." She turned several pages and stopped at another. "This one is for Maman Brigitte. She is a death loa and is married to another loa, Baron Samedi. Maman likes her hot peppers and swears a lot. There are more. They are the diagrams a practitioner would draw to attract these gods—or their attributes—down to earth to help with a wish or to fend off danger."

Each veve was given an entire glossy page in the coffee-table book. They were intricate, lacy, complicated designs that reminded Anna both of snowflakes in the high country and the wrought-iron work that proliferated on the balconies, fences, and doorways in the French Quarter. As Racine paged through the book explaining the loa the veves called into action, Anna could feel the pull of the intricate drawings. The ancient symbols brought together sharp points and gentle curves in sinuous patterns, shapes that indicated fish as well as stars, heaven and earth, fire and water. Looked at one way, they would evoke terrific strength, then, as a cloud formation can turn from a castle to a menorah and back again as brain and eye form and re-form it, suddenly remind her of the fragility of fading spidery handwriting on a crumbling document.

Anna wasn't sufficiently ensorcelled by these nuevo–dark continent runes to grant them independent powers, but she had to grant them the respect due to well-made tools. It was easy to see how a person with a strong godly—or ungodly—personality could invest them with the forces of the gods they summoned. If not enough to fool all of the people all of the time, then at least enough to make a decent living, as W. C. Fields said.

The intricacy that lent the veves their ability to fascinate also made it difficult for Anna to ascertain which one had graced her namesake's burial rag. Put side by side with the drawings in Racine's book, her sketch was simple and clumsy to the point of being virtually useless.

Closing her eyes to shut out the confusion of reality, Anna breathed in and out slowly, blowing detritus from her mind. When it was relatively free of dust and fur balls, she allowed herself to remember that first moment she had moved the dead bird and seen the figures on the cloth.

At the time, she'd been more focused on the carcass than the fabric it was wrapped in, and her mental picture was blurred as a snapshot taken by impatient hands is blurred.

"Damn." She opened her eyes to see Racine looking at her with an expression of alarm—if the infinitesimal lift of one eyebrow could be called an expression. No wonder she didn't have any lines on her face. "I wish I'd hung on to the thing," she said.

"Hung on to what?" Racine asked as she turned to the next image in the book of veves. Maybe her voice had iced over a tad. Maybe she was thinking of the cloth because she'd wrapped the pigeon in it or knew who did. Maybe she was just tired of Anna's staying and gobbling up free information and not buying.

"Nothing," Anna replied, waving away the need to retell the whole garbage can saga. "Wait, stop." The page facing her, Racine's neat fingers with their unpolished nails poised to turn the leaf, had a drawing as close to what she remembered as she'd seen. "Who is that? Whose veve, I mean. What powers does the loa supposedly have?"

Racine's hand slammed down on the page with such force Anna squeaked and jumped like a rat just saved from the cheese.

"Get out!" Racine hissed.

At the same time, Laura cried, "Mama!"

Both were looking at the entrance to the shop. Through windows in the door, Anna could see what had caused the eruption. Standing on the other side of the glass was Jordan, his lean frame curled into the shape of a crone, his hands limp at his sides. He was looking at Laura in her play area.

On his face was a look of such naked hunger it made Anna's flesh shrink back against her bones.

THIRTEEN

A clap of homemade thunder loud enough to penetrate the glass tore Jordan's gaze from Laura and dragged it to the counter where Anna and Racine stood. Even at a distance of thirty feet and through a window Anna could feel the heat from his eyes. Eyes like burning coals, like embers, like pools of desire—the clichés dropped into her mind and, made real, ceased being clichés.

Air was leaking out of the world. Hissing. The thoughts rattled through Anna's head and were gone in an instant. The paranormal had not stepped into the magic shop, at least not yet. Racine was hissing like a snake. Her empty moon face altered, the eyes narrowing, the lips drawn tight and thin down over the teeth the way children's do when they're playing as toothless old crones. Racine looked like a snake. Like she was becoming a snake. Or a snake inside her was allowing itself to be seen.

Jordan must have glimpsed the snake as well. The

eyes that so troubled Anna were immediately hooded. He turned, stumbling, regained his balance, and walked slowly toward the levee and the river, his gait as uncertain as that of a man three times his age. It was as if the snake loa Racine had called down had sunk its fangs into him and poisoned him to the marrow of his bones.

"What was that about?" Anna asked.

Racine's humanity was back; no trace of the serpentine face remained. Anna didn't believe it was truly gone, and she was no longer crazy enough to believe she hadn't really seen it. The sense she was left with was that of newly stilled waters where a monster, risen briefly from the depths, had resubmerged.

"We close the shop for lunch," Racine said calmly. The book of veves was clutched to her chest. That had been the clap of thunder that had changed their wee scrap of world. The proprietress had slammed it shut with enough violence for the sound to penetrate walls.

Anna stood her ground. "Has that guy threatened you, pestered Laura?" she asked.

"We reopen at one," Racine said.

"If he has, you should call the police."

A hint of snakiness played around Racine's mouth. Book still held to her chest, she came around the counter, walked to the front door, flipped the OPEN sign to CLOSED, and, one hand on the knob, looked pointedly at Anna.

Admitting defeat—at least for the moment—Anna thanked her for the information on veves and left the

shop. Her butt had scarcely cleared the lintel when she
heard the chunk of the dead bolt sliding into place.

Jordan, a block ahead, was crossing North Peters
against the light. A white SUV stopped politely; a green
sedan honked. He seemed unaware of either but continued his shuffling progress till he reached the far
curb and went on toward the art gallery, past the fountain, and through the floodgates to the trolley tracks
and the river walk. Anna glanced back into the voodoo
shop. It was deserted, the door to the upstairs firmly
closed and, no doubt, locked.

Anna's mention of the police had bounced off Racine's hard shell. Was it because, in New Orleans, the
police were not trusted to protect and serve? Or was it
because she had reasons of her own not to want police
looking too closely into her life? Like, say, skewering
live pigeons and delivering them door to door?

Anna knew she should leave it alone just as certainly
as she knew she wouldn't. For the best part of twenty
years she'd been in the business of rescuing things and
people from other things and other people. The habit
was too strong to break at this late date. Added to force
of habit, Helena, a baby she'd helped to keep alive in
Big Bend, Texas, had forever removed the insulating
idea of "children" and replaced it with a dear little face.
Since Helena, every baby, every child, was personal. If
Laura was in danger from Jordan, Anna would put a
stop to it. One way or another. It was the only way she
would be able to sleep at night.

Besides, she thought with a wry smile, Jordan was so wasted and frail she could probably take him two falls out of three. It was rare in the life of a female law enforcement officer to face a criminal who was physically weaker or smaller than she. She doubted most men would be as comfortable facing a world of foes that outweighed them by fifty to a hundred pounds. Women cops, rangers, and border patrol officers did it every day, all day.

She thought about calling the police, her brothers in blue. Except rangers didn't have brothers in blue, not the way real cops did. She'd probably get more attention as the wife of an Episcopal priest than as a ranger from the Far West, and one on administrative leave to boot. Besides, what could she tell them? That she'd found a dead bird in the trash and, thus, decided her neighbor was a pervert?

"Anna, you don't have to do anything. You're on vacation, remember? You left home and husband because you were working too hard doing nothing."

"This isn't nothing," Anna said.

"I know it isn't, love."

Paul's voice, a sweet tenor at the worst of times, said the word "love" with a tenderness that annoyed Anna because there was no defense against that kind of wonderful.

Too many years of risking whatever was hers—health, youth, charm, good looks, money, time, and sanity—in the pursuit of an idiosyncratic sense of justice wouldn't let her feel more than a passing gratitude for the man who wanted to keep her safe. "Geneva told me he's got a job, a night job. He leaves for work around ten o'clock most nights."

"You don't know where this guy works. You yourself described him as chased by demons. Maybe he's chasing the demons instead. You could follow him right into the middle of something that would be tricky to get out of. To say the least."

The last bit was almost a whisper, and Anna smiled in spite of herself. Paul had been at her side when the shots were fired in Big Bend. He'd handed her the knife to try to save a dead woman's unborn child; he'd wrestled a man eight inches taller, forty pounds heavier, and fifteen years younger to the ground and bashed him on the head with a stone because he looked as if he were going to hurt her.

"Geneva said he doesn't smell half bad when he's going to work," Anna said.

"And this not recking guarantees he works in an OSHA-approved place?"

Anna said nothing.

"Could you get one of the rangers there to go with you? Preferably one who can see?"

"They're musicians," Anna said. She thought she heard a minute sigh from Port Gibson, Mississippi.

"Could you at least wait till I can come down to serve as your backup?"

Again she said nothing. This time the sigh was quite audible.

"Promise me you'll be careful," Paul said.

"I will."

"Really, really careful."

"I promise."

Paul laughed, a sound of both love and exasperation. "Your definition of 'careful' is vaguely analogous to most people's definition of 'damn the torpedoes.'"

"I'm careful," Anna said. "It's just that occasionally my luck runs out."

"From the way you describe him, he sounds like a man who has it all: scabies, crabs, AIDS, gonorrhea, hangnails. If, God forbid, you have to take him down, promise me you'll wash your hands afterward."

Anna laughed. "And use sanitizer."

"Call me the minute you get back. No, call me the minute you get to wherever it is that your not-too-stinking, occasionally violent, demon-ridden little friend goes to work in the middle of the night."

"I'll do my best," Anna said. Cell phones were not a favored tool of hers. She didn't like conducting private conversations in public places, didn't like phone calls emanating from her pants pocket pushing their way into places where conversations—or those instigating them—didn't belong, like bathroom stalls, grocery aisles, fist-fights, and just about anyplace else she could think of.

"Am I going to have to settle for that?"

"Pretty much," Anna said honestly.

"I love you."

"And I you."

Anna closed the phone, then opened it again and

turned it off, watching the gray and white "Good-bye" fade from view on a Star-Trekkian whoosh of electronic noise. There were a lot of people who'd rather see her alive than dead—most, she liked to think—but, other than her sister, it had been a long time since there was anyone who was so hell-bent on keeping her alive and in one piece that it could be a pain in the pasta fagioli.

She would be careful, really, really careful. Her survival instinct had pretty much recovered from previous adventures; that was part of it. Mostly, though, she knew for a fact, knew with every gram of gray matter left in her cranium, that her death would devastate her husband.

Love was a grand burden.

Clad in black Levi's and a red tank top, lights off, she sat inside the open doors to her abbreviated balcony and waited. From the bedroom of the guesthouse she couldn't see Jordan's door, but she would hear when he opened it, would hear his feet on the brick, the squeak of the gate on his side of the apartments. The small deep courtyard funneled sounds up from below with such efficiency she heard even the faint scratching of insects in the leaf litter around the turtles' pond.

Most cities Anna was familiar with began to settle after the evening rush hour. Even on Friday and Saturday nights, there was a slowing and a sense of drowsiness that came over neighborhoods as breadwinners arrived home, suppers were cooked, children kissed and put to bed. Perhaps that was true in other parts of New Orleans. Not so in the French Quarter.

As the hour grew later there was a sense of waking up, the sound of laughter from the street, scraps of conversations drifting up from stoops and balconies, the crush of automobile tires as cars negotiated the narrow, one-way streets. On Ursulines, a few blocks from Bourbon, Royal, Chartres, and North Peters, where the bulk of the night tourists found entertainment, the coming to life wasn't hectic or edgy, just the waking of a nocturnal world as at home in the darkness as bats and cats and owls.

Since Geneva had given her Jordan's customary time of departure, Anna hadn't been listening for more than a quarter of an hour before she heard Jordan's door open, then shut, then the snuck-chunk sound of the lock.

When she heard his footfalls moving toward the iron door that let onto the street, Anna rose.

She didn't change into dark clothes, or mute the paleness of her flesh, or any of the things she might have done had she been going to track a possible malefactor through the woods at night. She didn't pull a ball cap low over her eyes or wear dark glasses to avoid being recognized as one might in other cities. This was New Orleans. On her way downstairs she pulled on a mask bright with red feathers and black sequins that she'd picked up in a souvenir shop on the corner of North Peters and Dumaine after Geneva finished her set, then wrapped a red and gold boa obtained at the same emporium of the tacky and predictable around her neck. All she need do was add a brightly colored hurricane in a shapely plastic two-foot-high glass and she would be just another tourist, all but invisible to the locals.

FOURTEEN

A silent descent made impossible by the old cottage's xylophone stairs, Anna trusted to distance and ambient noise to cover her, pattered down the three flights, and let herself out the front door. Once on the brick, she moved as silently as a cloud.

She didn't trail Jordan down his side of the house. The iron gates to the street were locked with a dead bolt and needed a key to open from either side. Geneva had given her a key to her gate; Anna had neglected to check whether it worked on the second gate. A task for another day, she thought as she stood quietly behind the iron, head cocked, ears straining for the sound of Jordan's retreating footsteps. Keen as her hearing was, she couldn't separate his footfalls from the general murmur of the Quarter.

She gave it a slow twenty count to let him get far enough that he wouldn't hear the lock unlocking, then let herself out onto Ursulines. He was a block and a half away, heading toward the river. Anna closed and locked

the gate behind her, then crossed the street to make
herself less obviously connected to Geneva's house and
followed.

At Bourbon, Jordan turned right and disappeared
from sight. Anna jogged half a block and turned right
as well. Bourbon smelled faintly of vomit and urine,
but, according to Geneva, it was positively aromatic
compared to before Katrina. One of the good things
the storm heralded was a cleaner French Quarter.

The street was well lit by streetlights that mimicked
gas lamps from the turn of the twentieth century and
by light spilling out of bars and shops. All was made
deliciously lurid by neon.

It wasn't crowded, but there was a sufficiency of
people and noise. Anna didn't worry about being noticed tailing Jordan. Not many people were wearing
masks—Mardi Gras had come and gone—but there
were a few. Two large-bottomed women in shorts and
flip-flops had on cat masks. Feather boas were fairly
common. There was a peculiar hat here and there. Three
young men were talking and laughing around the front
of Lafitte's, one shirtless wearing black leather short-
shorts and a pirate hat with a great white plume, one in
a black leather miniskirt that complemented his tattoos
and silver pumps, and the third in khaki pants, loafers,
and a madras shirt.

Anna, in red feathers and black sequins, did not
stand out.

Jordan was all in black: shoes, trousers, and a long-
sleeved shirt with a collar. That much she'd ascertained

from the dimmer view on Ursulines. Now she could see that the clothes were nice—at least compared to the garb he wore when he was hanging with the gutter punks. The pants were clean-looking and not too wrinkled, as was the shirt. He wore a black leather belt and black running shoes. His hair had been slicked back and greased—or was still wet from the shower. That, combined with the smudge of beardlet beneath his lower lip and the crown of thorns, gave him the look of Druggie Number Two in a B movie.

New Orleans residents tended to avoid Bourbon. The famous street was always in party mode. Locals looking for a bar open late or just mingling for the fun of the night scene came, but, for the most part, the party was for out-of-towners. Maybe at one time New Orleans had been a hotbed of sin. Now it was merely tolerant of it. Bourbon was about the only place that overt, commercial sin could be found, and much of that was "sin lite," more show than anything. The draw was the nudity and the booze and the illusion of walking on the wild side. Or maybe Anna had seen too much of the world. Maybe for normal people, pole dancing and pasties, thongs and booze and lap dances, were the wild side.

The street was home to the city's strip clubs, Larry Flynt's, Rick's Cabaret, Crazy Horse, and others less well known and less well funded. Jordan passed the higher-end joints and turned into a black rectangle of doorway in a seedy-looking building sporting the signs LIVE GIRLS LIVE and LIVE SEX ACTS.

Better than dead girls dead and dead sex acts, Anna

supposed. Still, it struck her as prurient and adolescent, not a fitting lure for a grown person. Here, she was in the minority. Beside the door was a box, like a speaker's lectern, with a handsome young barker extolling the virtues of the establishment to passersby. On the front of his box was a list of prices for drinks and other services offered within.

Anna stopped in front of the barker. He was a lovely creature with wavy hair the color of old honey and a smile full of fun and fine orthodontia. "Hello, beautiful," he said cheerfully. "Please tell me you are going to add a touch of class to our humble establishment tonight."

"I am," Anna said. "How much do I pay you for the privilege?"

He laid his hand over his heart and looked stricken. "Darlin', do I look like a man who extorts money from lovely ladies? For you, free." Then he added conspiratorially, "There's a two-drink minimum, ten bucks a drink. Don't waste it ordering water."

"I won't," Anna assured him.

He winked and said, "Our girls won't be able to take their eyes off you."

"That's the idea." Anna winked back. It was good to be a lesbian for the evening. Had she thought of it, she would have played that aspect up, though she really couldn't think of how. Butch haircuts and men's clothes were a bit out of fashion. Sedans and children in soccer camp were closer to the mark. Then again, that might merely be the age group of Anna's girlfriends.

These thoughts trailing as she stepped out of the night into the greater darkness of LIVE GIRLS LIVE, it occurred to her that a life spent in the woods wearing a duller shade of green than Robin's merry men was not particularly good training for what was new and happening in the rest of the world.

The club would have had to work hard to be any seedier. From the facades of the higher-end pole-dancing establishments, Anna guessed they had some of the amenities: carpet, mood lighting, and tables with matching chairs. Not the LGL. The room she'd stepped into was maybe twenty by forty feet and had been painted black—floors, walls, ceiling, stage, all flat black. Before this stunning transformation into nothing, it had been pinkish beige. Where the paint was peeling or had been scraped from the plaster walls by chair backs or bored customers, the previous incarnation showed through like bits of decaying flesh through a shredded burka.

Along the left-hand wall was a bar, also painted black. Jordan was behind it, his face a smudge in the gloom, tying a black apron over his clothes. There were no bar stools, and the bar itself was short and narrow and looked to be constructed of plywood.

To the left, six feet from the bar, creating a bottleneck in the middle of the long room, was the stage, also flat black, also built of plywood or something as cheap and uninteresting. Two silver poles were the only setting, one near either end of the three-and-a-half-foot-high, six-by-fifteen-foot rectangle. There were no entrances, no fly space, and no curtains. Just the box and the poles and two performers involved in the "live sex acts" part of the evening.

An athletic young man, dressed in leather cuffs and skintight black pants, had his feet and hands on the floor, face to the ceiling, creating a bench of his midsection. Astraddle the bench, in a tiny blue-and-white pleated skirt, like a much abbreviated Catholic schoolgirl's uniform, bare from the waist up, a woman in her late teens or early twenties bounced as if she were engaged in sex with the bench. Her thighs were taking the brunt of the action so she wouldn't drop her weight—which was not inconsiderable—on her fellow actor. The woman had a baby face as empty of emotion as a badly made doll's. The man looked so bored, had Anna ever wondered where the phrase "the old bump and grind" came from, she did no longer. Given the stunning lack of enthusiasm with which they went through the charade, she was unsure whether these live sex acts would indeed prove more appealing than dead sex acts. Or if there was even a difference in the LGI.

Relief swept through her, so sudden and unexpected it was unsettling, and she thanked any gods still standing that Paul wasn't with her. She found the proceedings sad and distasteful. Paul would have found the dehumanization of the girl and her bench almost intolerably painful.

On her end of the stage, the furniture in the sitting area consisted of thirty-inch wooden cubes for tables, each with a few molded black plastic patio-type chairs kneeing up to them. There were five of these clumps.

Two were occupied by college-age men with too many beers on the table and too many under their belts. A third was the temporary home of a balding middle-aged man as intent on the simulated sex act as the boys were on their beers. His clothes were the ubiquitous khaki pants and polo shirt. His stomach rested on his splayed thighs, his crossed arms on his stomach. The flesh of his face, dragged down by fast food and disappointment, was formed into an expression Anna could only describe as equal parts misery, ecstasy, and guilt.

No, she corrected herself with a second look, not ecstasy, avidity.

Sitting down at the empty table farthest from the bar, Anna adjusted her mask and set about getting to know Jordan.

Looking disgusted, he was wiping down the bar with a rag, scrubbing industriously at places his predecessor had left sticky. When he finished, he folded the rag into a neat square, then began picking up and fiddling with things that were invisible to Anna. As she watched, and her eyes adjusted, she realized he was gathering up black cocktail napkins and arranging them in neat fans. That done, he looked up, noticed the newcomer, and came out from behind the bar, moving toward her corner, his hands rubbing one another in the black of his apron.

For an instant, Anna thought he'd recognized her. Then she noticed the paucity of waitresses. He stopped by her table and said, "Two-drink minimum, drinks are ten dollars each."

"I'll take a Coke," Anna replied in a voice an octave lower than she customarily used. Either it fooled Jordan or he didn't care who she was or what she did on her time off.

"It's still ten dollars," he said.

"That'll be fine."

Jordan turned, continuing to rub his hands in a tortured homage to Pontius Pilate. Back behind the bar, he stooped; a light paled his face, then winked out, and he rose with a bottle of Pepsi in his hand. He returned to her table, put down a black napkin, set the Pepsi carefully in the middle of it, and said, "You need to pay for the drinks up front."

Anna pulled a money clip with several twenties from her pocket and peeled one off, plus a couple of ones for his tip. Ten percent. Usually, Anna overtipped. To work her way through college, she'd waited tables, and she believed if one couldn't afford a tip, one couldn't afford to eat out. Whatever Jordan was into, she suspected it wasn't something she wanted to help bankroll, but stiffing him would have called too much attention to her. Servers noticed people who stiffed them.

Pocketing the tip and closing his fist around the twenty, he went back to the bar, put the money under the counter, and began scrubbing the bar again, though neither drink nor food had touched it in the interim. Not once did he look at the stage.

The bench man slid from beneath the schoolgirl. Both clumped down stairs on the far side of the stage, wove their way between more box tables, and disappeared in the back. They were replaced by a handsome black woman in her mid-thirties wearing a high school marching band outfit—sans pants—and high-heeled red gladiator sandals. She took the stage as if she meant to do something with it and nodded at Jordan, who turned his back and put a CD in a portable player.

"House of the Rising Sun."

Anna couldn't remember ever walking through the entertainment district of any city in America where she didn't hear that song leaking out of at least one barroom.

After a few gyrations the band uniform came off with a ripping of Velcro. Jordan showed no interest in anything but compulsively cleaning his small corner of this dirty world, an activity Anna wouldn't have expected of him, given the way he smelled and looked in his free time. It reminded her of the clean lilac scent of his little black dog. Perhaps he'd learned to compartmentalize his filth in order to allow himself to live with it.

Compartmentalization was even better than denial. It was how the Baptist preachers who stopped at pullouts on the Natchez Trace to have anonymous sex with other men on the way home from church to family were able to live with themselves, the way brokers and bankers could defraud the public and continue to consider themselves righteous members of the community. People did it all the time. One compartment was not allowed to touch the other. Internal peace was maintained. To a point.

The woman on the stage had worked through bra
and panties and was down to G-string and pasties. The
boys with the beers were taking notice, and their excitement and noise level had increased accordingly.
The balding man in khaki was intermittently staring
and then closing his eyes as if the intensity of the sight
were too much to take in for any length of time.

Jordan disappeared into the back for a few minutes,
carrying bottles to tables beyond the stage. Everything
served, Anna noticed, was in the original bottles: one-
shot airplane-sized bottles of hard liquor, one-glass
bottles of cheap wine, Pepsi, bottled water. Not even
twisting the tops off, Jordan set them on his endless
supply of black napkins. The bald man had a plastic
glass with ice in it for his tiny bottle of bourbon. He
must have requested it to make this night even more
special.

A shape loomed from the darkness behind Anna
and became corporeal in the plastic chair at her elbow.

"Is this seat taken?"

Anna adjusted her mask so she could see. Being
flamboyantly incognito had its drawbacks. A woman
of about her age, maybe a little older, early fifties, with
the corded arms and seamed face of someone who did
hard manual labor for a living, sat smiling at her with
crooked teeth and a lascivious gleam in her eye.

"Hey," she said. She stuck out her hand. "I'm Betty."
Anna couldn't resist the rakishness of the smile and the
hard-knuckled, calloused hand. Rakishness, in a black-
out room full of sad addictions, was positively refreshing.

Naughtiness: the kind of misbehavior that still retained humor and fun.

"Anna," Anna said, taking the proffered hand. It crossed her mind to give a fake name in case Betty spoke of her to Jordan, but she didn't. If she did blow her cover, it wouldn't be a disaster. Indeed, it might be good for Jordan to know there were other eyes than those of the snake loa watching him.

Betty crunched Anna's knuckles in a steely grip. "I give," Anna said easily. "You're the strongest."

Betty looked nonplussed for a moment, then laughed, a happy cackle. "Believe it or not, that wasn't intentional. I work over at the docks. It's my job to crate and uncrate perishables depending on if they're coming or going. Bad news, good news: I got arthritis starting up in my knuckles, but there isn't a pickle jar in America I can't open."

The dancer left the stage, moving remarkably gracefully on the six-inch heels, and hip-chucked her way from table to table. The college boys laughed and flirted, and she laughed and flirted back until they had tucked a handful of bills in the string of her thong; then she undulated to the bald bourbon drinker's table and gyrated while he, looking even more miserable than he had earlier, tucked a twenty into her G-string, the backs of his fingers lingering against the skin of her belly till she wormed away.

"That's Tanya," Betty told Anna, gesturing at the dancer with the neck of her Budweiser. "She is too good for this dump. Way too good. You'd think Larry's or Rick's would snatch her up."

"Maybe she's the wrong color," Anna ventured just to see what happened.

"Could be. She's my girlfriend."

"Congratulations," Anna said. "I'd like to meet her."

"Oh, she doesn't know she's my girlfriend. Not yet," Betty said. "Right now she just thinks I'm a fan, but I'm growing on her. Like Paul Newman in that old movie? I grow on people."

She was growing on Anna. There was something so straightforward and good-humored about her that Betty felt like the only piece of genuine earth in the assorted filths of the club. Tanya wriggled her way past the long arms of the college tables toward where Anna and Betty sat.

"Shoot," Anna said. "All I've got is a twenty."

"Give it to her. You look like you've got dough," Betty said.

"Easy for you to say," Anna grumbled. "You get union wages."

As she dug out her money clip again, she felt Betty's hand trace lightly over her right buttock.

"Hah!" the dock worker crowed. "Calvin Kleins. Fork it over. My girl works hard for her money."

"And here I thought you just liked me," Anna said and peeled off yet another twenty.

"Nope. I'm a one-woman woman," Betty said. She snatched up Anna's twenty, added one of her own, and tucked it into Tanya's G-string. "You doing okay, baby. Any of these goons bothering you?"

"They wouldn't dare," Tanya said.

Betty laughed. "That's my girl!" The dancer gave her a bump on the shoulder with her hip and left to work the far side of the room. "Tanya tells customers she's paying her way through college on the pole, but she isn't. Tanya's got a son in college, Tulane. She strips because she digs it."

"Cool," Anna said, to prove she was listening. "What do you know about the bartender?"

Betty slammed her beer down on the black cube that served as their table and stared balefully at Anna. "Okay. You can tell me you're straight. I can live with that. But you tell me you're straight *and* interested in that little peckerwood and I'll go sit with bald boy over there."

"My interest is purely malicious," Anna assured her.

"That's all right, then," Betty said.

"Why do you call him a peckerwood?" Anna asked curiously.

"If I tell you, will you take off that ridiculous mask?"

"What the hell," Anna said. The thing kept slipping down her nose and blocking her vision anyway. She pulled it back, threaded her braid out through the elastic band, and laid the mask on the cube.

Betty looked at her, squinting a little in the odd dim yet glaring lighting design of house and stage. "Nothing to be ashamed of," she pronounced at last. "For an old broad, you're a stunner."

"Thank you," Anna said dryly and took a swallow of her Pepsi. "Peckerwood?" she nudged. The bench rider was back. She wore the same schoolgirl mini but had added a man's tie for some reason. As she worked the pole, Anna's attention was caught by the girl's middle and her breasts.

When Betty raised her eyebrows at Anna's sudden interest in the stripper, Anna said, "I'd bet a month's salary that child is pregnant."

"Good eye," Betty said. "Four months gone."

"It doesn't get much worse, does it?"

"You're not from around here, are you? That's Candy. I don't know her last name. I've had her do a couple lap dances for me, you know, in private." Anna didn't know, but she could imagine. "Candy has the IQ of about an eight-year-old, maybe ten. I told the owner he was a piece of shit, but he keeps her on. She probably works for beer and TV privileges," Betty said. "I never even tried for a feel, just tipped her good and hoped some bastard let her keep some of it. I may be an old dyke, but I'm not a sick old dyke." She took a deep swig of the beer.

"And I respect you for it," Anna said honestly. "Is she tied in with the bartender?"

"Not that I know of," Betty said. "He's not the owner. He's a peckerwood all by his little lonesome." For a long moment, Anna and Betty watched Jordan. Betty took another swig of her beer and held it up, the universal signal for "Bring me another." Jordan responded with a fractional nod and ducked under the counter.

Again the light hit his face. A small icebox under the counter, Anna guessed. He straightened up with a beer in his hand and came around the end of the bar.

"What do you know against him?" Anna asked.

"Nothing specific. He ignores Tanya and he's not gay. That is weird in and of itself."

"How do you—"

"Gaydar," Betty said. "He's not gay. He's just a freak of some kind."

Jordan wove through the cubes and chairs and put the fresh beer on a clean napkin in front of Betty. "Are you ready for your second?" he asked Anna.

The mask was off. Anna looked him square in the face for a second, waiting for him to recognize her. At first he seemed so lost in his haunted inner landscape he didn't. Then his eyes cleared, widened, narrowed, and, without waiting for her to reply, he turned and left, going not to the bar but to the dark recesses on the far side of the stage.

"What's it with you and the peckerwood?" Betty demanded.

"Malice," Anna repeated.

Betty sighed. "I'm here for love, not war. Go to the ladies' room."

"I don't have to," Anna said.

"Go anyway. Ah, beauty rises from the ashes!" Tanya was back, climbing the stairs to the poles, a silver cape and taxi cap over very little else.

Anna left Betty to her worship, elbowed her way through a gout of confused, overheated middle-aged

men who'd just come in, and headed toward the back of
the hourglass where the restrooms had to be. Jordan
passed her in the bottleneck between stage and bar. He
didn't make eye contact, but she could see his bones
stiffening what little flesh remained uneaten by demons.

Dead center of the back wall, between more cube
tables and plastic chairs filled with men and cheap
drinks, was a hallway as black and featureless as the
rest of the club. There being no other place to go, Anna
walked into it, feeling much as she imagined a cow
might feel walking into a chute at the slaughterhouse.
Three doors opened off the end of the truncated hallway, one to either side, one marked with a crude drawing of breasts, the other with that of a penis, larger than
life and erect, naturally. The third was at the end of the
hall, leading either upstairs or out to an alley. A faint
reek of urine emanated from the men's room; a stronger but not as repugnant reek of marijuana smoke emanated from the ladies'.

Putting her hand between the cartoon boobs, Anna
gently eased open the door and slid into the fog.

FIFTEEN

The happy lapping up of brains convulsed Clare's stomach one more time before she found the wherewithal to grab the little dog. Always willing to reassure his people, Mackie turned in her arms to lick her face. Blood discolored the white mustache and chin whiskers. Clare retched again but rose regardless, the dog clamped under one arm, and headed toward the small door that had to be either closet or lavatory. It was the lavatory. For this lack of delay in washing the vomit from her chin—and the blood from that of her dog—she actually felt lucky. After a night of ongoing misery, and a day promising more of the same, even this tiny easement was noted.

Mackie was dumped unceremoniously into the tub and the sink tap turned on as high as it would go. Water exploded out in a brown rush, splattering the front of her coat and the floor. The dog made a dash for the door and the irresistible delights that lay beyond.

"No!" Clare cried as she kicked the flimsy wooden panel, slamming the door almost on Mack's nose. The thought of him doing what he'd been doing even when she was not looking was intolerable.

The bathroom of the apartment was sufficiently cramped that one tub, one stool, one sink, a woman, and a small dog filled it to capacity. Mack sat between her feet as she washed her face. She could feel the cold trail of his bloodied whiskers on the insides of her calves as he licked her with a tongue that might still have the children's babysitter's brains on it. For a moment Clare thought she was crying—or perhaps vomiting again—but she was laughing. The confluence of events had come together with such stunning wretchedness that she couldn't contain the horror. It was cartoonlike, surreal, funny.

Damn funny. Too funny.

She was becoming hysterical or going insane. Neither was acceptable. Mackie began to whine. Clare raised her head and stared at herself in the mirror over the sink. The glass was old, the silver backing gone along the bottom edge, and the light over the bowl wasn't very bright. Even with this help, she looked a fright, frightening. Like a woman who could murder her own children. Abruptly she stopped laughing.

She had seen the small bodies. Against that, all she had was the knowledge—unratified by any living creature, including the dog—that Vee and Dana were not in the house when she came home. That, and the disparate facts of two dogs, one stuffed, one live, that were outside the house when by rights, if the children were within, the dogs should have been as well.

Staring at the face in the glass, the face of a woman much older than Clare's forty-two years, she said, "If they were dead, I would know it, I would feel it." Against the recommendations of those still in love with the Method, Clare had practiced the lines to more than a hundred plays watching herself in the mirror. This line sounded trite. Maybe she'd said it before onstage, read it in a book, heard another actor trying to make it fresh on a *Lifetime Movie of the Week*. Proof that simply because something was believed, or was true, that didn't make it good theater.

"I *would* feel it," she said again, putting the emphasis on the auxiliary verb. It had to be right. A mother was a *mother*, for God's sake. She would feel it if her children were dead.

When a child was taken, snatched from the sidewalk or school or the playground and spirited away, was this how the mothers felt? Like a great gaping maw of pain with only a microscopic flicker of hope to light their way back to life as it had once been? Did they, long after their daughters and sons were rotting in a shallow grave in some freak's backyard, still feel the life of that child like the whisper of a half-heard secret borne on the wind?

Sorrow so deep the only sensations were those of cold and dizziness enveloped her, and she grabbed the edge of the sink to keep from falling. Clearly her mind

was not a place she could afford to go alone anymore.
Moving to keep moving, she bent and snatched up the
dog. Mackie, sensing he had transgressed grievously
without knowing how, didn't fight her as she sluiced off
his jaws.

She was sitting on the toilet seat toweling him off
with an unadorned white Turkish towel when she heard
the apartment door open. Or thought she did. In apartment buildings it was easy to believe homey sounds
coming through the thin walls were actually occurring
in one's own abode. "Shhh," she said, though the dog
on her lap wasn't making a sound.

*Jalila. No. Jalila was dead. Whoever had made
Jalila dead? David?* Her short list of suspects—one of
whom had the perfect alibi and the other probably the
same—exhausted, Clare began to feel afraid.

It wasn't lost on her that, not too many hours past,
she'd wanted nothing more than to kill herself. Now
she was afraid for her life. A common enemy seemed
to be a cohesive force even when one battled only with
one's self. "Shh," she whispered again. This time Mackie
needed the reminder. His hearing more acute than
hers, he'd begun to growl, a thread of sound deep in his
chest. Not the sort of noise that would strike terror into
people's souls or make them hesitate to kick down the
bathroom door.

Door.

Clare reached over and turned the old-fashioned bolt.
The metal was sturdy, but the wood of the door wouldn't
withstand a strong breeze, let alone a determined foot.

She unlocked it, turned the knob, and opened it a foot or so. From a dramatist's point of view, an unlocked door was less interesting than a locked door, a closed door more interesting than one left slightly ajar. Secrets built tension. The unseen was more powerful than the seen.

Hoping she hadn't waited too long, she switched off the light. The bathroom was small enough that she didn't even have to disturb the dog. Bending over Mackie in her lap, Clare closed her eyes as if that would hide her or make her hearing more acute.

The front room's door banged back. Whoever opened it was not pleased or didn't know his own strength. Carpet swallowed the sounds of feet entering.

"Right where I left it." The voice was young, cheery, and, in some indefinable way, uneducated. There was a trace of an accent. Southern, but Clare couldn't tell from where. There were as many drawls as there were counties in the South, each a little different, depending on local culture and caste.

"Where the hell do you think you're going?"

Clare recognized this voice: the dark man on the cell phone who'd had the little girl by the hand. The man who'd said odd words: "Bourbon Street nursery," "magician," and something else she couldn't recall. There on the commode, his accent came to Clare. Cajun, the man was Cajun. There wasn't much call for that in the theater, but zydeco had been used as curtain music for *A Streetcar Named Desire*. Deemed too old for either Blanche or Stella, Clare'd had to sit that one out, but she

remembered the accent from several of the cuts on the
CD they'd used.

"I'm just gonna look."

"You think she put her head back together and
moved? Come on. Get away from there."

"I gotta take a leak." The young voice, the lighter of
the two, had come closer. Clare guessed he was in the
bedroom where Jalila lay—or at least standing in the
doorway. She didn't dare look.

A long silence wound out. Clare felt her nerves
winding out with it. A scream sang along the distance,
and she feared it would come out of her mouth if
something didn't break soon. These were the men who
had murdered Jalila. Probably the men who set fire to
the house. These men knew what had happened to her
children.

She didn't know if the scream was because she might
be found, and her corpse and that of her dog added to the
carnage, or because she knew she could not step from
the bathroom and pull the information she craved out of
these men along with their fingernails, entrails, and any
other part of their anatomies that might cause extreme
pain.

Silence dragged on.

Clare wondered whether the younger man was using the carpet beside Jalila's body as a urinal or waiting for the Cajun to give him permission to go to the
bathroom.

With a jolt her tired, shocky brain realized she was

in the bathroom, she and Mackie, in a space too small to hide even a rubber ducky, much less a woman and a dog. Years of ballet classes and fencing lessons allowed her to stand, dog in arms, and step over the edge of the claw-foot tub without making a sound. The shower curtain, white Egyptian cotton, hung from a metal ring suspended from the ceiling. The showerhead was an add-on, a long silver snake of pipe with a sprinkler set into a hook on the wall. The curtain was partially drawn. Clare eased back behind it.

David was a stickler for cleanliness and natural fibers. Much of the clothing he put together in the factory was made of polyester, rayon, and acrylic—the sort of thing one would expect to find in Target or Walmart for the most part. He himself would let nothing that had not once been living touch his skin. Till this night she'd thought it was because it was "natural"—whatever that meant anymore. Now, as she eased the 100 percent white cotton curtain along the track as quietly as she could with one hand, she wondered if it wasn't that he just enjoyed the sensation of something once living dead against his skin.

As with the bathroom door, she left the curtain open slightly. It would seem emptier that way.

"Let's get out of here," the Cajun hollered. He, at least, was still in the front room. Clare turned her back on the commode and closed her eyes. She knew there was little to the idea that people could feel eyes on them, feel themselves being watched. Over the years she'd watched hundreds of people, studying them for mannerisms, tics, postures, and walks she wanted to emulate for one role or another, listening in on conversations at neighboring tables, in the row behind her at the movies, on buses and planes and trains. People didn't feel her eyes upon them. Ninety-nine percent of the human race seemed to move through life in capsules, neither seeing nor hearing nor noticing other capsules unless they inadvertently crashed into them. Still, she turned away.

Mackie, already restless with fatigue and the anxiety boiling off his mistress, began to squirm. Clare tried holding him more tightly, but that brought the beginnings of a whine, and she had to settle for juggling a writhing dog. Having raised two daughters, she had experience in the exercise.

"I gotta go. Pleeeeeease." The man sounded younger even than before, like a kid no more than nine or ten. In her mind Clare saw him standing in the doorway near the murdered girl, his legs crossed, and his hand in the air with one finger extended. This time the layering of the absurd and the macabre didn't make her want to laugh.

"Make it fast." This from the Cajun.

She heard the bedroom door close and waited for the sound of the man's steps to leave the carpet and move onto the tile of her small prison.

Nothing.

Nothing.

Nothing.

"Hey, Dougie, you fall in?" The Cajun again, shouting from the living room.

From nearer Clare heard a low-voiced mantra. "Unh, unh, uh." Bile rose in her throat. The man wasn't taking a leak; he was beating off over Jalila. Maybe he was beating off. Maybe he was a necrophiliac. She bit down on her lower lip and buried her face in Mackie's fur so she would not see with her mind's eye.

A crash jerked her like a fish on a line. She may even have squeaked, but the racket from the other room drowned it out.

Something hard hitting flesh. "You sick fuck!" A thud as if a body hit the wall. "You sick son of a bitch." Another thump and a high injured cry. "Serves you right. Goddamn, you're a piece of work."

"Blackie, I didn't—" Slam.

A moment of quiet followed. Clare hoped the Cajun, whom she was warming up to simply because he exhibited a shred of human decency, had killed the other man.

There was a long silence. Then, "Somebody's been here." It was the Cajun again, but all anger had gone from his voice. It was as hard and packed as January snow.

Clare no longer trusted in his human decency.

SIXTEEN

The smoke was so thick it made Anna's eyes sting. Breathing in, she remembered the pot she'd smoked in college. At the tender age of twenty she'd taken a single hit of windowpane acid and hit the wall. After that her drugs had been limited to wine and, if it was hot enough and there was Mexican food in the offing, a beer now and then.

Stepping into the narcotic cloud, Anna closed the door behind her. Since Live Girls Live wasn't an establishment that catered to women clientele—Betty and Anna notwithstanding—little time or money had been allotted for the women's restroom. The tawdry space served double duty as public toilet and dressing room for the entertainers.

The pregnant, mentally retarded schoolgirl and an older stripper, so gaunt in her abbreviated costume of tap pants and matching bra that Anna could count each rib and see where it connected to the sternum, sat on folding chairs in front of a one-by-six piece of pine cantilevered out from the wall on metal shelf holders and littered with lipsticks, eye shadows, brushes, curlers, ashtrays, half-eaten bags of chips, and various other substances. Screwed to the wall above the narrow shelf was a cheap framed mirror. The only light in the LGL's rendition of a makeup area was an overhead bulb. A third woman, college age, thin, with augmented breasts and a plain face, leaned against a pedestal sink. The three of them crowded the room nearly to overflowing.

A single toilet stall with a black plywood door of the same tone and vintage as the bar and stage took up the remainder of the space. Anna stood with her back against the door because there was nowhere else for her to be.

The women looked up at her disinterestedly. The gaunt woman took a hit off the joint and passed it to the pregnant girl. In the odd voice of those trying to keep the good smoke trapped in their lungs while speaking, she said to Anna, "You want to use the toilet, knock yourself out."

"Thanks," Anna said. She bumped and apologized her way past knees and elbows and shut herself behind the stall door. Once there, she figured she might as well make good on her excuse for barging in and use the facilities.

Sitting in her partitioned box, listening to the desultory chat of the strippers, Anna wondered how she was going to pry her way into this group to ask her questions about Jordan. Information from the employees was the only thing Betty could have thought a trip to the loo would provide. As she dawdled, trying to stretch out an acceptable amount of time to be on the toilet, it occurred to her there was no way to finesse this one.

Having made herself once again presentable, she eeled out of the stall and leaned back against the plywood door. It creaked and moved a tad but held. "My name's Anna," she said. "I've got a proposition to make you."

"We're together," the gaunt woman said, indicating the artificially endowed woman by the sink.

"I don't go with girls," the schoolgirl whispered timidly as if Anna would take a belt to her for the rebuff.

"You ought not go with nobody," the gaunt woman said. "That's why you're getting fatter and fatter." To Anna she said, "I'm Star. This is Delilah," she nodded to her partner. "And this baby here is Candy."

"I'm not a baby," Candy said.

"Tanya might be interested, but I doubt it," Delilah said.

"Not sex," Anna said. "Information."

"Sex is cheaper," Star said. The three of them laughed, though Anna wasn't sure Candy knew what she was laughing at. In such close proximity, she looked younger than she did under the harsh lights of the stage. If she was of legal age, Anna would have been surprised. The skin of her face and breasts was flawless, the flesh around her eyes plump like that of a child, and her hair was baby fine. At a guess, Anna put her at no more than fourteen, maybe as young as eleven.

Delilah offered Anna the joint. She took a hit to prove she wasn't a narc, but the smoke exploded in her chest and she went into a paroxysm of coughing, much to the amusement of the strippers.

"Sorry," she gasped when she could catch her breath. "Out of practice."

"When were you in practice?" Star asked.

"When they came in lids and were fifteen dollars apiece," Anna said.

"Historical," Delilah said. "Hold on to your head. This isn't your grandma's weed, Grandma."

"You got that right," Anna admitted. The drug was already hitting her, and she wondered if she would remember anything she learned here. If she learned anything here.

Taking the joint from Anna, Star passed it to Candy, who pinched it expertly between thumb and forefinger and, narrowing her eyes against the smoke, took a hit.

Star watched Anna watching Candy suck marijuana smoke into her—and thus the fetus's—lungs. Anna returned her stare and shrugged infinitesimally. Candy's baby had so much going against it, Anna's ruining one toke wasn't going to get the poor little bugger into Harvard.

Evidently that giving over of judgment was what Star was looking for.

"Tell us what you want to know and we'll tell you what it'll cost," she said. "What we don't know, we'll make up."

"What if she's a cop and starts asking about . . .

things?" Delilah asked. Anna's one choking drag from the joint had not impressed her overmuch.

"Then we lie," Star said easily. "So, what do you want to know?"

Breathing in the confines of the smoking-room-cum-toilet was getting Anna high. The feeling wasn't one she particularly relished. Too close to crazy, too close to out of control. Claustrophobia was licking at its heels, and Anna had to force herself to concentrate.

Why had she come? What was it she was so all-fired desperate to know that she'd put on a cat mask, then paid twenty bucks to a pole dancer and twenty more for a lukewarm Pepsi? In the john of a shabby strip club, filled with a brand of courage and a flavor of despair she couldn't quite come to terms with, one creepy little bartender putting pigeons in garbage cans and freaking out over her catching his terrier didn't seem to matter much in the scheme of evil.

Before she could talk herself into saving her lungs and what was left of her cash, Anna remembered Laura and the look Jordan had burned through the window of the voodoo shop when he'd seen her playing with her prince and princess dolls.

"What do you know about the guy tending bar to-night?" Anna asked.

"Oooh, you're interested in that little pissant mother-fucker," Star said scornfully.

"He's not," Candy protested.

"Yeah, right," Delilah said as she tore open a bag of gummi bears with her long blue acrylic nails. "And the pope's not Catholic. Believe me, Jordan is truly a pissant motherfucker. Listen to your wise Auntie Star on this one, baby."

"You're just jealous because he only likes me and doesn't care about your new boobies."

"Yeah," Star said, smiling at her girlfriend. "For what we paid for those beauties, any cock that doesn't stand up and salute when they come out oughta be buggy-whipped."

"She is, too, jealous," Candy insisted. "Jordan likes me a lot. He takes care of me. We're like boyfriend and girlfriend."

"That's what got you in trouble in the first place," Star said. "This boyfriend stuff got you a baby. You got to get rid of it; you know that, baby doll. Ain't no way you can be bringing up a kid."

"I'm gonna get rid of it," Candy said. To Anna she looked scared. Not sad at the loss of her child, but scared of what it was going to take to lose it.

"How long has Jordan worked here?" Anna asked.

"Not long. Maybe a week, ten days."

"And he likes you best," Anna said to Candy.

"Better than Star or Delilah or even Tanya, and she's real pretty." If either of the other women in the dressing room minded Tanya being called the pretty one, it didn't show. "He doesn't call me a baby. He likes it that I'm not old."

"Motherfucker," Star muttered.

"Short eyes," Delilah said succinctly. "He's been ask-

ing everybody where you can find that sort of thing."
She wasn't being coy or evasive by not spelling it out,
Anna realized; she was being sensitive to Candy's feelings. Another wise old auntie, she guessed. Candy could
be worse off.

"We told him to fuck off and die," Star said. "But we
said it real nice." Both she and Delilah laughed. Candy
laughed, too, and this time Anna knew why she joined
in; she wanted to belong.

Star held the roach out, now in a gaudy beaded clip,
offering Anna the last toke.

"No thanks," Anna said. "I'm trying to cut down."

Star took the last hit and dropped the last bit into
the ashtray. Candy retrieved it and popped it into her
mouth.

"Then he falls for our Candy girl," Star said. "And
he's all interested in where she's been and if there are
other girls like her but younger and if any of her 'little
friends' are in the business and where they might be
working and shit like that."

"It's not shit!" Candy said. "He's interested in me.
He likes me." She was about to cry.

Star said, "I know he does, baby girl. You're an interesting person. Jordan might be a pissant mother-
fucker, but he's got good taste. We just think you're too
good for him, that's all, baby. Don't you cry, or Delilah's going to have to do your makeup all over again,
and there ain't time before your next act."

Delilah shook a Marlboro Light out of a pack, lit

it, sucked in a lungful of smoke, and then blew it out slowly. Anna felt like she was about to pass out from lack of air and space.

"You guys know where he's from? What his last name is? Where he worked before he came here? Anything like that?" Anna asked.

"Nope," Star said.

"And don't care to," Delilah said on another stream of smoke.

"How about you, Candy? Does Jordan tell you about his family or his home?" Anna asked.

"He's got a dog," Candy said. "He let me pet it. I like dogs a lot."

Anna wasn't going to get anything more—or, even if she was, she doubted she could survive in this alien atmosphere long enough to make use of it. She took the money clip out and emptied it onto the board that served to hold their cosmetics and ashtrays.

"Forty dollars is all I've got," she said. "Thanks a million. Have a good night. Uh, break a leg, I guess," she said as she weaseled her way back through the naked limbs to the bathroom door and out.

The club smelled of sweat and beer and cigarette smoke and, where she was, stale urine. Still, it was a breath of fresh air after the ladies' lounge, and Anna breathed deep of the lesser miasma.

As she began to walk toward the dim light at the end of this particular tunnel, a hand closed hard on her upper arm, and she swung around ready to clock some guy. It was Delilah holding her bicep in a pincer grip. Fighting the urge to deck her and run, Anna stopped docilely in the black-walled fun-house hallway and waited.

"Don't go getting your panties in a wad and telling anybody Candy's knocked up, not eighteen, and not Einstein. Guy owns this place is okay. She's got nobody. Nobody. She was hooking at ten bucks a fuck to anybody who came along. Which was at least ten bucks more than she got from her last joint. Here all she's gotta do is dance, and she likes it. It makes her feel important and cared for. You tell some agency, and they take her, and she's going to run away and be back on the streets or dead."

"You and Star look after her?" Anna asked.

"We try."

"Will you keep Jordan away from her?"

"Shit, there's always a Jordan. You can't keep them all away. If it makes you feel any better, we're pretty sure he's not fucking her."

Anna did feel better, at least till Delilah added matter-of-factly, "Not yet, anyway."

SEVENTEEN

Clare had heard the phrase "her heart turned over in her chest" and thought it merely a case of undeserved poetic licensing. When the Cajun said, "Somebody's here," she realized it was an anatomical reality. Whatever muscle worked its magic beneath the left side of her sternum twisted. Breath, intentionally hushed, whistled between her teeth. Blood banged in her ears, so loud it was surely audible outside of her skull.

"Did you get to the toilet or just . . . Jesus effing Christ. Check the goddam toilet and we can get out of here," the Cajun said.

In the sere corners of Clare's eyes, new tears formed. Terror, fatigue, guilt at being alive and at wanting to stay that way, turned to saltwater and flooded to lash line.

"Look, dickwad, if you didn't puke, somebody else did," the Cajun explained as if his companion were an idiot.

"Who'd do that?" Dougie asked, proving the Cajun right. "This isn't like Grand Central Station or nothing."

At the mention of the New York landmark, it struck Clare how incongruously close a Brooklyn accent was to Dougie's speech pattern. Close but not the same. To a trained ear the Cajun-French cadence was marked.

New Orleans.

The French Quarter.

Bourbon Street.

The Bourbon Street nursery.

They were taking the little girl to the "Bourbon Street nursery." Clare doubted these two were the child's god-fathers. Why did they have a four- or five-year-old girl with them in the first place? What had David done to condemn her own children?

With a fierce spike of need, Clare prayed to the dark gods that the charred corpse from the house fire was not her husband. She wanted to kill him herself, wanted it in a way she'd never wanted anything in her life: a visceral need, a druglike jonesing for the feel of her teeth ripping into the flesh of his throat.

"There's a wife." The Cajun cut into the false euphoria of Clare's revenge fantasy. "The wife wasn't in the house. It was the middle of the damn night. Where was she? Doing the lawn boy while he does the nanny? Maybe she's got a key to this place. Maybe she knows everything. Maybe she's in on it."

"He got a wife?" Dougie brightened at the mention of a woman, but not by much. Evidently living females were not to his taste.

Footsteps whispered over David's white-on-white vomit-on-blood-and-brains carpet. Clare cringed, her very bones feeling as if they telescoped with her wish to disappear. Curling down over Mackie's head, she wept for herself. Beneath her chin, the dog's silky neck hairs stiffened, and he emitted a faint and ludicrously dangerous growl.

The Lhasa, all sixteen pounds of his short-jawed puppy-fuzzed self, was willing to do battle with armed men to save her. His courage shamed her. Shame's heat dried her tears. She was to be slaughtered cowering and whimpering in her philandering husband's claw-foot tub by the men who had butchered her babysitter and burned her house to the ground. That they might also have murdered her children was not a concept she could factor in and stay sane. The pain, the rage—the helplessness— would melt her very bones, freeze her soul.

Strength born of the desperation said to give mothers the power to lift tractors off infants coursed through her with such force she was surprised she did not levitate. Before she had lowered the brave terrier to the porcelain tub bottom this superhuman power had gone, but a bony courage remained. "Hush," she whispered. Mackie obeyed, sitting in the middle of the tub. Looking around the tiny space for a weapon, she stepped silently from behind the shower curtain.

"Shit," she breathed with unthinking irony and snatched up the toilet brush. In his quest for purity or, as she had long suspected, his quest to suck the life out of Life, David had installed stainless steel accoutrements in their home, his office, and here. One of the rare moments of genuine merriment he had afforded her was when, on surveying a kitchen he had robbed of humanity, he'd said with all sincerity, "Accessorizing is so important." Her amusement was short-lived. David did not like being laughed at.

With two killers on the far side of a flimsy door, Clare finally appreciated her husband's love of heavy metal. In the great pantheon of weaponry a toilet brush might seem absurd, but at least David Sullivan's had heft. Filling her mind with Sammy Sosa, Babe Didrikson, and Geena Davis in *A League of Their Own,* she widened her stance, straightened her spine, choked up on the handle of the brush, and waited.

Lines, ever floating in the actor's personal cyberspace, spat out three words: "Go down swinging."

The muffled footfalls came to a stop. Dougie's voice, closer now, two or three feet from the bathroom door, slewed in Clare's ear as he turned back to address his companion. "We gotta get back. That little wiggler'll be as dead as those first two. Smother her own self," he yelled. The Cajun must have gone into the other room.

"Smother *her own* self," the Cajun repeated snidely, his voice low yet clearly audible through the walls. "You never *do* nothing, do you, Dougie? Guns 'go off,' things 'happen,' kids smother their *own selves*. You're not responsible for nothing, are you?" He waited as if for a reply, then sighed as if he'd been a fool to do so. "Did you go to the toilet or did you just—" His voice trailed off wetly as if he gagged on his own thoughts. "Fuck. Just check the toilet. Jesus. Fuck."

Clare rolled her head, trying to relax, to focus. *It's showtime,"* Bob Fosse from *All That Jazz* whispered in her ear.

"No, no, I did. I mean I checked the toilet," Dougie said, and Clare wondered why he lied. He wasn't scared, she was pretty sure of that. Then it came to her. He lied to make Blackie think better of him, like him a little bit. Sure, he did unspeakable things to the corpses of women he'd bludgeoned to death, but he really did take a leak when he said he would. And he lied because he could, because it made him bigger than the fools who believed him. Lies were power and currency to the world's Dougies.

Another thing the Dougies had in common: They could never leave well enough alone. He hurried on, "You see, it was like this, I did take a piss, see, then I was coming back quick as a bunny and she's laying here legs all spread like some kinda whore—"

"She's dead, you fuck." Another dull thud, knuckles on bone and the ubiquitous "Fuck," Dougie's head evidently proving harder than the Cajun's fist.

"Move." A crash. "Move." The sound of a body stumbling into something. "Move." The Cajun was herding the pervert from the front room with kicks to various parts of the latter's anatomy. The apartment door slammed open. Smashed shut. A metallic swallowing sound came as the dead bolt slid into place.

They were leaving. They'd left. Clare didn't have to fight for her life with a toilet brush. She wouldn't be beaten, raped, clubbed to death.

She didn't lower her erstwhile weapon, nor did she relax her vigilance.

These men, these monsters, had a key to her husband's pied-à-terre; murderers, smotherers of children, had a key to an apartment David's own wife didn't have a key to.

David's business partners? David's *friends*?

"Fuck," she quoted the Cajun. Still she didn't move. Finally her faint imaginings of their footsteps in the hall, on the stairs, passed. Secure in what his nose was telling him, with a hitch and scrabble, Mackie bounded out of the tub. Clare loosed the toilet brush. Her joints had stiffened, welding her fingers into the shape of the handle. She shook them, working out the tension the way she did each night before going onstage.

Mackie headed for the door. Remembering the macabre happenings that had driven her into the bathroom in the first place, Clare scooped him up before he made good his escape and, dog in lap, sat on the seat of the commode.

Heart rate and breathing quickly returned to normal—the rewards of half a lifetime of practicing yoga, meditation, dance, fencing, and half a dozen other disciplines that might, or might not, help an actress remain gainfully employed. Fear still clawed at her belly and brain, but this fear tasted a bit different. In her forty-two years she'd seen exactly two dead bodies. One was her ninety-seven-year-old grandmother, vain to the end, who'd insisted on an open casket so the Dior gown she'd been hoarding against that day for twenty-odd years could be shown off to best effect. The other was a young woman the paramedics had laid out beside the scene of an automobile accident. Clare had driven up just as they covered her face.

Today she had seen four. Two she'd believed to be her own children. Today she had wished and prayed that she, too, would die—but she had lacked the nerve to do it herself and had chosen to wield a toilet brush rather than let someone else do it for her.

Hence Clare Sullivan was alive.

Clare Sullivan was going to be tried for the murder of her daughters, her husband, and his mistress.

While Clare Sullivan was in jail, the men responsible for the carnage were going to get away with the murders and with the small dark child, the child who had whispered "alive" in Arabic. Maybe they were getting away with Dana and Vee. And Clare Sullivan wasn't going to be able to do one damn thing about it.

It was time for Clare Sullivan to vanish.

She had spent three of her four decades slipping into other people's clothes, their words, their worlds, their skins. There was no greater escape than to walk in someone else's shoes. For a long while she sat on the commode lost in thought. Several times Mackie tried to make good his escape, but the memory of his past transgression was still sufficiently vivid that she held tightly to his collar.

Though not yet committed to her next role, the act of stepping away from herself, a mental divesting of the trappings of Clare Sullivan, allowed her brain to shift gears. Grief, guilt, and survival were left behind in the abandoned psyche. The new one, the one that had never been written on, opened up with freshness and clarity of thought. Darkness lapped around the edges, the former life too strong for its losses to be banished entirely, but at least, here, she could think.

The dark-haired child whispered "alive." The little girl was Arabian, maybe Iranian, perhaps Saudi, Iraqi, or Kuwaiti. Possibly even Egyptian. Clare could speak and understand a good deal of Arabic but was not capable of distinguishing dialects or accents from one region to the next. Or even from one nation to the next.

The man who had jerked her arm and called her "brat" was Cajun. Unless it was Bring Your Daughter to Work Day, he had no business with that little girl at an arson/murder site. Unless the child was not his daughter but somehow connected to the fire and the killings.

The sun had risen into a clearing sunny sky, unusual for Seattle in the spring. Behind the white shower curtain a window brightened, throwing Clare's shadow against the glossy white enamel on the wood. Beyond that door was more white-on-white, painted-on purity that David had required to cover . . .

To cover what?

Clare let that question go for the moment.

The stark white beyond had been ruined by the colorful spent life of the au pair. Dead, Jalila was of no use to Clare. She could not answer the questions: why she and David had run out of the house, why only David had returned, why they'd both been killed, why two murderers from Louisiana had a key to David's apartment.

Clare pushed her head between her hands, fists closing tightly in her thick hair. The dog jumped from her lap, and she was wrenched out of her self-absorption. Having recaptured Mackie lest he be tempted beyond his small canine will to resist the edible, she walked through the defiled bedroom, careful not to look at the body, careful not to note whether the skirt or the panties or the legs had been disarranged, and into the living room. Still clutching the dog, she closed the bedroom door firmly behind them.

As she got a bowl of water for Mackie and crumbled outrageously expensive gourmet crackers onto a plate for his breakfast, she cast and recast herself.

A suspected child murderer; the search would be nationwide and intense. She needed money.

She needed to become invisible to the police.

EIGHTEEN

L ord," Paul breathed a word and prayer. "And I
thought carrying a bunch of vomiting boys from
Alcorn to jail was vile duty."

"Odd thing was," Anna said, shoving her toes down
into the corners of the bed where the sheets were still
cool, "I liked the people. I mean Betty and Star and
Candy and even Delilah."

"Not the men?"

Anna thought about that for a moment, not wanting to
damn her beloved's gender unnecessarily. "I didn't know
them. The women, talking, I knew them for people, I
guess. Maybe not the folks I'd necessarily gravitate to,
but if you cut them, they'd bleed, as the bard said. The
men . . . I don't know. They all seemed so *bent*." She
shifted the cell phone to the other ear. Two hours past
midnight, and the murmur of the Quarter had dulled to
a lullaby; still, cell phones always gave her the sensation
she couldn't hear, even when the reception was good.

"Not the college boys. They were just your basic run-of-the-mill sowers of wild oats."

For a few moments they were safe in companionable silence. Over the phone silence was like dead air on a radio; it was a testament to their connection that they could sit, each in his or her own space, miles and miles apart, and be together quietly.

"The bald guy and Jordan were the creepy ones," Anna said. "The way the dancers spoke of things lent an ambient creepiness. That and the black, black hole the owner had built for perverts to crawl into and indulge." Before her visit to the strip club, Anna would have referred to the women as strippers. They were strippers; they stripped off their clothes professionally. After talking with them and sharing their smoke, albeit unwillingly, she gave them the courtesy of the title "dancers," though she'd have hated to excuse it to Alvin Ailey or Martha Graham.

"It's good I wasn't there," Paul said, breaking the silence. "You wouldn't have gotten anything if I'd been there."

Paul not only took responsibility for his actions, he made a point of letting others know when they'd been right and he'd been wrong. It was a generosity of spirit that made Anna respect and love him a little more each time he did it. Lying there, naked and alone, it occurred to her that it was an unbelievably manly thing to do. A quiver went through her.

"I wish you were here," she said and laughed because her voice was slightly husky.

"Me, too. I'm dead on my feet. I always sleep better with you."

"Not tonight you wouldn't," Anna said. They held that thought for a few seconds.

"What do I do now?" she asked. She wasn't in a park, she wasn't in uniform, and she wasn't in the back-country. Urban nastiness wasn't unknown to her, but her brushes with it had been few and far between, and usually she'd worked with other law enforcement, real cops, not tree cops.

"Leave it alone?" Paul suggested hopefully.

Anna knew he didn't mean it. Had it been drug dealers, car thieves, or jaywalkers, he would have urged her to leave it to the NOPD. Where children were concerned, a different set of rules applied. This had been true for Anna even before baby Helena had come into her life in Big Bend. Occasionally she'd noticed the same sort of thing with animals. An old tomcat a friend of hers had, a beastly creature, who, given the chance, would shred the hand that fed it, let the new baby chew on its tail without complaint. When things went too far, the raddled old cat would merely levitate out of the baby's reach. If there was an altruism gene, this was probably its manifestation, a tendency to let the little ones live.

"With the highest murder rate per capita in the nation and, from what I hear, a lousy public response record, I don't think that the police will be of much help at this point," Paul said. "Being a pervert, asking about where to be a pervert, and thinking perverted thoughts—none of that's illegal. You'll have to catch this guy acting out before you'll get any juice with law enforcement."

"That's what—"

Paul spoke over her words, unusual for him. "I don't mean following him down the mean streets in the dark of night. Just keep an eye on him. These guys usually screw up. Most of them don't think what they're doing is wrong, just politically incorrect. They have support systems—not 12-step—fellow perverts that reinforce their belief that they're normal. Good for their psyches, I suppose, but it is bad for their freedom. They forget they are criminal and act out more in the open. Then we catch them."

"You sound tired," Anna said. His voice was hollow enough that he could have been giving a speech he'd given a thousand times to a painted audience.

"Dog tired."

"Why don't you get some sleep? You have another long day tomorrow?"

"Yeah. I've got two guys coming in to interview. Maybe I'll get somebody to help out by the end of the month."

"Priests or cops?"

"One of each."

"Love you," Anna said.

"And I you," Paul replied. The phone went dead. Her husband was probably asleep before the plastic had cooled.

The lateness of the hour and the excitements of the

day were telling on Anna as well, but she wasn't sleepy.
The fun-house feel of Stephen King–like clowns and
pregnant children lay in the pit of her stomach, a buzz
that mimicked nausea. In a city she was not familiar
with—at least not in any but a surface, tourist sense—it
would be too easy to stumble into organized crime networks and get hurt or killed. When people thought of
organized crime, it was the Mafia or the tongs or, in
recent years, the banks, careless of whom they destroyed in their grasping for money. The big guys were
scary, but the networks most regular people ran afoul
of were the small-time franchises, pimps who "owned"
prostitutes and prostitutes who "owned" street corners
and drug dealers who "owned" territories. The criminal equivalent of mom-and-pop stores. Every city, and
a lot of small towns, were riddled with them.

In New Orleans the streets were littered with the
bodies of gang members. Drug dealers, who'd moved
back to town and were trying to reclaim the patch
they'd had before Katrina, stirred up the muck on the
city's floor. Anna knew most of the black drug crime
was in Center City. Geneva had told her a brand of violent gutter punks had moved into the Marigny east of
the French Quarter. Anybody with a brain knew that,
as squeaky clean as the more famous strip clubs on
Bourbon were, some of the women were hooking some
of the time. There'd be whorehouses and pimps, and so
more territory worth defending.

In a way, Anna was less frightened of Organized

Crime with capital letters than she was of small-time local thugs. Hit men had a lot to lose, a reason not to kill or rough up anybody they weren't paid to.

Local boys often didn't care whether they went to prison or not. Life was short and brutal, and they would kill you for the laces in your shoes if the mood was upon them. Under duress, Anna had been known to attack creatures larger than she, take on burdens too heavy for her frame or mountains too steep for her skill. Now she wasn't under duress; she was on vacation. One of the tenets of a good vacation was that the holiday-makers all come back alive.

So, no sticking her nose into the dark underbelly of this particular beast.

As a private citizen there were things she could do that law enforcement could not, fairly safe things. A member of law enforcement could not break into a person's house and expect any judge in the nation to rule the evidence found there as admissible in court. As a private citizen, Anna could. If she found anything of note, she would call the police. An anonymous tip would do it. Given this was the New Orleans PD, maybe several anonymous tips and a trail of bread crumbs. Or cash, she thought uncharitably.

She picked up the cell phone from beside her on the bed and poked a number to make it light up: 2:23 A.M. In less free-spirited cities the bars closed at midnight or two in the morning. Bourbon Street partied till 4:00 A.M.

No time like the present for a little B and E.

She rose and dressed in the dark. The easy way to accomplish her objective would be to wake Geneva and ask for the key to Jordan's apartment, but Anna hated to drag her friend into the middle of her sleuthing. Besides, she didn't know the legalities of a landlord discovering evidence of a crime in a rental and reporting it. Especially with Geneva. The plain sight ruling might not apply to a blind woman.

If the lock on her cottage was any indication of the state of affairs on Jordan's door, she shouldn't have any trouble getting in. Armed with a flashlight and her library card to jimmy the lock, she descended the stairs and slipped into the courtyard. In the city it was never truly dark. She had no need of a flashlight to find her way, but, once inside Jordan's apartment, she'd feel more secure with a flashlight than if she turned on the overheads.

The alleyway on his side of the house was slightly wider than that on Geneva's, but paved with the same style old brick and verdant with things that loved heat and moisture. This included mosquitoes, and Anna cursed the whining bloodsuckers as she studied the door and window into Jordan's rental. There were no double French doors as on the owner's side. Here was only a plain window, six by four and paned and blinded by closely drawn shades, and a cheap wooden door the previous owner had bought at Home Depot or Lowe's and hung in place of the heavy one that had come with the original house. The window was dark; no light leaked out around the shades or under the door. Emboldened,

Anna stepped up to the lock and took out her library card, hard plastic like a credit card, and slipped it into the generous crack between door and frame. An easy snick let her know the plastic had eased aside the lock just as a sharp yelp froze her in place.

Jordan's mutt. She'd forgotten about the little black dog. Because he was little and soft and smelled of lilacs didn't mean he wouldn't take a bite out of a burglar in the wee hours of the morning. Anna steeled herself to kick the dog if she had to. It took more effort than readying to kick a member of her own species. Animals, by definition, might occasionally be guilty, but they were never culpable.

Slowly, she opened the door an inch or two to see if slavering hound's teeth would Cujo through. Only the sound of panting and another low moan, like a teensyweensy wolf howl, trickled out.

"I'm coming in, little guy. Don't be afraid," Anna said softly as she toed the door open another foot, then two. The inside of the apartment was as dark as human paranoia could make it, the windows not only shaded but draped. Ambient light from the city night drifted around Anna and cast a pale green square on the floor. In the middle was the dog, black as a Rorschach test, tongue hanging drunkenly from one side of its mouth, black feathery tail sweeping enthusiastically across the oaken planks.

"Not much of a watchdog, are you?" Anna asked as she squatted and petted him. Again the funny little howl. "But cute as all get-out," she said. "If I've got to send your daddy to jail, I promise I'll find you a good home. Maybe right here with Sammy and M'Boya. A pack. How would you like that?" The dog looked at her happily. Dogs were so easy to please.

In the precise beam of the flashlight she could see the dog wasn't truly black. As she ruffled his short fur, white showed at the roots. Punk to the bone, Jordan had dyed his dog's fur black. "Lucky you," Anna said. "It could have been tattoos or piercings."

The dog wagged his tail.

"Time to ransack," she told the little beast, and, with a last ruffle of his silky ears, she stood and shined her light around the room. "Holy shit," she whispered.

The room was tiny, eight by seven at best, with only the one window and a door in the back wall leading to either bath- or bedroom. The furnishings consisted of an old desk that had probably been rescued from the street on garbage day or dragged out of the maze of salvage that clogged most of Geneva's property, a chair of the same vintage, a few dishes on a counter with a sink and a microwave, and a laptop and printer. There was nothing to suggest comfort: no couch, rug, television set, or upholstered chair.

There was, however, wall decoration. As she played her light over it Anna wanted to weep and gnash her teeth. Most of all, she wanted to tie Jordan into a granny knot and lock him away for all eternity. Nearly every inch of space was covered with pictures downloaded from the Internet, printed out, and thumbtacked to the walls. Hundreds of pictures of children—little girls mostly—in sexually explicit poses. Some of the children were photographed having sex, with one another, with adults, with animals. Two were of babies, not yet two, being used.

"Goddamn it," Anna hissed. "Goddamn it!" She clicked the flashlight off so she could breathe. Still she could feel the images pressing in from the walls. Anna might have spent most of her adult life with squirrels and pine trees, but she, like every other American, was aware pedophiles stalked playgrounds and the Internet. What she hadn't wrapped her mind around was the sheer magnitude of the horror. In her brief and truncated passage through the photographs Jordan lived amid, she'd been drenched with the cruelty; hundreds of children being used like objects. Did the monsters not see their victims' eyes in the pictures? Dead eyes in five-year-olds, frightened grimaces, terror, dull acceptance, frozen smiles? How could anyone see past those to the point of his perversion? Or was the palpable misery part of the payoff for the pervert?

"Goddamn," Anna whispered, and it wasn't an empty curse; it was a request for the Almighty to put each and every one of them into everlasting hellfire.

She had no desire to crawl deeper into Jordan's lair. She had all she needed. She would call the police and tell them she'd peeked in the window and seen what she'd seen. Regardless of the murders perpetrated in New Orleans on any given night, there wasn't a policeman in a thousand who wouldn't jump at the chance to put a bastard like Jordan away.

Anna backed toward the door as if, in the black pitch of the hole, should she turn her back on the images, the very walls would pour forth sufficient blood and tears to drown her. The dog, invisible in the ink she couldn't bear to disturb with her light, woofed. For a moment she was overwhelmed by a desperate need to rescue the little guy. Surely even a dog did not deserve to live with images like this poisoning the air around him.

Another woof, and she felt the silk of his fur brush her calf. The dog was headed for the door as if he, too, needed to get away before the lights came on and the tragedy on the walls filled the room like concrete. Then he was barking a happy bark and scratching at the wood.

Welcoming his master home.

A key struck the lock with a metallic click. The slimy wretch had come home early.

It was just the sort of thing a prick like Jordan would do, Anna thought.

NINETEEN

The sun was well up by the time Clare had gathered together the tools of her trade—this time a trade of her life for that of a man. Laid out on the counter of the kitchenette, like all else white-on-white but for stainless steel drawer pulls, were the items she had walked two miles to the Walmart to buy with David's money. The bathroom would have been the logical place for the transformation, but Jalila had exclusive use of the bedroom and Clare hadn't had the courage to commute through it to the bath except as nature demanded.

The hair dye was dark brown—almost black—the stage makeup was the cheapest kind, stocked in children's toy departments for face painting and dress-up, but it would do. People saw what they expected to see. To pass cursory inspection, Clare need only provide the expected clues: hair, clothes, roughened skin, facial hair.

Picking up the scissors, she stepped back into the living room, where Mackie slept under the glass coffee table. David had hung a mirror beside the front door as was his habit. Before exposing himself to the eyes of the world, he always checked his looks. That or admired himself one last time. Over the years Clare had come to suspect the latter.

Using the Walmart shears, she began hacking off her hair.

The Fugitive. Harrison Ford in a gas station bathroom.

Only she would do the last part in reverse. Where he had cut off his beard, she would glue hers on. Her hair was collar length, thick and light brown. There was enough natural wave to cover the butcher job she did with the scissors. When she'd finished, the effect wasn't impressive, but it would pass. The back looked as if Mackie had chewed it off, but a ball cap—the ubiquitous head wear for American men—would cover most of it anyway.

Bending at the waist, she shook her fingers through her hair to get out the pieces. At her feet was what looked to be a sea of hair. DNA. Hers. Strands of it pushing into the carpet, wriggling down into the weave. Could they get DNA from hair, or did they need to have a bit of skin or root with it? She'd never played a forensic anything and so hadn't bothered to learn about it.

"You're a criminal now," she said aloud. "You better learn to think like one." Already her voice had slowed and cooled, deepened. Without conscious effort on her part, her careful articulation had gone; in its place was a rough edge of anger.

Letting the criminal mingle with the ghost of whoever she was becoming, Clare cleaned up the hair with a vacuum she found in a narrow closet in the kitchenette. David did not do housework. Ever. Not so much as put a dirty cup in the dishwasher or the milk back in the refrigerator. It was a matter of pride and entitlement that this was done for him and done by women. Women who were not paid. Clare's husband knew it was the wife's duty or, failing that, the daughter's. He would not allow "a stranger in to do work that is yours." Jalila must have cleaned for him.

Clare emptied the contents of the vacuum into the garbage disposal, wiped her prints off the vacuum, and replaced it in the closet. At some point she would need to wipe down the apartment and clean up the vomit by Jalila's corpse.

"Don't think about it now," she told herself. Mackie rolled a brown eye up at the sound of her voice. White showed beneath the dark iris. The dog was worried.

"I'm rehearsing, not insane," she said. When he continued to look at her with concern she added, "I don't think you are in any position to judge me. You consumed the brains of the au pair." The callous words startled her. They weren't hers. They were the words of whomever she was becoming, a man without much to run on but hatred.

At some point the character she played would begin to sink down through the skin to the bones beneath, changing her stance and, to a lesser extent, the way she thought. Sometimes. Sometimes the magic worked and sometimes it didn't. Between that avenue of escape and the life of Clare Sullivan was a great black place. Not a hole any longer, with its burned-out feel, like the smoldering hulk of a building destroyed by fire, but a huge obsidian mountain. A chunk of grief so solid and heavy it was difficult to breathe around it, difficult to stand upright.

The angry strength of the borrowed voice was a sham, and, as Clare moved into the tiny kitchen to begin the process of dyeing the remaining stubble on her head, she stopped and stood motionless, unable to move forward or back, too stony even to fall down. "The Fugitive," she said to bring herself back to center, to remember her lines, the role she was playing. "Running from the law." She had forgotten why she was running.

"To fight for Truth, Justice, and the American Way," she whispered. *Superman.* Long ago and far away she'd auditioned for the part of Lois Lane, long ago and far away when she was trying to make it in the movies in Los Angeles. There was a chip in her front tooth, the legacy of a wild ride on the Giant Stride when she was in the fifth grade. The director—casting director—had eaten a cheeseburger while she read. When she'd finished he'd said, "Get your teeth fixed. We're not casting *Green Acres.*" They hadn't called her back.

Then it came to her. "Aisha." Alive. Sleepy Dog. Vee alive. Maybe. Maybe was enough.

Freed from paralysis, she finished her journey into the kitchen and gobbed on the dye. For twenty minutes while it colored her hair, she sat on the white sofa staring at the blank television screen. In her mind she rubbed her hands through her hair, then smeared the dye over the couch and the walls, rolled on the white carpet like a dog, leaving inky smears on the artificial purity with which David had surrounded himself. In her body she was still as death, knowing that even a drop of the dye would tell someone—the police presumably—that she had been here, had colored her hair. If they found any remaining hairs in the carpet, they'd know she'd cut it. Her cover would be blown.

"My cover would be blown," she said to see if she could say it convincingly. The words sounded as foolish in the air as they had in her skull.

"The goddamn bugs whacked us, Johnny," Clare said. It was a line from the movie *Starship Troopers*. The worst line an actress had ever been made to utter. Meryl Streep would have a tough time making it work. Clare said it sometimes to amuse herself. She didn't know why she said it now.

When the allotted time had passed, she stood and took two paces toward the kitchen and the sink. She didn't so much stop as cease to move. What would she do when she had transformed herself? How might she begin with only a stuffed dog, a flesh-and-blood

dog, and a connection she'd made to the words "Bourbon Street Nursery"? A connection she'd feared might
exist only in her mind.

God bless the Cajun.

He proved the relationship between the two was
not of her imagining. He'd come to the house; then he'd
come to her husband's hideaway. From the byplay between him and his boy-voiced pervert pal, it sounded
as if they were the killers of Jalila. Then, too, they were
the killers of her family, her house, her life.

There was the dark child, the girl who'd said "Aisha." Alive. Because she'd wished to, Clare linked that
with the salvation of Sleepy Dog and the narrow escape of Mack the real dog.

She had told the Donovan children she was going to
find her daughters. A part of her knew that wasn't entirely true. This part knew she was going to follow the
voices she'd heard and she was going to kill the men
who uttered them.

It wasn't like she had anything else to do.

Clare was a woman who rescued baby birds, put
spiders out rather than killing them, nursed and placed
or adopted every creature her children dragged home.
She'd never killed anything but the occasional cockroach, and even that she avoided when possible. But
she would kill these men. It would feel good, like lanc-
ing a boil.

She was sinking into dreams. The sensation was of
curling inward till all that remained was a dark stage

with a voice in her ears and a narrow play of light where thoughts were acted out, then vanished. A brown study, but with her it was more than that. A black study.

"You're going under," she whispered so the physicality and the sound would tie her to the world outside. The pull of the dark lessened. In a scratchy sweet contralto she began to sing: "Wake up, you sleepyhead, get up, get up, get out of bed." It was the song she sang to Dana and Vee when they overslept. That memory smashed her back into the white-white of David's room.

Eyes clear, she noticed several things that had passed her by. The canary yellow coat was gone from the back of the sofa. Either the thugs had stolen it or they'd left it behind and came back to fetch it. And there was a door. At the end of the sofa nearest the kitchen was a door. A closet, Clare told herself, but she could not stop her heart from leaping in her chest—another anatomical reality—as, instantaneous with seeing the door, her mind grabbed onto the hope that behind it would be her children, alive and well. Was that how she would go through life now, yanking open doors for the lady or the tiger and getting, always, the tiger?

Clare turned the knob slowly and pushed. David kept it locked. Of course. A flash of anger, so sudden she was blind with it, raged through her. Weight back on her left foot, she smashed the sole of her right sneaker into the door above the lock and heard the wood splinter. A second kick opened it. Kickboxing. Years of it to keep slender and lithe after more than forty years and two C-sections.

No children waited. Though she'd known they would not be there, pain flared beneath the granite grief in her chest.

A computer desk, an executive's chair, file cabinets, and two bookshelves crowded the tiny windowless space. David's office. The one he'd had at home had been spacious and light, beautifully appointed, with a lovely view of the front garden. In his parallel life it was a co opted pantry.

Forgetting the muck in her hair, Clare switched on the light and stepped over the threshold. If her husband had a secret life—and apparently he had a much more complex one than she had suspected—this was where he conducted the business arm of it. Forgetting the dangers of fingerprints and DNA, she pulled open the first of the file cabinet drawers.

In another movie she would have gone for the computer and clicked her way miraculously through firewalls and passwords. In this movie she knew the villain—and by now she was sure David, if not a murderer of innocents, was a villain of some stripe—and knew he neither liked nor trusted computers. It wasn't the machine that offended him; it was the lack of secrecy, the sense that anything put on a computer could be stolen, read, posted, shared, infiltrated, hacked. Secrecy was power in David's mind, and he shared only what he had to to keep the bills paid and the business in the black.

Though she'd never dared—nor, till now, cared—to snoop through his home office, she doubted he would have kept anything of import there. The same was true with his office down at the warehouses. Both places were too public. Here, in this locked, claustrophobic pantry, in an apartment not even his wife knew about, would be what he considered "sensitive information." With David that could be anything from illegal activities to the results of his last colonoscopy.

The file drawer was so neat it could have been used as an ad for hanging files. None was off the runners; each was separated from each by a sixteenth of an inch. Subject matter was color coded. Each colored hanging file was labeled in David's hand. In Arabic.

"Fuck!" Clare exploded. Grabbing a handful of files in sheer frustration, she flung them to the floor. "Fool!" she said more quietly. The tabs were in Arabic, but the contents were in English; business was done in English. Kneeling amid the scattered papers she began to look through them, trying to piece together what David had done or been or said or not done that had resulted in the bombing of her home and the vanishing—not death, please God—of her children.

As luck would have it, she'd snatched and tossed most of the green folders. Finances. David was not imaginative. Bank statements told her David, and so she and the girls, were quite well-off, rich in fact. His admitted monies, those he'd trusted to Merrill Lynch at least, valued his investments at three million seven hundred thousand dollars and change. The house was paid for—now it was ashes, but it had been appraised at another million two. In the folder for the local bank was an ATM card and a MasterCard. There was no

way in the world Daoud Suliman would write down a
password. Ever. Clare left the ATM and pocketed the
credit card.

There would be a short window of opportunity
when she might be able to use David's card. Then it
would only serve to tell the authorities where she was
and what she was buying. The rest of David's investments she couldn't touch. She glanced through the next
green file. Invoices and receipts and memos regarding
fabric prices and shipping information, thread purchases
and sewing machine repairs. She took a moment to look
through the hotel bills. David had gone to New Orleans
three times in the previous seven months. Reassured
she was on the right track, she tossed the hotel receipts
aside, as she did insurance, rent, taxes, interest, utili-
ties, fuel, wages, and most everything else to do with
the expenses of David's garment manufacturing business. She did note, in the wages and insurance, there
was no mention of Social Security or workman's comp
or overtime or medical, dental, or any other kind of as-
sistance for the employees. David must have thought
that in bringing them to America he'd done them one
hell of a favor and now it was payback time.

Clare's peripatetic brain stumbled over *Norma Rae,*
but she wasn't cast in that role today.

The little girl, Aisha, had been Arabic; Clare had to
believe that, because that was all she had to go on.
David brought workers in from the Middle East: Pakistan, Iraq, Iran, and Afghanistan. Though they'd never
discussed it, nor would he have discussed it with her,

she was pretty sure they were undocumented. Had David brought in the little girl? There had to be a connection with the Cajun and David and the bombing. Why else would the Cajun have been at the house when it went up? It would be too much to believe this guy from Louisiana, who was connected with a guy from Saudi Arabia, who happened to import women from Arabic countries, had an Arabic child with him in the middle of the night at a fire. The importation of women was in the mix somehow. David must have crossed some line, gotten on the bad side of the wrong people.

A thought banged against her brain with painful force. Had her husband been importing not one little girl but many? Was he participating in the ever-growing sex slave trade? Were Dana and Vee in the hands of monsters like the one who'd jerked off over Jalila's corpse?

"Don't think," she told herself sharply, and, moving fast, she rifled through the rest of the green folders. She didn't find out where the women came from or how they got to Seattle. The fabric came in by sea in shipping containers and was unloaded at the docks. Surely he didn't bring the women over the same way? Crated like cattle?

In the last folder in the financial section was a white legal-sized envelope containing a sheaf of crisp, new one-hundred-dollar bills. David's security blanket. This Clare would take. Cash left a less obvious trail than credit cards.

The red folders were three in number and contained personal information. David's passport was there; so were Dana and Vee's birth certificates, both those in

English and certificates in Arabic that David had gotten for them.

Clare had seen the certificates—the girls were proud of them—but had no idea whether or not they were legal. There was her and David's marriage certificate, and David's citizenship papers. At the time they'd wed, the idea he married her to become an American citizen didn't cross her mind. She was lost in his matinee idol looks and his charm. Since, it had crossed more than once. Below that was the marriage certificate they'd been given when David's mother insisted they marry again in Saudi.

For a moment memory took Clare, and she sat on the office chair by the computer with a thump. She'd liked David's mother and sisters. She spoke no Arabic, but they were fluent in English. It had taken her by surprise how much fun they were, how witty and mischievous. David's dad undoubtedly spoke English as well, but he never did in Clare's presence. He had cloaked himself in righteous disapproval and ignored her.

Shaking herself the way Mack did when he woke up every morning, as if he needed to shake sleep from him like water, she bent again to her task and opened the second of the three red folders. This one contained a document identical to one in the first folder. It was all in the beautiful and, to her, indecipherable Arabic writing, but she recognized it immediately. It was a marriage certificate just like the one she and David had been issued in Saudi. The only thing different was the name of the bride. Where Clare Flaherty had been written was the name Jalila. Jalila, Victoria, and Dana were the only words Clare could read in Arabic. The au pair had taught the girls to write their names, and she had written hers. The three had been stuck to the refrigerator with magnets for six months.

Jalila wasn't David's paramour. She was his wife. By Islamic law David was allowed four. Clare was a co-wife in a polygamous household. As repugnant as that should have been to her, it made her like Jalila better, pity her less. Oddly it made her like David better. Certainly he was a lying, cheating, misogynistic pig, but he wasn't taking advantage of the babysitter. That was something to his account.

The second document looked like Vee's and Dana's Saudi birth certificates. Just exactly like. Clare could make out the mother's name, Jalila. The child's was as much a mystery to her as the rest of the document. Aisha? Could Aisha—*Alive*—be David and Jalila's daughter? That was a broad jump to a conclusion, but the idea made Clare so happy she couldn't let go of it. If. If that little girl with the doll . . .

"Holy shit!" she said so loudly that Mack jumped to his paws and whined. "The little girl had a doll, a fancy doll, Mackie, like Vee and Dana had. The kind of doll Jalila made for them. Of course she was Jalila's daughter. Mackie!" She scooped the alarmed dog up and hugged him and kissed him, then apologized when she saw she'd gotten brown hair dye on his head and ears.

It reminded her she'd best rinse the dye out of her own hair before it began falling out in clumps.

Having steeled herself to what lay in the bedroom, she picked Mackie up so she could rinse off his ears and hurried past Jalila's body to the bath. If the Cajun had one of David's daughters and was taking her to the "Bourbon Street Nursery," was it so far-fetched to believe he might have David's other two daughters and was taking them there as well?

Maybe. Maybe. For now that would be her truth.

Clare's only thought had been to wash the dye out of her and her dog's hair, but hot water sluicing ash and the stench of smoke from her skin fell like a blessing. It felt good.

That brought her up short, and she turned the water off with a vicious twist. Clare Sullivan had no right to feel good. The man she was becoming didn't either, but he wouldn't care. She had to practice not caring. About anything. Caring nothing for everything. Taking her soul out and burying it in sterile earth, the Nevada desert perhaps, where the bombs had been tested for so many years.

Once one was truly indifferent, life would be easy. Choices were easy when the outcome was of no consequence. Guilt would be a thing of the past; hope, a joke upon others. Once truly indifferent, would one be a god or a monster? Clare doubted she would ever find out. By the time she ceased caring for Vee and Dana, the earth would be a cold, still, lifeless rock drifting away from the sun.

She toweled off and dried Mack as best as she could. Where he had been white and black before, he was ecru and brown and black. "We both have a role, Mackie," she said.

Dye ruined David's expensive towels, and that pleased her till she remembered she didn't want to advertise the change of appearance. When she left, she'd take them and give them to the homeless people who gathered under the freeway overpass down by the docks at the end of this street. Police didn't see homeless people, or at least not as clearly as those more affluent.

Showered and dried, she dressed in the shabbiest of the clothes in David's closet: a pair of immaculate Lacoste linen trousers in black and a collarless silk shirt with a DKNY label, silk boxer shorts, white cotton T-shirt, and black cotton socks. David was the same height as she, so the length of the inseam and the shirt-sleeves was okay. He was beefier, and the clothing hung on her. Good. Her breasts, never large, were still significant.

Thoroughly Modern Millie. Julie Andrews's breasts popping out of their bindings and sending the necklaces swinging. Julie Andrews in *Victor/Victoria*.

The trench coat would have to cover Clare's until she could find something to strap them flat. Shoes were never going to transgender. David's were so big she'd walk out of them, and she might have a lot of walking in her future. Careful to keep her back to the corpse of her husband's other wife, she sat on the edge of the bed, put her running shoes on, and laced them up.

Having freed Mackie from the bathroom, she carried him past Jalila's body into the front room and closed the door. At the kitchen counter she took the Halloween makeup from the bag. It was crude. If the charade went on for any length of time she would have to find a supplier and replace it. She darkened her skin a half tone, enough to make it look coarser, thickened her brows, and used the pencil to suggest a hint of sideburns, nothing obvious, just a place missed while shaving. Her disguise would never pass close inspection—she didn't have the time or the tools—but it should suffice for the moment. Below her lower lip she put a bit of double-sided tape and used the hair cuttings to create a tuft.

Finished, she surveyed herself in the long mirror. The hands were wrong. She bit the nails to the quick and darkened the knuckles and nail beds. The total effect wasn't bad. To the casual observer she'd look like an underweight man of indeterminate age, with a bad haircut and nervous habits, dressed in expensive clothes.

Next would come the cleaning: wiping her fingerprints from every surface, scrubbing her vomit from the carpet, vacuuming up every bit of hair and fingernails she'd missed.

Suddenly she was so tired she could scarcely stand. Letting gravity do the work, she sat hard on the couch. Mackie jumped up beside her to give moral support. "I don't know if I can do this, little guy. I don't know if I can do anything." She started to cry, then stopped herself lest she wreck her makeup. Mack licked her face, then, evidently deciding she tasted too vile to kiss, laid his chin on her lap and sighed loudly.

Resting her head against the sofa's back, Clare closed her eyes. In the semidarkness behind her eyelids she saw time running out, a comet tail vanishing over the horizon. "Okay," she said and sat up with a suddenness that dislodged the dog. "Screw DNA. I'm up for three murders. Who cares if the law knows I was here, right, Mackie?" With speed born of the necessity of not thinking and not stopping lest she never start again, Clare cleaned up the evidence of her sex change operation and left the rest of the apartment as it was.

"Maybe our visiting freak left semen by Jalila's body," she said to the dog. "That's one thing they'd have a hard time pinning on me."

The money she'd found went into the pocket of the trench coat; the cell phone she left on the counter. Mackie she leashed with the coat's cloth belt. The nightgown and women's underpants she'd arrived in she balled up and stuffed into the Walmart bag along with the towels, leftover makeup, and the hair dye bottles and instructions.

"Is this an adventure, Barnaby?" she said to the dog as they left the apartment. If Mack recognized the line from *Hello, Dolly!* he didn't say anything. She closed and locked the door and started down the stairs, headed for Bourbon Street, New Orleans, Louisiana.

Flying was out; the airports would be on the lookout for a murderess of her stature. The same went for bus and train stations. Without a doubt there would be a cop or two watching David's SUV and her Honda. That left hitchhiking. She'd walk to the edge of the city, where cops would be less likely to stop and take a hard look at her, and stick out her thumb.

On the street, in the harsh light of midmorning, Seattle failing her and not providing its usual drizzle, Clare looked up and down. David's apartment was by the docks, near his factory and warehouses. Up was toward civilization. Down was toward industrialization. Guessing the police would be less likely to look for a woman in the rougher climes of docks and boatyards, and needing to get rid of the towels and other signs she was now male, she headed down.

Beneath a tangle of overpasses and raised train tracks was a scattering of the homeless. As was the American way, Clare moved a little more quickly and kept her eyes straight ahead. Sitting on the curb, unavoidable unless she crossed the street, was a scrawny old man, ratty beard halfway down his chest, cradling a bottle of orange juice. He was wearing an army surplus coat.

It occurred to her that she had to get rid of David's trench coat. The police knew she'd been wearing it, and, in the light of day, turning it inside out would call attention to her.

She stopped when she reached the old man. "Will you trade coats with me?" she asked bluntly. "This is a Burberry, warm and water repellent. I've also got some towels if you want them."

The man looked up with bleary eyes, bleary but not blind. "You running from the law?"

"The dogcatcher," Clare said.

He looked at her another minute. A minute onstage with no lines is an eternity, and Clare felt the flop sweat start between her breasts. She was about to move on when he said, "There blood on anything?"

"No. Hair dye."

"Sure, I'll take the stuff and your coat, if it fits."

Clare remembered the money about two seconds before handing him the trench coat and slipped the envelope unobtrusively inside her T-shirt. The army coat was filthy and stank of tobacco and rancid fat and despair.

That was good, she realized. Like her, most people didn't want to see homeless people. They were scary, tragic, and dirty; they smelled bad. As she slipped the coat on, the world boiled into noise so loud it made the air shudder and the viscera quake. A freight train was passing overhead.

Three men and two women—too young to be homeless, maybe runaways—stood up from where they'd gone unnoticed in the deep shade of a concrete pillar. They were gray with filth, their hair chopped off or in dreads achieved the old-fashioned way for white men: by never washing it. Two dogs were with them, one black with a white blaze on its chest, one probably yellow when it was clean, and both mutts. They watched the train with interest, then, when it had gone, sat down again.

"Travelers," the old man said and spat on the sidewalk. "Rich kids dropping out and riding the rails. Punks. That bunch is mean. Ugly mean."

Hopping trains.

With dogs.

"You want to trade shirt and pants, too?" Clare asked.

TWENTY

Anna's left hand touched the back wall as the door swung open to happy barking. Her other hand hit only empty space. Moving to her right she slipped into the bedroom, or whatever the room was, and stepped out of the frame and pressed her back against the wall.

Light came on in the front room. A bright square fell through the doorway she'd just vacated, and she could see it was a bedroom in the barest sense of the word. A single mattress lay on the floor. There were no sheets, just a ratty sleeping bag and a pillow without a case. These were arranged neatly, the bag straightened, the pillow centered at the top with a gooseneck lamp next to it, the cord snaking across the floor to an outlet by an open door to the bathroom. On the pillow, as if awaiting a child, was a much-loved bedraggled stuffed dog. There was no dresser, no rugs, no chair, and the walls were bare. Evidently even monsters didn't like their monstrousness gazing down at them as they slept.

"What a good boy you are. Did you miss me? Love my little dog." Crooned endearments drifted in with the illumination, the doting voice at odds with the man who could decorate his life with the ruins of childhood.

"Want some dinner? How about dog food? I know how you love my dog food."

The cloyingly sweet voice grated on Anna's ears, cutting like razor blades hidden in candy and given to trick-or-treaters on Halloween. This was followed by rummaging sounds as Jordan dug into the dog food bag.

Along the wall to Anna's right was another small door, this one firmly closed. The closet, probably. Unsure of what else she could do, she crossed the room quietly and opened it. One black shirt and one pair of black trousers, the cheap polyester kind one finds at uniform stores or Walmart, hung on plastic hangers. The shelf above held a pair of folded jeans, a T-shirt, running shoes, and an Ace bandage folded into thirds. On the floor was a black garbage bag lumpy with whatever was sequestered inside.

Anna stepped through the door, then closed it till there was the merest crack between her and the room. There was no knob on the inner side; if she closed it completely, she would be locked in. If Jordan closed it, she would be locked in. That thought nearly sent her crashing out and taking her chances.

The closet was old-fashioned; there was barely room for her and the black ensemble. Her foot nudged the garbage bag, and a vile odor puffed out. Anna felt her innards drop an inch. Was she sharing this tiny prison with the rotting corpse of a child? With only parts of a child? With a store of dead pigeons awaiting voodoo duty? As the stench thinned it occurred to Anna that, as Geneva had said, the apartment did not stink in general. Jordan, the gutter punk, smelled like he'd slept in a cellar once used to store old sewer pipes. Why would his apartment smell only of old wood and clean dog?

"There you go, little buddy. You've got to keep your strength up. We've got little girls to find."

Jordan used his dog as child bait.

Maybe that's why he kept him clean and good-smelling. *Come pet the doggie, honey, he won't bite*. Jesus, Anna thought. Candy from babies. Puppies to pet. She very much wanted to tear this man into little pieces and flush the pieces down the toilet. She also wished very much she'd thought to bring her cell phone. Dialing 911 would be such a fine thing. Despite her unkind thoughts about the New Orleans Police Department, she would dearly love to see a great big cop with a 9mm and nightstick about now. A double-barreled shotgun and a baseball bat would be even better.

After the dog ate, Jordan would take him out for a walk, Anna reasoned. At that point she would make good her escape.

The dog ate. Jordan babbled. Anna tried not to think about what might be in the plastic bag at her feet, tried not to think about quietly killing Jordan as he slept and dumping the body in the river lest he slip through the legal system.

"Good boy," Jordan crooned. "Out you go. If you see Geneva, tell her I'll scoop tomorrow. Tonight I can't stand the thought of handling any more shit." Anna heard the door open, then shut. Jordan wasn't going to walk the pooch; he was going to let him use the court-yard for a toilet. Just the sort of thing a prick like him would do.

Hatred of the most corrosive kind was eating Anna from the brain stem out. Bad guys were bad guys, and they kept her in business. The destroyers of nature and history, the builders of campfires out of bounds, the dogs off leash in the wild places: Anna didn't hate them. Her job was to correct and educate.

The vacationers who beat up on their wives, the con-cession workers who raped a waitress—these she dis-liked. Twenty minutes earlier she'd have said "hated." Now that she knew what hatred was, she wondered how the people who hunted down the Jordans of the world kept from being destroyed by it.

Scratching. Door opening and closing. Minute snick as Jordan pushed the button lock in the knob.

The sliver of light in Anna's purview went black, then bright, as Jordan turned off the light in the front room and flicked on that in the bedroom. A click of claws on hardwood and the dog's nose poked through the crack, trying to push open the closet door and ex-pose Anna.

"No, you don't," said Jordan, still using the higher vocal register that he'd adopted to talk sweet nothings to the dog he'd dyed black and used to find little girls. Then a smack on the wood and the closet door closed and latched. "That wonderful smell in there isn't good for little dogs," Jordan said.

The baby corpse? The pigeon bodies? Whatever was in the garbage bag. Whatever Anna was now locked in with.

In a pinch, with the closet wall to brace herself against, she could probably kick her way out without too much trauma to her feet, but it would certainly blow the element of surprise all to heil. Maybe, after Jordan had gone to sleep, Anna would be able to slip the lock and let herself out undetected. Not for the first time, she was glad she never went anywhere without her library card.

Outside her charnel house/prison/closet the going-to-bed noises that were standard in homes all over America, comforting noises of showers running, toilets flushing, teeth being brushed, were made. The juxtaposition of what Jordan was and these homey sounds was jarring. When a perverted monster readied to lay his monstrous head down on the collective filth of his lair, there should be at least the crunching of fragile bones between big teeth, grunting and scratching and a fee or fi or fo or fum. It was wrong that Jordan sounded like a human being. Then again, the monsters that could pass for human were the ones that survived the pages of the storybooks to walk among ordinary citizens.

Other than the occasional word to the dog, Jordan

didn't hum ditties or whistle happy tunes. That was a help.

Each time foot- or paw-falls headed in the direction of the closet, Anna tensed for a fight. Each time, they turned another direction. After a while she began to feel silly, like the lover in a French farce, dressed only in his shorts, hiding in the armoire listening to the cuckolded husband make his toilette.

The old wood of the closet's door had shrunk and the house tipped till straight lines and square corners were the exception rather than the rule. Lines of white showed on both sides where the door had receded from the jamb. There was a dot, unpleasantly reminiscent of the red laser dots from high-powered scopes, on Anna's abdomen where light penetrated a keyhole. Had she not been afraid of kneeling on the garbage bag and loosing its contents, as well as its perfume, she would have put her eye to the keyhole like the classic sleuths.

As her vision adjusted, she looked around her tiny prison a second time, craning her neck rather than risking moving her feet or body. If sound came in, it would go out just as effectively. The weapon she hoped she had overlooked before did not appear. Her flashlight wasn't the marvelous club a six-cell aluminum patrol flashlight was, but a pretty blue Maglite no more than seven inches long and half an inch in diameter. There was the library card. She made a mental note to suggest to the Estes Park librarian that the cards be made with at least one good slashing edge.

The light leaking around the door dimmed. Jordan had turned out the overhead and turned on the goose-necked lamp by the bed to read.

Or look at pictures.

Anna promised herself that if she heard him mastur-bating, she would cast caution to the winds and kick the door down. No such luck. In keeping with the nor-mal noises the bastard had the gall to make, he said a sweet good night to the pooch, and the light went out.

Creaks settled the house. Scratching and turning circles settled the dog. Anna had just centered herself to listen for the deep, even breathing of sleep when the pastoral audio was burst by an "Oh, shit" and the light came back on.

Before Anna had time to adjust to the new circum-stances, the closet door was snatched open and Jordan stood in front of her looking absurdly shocked, his mouth a big O.

"Hey, Jordan," Anna said and shoved him hard in the middle of the chest. The man was half a foot taller than she, yet he weighed so little it took her off bal-ance, and she almost followed him over onto the floor. Recovering her equilibrium, she got her legs under her and ran for the front room.

"No!" Jordan screamed.

A shadow flashed in the corner of Anna's eye and then she was down. The dog, wittingly or unwittingly, had tangled itself in her feet. Before she was even on hands and knees, Jordan was on her back, straddling

her, smashing his fists down on the back of her neck. His
sudden weight pushed her face onto the planks of the
floor; his knees pinned her shoulders down. The blows
made it hard to think.

Gathering her hands beneath her breasts, she pushed
up and over, rolling him off the way an unbroken horse
will try to roll off a saddle. He fell to his side. Anna
scrambled to her feet and reached for the door. Jordan's
hand shot out and grabbed her ankle. He hugged it to
his chest and began to climb up, using Anna as a support. Unused to fighting—or just worn out from his
lifestyle—he was gasping for breath. Each gasp came
out on a "no."

Anna clubbed him on the temple with her fist. Instead of dropping him, the jolt gave him a last surge of
desperate strength. He caught her hand in both his and
began flipping over and over as if he were spinning on
the end of a rope. His weight greater than hers, Anna
could do nothing but go with him down onto the dusty
boards in a tangle of arms and legs.

He couldn't last; Anna could feel his strength going from him. His energy had gone into fighting his
demons, and there was little left for fighting even
small women he found in his closet of a night, but he
was bigger than Anna and driven by an inner fire. One
arm freed, he snatched a knife from the countertop. It
wasn't big, a paring knife, and it wasn't sharp; he'd
probably rescued it from the trash, but Anna knew it
would suffice.

She caught his wrist in one hand and with the other grabbed for his balls. Since Achilles had a heel, she wasn't averse to using it whenever necessity demanded.

Except there were no balls.

Jordan moved his other hand to the haft of the knife and pushed it down toward her throat.

"What are you?" Anna screamed just as Jordan cried, "What have I become?" and went as limp as if he'd been shot in the back of the head.

Knife still in hand, he fell sideways. Curling into a fetal position, he began to wail, his mouth an agonized square, his eyes shut so tightly the lashes disappeared. The dog started to howl. Anna scrambled to hands and knees, snatched the paring knife from his unresisting fingers, and sat back, her shoulders against the door.

"What the hell is going on?" she muttered to herself. The crying of man and beast continued unabated. Knife at ready, Anna stood. Beside the mess of pornography next to the computer was a half-consumed liter bottle of water. She uncapped it and poured the contents onto Jordan's face. Sputtering and gulping, he struggled to a sitting position and wrapped his arms around his dog.

"I was going to kill you," he said, and the horror in his voice was unmistakable.

"So it seemed to me," Anna returned. There was still too much adrenaline in her system to speak kindly. That and she hated being bested. It reminded her how short and fragile life was. "So, what? You're a eunuch? Transgender but for the plumbing? A cross-dresser?"

"I used to be a woman," Jordan said in a creaky

voice that threatened another noisy breakdown. "Now I don't know what I am."

Anna stared at him/her for a while, trying to make sense of the words. Jordan looked like he—she—was slipping toward catatonia. To keep him from going co-matose, Anna pushed. "What's with the kiddy porn? I didn't know it had much of a female audience."

Jordan said nothing.

Anna walked past her into the bedroom and, keep-ing an eye on the erstwhile woman and the dog through the doorway, banged on the wall, hard and long, then returned to the front room. Geneva had to hear. Her bedroom shared a wall with Jordan's apartment. The racket should bring her out.

Jordan looked up, eyes unfocused, as if the noise Anna had made had only just penetrated her fog.

"Geneva will come. What you're doing is not only freaky-vile, it's massively illegal," Anna said succinctly. Her revulsion for this creature was not lessened because it was female, nor was it made worse; it was simply stirred up into a confusing mental nausea. Unable to de-cide whether Jordan needed an exorcist, a psychiatrist, a jailer, or an executioner, Anna settled on the police. "She'll call the police for me," she finished.

"No!" Jordan screamed, and his—her, its—eyes flashed crazy. For a heartbeat Anna thought the creature was going to go for her throat again. Jordan thought it, too. "My God" came out in a whisper, and arms held the dog more tightly. "Please. You can't call the police. My daughters, my babies . . ."

Anna waited. Jordan seemed lost somewhere inside herself. The demons Anna had watched devouring her for the past few days were active. The woman probably hadn't eaten for a while, maybe not slept either.

With a wrench that must have hurt her skinny neck, Jordan jerked her head up and forced her eyes to clear. The strain it was taking for her to pull herself together was evident in the tension in her face and shoulders.

"My name is Clare Sullivan," she said with more firmness than Anna would have thought she could muster.

The name slapped across Anna's mind with the force of a backhand to the face. Clare Sullivan had been America's Most Wanted for two weeks. The newspapers and television were avid for details and, where there weren't any, made them up.

"The woman who murdered her husband, his lover, and both her children," Anna said slowly. "And this would change my mind about calling the police why?"

Intellectually, Anna knew she should be bolting for the door, screaming down the streets for 911, but, once the paring knife had dropped, all sense of threat had gone out of the atmosphere. The papers said Clare was a four-time murderess, and Anna'd thought her an addict of child pornography, but for some reason—maybe her love for the dog—Anna didn't think it was true, or at least not all true.

Clare was maintaining her grip on sanity. "If you call the police, I will be arrested and sent back to Se-

attle to await trial. It's possible I will be convicted. I
don't care about the conviction one way or another.
What I care about is my girls. Dana and Vee. I didn't
kill them. I didn't kill anybody. They were taken, and
they are here in New Orleans. Somewhere. They have
to be." This last was in the merest of whispers.

A banging on the door made the women and the dog
jump. Anna had forgotten about rousing Geneva. She
opened the door. Geneva stood foursquare on the narrow walk, her nightdress as white and flowing as that of
a Victorian damsel in distress. In her right hand she
held a staff not unlike the one Moses was often depicted
with.

"Hey, Geneva," Anna said. "Jordan's a woman."

"I told you that. You bang me up in the middle of the
damn night to tell me I was right?"

"Come in," Anna said. "Jordan's telling a bedtime
story." Geneva didn't question, or even seem to notice,
the bizarreness of the invitation. Anna rolled the computer chair to her, and she sat, looking like Judgment
personified.

Jordan, still on the floor, still holding the dog, was
changing. Her outline had softened, her mouth had grown
fuller, her hands more graceful, or so Anna thought,
watching her. Freed from the curse and burden of a lie,
she was morphing back into a woman. Anna wished the
Incredible Patty was here. This was voodoo at its best.
Glamour, the mist fairies can put in one's eyes to make
them see what the fairies want them to see.

"I read you were an actor," Anna said. Her first husband, Zach, had been an actor, and Anna had always had a soft spot for those who trod the boards.

"Yes," Clare said simply. Anna was willing to bet she'd been a very good actress but wasn't in the mood to give compliments so she kept it to herself.

"This is Mackie," Clare introduced the dog. Then she embarked on a tale so twisty and full of turns it had to be true. She finished by telling Anna and Geneva that she'd hopped a train with some travelers out of Seattle and, when she'd gotten to New Orleans, kept on being a punk because nobody saw them, not really, and she could hide in plain sight and watch Bourbon Street, try to find the "nursery." She landed a job at Live Girls Live and was trying to get information about who ran child prostitution in the city. She'd attacked Anna because of the yellow coat the man Mack followed was wearing. It was the same coat that she'd seen in her husband's apartment, the one the Cajun and his cohort had taken away with them. When he'd gotten away, Clare thought she'd lost the one chance she'd had to track down her children.

When she finished, the four of them sat quietly, letting the telling and the hearing settle into their minds. After a minute Anna asked, "What's in the garbage bag in the closet?"

It took Jordan a minute to follow the jump in the conversation. "Clothes," she said, sounding confused.

"It smells like a sack of dead rats," Anna said.

"My punk clothes," Jordan told her. "If I don't keep them in plastic, they stink up the apartment."

Anna nodded. One mystery solved. She'd still look in the bag for good measure before the night was done, but she was no longer afraid of what she'd find. No one spoke for a bit, and Anna turned things over in her mind. Clare was a wanted fugitive. Now that Geneva knew, she was sheltering a fugitive— a felony offense. Because Anna knew, if she did not report it to the police, she would be aiding and abetting a fugitive, also a felony offense punishable by jail time. Serious jail time. Even should she and Geneva be found not guilty for some reason, both would lose their jobs. The Park Service was not appreciative of rangers who broke, or even bent, the law. If she shared any of this with Sheriff Paul Davidson and continued not to report it, or convinced him not to report it, he, too, would be guilty of a felony offense.

Though Anna had a good feeling about Clare, whatever that meant, there was a great deal of impressive evidence—or so she read in the papers—that the woman had committed the crimes of which she was accused.

If Anna turned her in, Clare would be locked up immediately, her search for her children over. There was no evidence but the word of a woman accused of quadruple murder that her children were alive. The charred corpses from the house fire could be DNA tested, but Anna doubted there was enough proof on Clare's side to get that done. Either way, by the time the results were in and a search for the children was begun, too much time would have elapsed to have much hope of finding them alive—or finding them at all. It was possible, if what Clare said was true and not the ravings of a crazy woman, the children had been sold out of the country.

Anna was also aware of the fact that if she turned Clare in, she and Geneva would have to physically restrain her until the police arrived. Already she was eyeing the door, and Anna could see the need to run building inside her. Even if she could escape detection a second time, if she remained in New Orleans, it would not be for long.

Geneva pushed to her feet, using the staff as if she were as old as the prophet. "I'm going to bed," she announced. "Before I do, I'm going to take another Ambien. When I wake up I'm not going to remember a thing. I won't remember you banging on my wall, Anna, and I won't remember this little tête-à-tête. I tell you, when I take that stuff I draw a complete blank."

With that she found the doorknob and let herself out into the waning night.

"What are you going to do?" Clare asked Anna.

Anna got an anxious feeling in her belly. Prison would be hell on earth for her. The thought of losing her freedom gave her the cold sweats. The threat of incarceration might not deter a lot of criminals, but it worked for Anna. She wasn't going to risk it now for the woman on the floor.

She was going to risk it for two little girls who might still be alive. Three, she amended, remembering Aisha.

"You're Jordan," she said. "A creepy punk guy. If you're anybody but Jordan, I've never even suspected it. I'm a good neighbor. I'm going to help you find the murderess's children."

TWENTY-ONE

Anna and Clare sat in cute uncomfortable chairs on either side of a tiny café table in the courtyard, each with a mug of coffee. It was nearly noon, but neither woman had been awake long. Anna still wore her lounging pajamas, pink with yellow duckies—her nod to the decencies. She slept nude. Clare was dressed, her little beard in place. The tattoo across her brow—the crown of thorns, which Anna had figured out was made with Magic Marker and powder—had been retouched. Anna appreciated that Clare kept up the masquerade even in private. Plausible deniability was the only thing that was going to keep her out of prison if this thing went south.

After Geneva had left to commit amnesia, Anna and Clare had spoken little. There was too much to absorb, too many risks taken or contemplated, to want to be with strangers. When Anna wandered out the following forenoon with her coffee, it had surprised her to find the other woman waiting. She'd more than half expected she would have rabbited and taken her dog with her. Part of her had hoped she had. That would have spelled the end to Anna's moral obligation.

Sunlight filtered strongly through the live oak, casting sharp-edged leaf shadows on the brick. Mack lay between Anna and Clare, sharing his benevolence. "What color are you when you're not undercover?" Anna asked him as she rubbed the toes of her left foot behind his silky ear.

"Black and white, like a zebra," his owner answered for him. "When I was dyeing my hair, I got the idea that he might be put in the police be-on-the-lookout-for things. The cops that came when the house exploded knew he was alive and with me. He's got a worse problem with roots than I do."

Where fur met dog, there was a quarter inch of white in some places. It gave him an exotic, slightly out-of-focus look Anna found fascinating. She continued brushing his fur this way and that, watching the play of black and white.

Clare cleared her throat. Anna didn't look up or stop playing with Mack. The burden of this conversation was Clare's to carry.

"Last night I told you what I'd found out in Seattle," Clare began, her voice in its male incarnation. Anna preferred it that way. Not only because it reminded her to maintain the charade on her end, never call Jordan "she," "her," or "Clare," but because when Clare was Clare, the crazed mom, running on nicotine and hope, she was too fragile to deal with.

As Jordan, Clare seemed to genuinely be another person. Her acting skills were uncanny. It reminded Anna of when she was a kid watching Charlie McCarthy on television, seeing the wood being brought to life by the puppeteer. Jordan was hard-edged and full of anger; he smoked nonfiltered cigarettes and seemed fueled by rage. Jordan was still functioning on a level that Clare could not.

"I haven't just been jerking off since I got to New Orleans. I've been trying to find out where the major houses are—not the street corners or upstairs rooms where these assholes stand in line waiting to get a ten-dollar blow job, but the higher-end houses where they'd be more likely to cater to a specialized, richer kind of asshole."

Jordan's vocabulary was stunningly different than what she'd heard of Clare's the previous night. Anna doubted Clare swore. She was probably the sort of mom who would quietly but firmly take people to task for using foul language in front of her children. The script she was writing for Jordan was different. It wasn't Clare who had intended to cut Anna's throat, it was Jordan. That Jordan would kill if he had to—and found the strength to—Anna didn't doubt. What she didn't know was how schizophrenic Clare Sullivan had become, as if acting had begun to slide over into multiple personality disorder. She made a mental note to call and ask Molly if she'd ever witnessed such a thing.

"Candy—you must have met her in the women's john—before she came to Dick's Den—"

Dick's Den must be the actual name of Live Girls Live, Anna guessed. "Classy," she said.

"Yeah, real witty. The owner's playing on the contrast with his dump and Rick's across the street. Anyway, before Candy got on at Dick's she was on the streets. Before that, from when she was real little, she remembers she was in what she calls a 'fancy house.' Candy's retarded. You noticed?"

"Hard to miss," Anna said. She drank her coffee and watched the sun play across her knuckles and the rim of the cup. This time of year it was rich and gentle, a mixture of honey and aloe and eternity spilling onto the skin. In a month or less it would be closer to molten metal. The sweetness and cruelty of the Deep South allowed the inherent insanity of the human condition to flower in ways it didn't elsewhere. Artists, musicians, writers, alcoholics—creativity and excess and genius and decay found a home beneath the heavy branches of trees older than most American cities.

Probably in the clear cutting air of the Rocky Mountains Anna would not be having coffee with a crossdresser accused of four murders. In New Orleans it was ceasing to seem particularly remarkable.

"The kid's also been beat to shit more than once. She's clean now except for pot, but she's had her goarounds with coke and horse. Only being broke and stupid have saved her from that good night. She's also gotten cunning—and the mind of an eight-year-old, given the right circumstances, can be as cunning as that of a much smarter person. Almost a feral survival mode. Somewhere along the line, someone told Candy to keep the secret of the fancy house in such a way she's not only keeping it but has probably buried it.

"Since she likes me, I think she might tell me in time. I think she'd tell me now, but on some level she senses that's all I want; that's what this man is going to use her for, then abandon her like every other man in her life used and abandoned her. So she's holding it back, keeping me with her. It's not my style, bashing retards—"

Again the schizophrenic-vs.-professional-thespian question flitted through Anna's mind and left a comet trail of alarm. Clare Sullivan probably never used the word "retarded," much less "retard." Seattle, liberal theater crowd, she was far more likely to refer to the intellectually challenged or mentally handicapped. Jordan used the word without a flicker of self-consciousness.

"But the one thing I don't have is time. I can feel it running out. It's like bleeding to death; I know the life is leaking out and if I don't stop the flow, the girls will die."

"Or worse," Anna said without thinking.

"For Clare—for any mother—there is no 'worse.' If they're alive, there's hope. If they're dead, it's curtains. For everything."

"How do you plan to 'bash it out of the retard'?" Anna asked coldly. "Would you really do that?"

"I'll do what I have to," Jordan snapped. He threw himself back in his chair. His hand fisted and began beating a silent tattoo on his thigh. Sun flickered in the moving shadows and lit up his crown of thorns. For a second it looked so real Anna had to quell the urge to reach out and touch it.

The fierceness left Jordan's face. "I didn't mean bash it out in the sense of hitting or hurting her," he said with the ghost of Clare Sullivan haunting his eyes. "I meant something not physical but, given what the poor thing has been through, no less brutal—threatening to abandon her unless she lets me hypnotize her."

"Can you hypnotize people?" Anna asked, impressed in spite of herself. She'd always wanted to be hypnotized for some reason and was the first to volunteer when opportunity knocked, but she'd never even come close to going under. Molly said she was too guarded to let anyone in, that or she was too contrary.

"Anybody can hypnotize susceptible people," an unsettling hybrid of Jordan and Clare said. "We studied it for a while when acting classes were all about weird. I could put Candy under. She's been giving over control of her life since she was born."

"Or having it forcibly wrested from her," Anna said.

"That, too."

"Why would that be brutal?" Anna asked, genuinely curious.

"Because she would be doing it so we wouldn't leave her. That's the tacit contract she makes when she gives herself away. But as soon as we get what we want we will leave her, just like every other son of a bitch."

"Ah. There's that. What do you hope to get from her, if she'll go under for you?" Anna asked. She almost said "you guys"; the sense of two people sharing one skin was so powerful!

"Just from the way she talks about the fancy house—and she doesn't do it much, I think she was scared silent, born stupid, and has forgotten most of it—but some of the things she's said made it sound like she was really little when she was put there. There is no memory of life before the fancy house. It's possible she was born there, but I don't think so. I think she was dumped there when she was around eighteen months to two years old. The bits she's remembered start when she got in trouble for peeing in her 'date dress.' I'm guessing she was maybe three when that happened."

"Damn," Anna muttered, thinking of the photographs that stained the walls of Jordan's apartment, the youth of the children, some babes in arms. It hadn't been too long ago a preacher of some sort in northern Louisiana was arrested for the rape of a thirteen-month-old infant. The child died. Mostly these were things Anna didn't think about by choice. Now there was no choice.

"I think when Candy got too old for the fancy house—probably eleven or twelve, when she started looking like a woman—they put her out on the streets. Lucky she's a retard," Jordan said. "The fuckers probably kill the kids that can tell on them, that or sell them overseas somewhere."

"Do you think she's just blocked all memory of the fancy house because she was so miserable there?"

"Miserable compared to what? She'd never known anything else. She had pretty clothes and food and there were other kids to play with when she wasn't 'on dates.' Candy remembers being on the street like being cast out of Eden. From what I've been able to pry out of her the fancy house customers weren't allowed to hit. In Candy's world that's a huge job perk.

"Look at this." Jordan fished a well-worn photograph out of the pocket of his disgusting punk shirt and passed it to Anna.

She laid it on the tabletop where the sun wasn't playing games and looked at it. "The guy's got a doll?" Anna asked.

"It's Candy."

Anna looked closer. Jordan was right. The doll's face was familiar. Other than the breasts and the height, Candy hadn't changed much in the past months or years.

"She give you this?"

"No. I lifted it from her little bag. The girls all leave their purses behind the bar so they don't get stolen."

"Good idea in theory," Anna said dryly.

"Look at her clothes." Jordan pushed the picture closer to her. "The costume looks well made. I'm guessing Paris, turn of the century—the nineteenth, not the twentieth. It was the fashion to dress children like tiny adults. Even to tiny little powdered wigs and heavy makeup. This isn't easy and it isn't cheap. If they've got guys paying for this kind of fantasy, it's got money connected. If there's money, we should be able to find it. They can't move an operation like that around to a new place every night like a Joe's speakeasy.

"I've tried to talk to the women at Dick's—Tanya,

Delilah, and Star—but they treat me like I've got every disease known to mankind."

"They think you're a pedophile," Anna said.

All trace of Jordan disappeared, and the stunned face looking at Anna was that of a shocked, middle-aged actress from Seattle. "You're kidding! My God! Why would they think that?"

"You cozy up to a child and pump her for information about where children are sold for sex, what are they supposed to think? That you're simply a murderess seeking her daughters?"

"Gosh," Clare said and slumped in her chair. "The woman who runs that voodoo shop, the blonde, does she think so, too?"

"That's my guess. Do you remember that dead pigeon, the one you put in the trash?"

Clare looked blank for a moment, then nodded.

"I dug it out. I thought you'd voodooed a pigeon to curse me. After talking to the Amazing Patty at Vieux Dieux, I figured her rival was putting the curse on you."

"Poor thing," Clare said. "She must have been afraid for her little girl."

Anna sipped her coffee and watched as Jordan seeped back into Clare's face and body.

When the transformation was complete, Anna said, "This is too big for us. We've got to bring in the police."

Jordan snorted. "See the guy in the picture?" Anna looked at the man on whose lap the Candy doll sat. "That picture was taken a few years ago—at least that's my guess. If Candy's in her early teens now and was about nine or ten then, three years would be about right. Well, that guy grew up, too. His name is Walter Le Beau. For the past five years he's been New Orleans's chief of police."

New Orleans had been making headlines with corruption in high places since Huey Long, but still Anna was shocked. "The FBI, then," she said.

Jordan puffed out a breath full of exasperation and disgust. "And tell them what?" he demanded. "That we've got an old picture of a guy who might be the police chief with a doll on his lap who might be a little girl and that this means there's a high-end child prostitution ring? Don't be an ass."

Jordan leaned across the table, so close Anna could smell his punk homeless reek. "And say we got real lucky," he said. "And they started an investigation. They were down here investigating prostitution for eighteen months. Eighteen fucking months! You know what they found? Three hookers. Bozo the clown could find a dozen in thirty minutes on a Saturday night.

"Are you going to help me, or are you going to sit around with your head up your butt?"

Anna was stung. She didn't like Jordan. He was a vicious, violent, foul-mouthed twit. Clare was a different thing. Clare she would help.

"My head's out," she said evenly. "What now?"

Anna's coffee was gone. She wanted another cup, but she didn't stir to fetch it from the cottage. Mack was licking her foot, and, though she was aware the gesture was meant to be kind, she didn't particularly relish having dog spit all over her toes. Still, she didn't bother to move her foot.

Sitting there in pink jammies and flip-flops, her red and silver hair loose around her face, her hands looking old and small on her coffee cup, she felt more or less helpless. Not only did she not have the color of law behind her, she didn't have Paul's advice and strength.

Lying to him was going to damage them both in some indefinable way. She wasn't fool enough to believe not telling wasn't the same as lying in a marriage. There would be omissions and evasions and, ultimately, an erosion of trust. Even if Paul never knew why. For a moment she considered backing out of the whole thing.

One look at Jordan and she knew she couldn't. He, too, was feeling lost and helpless, and bits of Clare were beginning to show through. The demon that was devouring Jordan, robbing him of physical mass and mental control, was the mother of two, her desperate need consuming them both from within. They didn't have much in the way of resources left. Anna had seen people go crazy before. She was seeing it again.

"Let's lay out what we've got so far," she said briskly.

TWENTY-TWO

*W*hat now? Clare echoed Anna's question in her mind as she rose from the ashes of Jordan to the misery that was Clare Sullivan. What could they do? How could they proceed? Picturing Vee, then Dana, on the knee of the man in the picture, their sweet faces caked with paint, the supple little bodies tarted into a sick fantasy, she felt she could claw her way through walls to get them—but crazy murdering mothers were never even allowed near those walls. Crooked cops, velvet voiced boys who jerked off over corpses, all the machinery of a man's world stood between her and her children. If they were still alive.

They're alive, she told herself. *If they were dead I would know it.* That had been her mantra since the night of the fire, and it was growing thin, sounding more and more like a pathetic lie.

Shaking herself the way Mackie did when his fur was wet, she blasted apart that train of thought. That way madness lay. Her eyes slewed toward her tablemate.

Sitting in the sun, the shadows of the leaves flickering hypnotically, the ranger was playing footsie with Mack like there was all the time in the world. Pink flannel pajamas, red and white hair falling in witch waves around a face that had been left out in the sun too long, didn't strike Clare as much of a federal agent.

Clare felt a bubble of hate and fear boil up inside her and looked away, resting her eyes on Geneva's French doors, so Officer Pigeon wouldn't see it. Whatever else the woman's faults were, she saw things. She saw Jordan when he was invisible to everyone else, saw the hatred people felt for him, saw the demons and the wrongness in everything he did.

She saw it, but she wasn't smart enough to figure it out, Clare thought. The possibility that she was a good enough actress that no one, regardless of IQ, would have figured it out didn't cross her mind. There had been a time she had pride and a sense of self, a sense of achievement, but that time was so impossibly long ago Clare had forgotten she no longer remembered it.

Clare knew she ought to be grateful: grateful that maybe the pigeon wasn't going to be a stool pigeon and call the police, grateful that Ms. Pigeon promised not only to remain silent but to help, grateful that she was no longer alone, that someone believed she didn't kill her children. But she wasn't.

Anna Pigeon had allowed in an evil so virulent that it could scatter Clare's mental house of cards to the edges of the universe: hope. When Anna said she would help, Clare had felt hope. It weakened her, made her afraid. If she could hope, she could lose hope. Better to be Jordan running on adrenaline and revenge; better to be a man who had no children, only a dog. A man who might not believe Dana and Vee were still living but had every confidence he would rip out the throats of the men who took them with his teeth if he got a chance.

Clare gathered herself together, whisking into a pile the debris of mother and actress and wife, then pulled Jordan over the detritus of herself like a cloak, wrapping the punk tightly around her bones.

If the bitch turned on them, he could always kill her, Jordan thought as he narrowed his eyes and addressed the pajama ranger.

"This is what we've got so far," he said. "We know David and the Cajun are connected. The Cajun had David and Jalila's daughter. The Cajun was at the explosion of the house; he had a key to David's apartment and was there with the man who killed Jalila—if the Cajun didn't kill her himself.

"We know the Cajun and New Orleans are connected. He was bringing Aisha to the 'Bourbon Street Nursery,' the yellow leather jacket that went missing in Seattle is here in New Orleans, and Mackie knew the smell of the guy wearing it.

"We know David was also connected to New Orleans," Jordan continued, finding power in cataloging what he knew, what Clare knew. "David visited here a number of times. Clare—I—didn't pay much attention to the bills regarding his garment business, but I think she remembers seeing he had dealings with a clothing firm here; he bought or sold something to do with fabric or machines or whatever."

Jordan watched the pigeon tilt her head and look a little sharper when she heard the third-person references. They made her uncomfortable. That was too damn bad. They made Clare uncomfortable as well, but Jordan didn't worry about it.

At the end of the day, Ms. Pigeon would reconcile Jordan and Clare and sit happy in her own sanity. Whether Clare could or not, Jordan didn't much care. If her children—or killing the fucks who took them—didn't make her whole, Jordan was going to be as good as she got.

"We know David imported undocumented workers from the Mideast, women to sew and cut." Jordan went on with his list. "You've got to figure some had kids. Maybe David's undocumented workers—or their kids—were connected with the sex slave trade.

"That's it. I don't know where the Cajun is. You screwed up me catching the yellow jacket. I don't know where the major whorehouses are, don't know if they still do kids in a big way. I don't know fuck-all. You got anything better?"

"My brother-in-law, Frederick, is ex-FBI," the pink ranger said after a moment. "He runs a computer detective business from New York, cyber-sleuthing. He might help. I'll think on it. See you tonight."

With one last pat to Mackie, she picked up her empty coffee cup and moseyed back to her cottage.

Jordan sat for a minute seething. Left to himself,

he'd have yelled, "Make your fucking call," but Clare held him back. Clare, too, had hoped for more, hoped for a miracle, hoped for magic. It was the hope thing again. Anna Pigeon had opened a box worse than Pandora's and into a world of horror released hope.

Clare had had a two-episode role on *Law & Order: Special Victims Unit* when they were shooting a sequence in Seattle. She'd played a computer whiz. Though she didn't know how it was done, she did know the FBI cyber-sleuth brother-in-law might be able to find out details about Police Chief Walter Le Beau and the garment trade in both Seattle and New Orleans. He might also be able to access information on David's finances, import/export patterns, business partners, and travel. Given that David—Daoud Suliman—was a Middle Eastern man living and working in the United States during the Bush years after 9/11, he'd probably been monitored by more than one federal agency.

For all she knew, their phones could have been tapped and their computers hacked. What was deemed "national security" and what "right to privacy" had become very hazy. For the first time in her life, Clare was grateful for the taste of fascism America had gotten. If it helped her find Dana and Vee, she didn't care if Big Brother peeked through the bedroom blinds at night.

"Fuck her," Jordan said suddenly, and, with a sense of relief, Clare started sinking into his ready anger.

Mackie whined, and Clare's abdication was interrupted. "What is it, little guy?" she asked in her own voice. Mackie's face was round, and his eyes so like those of an Ewok that Clare'd always thought George Lucas must have had a shih tzu or a Lhasa when he was a little boy. Mackie tilted his head the way he did when he was listening to her, as if, could he only get the angle of his ears to her mouth just right, he would be able to make out what she was saying.

Clare was all the family Mackie had left—and, but for the grace of whatever, Mackie was all Clare had. Not Jordan, Clare.

Talking with Anna Pigeon, she'd lost the sense that Jordan was a character she created, that they were two separate individuals. His domination had seemed natural, inevitable, like it happened in every body, this fight between good and evil, hope and despair, violence and sense. It had felt *normal*. Was this how people went insane? One day the most natural thing in the world was to let an entity, an "other," slide into the skin and push out the original personality?

Clare shuddered, as part of her made note of the sensations should she ever play a female Dr. Jekyll. Given how thin and wasted she had become, it brought out sweat on her forehead. Softly, so Geneva wouldn't hear and Mackie wouldn't howl, she began to cry. Folding in half, arms trapped between her torso and her thighs, she rocked herself and wept until tears dripped from her face to the bricks and Mackie began to lick her cheek with concern.

There came a crack and a fog and a cold that froze Clare's despair. With a jacknife jerk, she sat up, vacant-eyed.

Then, "Come on, Mackie," Jordan said, twitching Clare's body into action. "Let's go visit our gutter punk pals. Maybe Dan'll know something about the city's leprous underbelly."

TWENTY-THREE

The trains Clare had jumped with the punks on the trip south from Seattle were a blur of soot and fear and noise. She'd spent most of the time holding on to Mackie for fear he would jump from the train or not be firm under her arm when she ran for a moving boxcar. In the absence of her daughters and her home, the little dog had become the grail in which what remained of her heart was carried. If anything happened to him, Clare knew it would be the last straw she would ever feel strike her back.

By the time they landed in New Orleans, she'd known the punks' names—or the names they had given themselves: Danny, Rain, Darwin, Peter, and Stacy. When they detrained she'd gone with them. Along with five others, they'd bedded down in an abandoned house near South Claiborne, almost under I-10. Even all these years after Katrina there was no shortage of abandoned houses that either no one laid claim to or no one bothered to tear down. Mecca for squatters, runaways, and druggies.

Despite all this quality time, Clare had not bonded with the punks. At first, she hadn't spoken but simply followed them, did as they did, always a few yards away, a little behind, immersing herself deeper and deeper in the character of Jordan, creating his backstory, something she'd done a hundred times.

Once the punks figured out Jordan wasn't going to hurt or rob them, they accepted him. When Jordan shared his cigarettes, then bought a couple of joints and shared those, they let him sit closer. Jordan did, because the known was safer than the unknown and most of Danny's little gang was young and seemed nonviolent.

Because Jordan didn't fit the profile of a pierced and tattooed traveler or hardcase old-timer, they figured he was on the run from the law for something serious. Which, in fact, was the case. To Clare's surprise, this lent Jordan stature in their little group. Still, there were no beginnings of friendship, just a mutual understanding of sorts.

Though she hadn't thought it possible to feel more miserable than she did, she found the squat depressing, the filth, the drugs, and the vermin—two-, four-, six-, and eight-legged—too frightening. Her third night in the city, she hadn't gone back but slept on a bench on the river walk. A schizophrenic man—that was her take on his mental state—had chased her off his bed with a broken bottle. There was a protocol to being homeless, and

Clare did not know it. If it hadn't been for Jordan's reflexes, she might have been cut.

The middle of the next day she saw the FOR RENT sign in Geneva's window.

Clare bought a secondhand laptop and a cell phone and started surfing the Web for any hint of her children. Jordan spent a lot of time with the punks. They hung out on Bourbon Street, panhandling for the most part and occasionally dragging out a guitar one had found in a squat in another town and learned to play a few chords on. It was a way to stay on the street and watch without being noticed by anybody. As odd as the punks were, they were human and they were company.

Jordan found Dan and his gang on Chartres behind St. Louis Cathedral, leaning against the iron fence, enjoying the scowls of the artist who had set up there to sell her wares. Danny was the accepted leader. He was tall and bearded and in his thirties. Of the five of them, Danny was the only one who gave off the vibe of someone who would kill. The others, Jordan figured, would do violence only as a group. Taken one by one they were weak and pathetic and trying to cover it with rudeness and vandalizing their own bodies to spite an indifferent public. For them, Jordan felt little but disdain.

"Got any smokes?" Danny said by way of greeting.

Jordan slid down the fence till his bony butt rested on the sidewalk, fished a crumpled pack out of the pocket of his shirt, and shook one out. Danny took it, bummed a light, and then took the rest of the pack as if it were his due.

"Fuck that shit," Jordan said and snatched it back. He and Danny smoked in silence, letting the sun soak into their faces and the nicotine into their brains. Rain—not her real name, Jordan figured—played with the newest puppy.

The bulls the railroads hired to keep the yards secure didn't like to mess with punks with dogs. If they busted a punk with a dog, a city ordinance made them take that dog to the pound and, if it bit them or anybody, do a long rabies thing. Bulls didn't want to do that much work. So the travelers collected dogs. When they left a town, sometimes they took them. Mostly they left them behind to fend for themselves.

Rain had lost a dog in Sacramento when they'd jumped. It had fallen under the wheels of the train. At the squat she'd picked up a new puppy and was happy as a little girl playing with it, getting it to bite at a weed she'd pulled up. Rain was fifteen and had seven piercings in her face: both eyebrows, two through her lower lip, her tongue, her nose, and one through the middle of her left cheek. Her body and her hygiene were not able to support so much metal, and the nose and cheek wept all the time.

The new dog couldn't have been more than eight weeks old. It was a mutt, a bit of black Lab, Airedale mustache, retriever tail, paws that could have been given it by a St. Bernard. The paws were so big he tripped over them, and both girl and puppy grinned hugely.

Darwin, Rain's boyfriend and so called because he looked kind of like the missing link, was totally ripped on something and examining the end of one of his dreads. Jordan didn't know where the other two were.

"Where're Peter and Stacy?" he asked, letting smoke trickle out with his question.

"You working for the fucking Census Bureau now?" Danny asked.

Jordan let it go. It was just noise. "I'm looking for a guy," Jordan said finally, grinding out his cigarette on the cement, then tossing the butt into the gutter. Jordan hadn't told them why he'd come to New Orleans; he hadn't told them much of anything and didn't plan to.

"Peter swings both ways," Danny said. "If you're looking for an ugly guy."

Jordan didn't laugh. With Danny's punks laughing was a sign of weakness.

"Give me another smoke," Danny said.

Jordan shook one out and another for himself. This time Danny didn't try to take the pack. They both leaned back their heads and pulled in deep lungfuls of smoke.

Clare hadn't smoked for so many years she'd thought the addiction was gone. It wasn't. It had been waiting for that first drag. She'd only quit because she knew it would be bad for the fetus, then for the children. Unless she could again be a mother, there was no need to live a long life.

Smirking, Jordan took another drag. "This guy I'm looking for was on the river walk the other day, the one with the yellow coat that my dog ran after."

"That why you cut out? I thought you had the runs."

"Maybe it was something you ate," Rain said, still teasing the puppy with the weed.

"I followed him to an alley off Dumaine—I think it was Dumaine. He pulled a knife on me and I lost him," Jordan said.

"Sounds like you got lucky." Danny scratched in his beard with a thoroughness that bordered on lewd.

"I was wondering if you guys would watch for him, let me know if you see him, maybe where he goes."

Danny and his punks never asked for anything but cigarettes and money, not even so much as "Please pass the salt" or "Will you watch my dog?" Whether it was an unwritten rule or nobody had needed anything in the time Jordan been in their company, he didn't know.

"That's what you were wondering?" Danny asked, pretending to care. "You were wondering if we'd hang out and watch for some dude in a yellow coat? Maybe call you on a cell phone if we see this dude? Oh, right, we don't have a cell phone. So maybe you wondered if we'd jump up and run you down and tell you we see this guy? You spent all that time wondering this?"

Jordan guessed not asking for things was a rule.

"And you thought we'd do this why?"

"Money," Jordan said succinctly. "Drugs. Whatever you want." Jordan wished he hadn't added the last. He was negotiating in a world where seeming to have too much to bargain with could get a guy killed. Why jump through hoops when a brick to the back of his head and Danny could take it all?

Danny didn't miss it either. "Whatever I want," he said slowly, drawing the sentence out as if he were taking the time to dream a hundred sumptuous dreams in the duration of three words. "World peace? Nah, too easy. A million dollars?" He pretended to think about it for a while, then shook his head. "You know, a million used to be real money. Not so much these days."

Clare was getting scared.

Jordan was getting pissed off. "Forget it, man," he said and pushed his thin shoulders up the iron stakes. "I can buy half a dozen assholes for a six-pack of beer. I don't need your shit." Hands shoved deep in the pockets of his pants, spine curved in a slouch that was both lazy and cruel-looking, he headed down Chartres.

"Jordan!" Danny called after him. Jordan stopped and turned slowly enough that it could have been taken as an insult.

"Don't be such a sensitive prick. You travel with us, we help you. Right, Rain? We're family." Rain had picked the puppy up, and they were nuzzling each other, both strays finding joy in what love came their way.

"Bingo's family," Rain said, and she held the puppy's paw and waved it at Jordan.

Clare froze for a moment. She saw Dana and Vee and Mackie when he was no more than two pounds of fluff and bark. The girls were dancing around the new puppy, he was dancing around them. They were singing, "B-I-NGO, B-I-NGO, and Bingo was his name-O."

Jordan narrowed his eyes and the vision was blinked out.

"Get your ass back here," Danny said.

Jordan would have flipped him off and kept on going, but Clare made him slouch back. The return was out of character, but Danny'd never notice. Clare and Jordan didn't sit but stood, hands in pockets, looking around as if waiting for the Luftwaffe to begin their daily bombing runs.

"B-I-NGO, B-I-NGO, Bingo was his name-O," Rain sang softly to her puppy.

Clare felt hollow and strange, as if her memory of her daughters had been channeled into this damaged girl, as if the dead spoke to her through pierced lips. Tears started in her eyes. Jordan shook out another Camel and lit it.

"What do you want to find this guy for?" Danny asked.

"What the fuck do you care why I want to find him? I want to thank him for polishing my pew at church. That suit you?"

"You're all heart, man." Danny laughed. He didn't care, he was just making conversation. "And this Samaritan's got a yellow leather coat? Like in butter yellow or sunshine yellow or *Yellow Submarine* yellow?"

"Submarine on acid," Jordan said.

The smoke had cured Clare's tears. Clare had forgotten that. When she was young, not married, no kids, and smoked, she could always count on nicotine to stop tears. Odd but true.

"He's maybe thirty. Dark and wiry with hair greased like a fifties lowrider," Jordan said. Danny looked blank.

"Like the Fonz on *Happy Days*." That didn't do anything to clear it up. "Jesus, fuck, you some kind of cultural black hole, dude? Like that pimp that hangs around outside Dick's sometimes; the one that runs the old black whores, five bucks a shot."

Now Danny saw the light.

"He wears pointed shoes that should be shined but aren't and pants too tight with nothing in the package to show off."

Clare was startled at how much they remembered about the man Mackie had followed, the man the pigeon had chased into the alley. But he was there, as clear as if they'd spent hours studying him. Without pride, she knew she could step into his pointy shoes and play him down to the knife. Ratso Rizzo, but without heart.

"Sure, *dude,* we'll be on the lookout, punk BOLO for slimebag in pimp clothes. We should have about fifty-seven sightings before . . . oh, hey." Danny looked at a wristwatch that wasn't there. "Say fifteen minutes from now."

He and Rain laughed. Rain sat cross-legged in her short denim skirt. Bingo was asleep in her lap, his funny, fuzzy body the only thing keeping her from flashing the dead people behind St. Louis Cathedral.

"You're fucking useless, man," Jordan said easily.

It had been a long shot. Clare could see the guy Mackie and the pigeon had followed so clearly that if she'd been an artist, she could have drawn him, but words were paltry things, and she knew Danny had no idea what he was looking for.

"A thousand bucks if you get him," Jordan said. "Fuck-all if you don't. I gotta go." Jordan stooped. Clare petted the sleeping puppy. "Feed him," she said and slid up into Jordan's stinking clothes to walk down Pirate's Alley and out onto Jackson Square where the tarot readers and living statues and artists were trying to make a buck off the tourists.

CARICATURES $5.00. AN EXTRA DOLLAR IF YOU'RE UGLY, an artist halfway down on the shady side advertised. On his chunk of the iron fence around the square were a slew of not-half-bad caricatures of famous faces: Elvis, Michael Jackson, Cher, De Niro, Shirley Temple, James Brown, Bob Dylan.

Jordan stopped. He shook out another cigarette and lit it. At six bucks a pack and counting, David Sullivan's cache of bills was going to go up in smoke. "You ever watch *Law & Order*?" he asked the artist, a saggy bean-bag of a man who looked tired and cranky, with eyes that saw too much too often.

"Which part of the franchise?" he asked.

"The one where they have a police artist draw the bad guy from a description."

TWENTY-FOUR

Anna called her brother-in-law, Frederick, late of the FBI. Her main concern was the questionable ethics of asking him to help her while keeping him in the dark for his own safety. She had forgotten how quick the man's mind was.

"David Sullivan, Daoud Suliman, the slain husband/ father in Seattle?" he'd asked.

"The same," Anna admitted.

"And you want me to trace his business with a special focus on dealings with New Orleans."

"I do."

"You are in New Orleans on business?"

He knew she wasn't. Molly had been her favorite ear in the early days of her separation from the NPS, before she'd grown ashamed at her own whining and shut her out for a while.

"Vacation," Anna said.

"So, on vacation, wanting information on victim

Sullivan . . . you've got a lead on where his wife is, the prime murder suspect."

Anna said nothing.

Frederick groaned. "No. Don't tell me you've actually got the wife?"

Again Anna said nothing.

"Is she . . ."

There was a sudden silence. As it ticked by, Anna resisted the temptation to say "Are you there?" into her cell phone.

Frederick came back on the line. "Right, never mind; tell me no more. But, and you listen to me this time, doggone it, what you are doing is so very dangerous. Not only knife-in-the-back kind of dangerous, but thirty-years-to-life kind of dangerous. Let's not discuss it further. I'll e-mail you."

"Thanks, Frederick," Anna said, relieved. Since the Bush administration had bent or broken all the rules about right to privacy, paranoia was the norm. If one didn't want it recorded, one didn't say it over America's phone lines, or airwaves, or whatever it was cell phones sent things over.

"I owe you," she said.

"Oh my yes, a bunch, a whole bunch. I'm talking you come to New York for Christmas and stay with your sister and go shopping with her," Frederick said without a trace of humor in his voice.

"Shopping?" Anna quailed. "At Christmas?"

"Put it on your calendar. Bring your Paul. We'll run

background checks on each other and play chess."

"I will," Anna promised.

"Yes, you will," Frederick said. He added, "We love you. Stay out of dark alleys and the federal penitentiary." Then he hung up.

Walking down Bourbon, the sun long set and Friday night partiers thickening like soup left too long on the stove, Anna wished she'd been able to do more than she had. Clare's sense of time running out was contagious, she thought as she stepped into the street to cede the sidewalk to a knot of men too drunk to be trusted not to fall on her.

At CC's she'd accessed the Wi-Fi and gleaned as much about Clare, her husband, her children, the murders, and David's business from Google and Wikipedia as she could—whatever was public knowledge.

Clare had a Facebook account. Not being a hacker, Anna was limited only to the first page. It was about actors and acting and theater shoptalk. Her daughters weren't mentioned. Whether this indicated she was not a good mother or was an exceedingly good mother, Anna didn't know.

David's business had a Web site, but it was sufficiently boring to dull her senses. Again, she could only access the first page. The business was strictly wholesale, and without a vendor number she was locked out.

Newspapers and magazines were more forthcoming. The murders were covered from every angle and rehashed from the *Times* to the tabloids. Clare Sullivan had murdered her sleeping spouse and his mistress and then set fire to the family home, killing both her children. Since she'd disappeared the night of the crimes and so could not be tried and convicted, the better rags were careful to say "alleged" murderer. The others didn't bother.

Information made public by the Seattle police and coroner's office made it look like an open-and-shut case. Anna's instincts told her Clare was innocent, but Anna's instincts, when it came to judging character, were notoriously untrustworthy.

Without using any names, she had talked with Molly about the schism in Clare, the part of her that seemed to be becoming Jordan.

"We all do it to some extent," her sister told her. "Just look at the headlines. Family values politicians having affairs, antigay preachers going to male prostitutes. We aren't the same person to our grandmother as we are to the cop who stops us for speeding. It's when we force a divide between these seemingly disparate parts that mental illness comes in. Most of us compartmentalize, make excuses, or suffer guilt, but we hold the good and the bad together in our skins and our skulls. Your nameless person has taken it to a new level, but I doubt she's crazy. Yet."

The "yet" haunted Anna. If Clare was not a murderess, there was still Jordan. Anna believed Jordan could easily become a killer, if he wasn't already. Her gut told her, if and when this happened, Clare would step over that line from knowing she was behaving bizarrely to simply being that other bizarre person. Should Anna be in the vicinity when that happened, there could be deadly consequences.

Shaking off logical thoughts and sensible behavior, she cleared her mind. For whatever reasons, she believed in Clare. She had promised to help her as far as she could without committing any crimes—any more crimes. Second-guessing her decision or, worse, psychoanalyzing why she made it was a waste of time and energy. Opening her eyes to her surroundings, she soaked in the color, music, foolishness, and overindulgence that was Bourbon Street.

Without turning her head she could count half a dozen examples of Molly's contention that we all harbor other personalities within: the Minnesota businessman, sporting a new tattoo, a fleur-de-lis, that he would have to keep covered for the rest of his professional life; the acne-scarred middle-aged man in denim and flannel, flirting with a lovely boy when, at a guess, he was straight as an arrow when he was home; two women in their forties or early fifties, showing lots of leg and cleavage and having a wonderful time when, back in their normal skins, they probably wouldn't dream of wearing skimpy clothes and cavorting in high heels.

There was a part of Anna that occasionally had a yen to slither around in silk and heavy mascara, but she hadn't succumbed for some years. There was always a reason she wanted—or needed—to be comfortable, to be able to move freely, run quickly, and scramble through and over things that a dress could catch on. Tonight, for

all the usual reasons, she was in baggy linen trousers—
growing ever baggier in the humid air—a tank top, and
Tevas. Her hair was in its customary braid. It occurred to
her, should she make the Deep South her permanent
home, she'd probably be driven to chop it off. It was a bit
like wearing a coonskin cap in the middle of August.

Paul had fallen in love with her while she was in
uniform and carrying a gun. Perhaps, before she left
New Orleans, she would buy something sensuous and
surprise him. Though he loved her in the green and gray,
she didn't doubt for a moment he would love her in silk
and heels just as much, and, probably, suddenly. She
smiled thinking of his touch.

A thicket of boys on a wrought-iron balcony, each
holding a beer, green and gold and purple Mardi Gras
beads around their fists and necks, hollered down, "Show
us your tits!" Never mind that it wasn't Mardi Gras and
Anna was old enough to arrest their mothers. Anna
smiled and waved, amused to be included in their rev-
elry. She did not, however, flash her breasts.

Bourbon Street, New Orleans, a historically sinful
tourist destination, reminded her of the carnival that
Pinocchio was lured to, the dark place of noise and light
and lurid shadows where bad little boys turned into
animals. The main difference was that the carnival of
animal-children in Pinocchio's colorful hell scared the
bejesus out of the tiny Anna. She still couldn't recall the
scene without a modicum of shiveriness visiting her
spine. Bourbon Street did not have that same sense of

true evil, of no turning back, of consequences that creep up on one unawares and, when one finally realizes what's happening, it's too late.

Dick's was the same gray and dreary bunker of the night before. The young barker behind the lectern was chatty and charming and welcomed Anna back with "Why am I not surprised that such a beautiful woman got lucky? May Bacchus bless your evening, darlin'."

Anna thanked him politely and stepped into the grimy darkness of the strip club. Star was onstage with the same young studly sort that had provided a hobby-horse for Candy the previous evening. She was down to pasties, panties, and turquoise cowboy boots with matching hat. Her implants, tools of the trade, though seemingly not the requirement Anna would have expected, defied gravity as she lay on her back across a miserably uncomfortable-looking chair while her young costar did his best to keep his weight off of her and the rickety-looking set piece.

The plastic chairs around the battered black cube tables were full. Mostly men, mostly young, but a healthy smattering of guys in their forties and fifties. Too big for the knee-high cubes, they looked like huge toddlers hulking on playroom furniture. To further the illusion, most of them were sucking on a bottle.

Anna hesitated inside the short artificial hallway from the street, designed, she supposed, to give the customers a greater sense of having entered the devil's den.

Her eyes adjusted quickly, and she saw Betty at a table in the back of the room, past the bottleneck created by the bar and the stage, waving to her. Having threaded her way through the clumps of men, Anna sank gratefully into a chair beside her.

"Big crowd," Anna said just to be saying something.

"Southern Baptist convention's in town," Betty replied as if that said it all.

"Ah."

Betty watched the stage, and Anna watched Jordan hustling drinks. Dressed in black, emaciated and expressionless, it wouldn't be too hard to believe he was one of New Orleans's celebrated vampires. In a way he was, Anna thought, sucking the life out of Clare, turning her into a creature like himself.

Dramatic as these images were, Anna believed she could see the desperate woman beneath Jordan's skin in the shaking of the hands as beers were set down, the jerk of the shoulders at a sudden noise from the stage, the careful way of never looking at the dancers, as if that would somehow demean them.

If Jordan had seen Anna come in, he was ignoring her in an impressive fashion. Had she wanted a drink, she would have had to flag him down, and his eyes were always carefully elsewhere.

"Who all is working tonight?" she asked Betty after a few minutes had elapsed.

"Hah! Don't tell me you fell in love in the ladies' john last night?" Betty leaned across the table, her beer corralled between her hardworking hands, and grinned at Anna. The grin winked out. "Don't tell me you fell in love with Tanya," she said warningly.

"With you in the wings, I doubt I'd have a chance," Anna said gravely. Betty's grin returned. "Do you come here every night?" Anna asked. Perhaps Betty would know a thing or two about a thing or two.

"Most nights," Betty said, relaxing back as far as she was able in the stingy plastic chair. "If I'm going to grow on her, I've got to be around. And for little things to grow, they've got to be fed and watered." She rubbed her thumb and fingers together in the sign for cash. Betty was nobody's fool.

"As to who's working tonight, Candy's here—she's here pretty much seven days a week. I don't think she's got anyplace else to go, and she really likes the stage work and the people. She's a big star in Candy World. Uh, let's see, Star obviously, and my adorable Tanya— she has Mondays and Tuesdays off, so I'm not here those nights. I haven't seen Delilah, but I haven't been here all that long. She could be in back getting made up. Mostly she and Star don't work together, which is too bad. They've got a hot little girl-girl act they do once in a while. It goes over big. All the bozos picture themselves as the welcome third. Like that would ever happen. But they try and work different nights. Star's got a kid about nine, and they don't like to leave him with sitters if they can help it."

"Who's up after Star?"

"The single most beautiful woman ever about to fall in love with a wharf rat," Betty said and smacked her lips. Not metaphorically but literally, like a toothless sommelier trying to remember an exquisite vintage.

Betty was a font of information, and Anna was grateful. As Star finished her act and clumped off the stage, leaving the energetic young stud muffin slouching in sexy—and to Anna's eye totally gay—insouciance against a pole, Anna rose and followed her toward the ladies' toilet.

Some goddess or other had taken pity on Anna, and the cramped space was relatively free of smoke. Probably because Delilah wasn't there to add her nightly pack of Marlboro Lights to the dope smoke.

"You guys got a minute?" Anna asked. Star collapsed into the unpadded metal folding chair that she'd occupied the previous night.

"Geez, woman, how many minutes you need? Didn't you get your fill of bullshit last night? Whatever you're after, we're fresh out," Star said wearily. Shoving aside a blue towel that was probably older than her co-worker Candy, Star opened the lid of a plastic cooler and pulled out a beer. "You want one?" she asked.

Because breaking bread —or, in this case, yeast— with another was good for developing trust, Anna accepted. Being a woman of manners, Star unscrewed the cap and wiped the mouth of the bottle off on the old towel before handing it to her uninvited guest.

Candy, slumped in the other chair, *US* magazine open in her lap, her tummy looking bigger than it had the night before and her face rounder and younger, said, "Can I have one?"

"How many've you already had?" Star asked, eyes narrowed like a faro dealer peering through smoke.

"Just one. Honest," Candy said and crossed her heart with her fingers.

"Okay, but you go slow. You've got the rest of the night to get through, and the boss doesn't like it when you get too silly onstage." Star pulled out a third beer, twisted off the cap, wiped the mouth of the bottle, and handed it to the pregnant teen. She shot Anna a look that said as clearly as if she'd shouted it, "I dare you to say one thing, one fucking thing."

Anna didn't dare.

"I got somebody I want you to meet," Anna said.

Star groaned. "Everybody's got somebody they want us to 'meet.' We don't hook. Not even for 'sisters.' Got that? Didn't we go through all that last night? What part of 'fuck off' don't you understand?"

"Yeah, what part?" Candy echoed without malice.

"No," Anna said, feeling a fool for not knowing this was how her innocuous statement would be taken in the ladies' room of Dick's. "Not sex stuff. Serious stuff. You wait here." Not trusting herself not to screw things up with more unintended insults, Anna set her beer down on the board near Candy's makeup and let herself out of the bathroom. One elbow on the black plywood, she waited beside the bar, enduring the bumping of inebriated men making their unsteady ways back to the john in the rear.

Tanya was reworking a high school wet dream for the audience, the one where the pretty girl doesn't snub the ugly fat boys. Finally Jordan delivered the last tiny bottle of booze on his tray and returned to the bar.

"Ready?" Anna asked.

"It's pretty busy," Jordan replied with a fretful look at the patrons growing ever more hot-eyed and thirsty as Tanya's micro-mini pleated skirt rode up her brown thighs to expose the threadiest of thong panties.

"And you care about that why?" Anna asked.

Jordan's lips curled into a sneer, and Anna braced herself for the onslaught of the four-letter words he was so fond of. Before the lips parted, she saw Clare come home. Pressed to describe it, Anna would have had a hard time. Anna's back was to the stage, and the slow strobe of pink lights Tanya used for her act was in Jordan's face, dying his skin the shade of a living person's, and taking the bloodshot veins from the whites of his eyes. In this glow of artificial health Anna saw the irises change as Jordan left and Clare returned. The pupils grew slightly bigger, the hazel less brown and more gold. Eyelids relaxed infinitesimally, and brows lowered. The sense was of an evil spirit departing and the body's original owner returning to look out through the eyes.

"I'm scared is all," Clare said. She untied the black apron from over her black pants and laid it neatly across the black bar, leaving Anna to wonder what had really been accomplished.

"Afraid a teensy-weensy little thing like believing you are a child molester will make them not like you?" Anna asked with what she'd meant to be an encouraging smile.

"No," Clare said. "Scared to death they won't know anything, won't help, won't be able to help. Scared . . ."

She let the word trail off and stared into the darkness at the rear of the club. "Let's go," she said and began walking ahead of Anna toward the ladies' room.

Watching Clare square Jordan's slouching shoulders, Anna guessed she wasn't scared they would know nothing of her lost children but was terrified they would know something. They would know the girls were dead.

Odds were against any of that happening. At best, Candy would remember something that was useful or Star would know someone who might know someone who might know something useful.

That was if, in fact, Dana and Vee had gone missing and not been burned in their beds by Mom.

The worst that might happen was that, eager to please or to seem important, Candy would make up information that would delay them with wild goose chases. The girls had been gone nearly two weeks. If they were not dead already it would be a miracle. Any trail leading to them or, more likely, their corpses would have cooled.

Much longer and it would be cold beyond the abilities of a park ranger and an actor to detect.

TWENTY-FIVE

W ait," Anna said as Clare reached the bathroom. "Let me go first."

Clare backed into the shadows so Anna could open the door.

The smoke was back. Star had lit up. Candy was planting kisses on the mirror in hot pink lipstick, then trying to match her mouth's reflection to the greasy lips on the glass.

Anna took her usual place in the space between the toilet stall and the sink. "This isn't Jordan," she said by way of introduction as the skinny black-clad woman pushed in behind her.

"The fuck it isn't," Star snapped. "Get your bony ass out of here." She started up from her chair, a hairbrush held like a billy club.

"Easy, Star," Anna said. She was about to lay a calming hand on the other woman's arm but decided she would probably get a black eye out of the deal. Star looked like she'd taken her self-defense classes on the streets and in the alleys of New Orleans. "It's not Jordan. Jordan is a woman. Her name is Faye," Anna said. They hadn't discussed a pseudonym, but the less the dancers knew about Clare, the less trouble they could get into for helping her. "Faye disguised herself as Jordan because she's trying to find her daughter. The little girl got snatched, and Faye was able to follow her as far as New Orleans. She thought if she got a job in the business she might hear something, and she couldn't strip—"

"That's for sure," Star said unkindly.

"And she thought men might talk more easily in front of another man. So she went for bartending," Anna finished in a rush, trying to get it all in before Star bodily threw Jordan into the hall and her after him.

At the end of Anna's impromptu speech there was silence. The pulse of Tanya's dance music came through the thin walls as faint and all pervasive as if it were the building's heartbeat.

Star stared at Jordan, then Anna, her eyes hard as she looked for the trick, the hoax, the hook that was hidden behind the words.

"Bullshit," she said finally. "You want to play games, do it in the men's room." Stubbing out her cigarette, she turned to face the mirror and began touching up her eyebrows, Anna and Jordan as dead to her as the sink or the bowl.

Clare unbuttoned the black shirt.

"None of that shit," Star said without turning. "I can whip both your butts and will."

Clare undid the last button and pulled open the shirtfront to expose the Ace bandage wrapped around her breasts to flatten her chest. "My little girls—" she began, then stopped herself. If she told them too much, if there were two missing daughters in her story, they might realize she was the woman on the run for a quadruple homicide and stop listening in their rush to dial 911. "My little girl," she amended, "is seven years old," she said softly, letting the shirt fall to the floor. "She loves animals and is a good swimmer. She beat the third graders at the last meet. Her hair is brown and soft as a kitten's fur. On windy days it looks as if it has a life of its own."

As she spoke in the quiet clear voice, she removed the butterfly closure and began to unwrap the bandage from her chest. "She calls me Momsy and loves me to French-braid her hair and recite e. e. cummings to her in funny accents." The bandage was off. She started unbuckling her belt.

"Her father is dead, and the police won't help me. They think I'm insane, and more and more I do, too."

Leaning her fanny against the door to the hall, Clare pulled off one shoe, then the other, dropping them to the floor with a thud. "The night she was kidnapped I heard a man say he was taking her to 'the Bourbon Street Nursery.' He had a Cajun accent. There was an awful boy with him, no more than twenty, but so sick he should be put down like a rabid dog." One leg was free of the trousers, and, balanced on one foot, she was easing off the other.

"I've seen the boy here in the Quarter. I chased him,

but he pulled a knife and got away. I think they've got my little girl. I think they are going to sell her into sexual slavery or use her for a while, then kill her."

The panties were off, and, naked but for a pair of men's black socks, Clare stood before the strippers. "Could you help me?" she asked, and she spread her hands in the universal gesture of supplication.

Star's mouth was pursed and tight, as if she were on the upslope of a roller coaster and they'd just crested for the fall. Tears were in her eyes. Before she had a chance to speak, Candy burst out sobbing.

"You're a girl, and I'm not a lesbian. I hate you! Fuck you! I hate you! You said you liked me!" She wailed like the child she was, makeup running down in the tears and the snot.

"I do like you," Clare said, dropping on one knee, her nakedness forgotten, her arms going around Candy. "I like you a lot, a whole, whole lot." Candy kept wailing. "I like you better than me cutlass," Clare said in a perfect pirate's voice. "Better than high tea," she said in tones Maggie Smith would have to work for. "Better than a leprechaun." This in a brogue.

Candy stopped crying to snuffle at her. Amazement had taken the place of betrayal on her face. "You're like everybody rolled up," she said with wonder.

"And every one of us likes you more than anything. Forgive me for not being a boy?" Clare smiled, and Anna realized it was the first time she'd seen a smile on either her or Jordan's face. It changed everything. Without the smile, Anna had believed in her innocence. With it, she was sure. Almost sure.

Candy looked at Clare for a moment longer, then turned back to the mirror, saying, "But you're not a boy." Candy's interests were limited, it would seem.

"I can do tricks, though. Magic. Want to see?"

"Beer!" came a roar from beyond the door. Then, louder, as more voices joined what was becoming a chorus, "Beer! Beer! Beer!" The chant was accompanied by rhythmic banging of bottles on plywood.

"Put your clothes on," Star ordered. "We'll stay after. Without booze and bare breasts those monkeys'll tear the place apart."

Clare jammed herself back into her black clothes. The Ace bandage she left on the floor.

As she left, Star laughed. "Half those jackasses are going to see those boobs under the shirt, get hot, and think they've started batting for the other team."

At twenty after four in the morning, Dick's was finally closed for the night. Customarily, Jordan would clean the men's room, empty and wash the ashtrays, stack the chairs, and sweep and mop the floor. Tonight, he didn't bother. Neither Jordan nor Clare was coming back to Dick's Den any time soon.

Clare had taken six beers from the refrigerator, paid for them, and set them on one of the cubes. Delilah, come to carry Star home, had joined them. Wondering what was going on, Tanya stayed. She sat on the edge of the makeshift stage near their table, her feet in canvas high-tops, her body hidden under an ankle-length gypsy skirt and a long white linen tunic belted with a print scarf. The rest were in plastic chairs crowded around two cubes Clare had shoved together. Star and Delilah were smoking. Candy was yawning and playing with the fringe along the edge of Tanya's scarf.

Beers served, Clare waited till everyone's attention was focused on her. Anna wondered if it was a trick she'd learned in acting school.

When everyone was looking at her, Clare said, "I'm not Jordan—"

"Yeah," Delilah said. "Star filled us in. You lost a kid, followed the snatcher to New Orleans. Pick it up there. Danny's going to be up in two hours, and I'm gonna be there to make him breakfast."

"Tanya?" Clare asked. She had morphed into the very heart and soul of sanity, warmth, and the smell of baking cookies and talcum powder. The woman was good. Who wouldn't want to help her find her little girl? If Anna, who'd had a lifetime of looking behind people's facades, couldn't see through her, what chance did the dancers have? The question had barely formed in her mind when she realized they'd undoubtedly had more experience in that quarter than she. Many of her clients were animals in the best sense of the word. These women saw animals in the worst sense most nights of their lives.

The stage set, Clare introduced what characters she

had: the young freak in the canary yellow leather sport coat, the Cajun with the thick black hair and hard-muscled shoulders, a little girl named Aisha with long dark hair and the eyes of a doe. Careful not to give away so much detail they'd guess who she was, she told them that her husband had a factory business, used undocumented workers, and, she believed, took the children they brought with them and delivered them to someone in New Orleans.

"The Cajun said 'Bourbon Street Nursery.' Maybe where the kids were taken. The man he was on the phone with, he called the Magician. The yellow-coated freak was called Dougie. The Cajun was called Blackie."

"Like half the Cajuns in the bayous," Delilah said. "It's the coon-ass version of Slim or Tex." She stubbed out her cigarette, then shook another from the pack lying on the cube. As if it were a signal to rally 'round a dying cause, Star and Clare dug out their own packs and lit up. Candy held out a hand for one.

"You can smoke or you can touch my scarf," Tanya said, "but you can't do both. This thing is silk and cost me two nights' tips."

Candy drew her hand back and returned to letting the slinky silk fringes fall through her fingers.

"So, big announcement: no dick, no daughter. What do you want us to do about it?" Delilah asked. There was no malice in her tone, only a desire to move the meeting forward.

"If any of you know who might be trafficking in

children, or anybody who spawns rumors of that kind of activity, it would give us somewhere to start," Anna said.

Waiting for the public life of Dick's to bump and grind to a close, she'd gotten so tired she could barely yawn. Now that there was a chance at information, she was wide-awake. "Has anybody heard of a Dougie or a Blackie or even the Magician in the context of illegal trafficking in minors?"

"They give traffic reports on the radio all the time. Why don't you just listen?" Candy said helpfully.

"Not car traffic, baby. Kid whores, you know, like you were before you started here."

"I use to know a bunch of working kids," Candy said, proud to be the center of attention. "They're probably dead or gone off." She seemed indifferent to both fates.

"I've got something special that only you can do," Clare said to Candy. "If you would help me, I'd sure appreciate it." She used her warm apple pie voice and added the sugar of a smile to it.

"How much will you give me?" Candy asked.

"How about twenty dollars?"

"Some nights I get more'n that for one dance. I had forty-three dollars stuffed in my string once."

Candy might not have been blessed with all the brains in the world, but she counted money just fine.

"Hmm, that's a lot," Clare said, pretending to consider. "How about a hundred?"

Anna knew she'd give the girl a thousand if it came to that. She'd probably known intuitively that a number that big might have scared Candy. Too much for too little.

Canniness had filled in for the baby stripper where intelligence should have been.

"Okay," Candy said quickly. She didn't ask what the favor was. For a hundred bucks she would probably do anything that didn't hurt too much.

"Good girl," Clare said.

"Wait a damn minute," Star said. "What are you going to have her do for her money?"

"Be hypnotized," Clare answered. "I want to see if she can remember more about the fancy house she was in before she was put on the streets."

Mollified, Star took another swig of beer.

"The law busts a few hookers now and then to prove they're on the job—"

"Or because they didn't get a free blow job," Star cut in.

"That, too," Delilah agreed, "but mostly they leave them alone. But kids are different. You don't hear much about it unless you're in that groove, if you know what I mean. Too volatile with the politicians and the media. Gets the moms in from the suburbs with torches storming city hall."

They sat with that thought for a moment.

"Dougie and Blackie could be anybody. Might not even be their real names," Star said.

"I might have heard of the Magician," Delilah said after more thought. "There's this woman, used to dance, then went to hooking because the money was better but quit and started reading tarot on the square after a john nearly killed her. Andi—you remember Andi," Delilah said to Tanya. "Did a pretty little Bo Peep deal, made more than anybody not hooking could with her private lap dances, got canned?"

"Right," Tanya said. "Larry Flynt's. Got turned in by a john that didn't want to pay for the extras he'd got."

"We talk sometimes," Delilah said. "Seems like I heard her mention a guy gets his reading done a lot. She could have called him the Magician. Then maybe it was the Musician. If I see her, I'll ask."

The leads weren't exactly coming fast and fresh. The long night and the poisonous air were beginning to tell on Anna. What optimism she'd brought to the table was getting harder and harder to hang on to. Clare evidently felt the same way, but as she sank, Jordan rose. He came into her eyes like a fever, into her hands till the knuckles seemed to grow harder and the skin coarser.

"Fuck!" A fist slammed into the plywood with such violence the rest of them jumped. "There's got to be something! The pedophiles find kids somehow, for shit's sake!" Jordan was back with his redundant vocabulary.

"You know Les Bonnes Filles? That five-star boutique hotel between St. Peter and St. Louis up toward Rampart?" Tanya asked slowly, as if reluctant to divulge the name.

Everyone but Anna and Clare nodded.

"I used to get work out of there."

"No shit!" Star exclaimed. "Our little college mama hooked for a living?" She laughed. "Now that was worth staying after school to hear."

"Not for a living," Tanya said.

"For pin money," Clare suggested.

"For fun," Tanya said and glared at them, defying anyone to pass judgment.

Nobody did. They were all denizens of the glass house in Dick's that night.

"The place has a high-end clientele—rooms run four hundred and up a night, and there's no gym and no parking to speak of. What they sell is service. I don't know if the hotel doesn't know about it or just pretends not to, but the head concierge has a thriving little referral business. I don't know what-all services he's got on his speed dial, but it might be worth a shot. Pervs come in all financial brackets."

"Thanks," Clare said sincerely.

"Don't use my name," Tanya said as she reeled in her scarf from Candy's fingers and stood to go.

"I won't," Clare said.

Anna wouldn't if she didn't have to.

Jordan might just for the hell of it.

Tanya left, twitching her scarf like a cat's tail.

"When are you going to do that thing to me and give me my hundred dollars?" Candy demanded.

"Tomorrow when we have had some sleep and haven't had any beer," Clare said. "What time do you get up?"

"Noon," Candy said.

"Try three thirty or four," Star said.

Candy stuck her tongue out.

"I'll be over in the afternoon," Clare said, and the meeting was adjourned.

Candy left with Star and Delilah. Anna and Clare remained where they were, sipping the last of their beers. Anna's eyes were so heavy and so gritted with sad lives and cigarette smoke that, if she listened carefully, she fancied she could hear the skritching when she blinked. The fatigue that earlier excitements had banished was back, but in the version where one is too tired to sleep. She had expected little from the dancers. As it was, Tanya had given them a direction to try; that was more than she'd hoped for. Still, the sense of letdown and the enormity of the task blossomed in the dregs of the night.

Clare dug another nonfiltered Camel from her pack of cigarettes. Anna watched as she went through the ritual of tapping and lighting, then pinched a piece of tobacco off her tongue. "You know a mistake a lot of actors make?" Clare asked.

Anna said nothing.

"When they smoke they flick tobacco off their tongues, but they smoke filters. No tobacco. Makes me crazy."

"Speaking of crazy," Anna said. "Who smokes? Jordan or Clare?"

"He smokes more than I do," Clare said defensively. If she found the question—or her answer—odd, Anna saw none of it in her face.

TWENTY-SIX

Anna and Clare left Dick's by the front door, Clare double-locking it behind them. Even at 5:00 A.M. Bourbon Street was not devoid of life. As the last of the revelers were staggering back to their hotel rooms and the bartenders and dancers were counting their tips, the Quarter's distinctive cleaning vehicles were launching an assault. Small, shiny black three-wheelers with silver-white Texas longhorns emblazoned across the sides, they invaded like an army of dung beetles, sweeping up and washing away another long night's ordure. They dropped down a block for the more pleasant walk along Royal.

Toward Dumaine, where the classic iron fence wrought in the shape of cornstalks kept guard over the gently decaying old hotel of the same name, a huge rat trundled down the gutter.

He was sleek and fat and unafraid, putting Anna in mind of Templeton in *Charlotte's Web*.

"God, I hate rats," Clare said. Jordan flipped his

cigarette butt at the little beast. "Did you hear a year or so back about rats eating that baby down here?"

"I did. Maybe the baby was dead before the rats came on the scene." She doubted that was true, but she shared it because, since Templeton was the only bona fide fur-bearing wildlife she'd seen in a while, she felt duty-bound to protect and defend him.

The farther from the tourist area they walked, the darker the streets grew. Vintage streetlights were right for the city but didn't cast much light, and what they did was absorbed into green-gold halos of mist around the lamps. Fog had come in off the river, bringing with it a glamour that cloaked the historic quarter in time-lessness, the illusion heightened by the distant clop of horses' hooves as one of the carriage drivers came into the Quarter to do whatever a coach driver might do in the predawn respite.

"Hey."

A whisper out of the dark. Whispers were almost impossible to locate directionally; too much air and too little sound for the eardrums to separate out the niceties.

To either side of the street were the houses New Orleans was known for: shotguns and shotgun duplexes with steps to raised doorways, deep porches, barred shutters, brick alleyways between the houses no more than a yard wide. Regardless of the city's ambient light, there were a whole lot of darks left.

Anna stopped Clare while they were at least a base-ball bat's reach from the shadows.

"Up here, shit-for-brains." The whisper had become
a croak. Rude as it was, the insult bespoke a familiarity
that allowed Anna to let her guard down a fraction of
an inch. She and Clare followed this slightly more ro-
bust vocalization back to the man making it.

"Hey, Danny," Clare said. At the top of a stoop,
crowded into a portico that would not have been deemed
spacious by a Labrador retriever, at least three of Jordan's
punk pals had crashed in a tangle of limbs and ragged
cloth and bits of metal poking out of inked-on skin.

"Step into my office," Danny said. A hand with long
broken fingernails and ingrained dirt floated out of the
darkness. A finger crooked, and Anna couldn't but ad-
mire the man's flair for the dramatic. Edward Gorey's
works as performance art. The steps were cement with
low cement banisters flaring into flat circles at the bottom. Clare sat on one; Anna propped her foot on the
other. She was not yet secure enough to compromise her
ability to run away.

"You have something for me or not?" came a snarly
voice, and Anna corrected her earlier assumption. It was
not Clare who'd taken a seat at the bottom of the stairs, it
was Jordan. Having witnessed again the seamlessness
with which Clare shed one skin and slipped on another,
Danny's act paled in comparison, somewhere south of
walk-on and north of chorus boy.

"Tinka here—" Danny's hand, a pale spidery smudge
in the nest of punks, lifted the head of a girl sleeping on
his lap. It looked as if he lifted her by the hair, but surely

not, Anna thought. "Tinka spotted your yellow jacket for you." Two black holes appeared in the gray oval as Tinka opened her eyes.

"Ungh," she said, and Danny gently lowered her head back onto his thigh.

"So you said we could have drugs, money, whatever we wanted," Danny said.

Jordan lit a cigarette. He moved his wrist as if to offer Danny a smoke, then changed his mind and tucked the pack back into his pocket. "What do you want?" he asked when he'd gone through his routine of breathing toxins and pinching bits of tobacco off the tip of his tongue.

Watching this process, Anna could understand why, back when sex wasn't dangerous and cigarettes were still sophisticated, so many actors in so many movies smoked so many cigarettes. The ritual of lighting and puffing gave the audience time to enjoy the nuances brought to the screen. Despite the dim light, Anna had watched Jordan slide from interested to deadly bored. Or maybe just plain deadly.

"Why, I want what everybody wants, man, I want it all. Drugs and money and money for drugs." Danny smiled. Anna caught the glint of his teeth through the beard and general dinginess. The guy had to brush regularly to keep his teeth that white. Maybe good oral hygiene was his only failing in his chosen profession.

"What have you got for me?" Jordan asked on an exhaled stream of smoke that curled up into the fog illuminated by the streetlight.

"I told you. Tinka saw the guy in the jacket. How many assholes can there be with leather jackets the color of a lemon?"

"Saw him where?"

"Money first, man." The hand drifted out of the shadows again, palm up, as if he were feeding the birds or checking for rain.

"You haven't given me shit," Jordan said in bored tones.

For once, Anna was glad Jordan, and not Clare, was at the helm. Clare would have been turning her pockets inside out, too desperate for any scrap of information to negotiate.

"When did Tinka see him?" Anna asked. Both Jordan and Danny ignored her.

After another minute of tobacco and testosterone, Jordan said, "When did Tinka see him?"

Anna would have rolled her eyes had anybody been interested enough to notice.

"I don't know. Midnight maybe," Danny replied.

"Where?" Jordan asked as casually as Clare would let him.

"End of Bourbon, near Canal. We'd been up there on the bikes—"

"Were you with her?"

"Nah. I'd—"

"Did she follow him?" Jordan asked. "See where he went?"

"Jesus, man! Back off. Tinka!" Danny took his annoyance out on the sleeping—or otherwise unconscious—

girl, jerking his leg until her head bounced off his knee. Tinka pushed herself up with unsteady arms, and the jittering leg smacked her hard on the nose.

"Whuh the fuh . . ." she muttered, struggling to a seated position and patting her nose. Her hands were encased in gloves with the fingers cut off, and in the shadowy entryway it created the disturbing illusion of white grubs congregating in the middle of her face.

"What'd yah hit me for?" she whined.

"Jordan asked me to," Danny said, and his clean white smile flashed in the dark. "Tell him about the yellow jacket."

Tinka blinked. A trickle of blood, black as tar, trickled from her nose. The punks were wasting their time panhandling, Anna thought. They could make serious money just lying around in dark corners along the Vampire Tour route.

"I saw him," Tinka mumbled.

"Did you follow him?" Jordan asked.

"Yeah. He went into the McDonald's on Canal."

"And after that?"

"I dunno. I was eating fries somebody left, and some fucking bitch threw me out."

Thrown out of McDonald's. Anna hoped the girl would find her way up in the world—at least to being tossed out of Applebee's or T.G.I. Friday's.

"You better take what we got, because you don't have much time to catch up with this jerk-off you're so hot on," Danny said.

Anna's flagging interest was doing its best to ally

with a sleepless night and fog her brain. This remark
brought her back to full alert. Jordan perked up, too, if
staring at the tip of a burning cigarette could be said to
show an increase in cerebral activity. Time was the
enemy Clare had nightmares about. Anna knew it ran
out fast for stranger-abducted children. Most were dead
within hours of the abduction. Few lasted days. It was
the rare child who was allowed to survive to adulthood
and, in many ways, not the luckiest.

"Why is time running out?" Anna asked when it became apparent Jordan was locked into a paralysis of
hope or fear, or simply the grip of Clare's fingers around
his esophagus.

Danny didn't look at her. Since the question was
clearly one he wanted to answer, he directed his reply
to Jordan. "It's getting hotter by the day. Eventually
even the toughest arbiter of bad taste is going to have to
leave his sartorial signature at home."

Anna wondered which Ivy League college Danny
had dropped out of when he became a traveler and why
he wanted them to know it.

Jordan flipped his cigarette butt into the street. Anna
cringed inwardly. Violent crime was one thing. Littering was another. There was no motive for littering, nothing to gain. Under certain circumstances crime could be
considered a career choice. Littering was just a character flaw.

Ignoring her as he'd been doing so stunningly since
Clare had subsided at the advent of the nest of gutter
punks, Jordan reached into the pocket of his jacket and

pulled out a square of white paper. Unfolded, it was about twelve by twelve inches. After smoothing it carefully on his knee, he held it up for Tinka to look at.

Interested, Anna scooted up her side of the steps until she could see it as well. It was a pen-and-ink drawing of a face, a pretty good likeness to that of the man she'd chased when Mackie followed him, the man Clare had guessed was the one called Dougie. It was a face that was easy to remember and easy to caricature. The hair was thick and jet black and slicked down against the skull. His features resembled those of Elvis Presley, but they'd all been compressed into a narrow band between a low forehead and a short jaw.

"This the guy?" Jordan asked.

"Yeah," Tinka said, squinting through whatever drugs clouded her vision. "Maybe. Yeah, I guess."

"Where did you get that?" Anna asked. For a moment she thought this question was going to be ignored as well, but Jordan decided to be civil.

"An artist on the square drew it from my description."

"It's good," Anna said.

Jordan folded the paper and slipped it back into his pocket; then he took out a billfold that looked as if it had been stuffed in hip pockets for a decade or more. Anna admired the attention to detail. Knowing a new wallet would clash with Jordan's persona, Clare must have stolen or found it. Jordan took out two twenty-dollar bills, folded them in half lengthwise, and, with two fingers, held them up toward Tinka.

Danny's hand intercepted the transaction, and the forty dollars vanished into the front of his coat.

"You gave me nothing tonight," Jordan said evenly. "The money's for nothing. Next time give me something I can use." With that, he stood and slouched off, leaving Anna to trail behind, feeling about as surreal as a ghost, a real live dead ghost.

Within a couple of blocks, Clare fought for and won supremacy again. Or, more likely, Jordan had abdicated for the time being. These changes of character were bothering Anna less and less. She wasn't sure that was a healthy development.

"We do have nothing," Clare whispered. The whisper was broken, the end ragged. The woman was crying. Anna had watched a lot of people deal with weeping. Paul gathered them to him, and they felt safe and comforted. Molly let them cry it out in a supportive and therapeutic environment. Lisa, a woman she'd become friends with in Texas, broke down and cried with them, and they felt understood and less alone.

Anna had never figured out what to do. She'd tried two of the three options, but it hadn't worked out all that well for her. Probably she was too prickly for the first and too impatient for the second. She'd never tried Lisa's method. It wasn't that Anna never cried; she just didn't like having witnesses.

So she did what she always did; she pretended it wasn't happening. "We've got your forty dollars' worth," she said as if Clare were sniveling over the pocket change and not the lives of her children. Anna began ticking off the night's gains. "We have a lead on a man called the Magician from Delilah. It's weak, but it's a start. We've got the name of a high-end procurer from Tanya—the concierge at Les Bonnes Filles. We know Dougie has been to the quarter twice in seven days and that he ate at McDonald's. That suggests pattern. Pattern gives us hope we'll see him again and next time we'll follow him.

"We've also got direction, which is more than we had when we started out this morning. Tomorrow, you'll hypnotize Candy and we may get something from that. Then you're going shopping."

"Shopping?" Clare asked, confusion pulling her out of her funk.

"Yes," Anna said. "We're moving Jordan uptown."

TWENTY-SEVEN

Anna woke just before eleven. It had been years since she'd slept past seven in the morning and, most nights, she was in bed by ten. The 5:00 A.M. quitting time and the long morning's sleep, so reminiscent of her college days, left her with a not unpleasant sense of walking on the wild side. Following on the heels of this taste of youth was the realization of age: Time was running out. She snatched her shorts from the floor, wriggled into them, and cinched the belt. Pattering down the narrow stairs, she pulled on one of Paul's old sheriff's shirts, the patches cut off, and buttoned it before she grabbed her laptop and let herself out of the courtyard.

At CC's, a hot latte on the table beside the laptop, she hooked into the Wi-Fi. Frederick had come through. She downloaded the files he'd sent and was home before noon. Sitting at the little patio table in the courtyard, she called 411 on her cell phone and got the number for Les Bonnes Filles. Clare had undoubtedly given Jordan not only a last name but a full history when she was creating the character. Anna had no idea what it was, so she made the reservation in the name of Jordan Sinclair. Maybe it was the name Clare that suggested it, but Anna thought it sounded like the name of a rich man, and she wanted the concierge to smell money.

That done, she called her husband and let his love and the magic of the Arabica beans of her second latte bring her gently into the mellow spring in Geneva's courtyard. Mackie, Jordan's color-assisted dog, was outside and amused himself by watching turtles watching him.

As she was saying good-bye to Paul, the complaining of the rusted gate on Jordan's side of the house cried across the bricks. By Mackie's exultant rush down the walkway, Anna guessed it was Clare returning from wherever she'd spent the morning.

"Back here," Anna called.

Clare, wearing Jordan's clothes but having cleaned up for her morning's work, came into the courtyard dragging a rolling suitcase with several bags hooked around the handle riding it piggyback. Her arms were filled with more bags, all with the Brooks Brothers logo on them.

"Holy smoke," Anna said. "Brooks Brothers? You must be hemorrhaging money."

"Five thousand six hundred forty-three dollars and eighty-seven cents," Clare said, dumping it all to the bricks and dropping her cheaply polyestered rump into the chair across the table from where Anna was nursing her coffee.

"There was no way around it. Concierges at the better hotels know more about men's clothes—and some women's clothes, too, for that matter—than a lot of tailors. What they know is money: what it costs, how much the guy wearing it is worth. If this guy Tanya turned us on to is procuring for high-end swingers, then he'll have an eye for who can afford his services. Would you believe I paid sixty dollars a pair for the boxer shorts in that sack?" Clare nudged one of the bags with the toe of her beat-up Payless shoes.

"You plan on showing the concierge your underpants?" Anna asked with a laugh.

"Maybe. I doubt he'll bother checking out the rooms of his customers, but you never know. He might be canny enough to rifle through a few suitcases and closets to see if he's being set up by whatever vice cops might be conducting investigations in the area, things like that. If he did, and my boxer shorts were from Walmart, he'd know something was up."

Anna felt like a fool for not thinking of that herself. "You're good at this," she said honestly.

"It's all theater," Clare said wearily. She leaned forward, put her elbows on her knees, and rested her head in her hands. Malnutrition, stress, and the fatigue of the weeks since the fire were evident in the curve of her spine. "You wear an eighteenth-century corset and woolen drawers, you move more like a woman of that era," Clare mumbled. "Clothes make the man in more ways than people think."

"Or the woman into the man," Anna said. She sipped

her coffee and watched the actress. Jordan burned, and that fire, though consuming him, gave him the energy to move forward. Clare's energy was derived from another source. She was not so much moving forward of her own volition as being driven by horrors that filled her waking—and, undoubtedly, sleeping—moments. If she didn't sleep and eat and do a few self-sustaining chores, she wasn't going to make it many more days. Anna considered suggesting food and rest but knew she'd go unheard. Clare might last long enough to find her children. If they were alive, they'd cure her. If they were dead, it wouldn't really matter.

All Anna could do was keep her company and lift heavy objects. "Come on," she said. "Let's get that stuff put away, then see what you can hypnotize out of Candy."

Standing, she reached down and hooked her fingers through the loops on the nearest sack. She'd gathered up two more and was reaching for the suitcase handle before Clare struggled up out of the chair. As if dazed by the sudden change in altitude, she stared vacantly around her. Her eyes lit on Anna's laptop.

"You want I should bring that?" she asked, sounding like a lost child.

"Yes," Anna said. "My bro—" She cut herself off. Had she told Clare that the FBI agent helping her was her brother-in-law? Anna couldn't remember. She hoped not. If the proverbial hit the fan, and Clare told anyone he'd helped them, he could be up on charges regardless of whether or not he'd officially known he was aiding a suspected murderess. Because he was FBI—even retired FBI—he would be held to a higher standard of conduct than an ordinary citizen.

"The guy who was looking into things for me e-mailed what he'd found. It's all on there. I haven't had time to go through it yet," she said. Leading the way, she took Clare's keys from her and unlocked and opened the door to her apartment. Taking the one chair from its home in front of the computer, Anna sat down and read through what Frederick had found while Clare unpacked the trousers, shirts, socks, shoes, and half a dozen other items of wearing apparel she'd dropped over five grand on.

Frederick had paraphrased what he'd discovered. For that Anna was grateful. Plowing through the agent-speak of official reports was time-consuming. "Daoud Suliman, name legally changed to David Sullivan June 2003," she read aloud.

"After 9/11 he thought it would be better for business and the girls if he wasn't so obviously Mideastern," Clare said.

"Ah. Wife, two daughters, under investigation from 2006 to 2009 for human trafficking. Suspected of illegally importing garment workers from Pakistan, Afghanistan, India, Nepal, and Lebanon. Suspected of procuring garment workers for factories in New Jersey, Seattle, Washington, and Los Angeles. Suspected of using undocumented workers in two of his own manufacturing plants. Suspected of paying below minimum wage, not providing health care, limiting workers' freedoms, and—oooh," Anna said. "Here's where he's getting into big trouble. Evading income taxes and channeling money to Muslim charities thought to be a cover for terrorists."

Clare had stopped moving and stood in the middle of the unfurnished bedroom holding a shirt by the collar with one hand, the other on its cuff out to the side as if she stood in the arms of an invisible dance partner.

"That sound about right?" Anna asked.

"Yes," Clare said without hesitation. "I chose to think he was rescuing women from situations that were worse than what they'd face here. For some, I think that was true, women accused of a crime or on the outs with their in-laws or breaking some religious taboo. Others, I suppose their families sold them."

Anna looked at her for a moment, not judging, but wondering what it was she, Anna, chose to believe that was untrue, what she hid from herself so effectively that she didn't even suspect she was doing it, what rules she lived by that were arbitrary and destructive.

"And Jalila," Anna said. "The second wife?"

"She was from Saudi. David felt Saudis were superior to people from other Muslim countries. He wouldn't marry a Pakistani, and never anybody from Afghanistan. Too *uncivilized*."

Anna forgave her the sneer. Until a country treated its women equally and fairly, it wasn't going to climb all that far up on Anna's list of civilized places either.

She went back to the screen. "The investigation stopped three months ago; that's interesting. No disposition, nothing. Frederick thinks that means, to keep himself out of jail, David went to work for the FBI, either by rolling on his buddies or by working under-cover in whatever scheme they had pinned on him."

Clare began moving again, hanging up the shirt she'd been dancing with.

Scratching Mackie's back absently and letting her mind float, Anna let the new information find and mate up with the other fragments she'd been told by Clare or gleaned from the gutter punks. It wasn't much, but it did hang together.

Clare took a wicked-looking knife from her trouser pocket, and Anna tensed, waiting to see if Jordan had sinister plans, but Clare began neatly cutting off price tags. "Best guess," Anna said. "Do you think your hus-band was selling kids into the sex trade—or women?"

"Best guess? No. David was a religious man. I don't doubt he'd stone a woman to death for adultery without blinking an eye or losing a night's sleep afterward, but he wouldn't prostitute her."

"Not even if she was sold to him because she was an adultress or whatever?" Anna asked.

"Maybe, but I don't think he would. For men like David, death is one thing—and not all that bad a thing, really—but desecration is another. Even if a woman had, by his standards, been desecrated either by choice or force, I don't think he'd want to have any part of it. He wouldn't save or harm her. She'd be dead to him."

"Same for children?"

"More so, probably." Clare snipped off the last tag from the clothes she'd hung in the closet and turned to

Anna, knife open. "But then I thought a lot of things. And didn't bother to think a lot of things. So I could be dead wrong." Anna could see the choice of the phrase flashing like lightning in Clare's mind as it did in hers. If Clare had been wrong, it wasn't her own death she'd earned.

"You are sure the corpse carried out of your house was David?" Anna asked.

"It had on David's pajamas," Clare replied. Back against the wall, she slid down until she was sitting on her sleeping bag, knees up to her chest, expensive men's undergarments scattered around her. Gathering the stuffed dog to her chest, she buried her nose in its back.

Anna waited.

"It was when I found Jalila murdered that I knew it was David on that stretcher," Clare said finally.

"Couldn't David have murdered Jalila? Maybe she was going to leave him, or turn him in to the law. Maybe she was having an affair."

Clare thought about that for a while. "Oh, God," she said, and, putting her hands to her head as if it was about to explode, she groaned. "I guess he could have. But there was Aisha . . ." Her voice trailed off and she appeared to be shrinking before Anna's eyes.

"Pack," Anna said to keep her moving. Clare heaved herself to her feet, using the wall for support, and dragged the suitcase to the middle of the room.

Anna went back to the report Frederick had sent. "It looks like David had at least two business partners, one in L.A. and one in New Orleans. Both port cities.

The one in L.A. was known only as Big Fish and the guy in New Orleans as the Magician. You got that right," she said to Clare. The woman needed to be re-inflated somehow.

Clare said nothing, just kept folding and stowing.

"Maybe because he could make people disappear?" The thin nature of the information they had was disheartening. Anna wanted to ask Clare if she'd run off to New Orleans on the strength of a Cajun accent and the words "Bourbon Street Nursery." She wanted to ask her why, if she believed the body on one stretcher was that of her husband, who she claimed had not been in the house when she'd come back from her night run to the pharmacy, she did not believe the two smaller corpses were those of the daughters. Why she was so certain the girls had been taken for the sex slave trade and not just killed and dumped. Knowing those questions might well render Clare useless, Anna changed tack.

"Let's get on with the hypnotism," she said and closed the laptop.

"Candy won't be up," Clare said dully.

"We'll get her up."

TWENTY-EIGHT

Candy was up but only just. She was still in her pajamas, a loose top and shorts, childlike in pink with white poodles. Her room, attached to a rambling old apartment shared by Delilah, Star, and their son, was cluttered to the point few of the original surfaces were visible beneath the tossed-off clothing and, to Anna the saddest and most poignant paraphernalia, dozens of Beanie Babies that looked much loved and played with.

"Hello, *Mrs.* Jordan," Candy said when Delilah let them into her bedroom. The baby stripper had yet to forgive Jordan for lacking family jewels. Sleepily, she combed the fine blonde hair off her face, still puffy from the pillow, and stared at them with a look of anticipation and alarm. "You come to hippopotomize me?"

"Hypnotize, baby girl," Delilah said.

"I changed my mind," she said sulkily. "I don't want any hippotizing." She swung her plump legs over the side of the bed, planting her feet on yesterday's Levi's.

Clare shot Anna a desperate look.

"You'll like it," Anna said. "It's fun."

Candy looked unconvinced.

"It's like knocking back three beers in a row," Anna said, feeling a twinge of guilt. For what, she wasn't sure. Maybe appealing to alcoholism in a minor crossed some internal line between right and sleazy.

Candy thought about that. "Can I have a beer first?"

"How about after?" Anna said. Again the twinge. "It'll be more fun that way."

Delilah had a sour look on her face. "With lunch," she said firmly.

One couldn't but respect a woman who wouldn't let the children drink before noon. Anna put aside her judgment. At least Star and Delilah looked after the girl; that was a whole lot more than anyone else had done.

"Okay," Candy said resignedly. "Do me."

Coming from a child stripper and, once, prostitute, the phrase jarred.

"Okay, then," Clare said. Her sweet motherly voice coming from Jordan's black-clad frame, a tattoo of thorns across his brow, seemed almost like reverse demon possession.

Clare settled Candy on the rumpled bed, her back comfortably supported by the headboard. She sat tailor style in front of Candy.

"Just relax, sweetie, and listen to my voice. We're going on a walk together, okay?"

"Don't you need one of those gold watch things on a chain?" asked Star, who'd come to stand in the doorway to view the proceedings. "You know, to swing back and forth?"

Clare shook her head, her eyes never leaving Candy's. Star took the hint and kept quiet.

Clare raised her index finger and said, "Look at the tip of my finger. See how pink it is, and the lines on it? Keep watching it." She began moving the finger in smooth arcs back and forth in front of Candy's face as if drawing a big smile in the air. As the finger moved she spoke in a near monotone, her voice low and soothing.

"You're snug in your room, in your own bed. All your friends are here. You feel so safe and so loved. The bed is soft and comfortable, and you can feel yourself sinking into it deeper and deeper."

Anna was fascinated. Candy's eyes were drooping and unfocused after less than a minute of the process. Even Delilah and Star were looking a little hazy. Other than interest, Anna felt nothing.

Another half minute and Candy was clearly transported into another state. Her facial muscles grew slack, and what few years she'd racked up were erased. She looked no more than ten and as innocent as if she hadn't seen the ugliest the world had to offer.

Gently, Clare led her back to Dick's, then to the streets where Delilah and Star had found her. At the strip club, Candy was happy, and the images were clear and detailed. The same wasn't true for her time on the streets, and Anna wondered if her mental disability carried with it a hidden strength, the ability to forget the bad times.

As Clare and Candy regressed through the fog of the girl's streetwalking days and closer to the information they sought, Anna's agitation began to make itself felt. Had she been sitting, she would be on the edge of her chair. Clare remained cool and measured, and Anna was impressed with the woman's self-control. She'd seen so little of it, it came as a pleasant surprise.

From the fragmented history Clare was eliciting, it looked like all of them had gotten Candy's time line wrong. Unless there was much she had forgotten or blocked, it sounded like she'd been on the streets no more than a few months, a much shorter time than Delilah and Star had supposed. They knew for a fact that she'd been a dancer at Dick's for four months. If she had been cast out of the "fancy house" when she turned eleven and her period started, as she'd intimated, that made her not thirteen but twelve, and the child she carried the result of hooking or rape.

Twelve and retarded and pregnant; Anna pushed a chunk of sadness aside and was surprised at how heavy it was.

"Come on, Candy, honey, let's leave the streets and go to the fancy house. Ready?"

"Yeah," Candy breathed, and the smile of a child expecting a treat teased the corners of her mouth up.

Clare glanced at Anna. Both of them were tense. Too much was hanging on the memories of a mentally challenged girl.

"Take my hand and take me to the fancy house,"

Clare said. She folded her fingers lightly around Candy's hand where it lay palm up on the wrinkled sheet. Candy's fingers twitched but didn't close. "Where are we going?" Clare all but whispered.

"To the fancy house," Candy murmured.

"Are we walking?"

"Uh-huh."

"Tell me what it looks like."

The description was sketchy and could have fit any street in the Quarter. Candy was not agitated about walking to the fancy house; she just wasn't observant. She came up with only one detail, and that was a big pile of dog poop in the middle of the sidewalk that she got on the edge of her shoe. Though that, in itself, wasn't of use, it was heartening to know she was in a specific time, the day she had dirtied her shoe, and not merely wandering.

Clare continued to let her lead her down streets, not hurrying, just softly interjecting a question when Candy slid off course or deeper into the trance. Anna clenched her jaw to keep from blurting out questions of her own. Delilah and Star were transfixed; evidently this was more information than they'd ever heard from their lodger in the months they'd known her.

Clare led Candy to the fancy house, but the girl was unable to describe it any better than big and nice and blind. Whatever that meant. Anna wondered if Candy had ever seen the outside of the house. Likely as not, she hadn't. She would have been brought in through another building or a back door or gate lest she escape and be able to lead someone back to the place. That's the way Anna would do it if she were abducting children and keeping them as slaves. She suspected Candy was still in the time of being a streetwalker.

Finally Clare gave up on the architectural aspects and said, "Good, good. Now we are in the fancy house."

Candy's voice lost the vague aspect it had when on the street looking for the building and perked up with, for lack of a better word, joy, the joy of homecoming.

What followed was a fairy tale, but one so twisted and sick that no self-respecting fictional ogres would dream of haunting it. The real ogres were too evil for those that merely consumed the flesh of princesses.

Candy described a bricked courtyard filled with fountains and lanterns. Wrought-iron benches were tucked into corners screened with blooming plants. The air was perfumed, and from somewhere music was piped in. The kind without words, Candy said, and Anna guessed it was chamber music or classical. All very high-class. All used to try to dress a heinous crime so it would seem a refined taste.

On one side of the courtyard was a vine-covered wall with a door but no windows. On the other was the fancy house. Three stories high with balconies where the patrons could smoke and drink and the girls could come when they weren't "entertaining guests." Flowers cascaded down one side in a curtain of "pointy pink"— bougainvillea, Anna guessed.

Inside, the fancy house was lit with "candles in boxes,"

and the walls were "red and fluffy" and the furniture "fat and soft." Probably a re-creation of somebody's idea of an expensive Victorian-era whorehouse. It seemed no men worked at the house, just girls and little boys and their "governess." The "governess," according to Candy, didn't get to wear nice things and went around in plain gray dresses and had to wear her hair pulled back.

Candy waxed nearly eloquent on the clothing she was dressed in. The dresses for the children were tiny versions of midnineteenth-century fashions, with low-cut bodices and lots of petticoats, lace, and cotton underthings. Their hair was piled up and decorated with feathers and bows, or covered with ornate wigs, and their baby faces painted. Candy was particularly enamored of the fans and the little gloves.

The boys had to wear "stupid pants that were short and stupid coats with buttons or diapers and nothing fun." Candy said she was glad she wasn't a boy.

The "guests" were "men who smelled good and weren't supposed to mark anybody." To Anna that suggested that some violence was allowed, just not the kind that would damage the goods.

"How did you 'entertain' the guests?" Clare asked.

Then Candy told them. As one horrible act after another was described, Anna felt sicker and sicker. Clare, her children undoubtedly on her mind, grew so pale Anna was worried she wouldn't be able to continue. Candy finished with "It wasn't so bad because I'd get ice cream after. Till I got fat. They liked me some fat but not real fat."

Pleasingly plump, Anna thought, and a tide of nausea threatened to send her running to the bathroom.

Blessedly, Clare changed the subject.

"Did you have any friends there?" she asked.

"Dolly was my friend," Candy said; then sadness aged her face. "She was real little and she got broke and they took her somewhere. A broke jewel got given away."

"Who were the broken jewels given to?"

"People. Sometimes to Dougie. He was bad. He sounded good, but he was mean."

At the name Dougie, Clare looked at Anna. That was the name the Cajun had called the pervert.

"I had a baby for a while. A real baby, and they let me carry her around and feed her, but she got broke so bad she was dead afterward."

Star groaned, and Anna thought of the infant Helena she'd cared for and was blinded by a white-hot need to kill somebody.

"Did you have any other friends?" Clare pressed on.

"No. Maybe Blackie. When I got broke he was supposed to give me to Dougie, but he said since I was a retard I could just go away and he wouldn't tell anybody."

Blackie, the Cajun; it was he who turned her loose on the streets to survive the only way she knew how. Charity of a kind, Anna supposed.

Interesting as this all was, it brought them no closer to the location of the house, if, indeed, it was still operating out of the same space it had been when Candy

was there. Since it had been less than a year since she'd
been turned out, it was likely, but not certain by any
means.

Despite the hypnosis, Candy was growing restive
under the questioning.

"Ask her if she could smell anything or hear anything from the outside world," Anna whispered.

Clare nodded and turned back to the girl on the bed.
"We're nearly done, Candy. There's just one more thing
I'd like to ask you. Let's go into the courtyard in the
morning after all the guests have gone and sit by our-
selves on a bench. Are we there?"

"I guess."

Anna didn't know if hypnosis wore off after a time
or if people could get bored or annoyed or scared and
bring themselves out of it, but it sounded like one or
the other was happening. Candy's voice was a bit more
distinct and her eyes active beneath the closed lids.

"Listen," Clare said. "What do you hear?"

Anna found herself listening so hard that, even with
the low hum of the city, her ears were ringing. For a long
time Candy said nothing. Clare's shoulders slumped.
Then Candy opened her mouth and sang. "Da, da, da,
da, da, da dah." Scales, sung in a clear sweet voice. She
sang them again in a higher register. Then again.

"Anything else?" Clare asked.

"A piano." This time Candy sang low, using the word
"dunk" to imitate scales being played on a keyboard.

Music lessons, singing lessons. For the first time since

the hypnosis began, Anna had hope they might learn something after all.

"That's good. That's good," Clare crooned. "Let's listen some more."

Candy quieted but for a tiny voice in which she sang the scales again. Just when Anna thought that well had gone dry, the girl erupted with a great hiss.

Crawfish dumped into boiling water? A steam cleaner? An industrial-grade iron for pressing sheets? There were too many things it might be.

"Thunk, thunk, thunk like big darts hitting, or a gun with a silencer," Candy said.

A child who probably didn't know the world was round—or care—lived in a city where guns with silencers were common enough for her to know what one sounded like when fired. Anna longed for her parks, her mountains, and her quiet home with her kind husband, her soft cats and silly dog. Cities were too grating.

Clare looked at Anna, and Anna shook her head. The sounds, the thunk and the hissing put together, brought nothing to mind.

Clare rubbed her eyes wearily. "One last question," she said. "Do you smell anything?"

"Perfume," Candy said. "Nice kinds."

"Flowers?" Clare asked.

"Uh-huh."

"Anything else?"

"Other flowers."

"You've done so well, Candy. I'm going to count

backward from ten, and you're going to come up slowly like you were floating, and when I get to one you are going to open your eyes. You'll feel real good and rested and happy."

Candy got her beer and her hundred bucks.

Anna and Clare got three vague clues and a memory of misery that would last a lifetime.

TWENTY-NINE

They walked the streets of the Quarter. They sniffed and listened for thunks, hisses, and scales being played on a piano. Clare put one foot in front of the other and fought images that slammed into her mind with the force of sledgehammers, making it a struggle just to remain upright. The swift dark Mississippi River called to her, and she wanted to throw herself into its deadly embrace and never think or feel again, but, until she knew her daughters were dead, that was a release she had to deny herself.

Anna Pigeon walked with her. She talked of the clues they had, of the names Dougie and Blackie, proof of the connection between the fancy house and Seattle, of the possibility that David had been killed because he learned what was happening to the children and turned to the FBI.

Clare heard her and knew the woman was trying to prop her up with hope. Clare wanted the hope but couldn't get hold of it. Each time she tried to grab on, it slipped from her fingers and was replaced by pictures of men's hands on her girls. The depth of the depravity shamed her, made her not want to be a human being anymore, if humans could do these things; made her hate men for what they did and thought and wanted; made her want to be a man that she might atone by killing herself.

They made copies of the sketch the Jackson Square portraitist had drawn from the description of Dougie. Anna kept one. Clare gave the rest to Danny and his gang of punks. Handling the page, seeing the lines coalescing into the cramped face of the man with the yellow coat, the words "broke jewels" cut into her brain like a razor blade held too tightly in the hand: children as commodity, as things, things that could be broken and given to scum like Dougie to use or kill or both, precious Dana with her olive and alabaster skin, dark eyes brimming with love; little Vee always moving, too full of fun to stay still; jewels, broken toys, used up and thrown on a trash heap to be picked over by rats like Dougie.

"Hey!"

Clare dragged herself from the chamber of horrors. Anna Pigeon was standing in front of her, her hazel eyes so penetrating they burned some of the fog from Clare's brain.

"What happened?" Anna demanded.

Had the fool woman been listening? Had she not heard what Clare had? Did she not see the fancy house?

"Are you a fucking idiot or what?" Jordan snarled.

Oddly, the pigeon didn't look offended, only concerned.

Clare was outside of herself, above and to the right, looking down from the space she inhabited when she was being her own director. What she saw was not Clare Sullivan the actor playing a role; she saw a man who had no conscience, no regrets, no ethics, no friends, no hopes or fears, a man who was as free as he was reprehensible. She envied him.

"Clare?" An iron grip closed on Jordan's arm, and Clare slammed back into the body and the costume. Metaphorically speaking, Clare had lost herself in roles before, becoming enamored of the accent or the time period or the internal workings of a character she played—but only metaphorically. Never had she confused herself with a fictional person. Never thought their thoughts but with full knowledge that she was merely walking a mile in another's shoes, not morphing into flesh of their flesh. The line between art and insanity was always clearly drawn. Actors were the world's great realists. One couldn't focus intently on what made humans do as they did and have many illusions left.

Jordan was different. More and more Jordan was the only person Clare could bear to be. He'd become more than pretense; he'd become her fate, what she was becoming, cell by cell, thought by thought.

When Anna asked what happened, she wasn't harking back to Candy's revelations. She was asking why Clare had stopped and was standing in the middle of the sidewalk staring at a construction Dumpster.

"Sorry," Clare said. Unable to say more, she began walking.

Mackie greeted them at the gate. For once the joyous little face, the tongue that would not stay in his mouth, the ears flopping and bouncing as he ran, his obvious delight in her existence, did not lift her spirits. In a way, she had seen what she had let happen to Mackie's kids, the little girls he'd slept with most nights of his life and every night of theirs, the girls who doted on him and to whom, in return, he gave complete love and loyalty, even unto allowing them to dress him in doll dresses and bonnets and wheel him up and down the street where other dogs might see. His unquestioning love only served to remind her that she had betrayed him; he trusted her to keep his world with its two suns, Dana and Vee, intact. Having failed, it physically hurt to be greeted like a returning hero. Jordan pushed at Clare, and she had to fight not to kick the little dog away, yell at him to get down.

This cruelty, on top of the others she had borne this day, knocked her to the ground. Her knees slammed into the brick, and the pain was welcome. She opened her arms and gathered up her children's dog, burying her face in the fur of his neck as he wriggled and licked and made small happy noises.

When she could let him go, she realized she'd blocked the way, effectively trapping the so-called federal law enforcement officer behind her on the narrow walk. The pigeon had waited patiently, not trying to comfort or rush her.

Grateful, but without the strength to express it, Clare pushed herself to hands and knees, then to a standing position. No more than a month before, she'd been able to rise fluidly from sitting cross-legged to standing without the aid of arms or hands. Now it was all she could do to pull herself upright by holding on to a swirl of iron decoration nailed to Geneva's fence.

"Go take a shower," the pigeon ranger said. She put her hand on Clare's shoulders.

Neither Clare nor Jordan had the energy to jerk free of her touch.

Clare allowed herself to be steered to her apartment door. The key fell from nerveless fingers as she took it from her pocket. She watched Anna bend down to retrieve it. The ranger's hair was red and white, salt and cinnamon. It was braided into a single plait down her back and so long that, as she took up the keys, the red tail of it coiled momentarily on the ground.

When Clare played her she would remember that; she would remember what it felt like to have hair that fell heavily and had a life of its own, that did things the head never realized it was doing.

"A long shower," the pigeon said as she unlocked the door. "With lots of hot water. Wash your hair. I'm going out for a little while—not long." She peered at Clare with those sharp greenish gold eyes, the skin around them wrinkled from too many days in the sun and too little vanity to do anything about it.

"Shower," Clare said.

"Atta girl!" Anna slapped her on the shoulder as if

they were old friends from the football field and left, pocketing Clare's keys as she did so. The water was hot and Clare was wet before she realized the ranger had effectively taken her prisoner. The gate could only be opened with a key.

She'd showered and washed her hair and was standing naked in the middle of the bedroom when the apartment door opened and Anna Pigeon walked in without knocking. She had two plastic bags, both of which she dumped on the table by the computer.

"I'm figuring you'll want to ask the concierge of Les Bonnes Filles to recommend a good restaurant, and then tip him lavishly to sort of break the ice," the ranger said as she took out a baguette, cheese, a bottle of wine, a carton of orange juice, and a jar of dill pickles.

"But I doubt there's any point in wasting time and money at a fancy restaurant. This should give you enough energy to go on." Anna took a Swiss Army knife from the pocket of her shorts, opened the corkscrew blade, and uncorked the wine. "Strictly medicinal," the ranger said with a smile. She looked around. Clare had no dishes. None. Surely she'd eaten in the last couple of weeks, she just didn't remember when.

"Well," the ranger said. "It'll be like camping." She took a genteel swig from the neck of the bottle, wiped the mouth on her shirttail, and offered it to Clare. "It is a proven fact no one ever got sick from drinking out of a bottle that has been wiped clean with a shirttail or a sleeve. Socks are another matter entirely. I knew a guy who had survived three weeks in Olympic National

Park in one of the worst blizzards to hit the Northwest in half a century. Died a week and a half later because his brother wiped off the mouth of a beer bottle with his sock."

Clare accepted the bottle and took a drink. Anna carried the cheese, bread, pickles, and knife into the bedroom and sat on the floor. There she spread the picnic out on the boards. Clare watched without moving. Her brain wouldn't engage, and though she felt vaguely impolite, she didn't know what to do about it.

The ranger looked up at her expectantly. When Clare didn't respond, she said, "Food," as if telling a being from a distant galaxy what lay before it. As proof, or to remind Clare how it was done, or because she was hungry, she cut off a bit of the cheese and put it into her mouth.

"Right. Food," Clare said. She padded over to where the ranger sat with the pickle jar and joined her on the floor. *"Naked Lunch,"* she said.

"William S. Burroughs," Anna said and handed her a chunk of bread and cheese.

"Yes." Clare held the rude sandwich. The smell made her sick.

"Eat," the pigeon ordered.

"I'll eat it later," Clare said. Anna Pigeon looked at her narrowly but didn't press the matter.

When the ranger had polished off a good bit of the food, she put the leftovers on the counter.

"Sleep," she told Clare.

Clare crawled to the sleeping bag and lay down.

"I'll wake you up in a few hours. It will probably be a longish night. At least I hope it will."

Clare closed her eyes, but cold panic shot through her and she opened them again. The ranger was still standing in the bedroom door.

"Don't worry," she said as if she were talking to a child. "I'm not going anywhere. I'll be right here in the next room."

Clare slept.

Anna didn't have to wake her. Two hours later she shot into a sitting position, driven there by a nightmare that was too like the reality Candy had painted to be let go of easily. From the other room she could hear the faint *tak tak tak* of fingernails hitting a keyboard. Anna had been as good as her word; she'd stayed and kept watch over her while she slept.

Having gotten up and brushed her teeth, Clare got the Ace bandage down from the shelf in the closet and bound her breasts flat. That done, she pulled on the fine silk boxers, a pair of pale blue silk-linen blend pleat-front trousers, an off-white collarless linen shirt, a snakeskin belt in light brown, and Gucci loafers without socks. In the shower she'd tried to scrub off her crown of thorns, but the ink left a ghost that was worse than the tattoo, so she refurbished it. Using spirit gum and a bit of hair, she replaced the patch beneath her lower lip. There was no need to darken and roughen her complexion with makeup. Stress and weight loss had aged and coarsened her skin.

The mirror reflected back Jordan Sinclair, and Jordan recognized himself.

Hair slicked back, he took a wad of twenties, fifties, and hundreds from his old wallet and folded them into a buttery soft leather billfold that he tucked in the inner pocket of the jacket hanging in the closet. Jordan liked the upgrade, the way the expensive clothes felt. He could do a pedophile with money to burn. Clare wasn't the only one who could pull off a scam. He dug out her last purchase from where she'd stuck it in the side pocket of the suitcase: a heavy gold signet ring, set with a diamond the size of a hen's eye. The weight felt right on his hand.

"Wow," Anna said, and he looked up to see the pigeon leaning in the doorway, legs crossed at the ankles, arms crossed on her chest. "Nice ring. It'll be good in a fight."

"Yeah," Jordan said. The pigeon blinked. Maybe she saw him, maybe she didn't.

"Did that set you back another five thousand dollars?"

"What do rangers get paid?" he asked.

"Not much."

"We get the fuckers who took the kids, you can have this." The ring was the cheapest thing on Clare's wardrobe list. She'd bought it for seven dollars in the French Market.

"Are you about ready?" Anna asked.

"Let's do it." Jordan slid into the sport coat—also

silk and light enough for spring in Louisiana—and grabbed the handle of the rolling suitcase.

"You may need this. It's prepaid. My cell number is programmed in."

Jordan took the cheap phone from the ranger's hand. He might need it, but he sure as hell was going to keep it out of sight. It screamed *LOW RENT*.

"Take these, too," the pigeon said. In her hand were two of the pictures from the wall where Clare kept the photographs of children from porn sites.

Clare flopped in Jordan's breast. Had Anna held out a rattlesnake, she couldn't have had a more visceral reaction of fear and nausea. Jordan swallowed her down.

"Right," he said, unzipped the bag, and put them under the boxer shorts. If the concierge did any snooping, Jordan might as well let him know exactly what he was in the market for.

THIRTY

Clare hadn't eaten "later"; nor had she slept long enough to overcome the weakness that had brought her to her knees outside her apartment door. Even so, as Anna watched her becoming Jordan Sinclair, a well-to-do pedophile in New Orleans for a good time, she was suffused with energy. She was Jordan running on his own toxic brand of fuel. Using Clare's key, Anna let him out the gate. Jordan had chosen not to carry the key because it didn't "feel right." Anna suspected that call was from the actress, not her alter ego. Jordan would call Anna on the cell if he needed to get in.

"Les Bonnes Filles is the other way," Anna said as, towing the suitcase, Jordan turned toward the river and the heart of the French Quarter. He looked back at her with such disinterest, had she not watched the man being constructed, she would have sworn he'd never seen her before.

The stare altered in some unfathomable way, and Clare's voice said, "I'll walk down to North Peters and get a cab there. I need to put some wear on the shoes and on the wheels of the suitcase." She—or somebody—sketched a salute and turned, continuing in the direction she'd chosen.

Anna watched for a minute, noting how gutter punk Jordan's slouch was gone, replaced with the sullen swagger of a man whose money can't buy him the respect of those he admires.

Closing the gate, she locked it and went back to her cottage. The day had been filled with the high-tech research of computers, the esoteric research of hypnotism, and the artistic use of disguise. Unfortunately for Anna, there remained only the tedious work every law enforcement officer depends on, whether the crime is bank robbery or the vandalism of Anasazi ruins.

Retrieving her backpack and the photocopy of the sketch of Dougie, Anna let herself back out onto Ursulines to walk door to door, show anyone who would look at the sketch, and say, "Have you seen this man?" Not particularly sexy, but the Boring Technique was the backbone of most police work.

On a spring evening the shops in the Quarter where she had followed Mackie and Dougie would be open till six, some till eight, and, of course, the bars and restaurants would be open for business. Given it was going on six already, Anna decided to start with the shops at the levee and Dumaine, then work her way up to Bourbon

Street. There, she'd have till 4:00 A.M. to wander around shoving her sketch under noses.

She'd walked four blocks when the cell phone in her pocket started playing "Clair de Lune," the ringtone she'd programmed in for her husband, Paul. The rush of pleasure and excitement contact with this beautiful man always engendered in her was soured as she realized, if she answered the cell, she would have three choices: She could lie to him, either by omission or commission; she could abandon what she was doing and leave Clare to do or die on her own; or she could endanger her law enforcement spouse by telling him she was aiding and abetting a suspected murderess. None of the possibilities was palatable. Not answering the phone wasn't palatable either. It was unthinkable that should Paul ever need her, she would turn away. Even if all he needed was to know she was alive and well and loved him.

Across the street was what had once been—and could still be, for that matter—a convent. The building dated from the late nineteenth century and was surrounded by a high brick wall. The wall ended at a parking lot separated from the street by a matching wall, modern and only thigh-high. Anna crossed, sat on it, and flipped open the cell.

"Hello, love," she said, feeling, through her guilt, the joy of having someone for whom pet names were not silly but secret and grand.

"Am I interrupting anything?" Paul asked. This had become their traditional first line over the time they'd been together. With both working criminal cases—him much of the time, and Anna when she had to—it was too easy to interrupt a sensitive moment with an ill-timed call.

At the sound of his voice, with all the warmth of his heart in it, Anna made a sudden decision. She had gotten in too deep to abandon Clare and her quest, even to the extent of turning her quest over to the police. Lying would start a cancer between her and Paul that nothing would ever be able to completely root out. Choosing the lesser of the evils, she decided to endanger him.

"You're not interrupting anything—well, you are, but I need to make a confession."

There was a brief silence; then he said, "Episcopal priests hear confessions, but we don't give out penance. We leave that to our Catholic brethren." His tone was light, but Anna could hear the worry underlying it.

Starting at the beginning, she told him everything she had done or said or found or suspected since she left Port Gibson to "find herself" in Geneva's backyard. When she finished, she waited. Paul said nothing for a bit, and she forced herself to relax her shoulders and unclench her left fist. After so many years of not caring a whole hell of a lot what people thought of her, caring so much was painful.

Finally, he let out a breath and said, "Oh, Anna . . ."

He sounded frustrated and scared and a little angry, but he didn't sound disappointed. Anna breathed a sigh of relief.

"I wish you weren't doing this," he said. There was a

weariness to his tone that let her know how much working two jobs without help was grinding him down. At fifty-seven Paul was fit and strong, with the body type her father used to describe as "built like a brick outhouse"—not too tall and powerful across the chest and shoulders with legs that could carry him up steep hills with ease. Still, he was fifty-seven, and Anna had noticed when fighting wildland fires that the middle-aged firefighters were tougher than the youngsters at the beginning of a twenty-one-day assignment, but by the end the kids had grown stronger while the older guys had only grown more tired.

"Yeah," Anna said, hearing an echo of his fatigue in her own voice. "I do, too, but Clare's right. Her stature as prime suspect would blind any law enforcement to what she was trying to show them. You know how it is."

"I do," Paul said. "Your brother-in-law knows what's going on?"

"Not officially, but he's been figuring out what evil-doers are doing for so long it didn't take him long to catch on."

"Molly?"

"I'm sure he told her. Molly could tempt secrets out of the Vatican."

"Well, that's good, then," Paul said. "We'll make going to the federal penitentiary a family affair."

Anna laughed, not because she was in the mood for laughing, but to thank him for trying to lighten the mood.

"You know what I want to do, don't you?"

"Yes," Anna said. "You want to jump in the car and rush down here to watch my back."

"And all other parts of your vulnerable anatomy," Paul said.

"Failing that, you want to issue a head-of-the-household dictum forbidding me to do it."

Paul broke out laughing. "Yes, but I won't because it would only serve to spur you on to do it further and faster and more often, just to prove you can."

"I love you," Anna said with a depth of sincerity that couldn't be watered down by distance or sketchy cell phone coverage.

"And I you," Paul said. "I will call you every three and a half minutes until we're together again, and if you don't answer, I will flood Sin City with good ole boys from Miss'sippi toting deer rifles. Make me one promise?"

Anna hesitated, then was ashamed of herself. "Name it," she said.

"Tell me *before* you do anything risky."

"Cross my heart and hope to die," she said.

"Not remotely funny."

At the gate in the levee wall between North Peters and the river where she'd first spotted Dougie wearing the infamous yellow leather jacket, Anna realized she was whistling "Dixie," a song as politically charged as the Confederate flag. She changed to "The Yellow Rose of Texas," realized that, too, was a touchy subject, and gave up altogether. She didn't give up being happy. Had she realized how heavily being less than honest with Paul had weighed on her, she would have put his freedom and his career in jeopardy days ago.

Smiling at her cheerful selfishness, she surveyed the bricked lane called Dutch Alley. The confectioner to the left was closed, but on the corner where Dougie and Mackie had turned was one of New Orleans's many art galleries. The sign over the door read DUTCH ALLEY ART-ISTS' CO-OP. Anna went in and began her canvassing.

The two artists working didn't recognize her sketch, but she didn't write the stop off as a waste of time. The gallery was one of the finest she'd ever seen—not that she saw many in her line of work—and she made a mental note to come back when she had time and money to throw around.

Settling into the patient, stolid mode of a magazine salesperson, she stopped in two of the main watering holes near the gallery. At Sydney's grocery, the woman behind the counter thought she might have seen him but, then again, probably not. Anna thanked her.

The bartender at Coop's said he'd never seen the guy with such alacrity that Anna suspected it was his policy never to see anybody. She thanked him.

Returning to the corner of Dumaine and North Peters, she began the chore of stopping at every shop along the route she and Mackie had chased the yellow jacket.

A young man at the tourist info center said the picture didn't ring any bells but he thought she'd like to try a Ghost Tour. The girl in the souvenir shop on the opposite corner knew the man in the sketch. Anna was thrilled with her luck until the girl began to tell her about all the secret police work she'd done and how if anybody knew she was working undercover, they'd sure be sorry they'd been such pricks. Anna thanked her.

She worked her way up the east side of Dumaine getting nothing and thanking everyone. The Amazing Patty at Vieux Dieux offered to read the tarot or the stars or the angel cards to find the guy. Anna politely declined, so Patty gave her, free of charge, a charm to find lost things.

Half past five, she turned at Chartres and headed down the west side of Dumaine. Stores were beginning to close for the evening. Soon she'd need to move into the nocturnally oriented businesses' territory.

At Authentic Voodoo she made her last stop. She paused in front of the door trying to remember the owner's name. *Racine.* As she reached for the door handle she heard a man shouting. Unashamedly, she leaned closer to eavesdrop. The words were unintelligible, Cajun French, she guessed. Racine—at least she assumed it was Racine—replied in English. Unlike the man's, her voice was not raised, but Anna could still hear well enough.

"You hate magic, you embrace work the devil would turn down, and yet you say you love me and Laura. There is so much dark in you, I wouldn't let you near her. Get out." The last was hissed. Anna was reminded snakes were an integral part of a lot of voodoo rituals;

she was also reminded of the snake she'd sensed beneath Racine's skin on their first meeting.

The man spoke again, still in Cajun French, but Anna
knew cursing when she heard it. Then he cried out as if
Racine had stabbed him with a knife. Anna jerked open
the door and walked in, making as much noise as possible, banging the door and stomping. It was not her intention to get cut in a domestic dispute. She merely wanted
to shatter the mood and distract the participants till things
settled down. Failing that she would run away, fleet as
any deer.

Again dressed in unrelieved white, a tiered cotton
skirt with eyelet trim and a tank top, the tall pale voodooienne stood behind the counter. Her hair was loose
and straight and fell from a center part. Her daughter,
Laura, was nowhere to be seen. In a bizarre tableau, the
slender blonde was holding a burly middle-aged man,
with wild black hair and muscles like the roots of an
old oak, at bay with what appeared to be a handful of
dried sagebrush.

"I call on Papa Legba. Come to me. Send me a war-
rior; send Ogoun." Her voice was louder now and had
changed pitch. The man threw his hands before his face.

"You goddamn witch!" he cried in accented English
and backed toward the door in such a blind rush Anna
had to jump out of the way or get trampled. He was so
anxious to escape the curse of the loa that Anna didn't
think he'd even noticed she was there.

Slowly Racine lowered the weeds with which she

had terrified the man. The elevated stare she'd adopted as she chanted melted down to a normal gaze, and her eyes locked on Anna.

"You," she said. "We are about to close, but if your problem is small, and I can help, I will."

Anna wasn't going to get a better invitation than this. She crossed the room and laid the sketch on the glass-topped counter. "Do you recognize this man, or does this sketch resemble anyone you know or have seen?"

Racine turned the page around and, holding her hair back with one graceful hand, bent over the paper. It occurred to Anna that the woman was nearsighted and too vain to wear glasses.

Suddenly, Racine jerked her head up as if the drawing were a scorpion about to strike and emitted a stifled gasp. Without looking at Anna, she spun around till her face was shielded from view and snatched up a pile of papers near the cash register, tapped them into line on the counter, laid them back down, and squared the corners as if it mattered.

"You know him," Anna said flatly, not wanting to give Racine time to work up a good story.

"I don't," Racine said, continuing to fiddle with the small pile of flyers.

"It matters," Anna said. "It matters a lot."

Racine took a deep breath. Letting her head fall back, she exhaled slowly. "I don't know him," she repeated.

"Nothing will come back on you. I don't need to know how you know him, and I don't need to tell anyone you told me."

Racine said nothing for a moment. Then, "I was about to close. Is there anything else I can help you with?" Her eyes were hard and her mouth determined.

Playing for time, Anna looked around the shop. Racine started toward the door to usher her out. Anna sighed. Meeting Racine's eyes she said, "I know this guy's name is Dougie. I know he's dangerous. I know he's connected to the business of harming children. Me, by myself, I might not stoop to threats. With little girls factored in, I might stoop to anything. So: I know your name, Racine Gutreaux, and your daughter's name, Laura. I know you're involved with—or married to—a man who speaks Cajun French. I'm guessing he's Laura's father and there is a dispute about custody. In this information age, just how long do you think it will take me to put these pieces together and find out how you know Dougie?"

Racine opened the door to assist in Anna's immediate departure.

Anna rubbed her face with one hand. A headache was starting behind her left eye. "It might take me a day, two days. That might be long enough for the little girls I'm looking for to die or to be shipped somewhere their mother will never see them again. Can you live with that?"

Racine looked at the floor. "Please go," she said.

Having been chasing wisps and scents and old clues from the mind of a child, Anna had no intention of letting something that resembled a solid lead slip away. Eliciting information from an unwilling witness was tricky business. Sometimes threats worked; other times they backfired. The same went for good cop and bad cop and every other form of manipulation. The only thing that was fairly dependable was payment, but what kind? Money wouldn't work on Racine, Anna was fairly certain of that. She stood silently for long enough that Racine finally closed the door softly and leaned her back against it.

"You know Jordan," Anna said suddenly. "I was in here one day when he stopped to look through your window at Laura. You thought he was a pedophile, and, being a voodooienne, you did something to him, didn't you?"

"Curses are not illegal," Racine said.

It was close enough to an admission of guilt for Anna. "Murdering harmless pigeons is."

"No it isn't. If they are not anyone's personal property and if they are not protected by state or federal statute or city regulations, they can be killed at will. You don't even need a license, and there is no hunting season as regards pigeons."

Anna hated it when people were well informed.

"What would you say if I told you Jordan is not, and never has been, a pedophile?" Anna asked.

"I wouldn't believe you. He's a pedophile. I should know."

"Ah. You should? And why is that?" Anna leaned back against the counter.

Racine said nothing. Her hands twitched on the

doorknob as if she couldn't decide whether to run or to try to bodily throw Anna into the street.

"Mommy?" came a tiny voice from behind Anna's shoulder. Laura had come down from the upstairs apartment and stood looking out at them from the gloom at the foot of the stairs.

"What is it, honey?" Racine asked, trying to watch Anna and her daughter at the same time.

"I heard Daddy's voice," Laura said.

"Daddy's gone, baby," Racine said.

Anna watched the interplay between mother and daughter, both ethereal with their long blonde hair and pale skin, eyes big and luminous blue in their smooth faces. Did Racine know about child molesters because her husband was molesting Laura? The idea of anyone despoiling such a frail and beautiful child made Anna's stomach clench. The idea of anyone despoiling any innocent made her stomach clench.

"He didn't say good-bye!" the little girl wailed.

Clearly she loved Daddy. That proved nothing. Abused children were dependent on their abusers. The attention and secrecy and "special" relationship, mixed with the natural love of child for parent, strangled the true meaning of love. Love was power and, in the hands of the corrupt, could be used in the most heinous of ways.

Anna's mind leapt from Laura to Vee and Dana, the lost girls of Clare Sullivan. Girls who'd not yet been removed from danger. "Dougie," she said to Laura. "Is that your daddy's name?"

Laura didn't say anything, but she scrunched up her nose and wrinkled her perfect little mouth into a moue of distaste. "Dougie's a stinker," she said. Anna got a sense that Dougie was not big enough in the child's mind to have monster status but was sufficiently odious to dislike.

Racine left the door and was crossing quickly toward the stairs, intent on snatching her daughter out of Anna's reach, when Laura said, "My daddy's name is Blackie."

THIRTY-ONE

Anna was invited upstairs, not, she knew, because Racine had come to like or trust her but because it was more private than the windowed shop. They sat at a tiny table in a kitchen the size of a closet, each with a cup of tea that smelled faintly like gardenias and had little more color than plain water. Laura was in the front room. They could see her through the open door serving tea to her dolls. Beyond the child was the door to the stairs down to the shop. Though it was an internal door, and the voodoo shop was locked, Anna noted there were three locks on it: a key lock, a dead bolt, and a chain.

"Is your husband a child molester?" Anna asked when it was clear that, once the tea and amenities were seen to, Racine wasn't going to speak further without prodding.

"Shh!" Racine hissed, her eyes on Laura.

Anna had spoken softly so her words wouldn't carry to the child, but the admonition didn't offend her. To even speak of these things seemed to taint the air in a room.

"No," Racine answered in a low voice. She lifted her tea as if to drink, then set it down again without taking any. "At least I don't think so."

In that sentence lay the end of the marriage. How could a woman live with a man she didn't "think" was abusing children? That she could even have the thought was trust's death knell and the beginning of fear.

"Dougie?" Anna asked. She suppressed an urge to glance at the doll's tea party. To look at Laura with Dougie in mind would be somehow damaging. Whether to her or the angels, Anna wasn't sure.

"I don't know. I only know him from meeting him three or four times. He gave me the creeps—the way he looked at Laura—and I asked Blackie never to bring him to the house again. Blackie doesn't like him either. Maybe even hates him, but they had to work together."

"At what?" Anna asked when Racine didn't go on of her own volition.

Racine lowered her face till her hair fell in a curtain, hiding her features. "Blackie worked for an import-export company. He drove a truck, picking up things off-loaded at different ports and delivering them to a buyer here in New Orleans. Dougie sometimes went with him when there was more work than one man could do by himself."

Again she raised the teacup, and this time it actually arrived at her lips; still, she didn't drink. Setting the untouched beverage down, she said, "I thought my husband was hauling art—the mass-produced stuff from China—that you see in shops in the Quarter. Even uptown there are a lot of antique shops that sell reproductions. Sometimes they tell the customers that they are. Sometimes they don't."

Getting the feeling that Racine wasn't telling the whole story, Anna leveled an open, expectant gaze on her and waited.

Finally the woman said, "I guess I guessed that some of it wasn't quite, well, kosher. Dougie was so creepy, and they called their boss the Magician instead of by his name—there were a lot of things like that. But I thought it was just maybe that some of the things Blackie was hauling were maybe stolen or contraband or the import duties hadn't been paid. And I love—loved—my husband, and Laura thinks her daddy walks on water, so . . ."

She let the thought trail out. It didn't need finishing. She'd done what most people do, hoped and ignored and made excuses and tried to keep her and her child in the life where they were comfortable, in their home, with their family. In a way, Clare had done the same thing.

"Then you found out something," Anna said to help bridge the gap between denial and realization.

"Yes," Racine said. "Blackie came home from one of his trips to pick up imports and he was really upset. He grabbed a bottle of bourbon that we've had around the house so long I don't know when we even bought it—neither of us drink all that much, and mostly wine—and he poured himself a half a glassful and took it like he was taking castor oil. He got in late—sometime after midnight—and he was tired. Laura was asleep, but I'd heard his van and gotten up. When I came into the kitchen he wouldn't even look at me. He filled the glass again and knocked it back. I think it was the bourbon that let him talk. If he'd been rested and sober and in his right mind I don't think he ever would have told me. But he wasn't, and he started to cry after the alcohol hit him.

"He said Dougie had killed a woman and her husband. From the way he said it, I think he didn't do it, but maybe he didn't stop it either. He said they'd had to make it look like an accident—or like the deaths weren't related to anything that could lead back to their boss—so they took the man's body to his house, put it in his pajamas, and burned the place down so it would look like he'd died in the fire."

That was in keeping with what Clare had told Anna. David had been murdered. It was his corpse the firemen had carried out of the house on Laggert Street in Seattle. "What did they do with the woman's body?" Anna asked.

"He didn't tell me, only that we were safe. By 'we' he meant me and Laura and him. Of course we never would be safe. Dougie is a rat right down to his little rat heart. If he saw a nickel in it, he'd rat out his own mother."

Finally teacup made a successful trip to tongue and Racine took a long drink. Anna hadn't touched her tea either. Though she'd seen Racine make it, she knew the woman was steeped in voodoo with its powders and potions and skewered pigeons, and she had no intention of swallowing anything she gave her.

They sat without talking for a moment. Laura had finished serving her dolls their tea and was now reading to them from a book about balloons and balls. Anna let her mind drift over what Racine had said; it appeared to her Racine would not have broken up her marriage over something as mundane as aiding and abetting in two murders, covering up felonies, and the illegal transport of bodies.

"Did Blackie tell you about killing two children?" Anna asked softly, her eyes unable to tear away from Laura.

"Blackie would never do that," Racine said and sounded sure.

"But?"

"But the items he hauled for the Magician weren't fake antiques or mass-produced bronzes."

"They were people," Anna said.

"Yes."

"Children."

"Not usually."

"But sometimes."

Racine nodded. After a moment she couldn't sit with that damnation on her husband's head any longer, and she said, "Blackie told me he thought they were orphans. Most of them were from the Middle East, but there were some from Central America, Mexico, and Asia. He said he thought they were going to be adopted—you know, those illegal adoptions for people who can't get a baby through legal channels or don't want to wait? There's big money in that."

Another silence came and went. Anna thought, *Given to nice people in the country that have a farm where Fluffy can run free*. She said, "But you didn't believe him."

"I wanted to. But I didn't think he believed himself. The bourbon had made it so he couldn't lie as well as he can sober, and I knew he really didn't think the kids were adopted. I still thought it was bad but not so bad, like they were going to be servants in people's houses or maybe do factory work."

She looked up at Anna and shook the hair out of her face. "I know you think that makes me a monster, too—to be okay with that—but there are worse things that can happen to orphans." Such was the look of defiance and sorrow on her face, Anna guessed she'd been one of those orphans and would have traded whatever her lot was for a little overwork and underpay. Even a lot of work and no pay.

"Yet you took Laura and moved out? When was that?" From the Amazing Patty, Anna knew Authentic Voodoo had been open for six months or more. Hardly on a time line with events of scarcely a couple weeks back.

"Two weeks ago," Racine said. "I'd had the shop for a while. Blackie didn't like it. Magic scares him. Even white magic. He grew up in the swamps, and he says that magic is magic and you can think it's white or black, but it is what it is in the end, and it doesn't care what you wanted it to be when you took it up. Blackie doesn't think it's like water or electricity—forces you can understand and control and use to create light or destroy cities.

To him magic is alive, and, like a wild animal, it might let you think you've tamed it, but you haven't, and it will turn on you. But he was gone so much he let me have the shop."

"Let?" Anna said. Racine didn't seem quite the type to ask a man's permission for much of anything.

"There might have been a suggestion of Gutreaux dolls and hat pins," Racine said with the first smile she'd shown since Anna had come into the shop. "The upstairs wasn't rented, so I took it, and Laura and I moved in."

Since Racine wasn't bothered by the possibility of her husband dealing in contraband and, though she didn't like it, wasn't suffering the tortures of the damned because he might be selling children into, if not slavery, then certainly indentured servitude, Anna waited for the last revelation, the moment when Racine knew or suspected he was selling little girls to whoremongers.

"And the straw that broke the proverbial's back?" Anna nudged when, instead of continuing her story, Racine got up and began fiddling with the teakettle.

Racine looked over her shoulder, her eyes meeting Anna's with such loathing that Anna got ready to run. "Dougie." Racine spat out the name, her lips twisted around the vile taste it left in her mouth. "Dougie's not smart, but he thinks he is. He texted Blackie about getting some broken 'jewels.' I heard Blackie's phone go off, and I read the text. The so-called code the fool had dreamed up didn't do much to hide the fact he was asking if he could use the little girls—or boys—that were sick, dead, or damaged in some way. He was asking my husband for permission to do it. Then I knew what happened to the children Blackie delivered to the Magician.

"He said he wasn't going to work for the man anymore—I just can't say 'the Magician,' it's too stupid!" Racine blurted out. Anna agreed but hadn't thought a woman who was a self-proclaimed voodooienne would have such a low tolerance for street theater. "He said he was going to go back and work in his dad's swamp tour business, but I left anyway."

"What happened to the kids?"

"My husband sold them into prostitution," Racine said with measured formality as if testing each word to see if it would hold, trying on each sound, knowing they were words she would be saying for the rest of her life either out loud or to herself.

"He told you this?"

"He said a couple of them had died—were dead when he and Dougie went to get them—and that he was glad they were dead because, if it was Laura, he'd rather see her half rotted and stinking than to see her after the Ma— the man's clients had done with her. I didn't listen to any more after that. I took Laura from her bed, and we came here. For a few days we slept in the shop. Then I rented these rooms."

THIRTY-TWO

R acine didn't know where Blackie took his imported "jewels"; nor did she know where the man who called himself the Magician conducted his business or what his real name was. She didn't know where Dougie lived, or his last name, and Blackie Gutreaux was not answering at either number Racine had given.

Anna took a cab to the Gutreaux house in Jefferson Parish, a small bungalow half a block from the levee. She told the cabbie to wait, then knocked and rang and peeked in windows, but the place was deserted. Having no way of knowing when, or if, Blackie was going to return to the homestead, and doubting she'd have an easy time catching a cab from his neighborhood, she rode back into town with her cabbie.

Racine said Blackie had quit working for the Magician after the murders. She had also said two children died. Anna spent a good bit of the time wasted on the cab ride debating whether this was news she should share with Clare. Had she been certain the dead children were Vee and Dana, she would have done it immediately, but the story Blackie told Racine contained the words "rotted" and "stinking."

If Blackie was an imaginative sort, he could have been speaking metaphorically. If not, he was describing decay, corpses more than a day or two dead, depending on the temperature where the bodies were kept.

Clare insisted she'd seen her daughters at 3:00 A.M. the morning the house burned down. Even if they had died moments after she left them to buy cough syrup, they would not have begun to smell for a while. It was possible Blackie hung around Seattle for a while after the killings and the bombing, but Anna doubted it. A man trucking cattle, whether two-legged or four-legged, has to keep to a tight schedule or he'll lose too many head before he gets to market.

Dana and Vee could have died, then Blackie took their corpses with him and Dougie in the van, and the bodies began to get ripe somewhere between Washington and Louisiana. Carrying bodies around was dangerous business. The most likely scenario was that he and Dougie had dumped them where they wouldn't be found, or at least not for a long time. If that was the case, they'd yet to turn up. The bodies of children always made national news.

If Dana and Vee still lived, as Clare and Mackie and Sleepy Dog attested, then whose were the little burned bodies carried from the fire? Had they been long dead when Blackie and Dougie stuffed them in the nursery?

Had the Cajun and his sidekick killed them along with David Sullivan because it was easier than dealing with them? Were Dana and Vee collateral damage? Or had something gone terribly wrong with the delivery and the children meant for the whorehouse had arrived dead, dead long enough to begin to decompose, and upon discovering two little girls in a house they intended to torch, Dougie and Blackie had simply exchanged the dead for the living, so they'd still get paid?

That was a miserable thought among a host of miserable thoughts. For a fierce vicious moment, Anna wished there were something to voodoo and that Racine would bring down a curse on her husband and Dougie that would peel the skin from their flesh and the flesh from their bones.

Arming herself with an aromatic muffuletta and a six-pack of Abita beer, Anna returned to Ursulines and knocked on Geneva's French doors. The sun had long since set, and, limned by the silver of ambient city light, Geneva manifested out of the inner darkness, the cat, so black mere ambient light would not serve to illuminate it, draped over her shoulder like a sack, and opened the glass door.

"I come bearing gifts," Anna said.

"Yes, I smell you. Well, one hopes it is not you but a sandwich," Geneva said and stepped back to let Anna and her gifts in. Clare's dog trotted in at her heels. Mackie had been in the yard sleeping somewhere out of sight but had materialized at the smell of food. The cat showed no interest in Anna, the dog, or the sandwich and Anna thought of Hobbes from "Calvin and Hobbes" and how he reverted to a stuffed tiger when alien eyes were upon him.

"I was hoping for a favor," Anna said as she set the sandwich halves, each enough to feed four hungry people, on paper towels on Geneva's coffee table and uncapped a beer for each of them.

"Why am I not reeling with shock at that announcement?" Geneva drawled.

For a second Anna was nonplussed. A fleeting thought of manners and small talk withered on the vine, and she said, "Yes, well, that's as may be, but I was hoping you could help me search for something."

"I'm all ears," Geneva said, emphasizing the word "ears," as she spread herself on the sofa and the black cat across her knees. "Ears and hands," she amended. "I am much more likely to grant favors if you put a beer in the latter."

Anna did as she was asked, then joined the woman and the cat on the sofa. The whole point of a muffuletta is the olives, but Anna plucked hers out and left them on the paper towel just the same. "In the conducting of the situation of which you know nothing, about a person you've never met, I've come upon three clues as to the location of a place which, should you ever be called upon to testify, you've never heard of," Anna said.

Geneva nodded, took a swig of her beer, and said, "I'm not listening."

God, but Anna loved musicians. "Okay. One: a place
that gives piano or singing lessons. Two: a place from
which the sound *pssssssst-chunk* emanates. Three: a
place in which you can smell lots of flowers at once."

"The flower stall by the subway grate down from
Juilliard," Geneva said without hesitation.

"Yeah. Like that. But here." Anna took a bite of her
sandwich. She'd forgotten Geneva had studied music at
Juilliard. She wondered if she'd ever seen the woman
in white by Saks. Well, no, she wouldn't have. She
might have heard her, though, and, ten to one, if she
did, the woman in white saw her. Geneva might even
have been the inspiration for the singer's blind/blues
shtick. Reminding herself to think about that later, Anna
concentrated on the issue at hand. There was little else
she could tell Geneva without compromising her even
further, so she said nothing, concentrated on her sandwich, and let Geneva mull over Candy's three fractured
memories.

"You can't spit in the Quarter without getting a musician wet," Geneva said around bread and olives. "A
lot of them do lessons on the side to make ends meet. I
know of four piano teachers for sure and three vocal
coaches—the one I go to and a couple of others."

Anna's musical skills were dedicated to being an appreciative audience member. She didn't even sing in the
shower for fear the soap would make fun of her. "Do piano teachers sing scales, or have the students do it?"

"They do, but not so you'd hear it through walls—
I'm assuming you are talking through walls or you'd

know where you were at. But I have no interest in it, so never mind," Geneva said and took a pull of the Abita.

"Will you show me where they are? Go with me so we can sniff and listen and, well . . . *sleuth*?"

Geneva laughed. "You are weird, Anna. With talent you would have made a fine musician."

"Oh, and my information is at least six months old," Anna remembered.

Geneva groaned.

After they'd eaten, the two of them finishing less than a quarter of the gigantic sandwich, Anna let herself into Clare's apartment, fed Mackie, tended to his important dog business, then shut him up for the night. The little guy wanted to go for a walk in the worst way and wagged his entire body and looked at her with beseeching brown button eyes, but Anna stayed strong. There would be enough distractions without Mackie along to pester Sammy and get underfoot.

She ruled out North Peters, Chartres, Royal, and Bourbon streets. The heart of the tourist district was noisy and crowded. The "fancy house" was the sort of establishment that would require privacy, and the four streets cutting through the heart of the French Quarter were alive with noise year-round. Candy would have heard more than scales and *pssssst-chunking*.

It was after nine when they began their odyssey, and, though the streets between Royal and Rampart were by no means deserted, Anna was on alert. As one resident had put it, in New Orleans you were never

more than two streets from trouble. It was a violent
city, the young men running wild with guns and pov-
erty and deep-seated anger. Even knowing this, it was
hard to maintain her edge. The somnolent hum of the
Crescent City, people talking quietly on their front
stoops, smoking cigarettes, walking dogs, the murmur
of a breeze off the river whispering in the palm fronds,
belied the danger.

Geneva led Anna to the piano teachers' homes, and
they stood on the sidewalk in the drift of streetlights
sniffing and listening. The smell of flowers existed, but,
for the most part, it was only a whisper behind the more
insistent odors of cooking, garbage, and automobile exhaust. Anna serving as guide dog for the night, Sammy
padded complacently along at heel and selfishly kept his
fabulous dog nose to himself, his main interest being in
the news other dogs had left on fire hydrants and light
poles.

Street by street and smell by smell, they left the residential part of the Quarter behind and were nearing
Iberville and Rampart streets on the northwest corner.
Shotgun houses had given way to industrial buildings
with bricked-in blind windows, gaping parking maws,
and dark doorways. On the far side of Rampart was one
of the city's many subsidized housing developments,
acres of three- and four-story brick buildings around
open areas that, one supposed, were intended to be green
spaces but had the stomped and neglected appearance
of fairgrounds after the carnival has moved on. The

apartments, built in the thirties and forties and fifties, housed generations of people with little hope for better and a lot of fear of losing what they had.

Two streets from trouble.

Slouching and pushing down the sidewalk from the direction of the projects was a group of boys in their teens. None was old enough to buy cigarettes, but that didn't make them any less deadly. All wore the uniform of the streets: a T-shirt so big it came nearly to the knees, shorts so baggy the crotch was at about a level with the hem of the shirt, and oversized sneakers with the tongues hanging out. The horseplay was limited to what could be done one-armed. Each had a hand that was apparently dedicated solely to keeping the trousers from falling around the ankles.

The noisy lads might be on their way to late, late choir practice, or to help a friend in need, but still Anna was thinking about turning around and calling it a night. Two middle-aged women, one blind and one too small to scare anybody, might be a greater temptation than nocturnal predators could resist, might even be sufficiently attractive to make, as she'd once heard an apologist claim, good boys go bad.

"Geneva," she said, laying a hand on her friend's arm.

"Wait," Geneva said and tilted her head back as if listening or remembering or, maybe, just about to sneeze. "Where're we at exactly?"

Anna told her.

"Okay, this is it. This was where the opera singer had a studio. Third floor. Piano. Nilla was her name.

Nilla something. Nobody could ever remember because she was so white everybody called her Nilla Wafer, but she had a big black voice. I think she went with an opera company out west. That was a year or so ago."

"The sound of scales sung loud. Good. That's one out of three of our clues. I'm not seeing a dry cleaner's— or whatever might be the *psssssst-chunk* part of our equation—and we're not exactly in a big flower-growing neighborhood," Anna said, her hand still on Geneva's arm. "Diesel, more like. Let's head back."

The boys had seen them and were focusing the way a pack of dogs will when a rabbit is scented but has not yet broken cover. They hadn't noticed, then ignored, the way most kids will when crossing paths with adults. They'd stopped shoving and closed ranks.

Had she been on her own, Anna would have taken to her heels and run for less isolated environs. If these were nice boys, out for a night ramble, they could have their fun laughing at her and she could have her fun not having to hear most of it. As it was, running wasn't an option. She glanced at her watch. It was after eleven. Was she hoping the violence hour had not yet begun?

"What's happening?" Geneva whispered sharply.

"Boys," Anna said succinctly. "Curb," she added as, taking Geneva's arm, she steered her into the street and toward the far sidewalk. Perhaps the boys would be happy with this evidence of their power; maybe they'd be too lazy to bother crossing. "Sammy isn't a Green Beret attack dog by any chance, is he?"

"Sammy is 4-F due to an amiable disposition," Geneva said. There was still most of a short New Orleans block between them and the boys. "They're crossing," Geneva said.

Anna glanced up. She'd been avoiding eye contact the same way she would with a wild animal or a paranoid schizophrenic. Eye contact was an act of aggression under certain circumstances. The boys were crossing. They looked older and bigger than when she'd first noticed them. The rodeo clown clothes no longer looked as funny as they had.

Gangs were not unknown to Anna. In New York they were white and Puerto Rican and black; in Texas, white and Mexican; in small towns, redneck white boys and whoever they found to fight. What she didn't know was how to stop the momentum of a gang event in the making. These kids might be mean to the bone, but she guessed they were more bored and drunk, egging each other on and out to have a little "fun." What defused a group who thought tormenting or robbing or killing was "fun"?

As the boys reached the sidewalk, they made sure they took the full width of it. To miss them, Anna and Geneva would have to step back into the street. They didn't. Given that showing humility—fear—in ceding the sidewalk hadn't appeased them the first time, there was no reason for Anna to think it would the second.

Stopping, Geneva at her side, Anna waited, letting the boys close the distance. A faint click, then a snicking sound, made her glance down. Geneva had taken

the leash from Sammy's collar, then pulled her seg-
mented and folded white cane from some pocket in her
skirts and flicked it into a narrow staff. Not much striking power, but the stings could be diverting.

Leaving her the cane, Anna took the leash with its
metal clasp from Geneva's hand and, surreptitiously
wrapping the strap around her knuckles, stepped a bit
away from her friend.

"Good evening, gentlemen," she said when the boys
were half a dozen yards away. "Geneva and I were hoping you could help us. Do you know your way around
the French Quarter?" She smiled as if she truly believed they'd come to earn their merit badges by helping a couple of little old ladies back across the street.

"You ladies looking for something special?" the boy
marginally in the lead asked. He'd taken an unlit cigarette from behind his left ear and, holding it between
thumb and forefinger, was stroking the length of it in
an unsubtle gesture.

"Yes," Anna gushed. "Friends of ours said one of the
city's best restaurants was on this street, but, gosh, if
it is we sure didn't see it. It's called Grandma's." Why
that name popped off her tongue, Anna wasn't sure.
Possibly because the kids looked like big bad wolves
and she was feeling Red Riding Hoodish.

For a moment, she thought they were going to play
the game, at least for a while. Then a shorter boy elbowed the cigarette stroker to one side. "What you got
in the backpack, bitch?" He snaked an arm out to try to
grab hold of the daypack Anna carried.

"Okay, then," Anna said flatly. "I guess we aren't going to be friends. What will it take to get you to leave us alone?"

"Oooooh," one of the wingmen crooned. "Tough mama! Maybe we got to tenderize your ass 'fore you go home to the hubby. Fact he prob'ly be thankin' us for breaking that broomstick you got up your butt."

So much for civilized negotiations. Her cell phone was in the daypack. She doubted she could dig it out and dial 911 before she was stopped, so she didn't try. Anna sensed Geneva tensing up. The singer hadn't survived childhood trauma and gotten to where she was by backing down or begging. Even Sammy came up from his obedient sitting position and lowered his head as if he were trying to remember where it was best to bite people he didn't like.

They were going to fight: a small middle-aged ranger, a blind woman, and an amiable dog, against five streetwise thugs coming into the strength of men. They would lose, of course, but now wasn't the time to think about that.

Headlights raked the seven of them, and Anna threw her arm across her eyes to keep from being blinded. A cab pulled to the curb under a streetlight fifty feet beyond the boys. A door opened, and a man climbed out.

"Hey!" Anna shouted, waving both arms. "Cabbie!" Sidestepping into the street, she kept waving. The cab's IN SERVICE light blinked out, and the car picked up speed. "Hey!" she yelled again, stepping farther into the street. The cabbie floored it, swerved around Anna, and cut the corner at the end of the block so sharply his tires screamed.

"I guess he don't want your sorry white ass in his pretty black cab," the speaker of the gang said.

"At least he veered," Anna grumbled. "Surely that means he had some affection for me." The sneers didn't waver, and she wondered if they knew what the word "affection" meant, wondered if they'd ever felt it under any name.

The man who'd gotten out of the cab was standing beneath the streetlight watching the drama as if it were being played out onstage. Anna started to raise her hand to holler at him, and then they locked eyes. It was Dougie, the yellow jacket, the man who had pulled a knife on her and Mackie. He was staring at her hard, and she wondered if he recognized her, if he knew she was looking for him. Then she realized that what had him transfixed wasn't the way she looked but the way she was looking at him, much the way a fox might look at a baby duckling.

Before she could move or shout, he turned and walked rapidly across the street and out of sight down Rampart.

The boys were grinning, and the loose chain they'd made around Anna and Geneva began to tighten.

Geneva leaned her head back and took in a great lungful of air.

She could scream all she wanted to, Anna thought. Nobody was going to hear her.

At least nobody who gave a damn.

THIRTY-THREE

Clare was standing in a narrow alleyway. To one side was a Dumpster, to the other a windowless brick wall. Just enough space remained between the two for a broad-shouldered man to stand without quite touching anything vile. Narrow as her frame was, she kept her arms close to her sides. The expensive leather shoes she'd been worried about looking too new when the evening started out now appeared as if she'd worn them for ten years and never polished them once. Her crisp linen slacks were limp and wrinkled, the cuffs taking on the color of the sidewalks she'd been tramping.

Behind her were three young men, almost boys, high school juniors or seniors probably. They'd been joking and smirking and generally bolstering each other's courage till one of them had vomited against the wall a few minutes back. Since then they'd been fairly quiet. Ahead of her two more men stood stolidly without much obvious joy. A third was out of sight ahead of

them. Now that the boys had quieted she could hear the
guy in front groaning like a man in pain.

All of them were in line behind a run-down conve-
nience store, pragmatically named Food Store, on the
edge of the Marigny, waiting for a twenty-dollar blow
job. Already Clare had seen enough female flesh and
enough male assholes to send her into a convent for the
rest of her life, but there was no quitting, no calling it a
night, no going back. Not ever.

The Jordan who stayed at the high-priced hotel and
wore Brooks Brothers clothing had gone somewhere.
Not gone, Clare corrected herself, turned his back for a
while. The relief at feeling in control was not as great
as the fear of being alone, of losing the strength she'd
found when Jordan joined her on the train she'd hopped
out of Seattle.

The groaning man had recovered and was elbowing
his way back out of the crowded alley, not meeting anybody's eyes. He'd done up his belt, but his fly was still
unzipped. Nobody told him.

The next customer vanished from sight around the
edge of the Dumpster, and Clare shuffled up a couple
feet in line. The alley was paved in brick, clean enough
because of the heavy rains this near the Gulf of Mexico;
clean enough she could easily see the two cockroaches
that ran for cover when she moved. Two months ago
she'd have shrieked and run for a can of Raid. Now she
simply watched her fellows with mild interest. Cockroaches didn't bite, didn't rape, didn't set houses on fire
or sell one another into slavery. The hero of Kafka's

The Metamorphosis might have had it better than he'd thought.

She'd come to join these cockroaches on the recommendation of the bouncer who threw her out of Hustler's Barely Legal. Time was draining from the world in a palpable way; Clare felt it as if it were blood draining from her veins, the lives of her children dripping away. Pushed by this urgency, she'd taken three different strippers to the private lap dance rooms upstairs and tried to bribe them into getting her somebody younger. A lot younger. To their credit, and her disappointment, they'd all turned her down. One of them had slapped her so hard her ears rang for five minutes. She was probably the one who told the bouncer there was a pervert on the premises, a real one.

Because she was an actor and because she was playing a pedophile, people believed she was a pedophile. This was what she wanted; this was how she might best find her daughters. It didn't change the fact that the revulsion on the faces of the strippers, and the way the bouncer didn't want to have to touch her to move her from the club, made her want to scream, "I am not one of them! They have my children!"

The bouncer, a burly fellow no more than thirty, escorted her to the street and said she might find something more her style behind the Food Store. He didn't say it nicely. He was probably setting her up to be beaten or killed, but she came anyway. She doubted his promise of something more in her "style" would turn out to be true. Mass-produced fellatio didn't strike her as having a direct tie-in with child abuse, since she was out of ideas, she stood with the roaches skittering over her three-hundred-dollar loafers, cursed Jordan for his untimely abdication, and listened to another guy getting his rocks off behind the garbage.

Shoving her hands in her pockets to keep them from straying too close to the Dumpster and the effluvia glistening on its sides, she felt the cell phone in her pocket with its one number: Anna Pigeon. Though she'd only been living without contact with others for a couple of weeks, till now it hadn't crossed her mind to call anyone. She could call Anna now, find out if she'd learned anything. Somehow Clare couldn't bring herself to drag another woman—even the pigeon, even by wireless—into this alley.

A grunt, a "Goddamn," and another man, looking at no one, fumbling with his trouser front, lumbered by, hitting Clare's shoulder as he passed. Next but one for a blow job, Clare moved ahead, watched the roaches run, and tried not to think too far into the future.

Then it was her turn. The energy of rage and shame and doing something that might by some stretch of a miracle lead to her children had trickled away with the vomit and urine in the alley. Had she not come so far and waited so long, had she anywhere else to go to, Clare would have turned and walked from this sewer where a poor debased creature plied her trade.

As it was she rounded the end of the Dumpster. She'd thought there was a wall there and, maybe, a kneeling pad. The bricks would shred the knees out of anything less than chaps if there wasn't. What she found was greater darkness, a square in the brick of the wall so devoid of light that it seemed like the entrance to a netherworld.

"Hello, handsome. Let me see what you got for me," came a voice so sultry it almost managed to make the fetid alleyway seem more mysterious than pathetic. Almost.

Clare stepped toward the darkness, and, as she did, she could see that it was a recessed doorway. In the room beyond, a single candle burned. Between the door and the candle, silhouetted against the feeble light, a woman sat on a low chair, a slipper chair, Clare remembered from the set of *The Importance of Being Earnest*. The back of the chair curved gracefully up behind its occupant, who sat with long skirts artfully arranged, long-nailed hands drooping languidly over the arms, one holding a burning cigarette. Clare could distinguish little, only that she had a wealth of long blonde curls and that, where the candlelight touched her sleeves, the gown looked to be a deep red color. The room smelled of cigarette smoke, perfume, and the slight metallic odor of what had to be nearing quarts of semen.

The woman rearranged her skirts, and Clare saw the bronze flash of the rim of an old-fashioned spittoon. The receptacle of ten thousand unborn babies. Of course she wouldn't swallow. At the rate she sold favors, if she had, she'd be as big as a garbage truck.

"Don't just stand there, honey, time is money, and, unless you want trouble, get those pants down on the double." Low throaty laughter followed this doggerel of house rules.

Clare stepped closer, fished the Bic lighter out of her pants pocket, and struck a light.

"Fuck, no," the woman growled and was out of the chair so fast Clare had no time to do anything but freeze in place. The lighter was snatched from her hand as fast, and the woman back in her chair.

"No light, baby. I got sensitive eyes."

In the brief flash Clare had seen what the intentional gloom hid. Ms. Fellatio was really Mr. Fellatio in a long gold wig and no teeth. An old fag down on his luck, but with a gig that paid for rent and dentures.

"You bring out your business," the sultry voice suggested. "I got a line outside."

Jordan came back on a tide of violence. He jerked out his wallet and brought out a hundred-dollar bill. "I wouldn't put my foot in your mouth, much less my dick," he said. "Want to talk?" He proffered the bill, and the prostitute took it.

"I love good conversation," the hooker said, then rose and called into the alley, "Y'all come back in half an hour. Lady Kneepads has got to take a break." Shutting the door on the groans and shouts of annoyance, he threw a dead bolt that sounded as if it could withstand Mongol hordes and turned to Jordan.

"What you need, baby? You got half an hour." He draped himself back onto the low chair, leaving Jordan standing. Fine; the less of Jordan's surface that touched that faggot's work area, the better.

"I'm looking for something a little younger," Jordan said and, forgetting Clare's lighter had been confiscated, shook out a Camel.

"Younger than Lady Kneepads?" the transvestite said as he leaned forward and struck a light for Jordan's cigarette.

In the glare, Jordan couldn't but notice the arch look in his eyes and the easy humor around the toothless mouth. He wasn't as old as Clare'd thought, probably forty, and, with his teeth in, could probably still get laid.

"I know, you thinking, what's a nice girl like me doin' in a place like this."

The light went out on the sexy chuckle.

"Real young," Jordan said. "Tender flesh."

"We talkin' legal tender?" Lady Kneepads asked.

Jordan said nothing. He took a drag and glanced back at the door locking the others out. Locking him in.

"You with vice, baby boy?" Lady Kneepads asked.

"Not a cop," Jordan said on a stream of smoke. "I just like my women young. And women," he added.

"No need to be insulting. A lousy hundred bucks don't buy meanness in my book. But you aren't talkin' *wimmin*, are you, baby? You're talkin' girls. Am I right?"

"Tender flesh," Jordan repeated.

"Now, you talking big girls or little girls? Barely legal high school or Parchman-Farm-here-I-come kindergarteners?"

"By the time they get to high school, they're all whores," Jordan said.

"And why do you suppose that is, hmmmm?" Lady Kneepads asked.

"You want another hundred or you want to blow every guy in that alley and still end up with a night's take worth half that?"

"Lady Kneepads would adore another C-note, but if you insist on being a royal shit, she will demand two."

The lady held out her hand. Jordan dug out another hundred-dollar bill but didn't give it to her.

All night Clarc'd dragged his butt around the underbelly of a city known for sex and sin and gotten nothing. He'd probably get nothing from this broken-down cocksucker, but at least their transaction was honest: money for information. It beat hell out of hinting to overpaid concierges, lap dancers, and bouncers.

"You got what I want?" Jordan demanded, flicking the bill in her face.

Lady Kneepads lowered her hand. "What you want doesn't go around advertising. That kind of thing gets the vice boys all hot and bothered, and they come shut down poor hardworking girls like Lady K. So I can't guarantee you're going to get what you want where I send you. Hearsay says if you go to the Bonne Chance— that's chance, c-h-a-n-c-e—you might hear the pitter-patter of little feet, but that's just what I said, it's hearsay."

"Hearsay." Jordan spat out the word in frustration.

"You keep your money. And why don't you take yourself off? I don't have much use for the likes of you anyway. I just took the money—"

"Because you're a whore."

"That's right, baby, and a girl's got to live. Bye-bye." Lady K rose effortlessly from her chair and glided to the door with dignity. She threw the bolt and held it open for Jordan. As he passed, she hissed, "You ever come to me for a blow job, I'm goin' to put my teeth in, you got that?"

Jordan got it.

Clare held tight to the name Bonne Chance.

THIRTY-FOUR

Geneva's diaphragm swelled, her throat opened, and she began to sing, "Swing low, sweet chariot, comin' for to carry me home," in her rich contralto voice.

The gang of thugs shuddered as if they'd been hit by a magic spell. Suddenly they were boys again. Whether it was the music/savage beast connection or the shock of having their victim break into song, Anna couldn't begin to guess.

While they were momentarily human, Anna said, "That guy that got out of the cab. He's a major pedophile. We've been trying to track him down. A hundred bucks to the guy who tells me where he goes." One of the kids at the end of the arc they'd been tightening around Anna and Geneva forgot they were going to steal all of the money anyway and sprinted off in hopes of earning the hundred dollars. After a brief hesitation, another boy took off after him.

"Ty!" the most vicious kid, the one who'd threatened

rape, shouted after them. The thrill of the chase was as much a draw as the money.

"Fucking pedophile," the biggest kid, the one Anna'd mistaken for the leader, said. Nobody liked pedophiles but other pedophiles. These kids might be murderers and thieves and God knew what else, but they weren't *sick*. He turned and looked—wistfully, Anna thought— after the two younger boys. Knowing the scene could go against her and Geneva in the time it takes to change a mind, Anna grabbed the singer's hand and started trotting toward the streetlight on the corner as if she'd never expected anything but cooperation.

Geneva, still singing but with a softer, almost lullaby sound, trotted obediently along, trusting Anna not to run her off a cliff or slam her into a wall. Sammy was not so sanguine. He darted around to get ahead of his mistress, woofed to let her know he was there, and then ran slightly ahead of them to make sure there were no incidents on his watch.

Behind them, somebody shouted; then came the thuds of sneakers pounding the sidewalk as the rest of the boys caught up. Or readied to run them down. Either way, Anna was neither slowing nor looking back.

When they reached the corner, the sidewalk was empty, but for the boys who'd chased Dougie. The two of them were standing half a block down, staring at a door in a wall of cinder block, the side of a four-story windowless structure used for storage or parking. Beside the smaller entrance was a closed steel garage

door out of sync with the rest of the wall, clearly an
addition in the last few years.

Anna slowed to a walk, and she and Geneva headed
toward the boys. The runners passed them in a cannon-
ade of rubber soles on pavement. For now, at least, the
target had been moved from Anna's and Geneva's backs
to that of Dougie. Before it could switch back, Anna
hailed the one cab rolling down the street and, when it
stopped at the curb, helped Geneva in. "Wait for me,"
she instructed the driver. "I just need to pay these kids."

Feeling that she had, if not backup, at least an escape route and a witness, she walked to where all five
boys had clustered, staring at a door that was painted
the same color as the wall and looked as if it had been
built to withstand battering rams.

"Dude went in here," the first boy to run after Dougie told her. "Door's locked." He pounded on it.

"What's this building?" Anna asked.

"Where's my money?"

Anna took out her wallet and removed the bills from
it, then slipped it back into the front pocket of her
pants. Holding the money, she said, "Warehouse? Or
what do they do here?"

"I want my hundred bucks," the kid said belliger-
ently, and Anna realized that the magic of gospel songs
and pedophiles was rapidly wearing off and that the
kid probably had no idea what the building was and
was damned if he was going to admit it.

"Twenty, twenty-five, thirty." Anna started counting

the bills into his outstretched hand, peeling them off slowly, making the count laborious. The quasi-leader of the gang snatched the cash roughly from her hand.

"We'll take it all."

"Suit yourself," Anna said and sprinted for the waiting cab. She hoped to be well away before they got around to counting it. At a guess, there was no more than fifty or sixty dollars. She hadn't meant to cheat them; she'd just said the first number that came into her head.

When the cab let them out in front of Geneva's home on Ursulines, Jordan was waiting for them, pacing the sidewalk, smoking a cigarette.

"I phoned," he accused Anna. "Where the fuck have you been? I must have called sixteen times."

"Sorry," Anna said evenly. She seldom turned her cell phone on, certainly not when she was trying to get work done. Old habits die hard, and she hadn't been in any mood to hurry this one to its death. It was not necessary that she be available to everyone all the time. Answering the phone at the ranger station had been a pain in the ass. Carrying one around to be answered in every conceivable circumstance was odious.

"Jesus fucking—"

"Good evening, Jordan," Geneva said pointedly.

"Yeah. Right. Open the fu— open the gate, Anna. We got something we got to do." Leaning down, he snatched up a plastic bag from the shadow of the wall and entrance.

There was no trace of Clare. Not deep in the sunken eyes, not in the knife-thin lips clamping on a smoke and a curse, not in the bowed shoulders, not in the ruined English of the streets.

Anna turned her back to unlock the gate, wondering if Clare was still in there at all, or if she'd killed herself in one way or another.

As soon as the gate swung open, Jordan pushed through, his shoulder bumping Anna's rudely. She held the gate till Geneva was in, then closed and locked it. "Get a move on," Jordan growled over his shoulder.

"Thank you for a lovely evening," Geneva said dryly as she passed Jordan's door, open now and spilling out light. Anna stepped into the small apartment.

Jordan closed the door with a kick, dumped his plastic bag beside the computer, and vanished into the bedroom.

Anna heard the toilet flushing. Mackie, unsure why his mistress had ignored him, stood in the doorway between the two rooms looking first at the bath, then at Anna, as if waiting for an explanation.

Tired from walking on unnatural surfaces for the past five hours, Anna dropped into the chair in front of the computer. Mackie trotted over, and she scratched his ears. At times like these she envied her fur-bearing friends. It would be so good to eat and sleep and live without complications.

Jordan reappeared, zipping his fly. "Put on the clothes in the bag," he said. "We've got to check out a place called Bonne Chance. It's a members-only sex club a hooker told me about. Membership can be bought at the door, but they don't like guys showing up stag."

"It's nearly midnight," Anna said. "Won't they be closed?"

He shot her a look of such scorn she worried Clare would never survive this night.

"Right," she said. "Party's just beginning."

"There're a dress and shoes in the bag. Put them on. Looking like you do will get us noticed. I'm thinking the old hippie thing won't play at a place like the Bonne Chance." He turned back into the bedroom, crossed to the bit of mirror above the battered bureau, and ran a comb through his hair. Then he did something that Anna found too creepy for words. He rubbed his fingers along the edge of his jaw as if testing to see if his beard had grown out enough that he needed a shave.

She glanced down at her baggy drawers, her cinnamon-and-pepper braid falling across her old shirt like a harbinger of age on Pippi Longstocking. She made no move to do as he asked; instead she said sharply, "Clare!" For a long enough moment that she began to worry, Jordan didn't respond. Finally he turned from his self-inspection and looked at her.

"Clare Sullivan?" Anna pressed.

Jordan shook himself the way a horse will when the flies are biting. "Yes," came Clare's whisper.

Anna told her about the boy thugs, the warehouse, the studio of the long-gone opera singer, Dougie, and the locked metal door.

Clare didn't move throughout the recital but remained standing in the middle of the bedroom, listening through the open doorway. Mackie, sensing perhaps that his mistress had returned in some indefinable way, trotted over and was sitting, his tail sweeping an arc in the dust on the floorboards, his eyes on her face. Even the dog couldn't reach Clare tonight.

"No perfume of flowers? No strange hissing drop sound?" Clare asked when Anna'd finished. "Just Dougie and a door?"

"And the apartment where an opera singer practiced when Candy was at the fancy house." Then Anna remembered the newer garage door cut into the side of the building. Construction. "The hissing thud could have been the sound of a nail gun," Anna said with sudden certainty. "They were doing construction near where Candy was kept."

"This is post-Katrina New Orleans. Everybody's doing construction," Clare said. "You've got nothing. A door. A creep." Anna watched Clare sink into the dark pools of Jordan's eyes, like the fading smudge of white as an undertow sucks a swimmer into the deep water.

Clare no longer had the strength to so much as remain on her feet without Jordan. Even with his fury and insolence, Anna doubted either of them had much more time. Anna'd yet to see Clare or Jordan eat. They lived on smoke and disappearing dreams.

"Change," Jordan snapped.

Anna stripped off her limp trousers and shirt. "Old hippie, my ass," she grumbled as she picked up the plastic sack from the table and upended it. A dress with straps and spangles and very little else was tangled up with a pair of red high-heeled shoes comprised mostly of more straps.

"Is this all?" she asked, somewhat dismayed.

"It's about sex, not coverage." The sound of a match striking brought Anna's attention back to Clare. Not Clare, Jordan. He was lighting up and looking at her in her underpants and little muscle shirt as if he were precisely as male and immoral as Clare had designed him to be.

Refusing to be intimidated, she peeled off the tank top and, wearing nothing but panties covering too much to be considered fashionable, stepped into the abbreviated dress.

"Is this yours?" she asked, threading the strappy top over her arms and arranging it so she was not visibly hanging out anywhere. "I mean, where did you get a dress and shoes in the middle of the night?"

"Delilah gave me the dress. The heels are Star's. Her feet are smaller. I figured they'd fit you better."

He was staring at her with enough heat in his eyes to convince the most discerning audience member that he harbored a Y chromosome.

"Would you stop pumping imaginary testosterone for a minute?" Anna snapped irritably. "I feel enough of a fool without a fake Lothario ogling me with fake lust. Save it for the matinee crowd."

"Hurry it up," Jordan said. "I'll wait outside. Do something with your hair. You look like a mountain woman after a bad couple of winters." He left. Mackie followed close on his heels, looking frightened and emitting low whining sounds.

Finding the insult amusing, Anna finished buckling on the high-heeled sandals, then went to find the mirror and comb he'd been using. The shoes couldn't be called comfortable by any stretch of the imagination, but they fit well enough. Once she suppressed the irritation at being crippled by fashion, she managed to walk with a modicum of grace. The braid she undid and combed out with her fingers. She'd done it up wet, and it fell in a silver and red rippling cascade.

It might have been sexy and it might have been Bride of Frankenstein, but that was as good as it was going to get. Wishing she had a purse for her key and cell phone, she palmed them and joined Jordan on the narrow walk.

"In low light you don't look half bad," he said.

"Thank you," Anna said dryly. Handing her cell and keys to him, she said, "Carry these, would you? Men think women have penis envy. Not so. We have pocket envy."

He stowed them in the pocket of his pants. "Come on, Mackie. Inside."

The little dog, usually friendly and obedient, was so anxious Anna could see the whites of his eyes gleaming around the brown irises as he skittered sideways and, tail down, ran away from Jordan's reaching hands.

"Come on, guy." A touch of Clare's sweetness softened Jordan's voice, but the dog wouldn't come. Jordan straightened up. "He'll be okay in the yard. Let's beat it."

Anna didn't argue. The yard was dog-proof and the

night cool and pleasant. There was even drinking water if Mackie didn't mind turtles swimming in it.

Jordan preceded her down the narrow overgrown walk and, with a rusty clanking, unlocked the gate. "Goddamn it!" he hissed as Mackie darted past Anna, between his feet, and out into the street. He made a grab for the animal, but Mackie was having none of it. He looked as if it pained him to run and disobey, and the angrier Jordan got, the more tragic the little dog's face, but he wouldn't be caught, and he wouldn't go back into the safety of the yard.

"So be it," Jordan snarled. "You're on your own."

Anna could tell Mackie was not going to give in, not for Jordan and not for her.

They walked down Ursulines toward Rampart looking for a cab. Mackie followed, but never close enough to risk capture. Anna wondered if he sensed danger or the nearness of his children or the pain of Clare hidden beneath the carapace of Jordan or if he was simply scared and didn't want to be left alone. "Phone," she demanded of Jordan.

"What—"

"Just give me the damn phone," Anna said exasperatedly. She punched the speed dial. Geneva answered, hoarse and cranky with sleep. Anna told her about Mackie, and the crankiness vanished.

"I'll try and get him," Geneva promised.

Past Dauphine, Jordan flagged down a cab. He didn't hold the door open for Anna, and she didn't expect him to. "Where to?" the driver asked.

Jordan told him.

If he knew it was a sex club, he didn't make any of the cracks.

"That your dog?" he asked after they'd driven half a block.

Anna turned in the seat, aware that her dress hiked up nearly to her crotch when she did, and looked out the back window. Mackie was chasing the taxi.

Anna started to tell the cabbie to stop. "No!" Jordan barked. He grabbed her wrist hard and muttered, "He'll go home on his own."

But he didn't. Stop signs at most corners in the residential area kept the cab from getting up any serious speed, and, whenever Anna turned, the dog was determinedly running after the car, sometimes a block behind, sometimes two. Finally they lost him.

Minutes afterward the driver stopped on a street that looked more industrial than anything else, the buildings high and without redeeming features.

"There." The driver pointed to a nice-looking young man sitting on a tall stool in front of a nondescript door into a windowless wall. The door was open, and faint light shone onto the sidewalk. There was no sign reading BONNE CHANCE, just the number 69 in silver on the side of the building.

Jordan paid the driver. Anna stepped out of the cab, flashing more leg than she was accustomed to, and oriented herself with difficulty. Spending the short ride looking over her shoulder worrying about a Lhasa apso, she'd lost her sense of direction.

"I think this is the front of the back where Geneva and I were," she said as Jordan came to the sidewalk.

"You're kidding!" For the first time that evening he sounded like a person who might not bite the heads off kittens if given the chance.

"No. I'm pretty sure the next street up is Rampart. This was the building."

"Kneepads said this club is legal," Jordan said. "Private clubs can do anything they want as long as the 'members' are over twenty-one and willing. What she gave me was rumors of other services to be had. Dougie, a sex club, and an opera studio. Gotta be something," he said with a cruel twist of his lips that Anna realized was his happy face.

"Welcome to Bonne Chance," said the young man on the stool. "Are you members of the club?"

Jordan stepped to the doorway. "We'd like to be," he said.

"Onetime memberships are very popular here at Bonne Chance," the man said smoothly. "But you'll want to come back, I can guarantee it. Right in there, and Jennifer will take care of your memberships." He smiled a lovely toothpaste-ad smile, beaming on them both equally. "I'll bet that dress comes off as easily as it looks like it will," he said politely to Anna, letting her know she was desirable, if old enough to be his mother.

"It's the shoes I want off," she told him as they entered the building.

THIRTY-FIVE

Inside the door was a small room with a ficus tree, a framed poster of New Orleans by night, and a reception desk. Behind it sat a lovely and exceedingly busty young woman in a low-cut but tasteful dress.

The desk had a green blotter, local brochures, a small potted African violet, pens, and a pile of papers. In short, it looked like any reception desk in any business anywhere. Anna didn't know what she'd been expecting, but this wasn't it.

"Welcome to Bonne Chance. My name is Jennifer," the woman said with what looked to be a genuine delight in seeing them.

"This is their first visit," said the young man from the stool. "They'll need a onetime membership."

He went back outside, and Jennifer set about the simple but expensive process of providing them with official access to whatever lay within. Jordan paid out another two hundred dollars; Jennifer put it in a cash box, then stood and, still smiling, said, "Right this way."

They followed her three steps to the door leading into the building, where she knocked gently.

"Whoa, little fella! Where do you think you're going?" This shout, followed by a scuffle of footfalls, came just as the door to the inner sanctum began to open and Mackie, tongue lolling, eyes wild, dashed in from the street. Before the agile young man could catch him, Anna scooped him up.

"No dogs allowed here, ma'am," Jennifer said politely.

"Mack's a therapy dog," Anna said, holding him more firmly. "He warns us when my husband is going to have an epileptic seizure."

Jordan trumped her appeal to the goodness of their hearts—or their naïveté—and pulled out his wallet. Without preamble he yet again pulled out two more one-hundred-dollar bills and handed one each to Jennifer and the stool man.

Jennifer hesitated a moment. The man said, "Whatever floats your boat," and retreated to his post outside. A third person, the guard of the inner sanctum, stood in the open doorway to the club. Jordan plucked a third bill from his wallet and gave it to him. "Long as the dog's over twenty-one," the man said with a wink. Absolved of responsibility, Jennifer poked the bill into the front of her dress and resumed her seat. Jordan, Anna, and Mackie were ushered inside.

The place was no different from many watering holes, though the décor left something to be desired.

They were in a large room crowded with patrons, a bar
at one end, a small dance floor, and a scattering of
tables with candles and couples. Music was piped in and
played loudly enough to make conversation difficult.
Corners and ceiling were lost in darkness.

"Is this your first visit to our club?" the doorman
asked. Anna looked at him seriously for the first time,
the drama of dogs and bribery having distracted her
when he'd appeared on the scene. Like the two young
people in the outer area, he was well dressed and good
looking and spoke with respect tinged with appreciation
for Anna's form and figure. It was flattering. It was also,
undoubtedly, company policy. It was uphill work to feel
sexy and gay if one was made to feel ugly and unwanted.
The Chance employees were so adroit at the subtle
compliment—one that didn't exclude either sex—that
Anna wondered what sort of training they went through.
Whatever it was, it had to be more interesting than the
annual forty-hour refresher courses law enforcement
rangers had to endure.

"First time here," Jordan said.

"Welcome."

So many charming people smiling and compliment-
ing and seducing her—even for a price—made Anna
feel rather like a blood donor at a vampire reunion.

"My name's Jason." Another lovely smile and appreciative look at Anna's cleavage. The effect was somewhat spoiled by the fact that her décolletage was covered
by a panting dog with black hair and white roots.

"Bar and dancing, as you see." Jason waved an arm to take in the room. "Upstairs is where the magic happens." He led the way to an elevator—not a bank of modern elevators but a single elevator old enough to have carried Otis himself, in a corner of the room so dark Anna had to gauge when the doors opened by the slight *thunk* heard through the blare of the bar.

The four of them crowded in, and the door slid shut. The ensuing silence lowered Anna's blood pressure a few points. "We have some house rules," Jason said. "Ask before you touch; no means no; and have fun."

The same rules as in kindergarten.

"Take off your belt," Anna told Jordan.

"That's the spirit!" said their guide.

Jordan did as he was asked, and Anna threaded Mackie's collar through the buckle and snapped the collar back around the dog's neck. That done, she lowered him to the floor, where he sat obediently on his new leash.

The elevator door opened.

The second—or was it third?—floor of the club was a different world from the noisy modernism below. They stepped out into what appeared to be a Victorian library. The ceilings were high and the walls lined with books. Though looking old and important, they were probably bought by the yard for decoration; still, Anna had the untimely desire to read the spines. She quashed it.

Arranged in the center of the room were two oversized leather chairs and a couch forming a conversation area. Tall lamps in faux alabaster—or, given the price of admission, real alabaster—lent the room a romantic glow. Potted plants that had to be silk or plastic, considering there were no windows, suggested a tropical feel appropriate to New Orleans. A fireplace with a fern in it finished the illusion. Double doors opened off one corner, and the dark maw of a hallway gaped in another.

Three couples sat on the couch and chairs. One was kissing deeply, the man's hand on his partner's breast. Two women, dressed in dominatrix leathers, boots, and bustiers, chatted together.

Anna, holding on to Mackie's leash as if, like Sammy, he were a guide dog and could hold her to a moral compass, passed them and was startled by a scrap of overheard conversation.

"So I dropped the kids off at piano lessons—you know, that new woman from the gym—and I see the perfect claw-foot tub for the guest bath. Perfect!"

The ordinariness of it was surreal, chitchat in Hades. Perhaps they were longtime members and the shocking had grown sufficiently mundane that home redecoration trumped wild orgiastic sex with strangers.

The third couple had gotten more into the swing of things. The woman, her skirt pulled up and her blouse unbuttoned, straddled the man's lap, rocking gently, while he sucked her. Two men, apparently without partners—or maybe the husbands of the dominatrices discussing porcelain finishes—watched the copulating couple with mild interest. Both were sipping drinks.

Jordan tapped Anna on the shoulder, and she flinched.

Being touched in this environment gave her the same willies as being offered food from dirty plates. "Nothing here," he said and jerked his chin toward the doors in the corner of this weird universe.

Anna went first, Mackie sticking so close to her heels that she bumped him when she walked.

The attached room was set up as a theater. A full-sized screen was on the far wall, and sumptuous leather couches formed three arced rows in front of it. Maybe the club preferred leather because it could be wiped clean of effluvia. The only light came from the screen. Several couples lolled and watched the porn, but there was little interest or action. Undoubtedly voyeurs didn't come to the Chance to watch what they could get on their computers at home.

"Not promising," Anna whispered and wondered what would be promising. A room full of toys and dolls? The sound of little feet scampering between sexual athletes? Surely that sort of thing would not be in the open. The women in the library might like leather and whips and home décor, but Anna guessed they would go ballistic if they saw little girls being abused.

Closing her eyes against the actors going through the motions with disquietingly bored expressions on their faces, Anna called up images of the back of the building where the boys had chased Dougie. If Dougie's door and that of the Chance shared the same structure, the building was a block deep and comparatively narrow. It was possible Dougie worked at the Bonne Chance as a bouncer or bartender—or whatever else perverts do as a day job. From what she'd seen of the club employees, Dougie wouldn't have a front job. He was too uncouth. There didn't seem to be a kitchen on the premises, so cook and dishwasher were out. That left cleaning or stocking liquor for the bar. There would be other jobs in an establishment this large, but Anna didn't picture the yellow jacket in management or laundry. The thought triggered a memory, Candy's *pssst-chunk*. Could it have been industrial steam irons ironing the many sheets a place like this might go through in a day? She shelved the thought for later.

Taking Jordan's hand, she pulled him close. Their noses inches apart, she whispered, "Let's take a walk into the bowels; see how deep the club goes, if there's another building behind it, or if it runs the length of the block."

Jordan nodded. "You want I should take the dog for a while?"

"No." Anna wanted the dog as close as possible. Mackie's innocence and loyalty were her talismans against the curse of finding herself totally disgusted with the race to which she nominally belonged.

They traversed the library toward the dark opening to what they assumed was the rest of the club. The fornicating couple had reached the moaning stage, and their observers, the drooling stage. One dominatrix was gone. Now that Anna thought of it, they might share decorating tips, or which whips were the best, but, given their proclivities, it would be tough for them to work or play well together.

The remaining dominatrix was allowing a woman, who hadn't been in the room earlier, to kneel in front of her and respectfully stroke her inner thighs.

Reminding herself it was okay to look, that they were doing it in public for a reason, Anna quelled the unpleasant feeling one gets when a guest fails to lock the bathroom door and sidled past to the dark doorway.

It opened into a hall. Walls, ceiling, and floor were painted black. Down the middle of this fun-house darkness ran a skinny carpet in harlequin black and white. To the left were half a dozen or more doorways obscured, or partially obscured, by heavy red drapes. Between each pair of the curtained entrances was a wall sconce. The bulbs in the shape of the Statue of Liberty's torch emitted enough light to pick up the crimson highlights and make the white squares on the carpet shine. The glow was pronounced enough that they might have been black lights.

The carpet was thick, and she and Jordan made no noise despite Anna's stiletto heels. The curtained rooms were mere alcoves, large enough to hold a double mattress covered in a white sheet. Several of the curtains were closed for privacy, but a majority were completely or partially open. The insides of the cubicles were lit with smaller wall sconces in the shape of seashells and giving off a flattering peach-colored light.

Anything flattering was a boon. Most of the patrons of the Bonne Chance weren't the sort of people one would cross the street to see naked. At a guess, the average age was mid-forties to mid-fifties, with a spackling of thirtysomethings. Anna saw no one who looked to be in his or her twenties. Body types were the kind filling the streets and malls on any given day: a lot of plump, a lot of bald, and a lot of gravity dragging things from pert to ponderous.

Mardi Gras was over and Jazz Fest yet to come, so the city wasn't as crowded with tourists as it sometimes was, but still the club was doing a good business. Passing the alcoves, Anna grew tired of views of a personal nature, but there was no relief to the other side.

There a doorway opened onto a room with salmon-colored lockers floor to ceiling, the kind one might find in old high schools. In the middle was a swing made of straps of leather woven into a seat and affixed to a chain hanging from the ceiling. A long black cord hung down next to it with a black box the size of a paperback book at its end. In the middle of the box was a toggle switch.

"If that's not for adjusting the height, I don't even want to know what it does," Anna whispered as they stopped. Jordan grunted. Mackie whined. Anna picked him up. She didn't want him to get anything on his paws, then lick them.

Beyond the swing were three doorways, one to the left and two, side by side, directly in front of them. Those were closed; Anna couldn't see what lay beyond the other.

"This way?" Anna asked.

"We'll come back if we have to," Jordan said and walked away. With the dog and Star's fancy shoes,

Anna had to hurry to catch up. She didn't relish being left alone. It wasn't fear, exactly. Except for being in various states of undress and/or masks and costumes and having public sex in groups, the people seemed well behaved and ordinary. There wasn't any doubt in her mind that the nice young people downstairs would let her out should she wish, nor did she really think she would catch some icky disease from the air. Mostly she felt like a stranger in a strange land, a fish out of water, a bull in a china shop, a rube in the big city, a park ranger in a sex club. It made her want to stay with her own kind, even if that kind happened to be a dog and a woman whose personality had been co-opted by an imaginary gutter punk.

She caught up with Jordan and fell into step beside him.

Beyond the locker-room-cum-swing-set were two rooms, each easily twenty by thirty feet and each paved in one gigantic mattress. Viewing windows were set into the walls so those in the hall might watch the events. Inside, groups and couples squirmed about amid cast-off bits of clothing, some hardy souls moving from group to group in hopes of joining in.

Past what, for lack of a better term, Anna mentally dubbed the orgy rooms were four more curtained cubicles, then a dead end. A wall of brick, painted flat black, ascended into the gloom.

"Shit," Jordan said. He balled his fists and uttered a low feral growl as if about to physically attack the brick and mortar.

Anna grabbed his arm, jockeying Mackie aside to do it. "We've got a few more places to look—the doors leading out of the locker room. We do that, if there's nothing, we go to plan B." Whatever that was.

For a minute she didn't think Jordan could hear her past the white-hot noise in his brain, and she braced to make a run for freedom with the dog if he snapped and brought the Chance's muscle down on them. His fists stayed white-knuckled, but he nodded, a sharp jerking down of the chin. When Anna started back past the orgy rooms and the fornication alcoves, he followed stiffly, moving as if the heat of his anger had partially welded his joints.

Clothes might not make the man, but they could certainly unmake him or, in this case, her. In the strappy high heels, no good for running or kicking, the dress built only to fall off at the least provocation, and the cascade of hair just begging to be grabbed by others or blind its wearer, Anna felt more helpless than had she gotten in the party mood and gone naked. It was no wonder women did a fairly rotten job of defending themselves. Not only were they smaller and less muscular by design, but they were willing collaborators in the bondage of fashion. Anna longed for boots and jeans and a good solid shirt: armor against the world.

The leather swing was now occupied by an ample woman in a cat mask and green high-tops being serviced by a geeky bald man in thick glasses.

Murmuring, "Excuse me, pardon us," Anna squeezed between them and the lockers to reach the far doors.

"Cute dog!" said the cat mask.

"Thank you," Anna said politely and pushed on. With nothing between people but air, good manners seemed a necessity.

The archway they'd noted to the right of the two doors opened into a smallish room that had been convincingly transformed into a medieval torture chamber. The walls were of stone the color of a stormy sky. Iron rings and belt restraints and chains were affixed to them. Opposite the archway was a rack the Catholic Inquisition would have been proud to own. Shackled to the rack was a naked man, a little fleshy around the belly but not too ugly by modern standards. The missing dominatrix was running her long acrylic fingernails down the side of his chest, leaving welts, but no blood, as he groaned with . . . pleasure? Pain? Whatever.

As Anna and Jordan entered, the man opened eyes bleary and bloodshot with sex or booze. "Cute dog," he said.

This time Anna didn't thank him. Backing into Jordan, the heel of her stiletto grinding into something softer than the floor, she turned to the other doors.

"They're locked," the naked, shackled masochist called helpfully.

Beside each was a keypad for the code.

Anna and Jordan stared at them as if they would tell them something, then, simultaneously, turned away, squeezed back around baldy and the cat-woman, and retreated to the far side of the hallway. Ducking into an unoccupied fornication alcove, Anna waited till Jordan joined her, then pulled the heavy drape closed.

Jordan dropped onto the edge of the low mattress, his knees up around his ears and his face in his hands. "What now?" he said.

"We wait and watch," Anna replied. The dog struggled, and she set him on the mattress next to his master/mistress. "Don't let Mackie lick up anything, okay?"

THIRTY-SIX

Anna took the first watch, squatting on the edge of the mattress, wishing her dress covered more of her behind, keeping an eye on the doors adjacent to the torture chamber. Couples came and went in the swing. Clothes became scarcer as the night wore on. Groups became more common. The level of hilarity rose with the blood alcohol content.

The doors with the electronic combination locks stayed closed.

Every twenty minutes she and Jordan switched off, more to have something to do than because they needed to stay alert for this particular assignment. Though there had been long hours and less sleep—at least on Jordan's part—than was ideal, neither of them felt any inclination to rest.

Several times revelers wanted to "join their party," and several times they were invited to join others. As far as Anna was concerned, these were not temptations but interruptions.

Finally, near three in the morning, the door nearest
the torture chamber opened. Jordan was on watch and
hissed at Anna to join him. A woman squeezed through
the door and closed it carefully behind her. She was
dressed in an ankle-length gray dress of muslin or linen
and wearing black boots. The dress's neckline was high
and finished in a Peter Pan collar. The sleeves came
down to her knuckles. Her hair was pulled back into a
neat bun. Juxtaposed with the rest of the denizens of the
Chance, she looked like a nun

The gray sister didn't come any farther into the club
than necessary but turned immediately to the second
door, punched in the code, and slipped through, disappearing from sight.

"What do you suppose that was about?" Jordan asked
when they'd returned to their alcove.

"The outfit?"

"The whole thing."

Anna didn't know. Shoulder to shoulder with him on
the mattress, she mulled the uneventful arrival and departure over in her tired mind. "The clothes—could be
the governess Candy described. Remember? A lady
that didn't get pretty clothes?"

"Could be," Jordan said.

No, Anna thought. It was Clare, or partly Clare. A
hysterical edge was cutting through Jordan's armor.
Mackie whined and rose from where he'd lain collapsed
for the better part of the night to walk over and drop his
chin on his mistress's knee.

They sat like that, man/woman, woman and dog,

until the second of the two locked doors opened and the governess reappeared, this time with an armload of paper towels. Juggling the loose rolls, she began punching numbers into the keypad by the door from which she had first emerged.

Before Anna could make any decisions, Jordan was on his feet, Mackie spilling unceremoniously onto the floor, and through the locker room. Scrambling up as quickly as she could in four-inch heels, Anna followed, afraid he—or Clare—was about to get them thrown out, if not arrested.

It was Clare, she was sure; Jordan wasn't as good an actor as his hostess. "Allow me," Anna heard Clare murmur with just a trace of highly educated drawl in her voice. "Looks like you've got yourself an armful." Such was the graciousness the actor had pulled around her, Anna would have sworn the chosen costume of Jordan became quite debonair, a kind oilman from central Texas out of his league in Sin City.

Anna hung back, poised uncomfortably between a very large, very naked woman in the leather swing and the grunting little man, naked but for a porkpie hat, between her ample thighs. The lady in the swing opened her eyes, cupped a breast in one hand, and, offering it to Anna, said, "Care to join in?"

"No thanks," Anna said distractedly. "I've already eaten."

Smiling, laden with paper towel rolls, the governess was thanking Jordan and backing awkwardly through the door he held for her. Then she was gone, and Jordan

still had the toe of his shoe between door and jamb. He jerked his chin at Anna, and, before she had a chance to weigh in on the advisability of rushing unarmed and ignorant into a black stairwell leading to Dougie's lair, he was gone as well, and the door was swinging shut. Running, she grabbed it and slipped through, Mackie, dragging Jordan's belt, at her heels.

After the strange dark opulence of the sex club, the utter utility of the stairwell had the effect of a cool breeze on a hot day. The single most stultifying thing about the club had been its sheer banality. The desultory sexual gluttony had had about it a tedium that made the revelers—if such they could be called—seem to be merely naked people so weighed down with ennui that even the forbidden was a chore.

The metal and concrete of industrial stairs, with work lights in metal cages, seemed positively life-affirming in contrast. Anna breathed deeply, but she didn't move. Jordan, despite his rush in, was still as well. Metal treads were wonderful instruments for making noise. Both in leather-soled shoes, and Anna in heels, the timpani of their descent would have alerted the governess.

Jordan picked up Mackie, lest his claws clack on the tread, and they waited until they heard the door at the bottom open and shut. Then they waited another minute to make sure the governess had cleared the area—in hopes the governess had cleared the area.

Jordan, still holding the dog, started to descend.

"Shoes," Anna said. Both removed their shoes. For Anna it was a blessing as well as a precaution. She didn't

bother to try to talk Jordan—or Clare, or whoever was driving the exhausted malnourished body at the moment—into waiting to make this assault until they were better prepared. She wouldn't be heard, and she wasn't interested in wasting breath she might need in the near future.

In bare and stockinged feet they descended. There were no windows and no doors. The stairs ended less than a flight down at a plain gray metal door like that above. Jordan grabbed the knob as if he were about to storm whatever battlements lay beyond.

"Stop!" Anna murmured. His hand twitched and his shoulder muscles spasmed, but he managed to keep himself in check. "Let me," she suggested and shouldered by before he could change his mind and barge in.

As she turned the knob slowly, she heard him setting the dog down. "Not locked," she whispered and eased the door open a crack. Mackie put his nose to it and Anna her eye. What she could see of the room was clear of human occupants. Opening the door wider, she slipped in. Mack and Jordan followed. The door clicked closed behind them. Like those upstairs, it had a combination pad to one side. "Did it lock?" Anna demanded.

Jordan tried it. "Locked."

"Well, that's just peachy," Anna fumed and turned to look at the room they must now deal with. It was long and narrow. At one end were racks of clothing; at the other, mirrors and hat stands with a collection of top hats and cloth caps. All of it was for men, and all of it looked as if it had been fashionable in the Victorian era.

The hats were tall and flared slightly at the top, the coats and trousers and vests were dark and staid-looking, the white shirts had detached collars, and there was a rack of cravats by the mirrors with pins of various kinds in them.

"It's a theatrical dressing room," Clare said. Anna turned to look at her. It was definitely Clare. As uncanny as it was—or as canny an actor as Clare Sullivan was—it was as if she and Jordan were, in fact, two different individuals, and only a fool or a blind man would mistake one for the other.

"Storage room?" Anna asked. "Mardi Gras costumes? This is a big costume town."

"No. Nothing is protected, no plastic, no mothballs. These are being used. Look." Clare crossed to the dressing table and held up a brush with hairs in it. She opened the top drawer, and there were perhaps a dozen more brushes, each wrapped in plastic so the next user wouldn't have to worry about hygiene.

"The photograph," Anna remembered aloud.

"That's what I'm thinking," Clare said. "The man whose lap Candy was sitting on, the man who's now chief of police, was dressed in an outfit like these." Mackie had moved to the door in the far wall of the room and was sniffing at the frame. He scratched once, whined softly, and looked back over his furry shoulder at Clare.

The blood drained from her face so quickly she swayed and might have fallen had Anna not steadied her. "He smells the girls," Clare gasped. "I know it. He knows they're here." Yanking free of Anna's fingers, she started for the door. Anna wrapped her arms around the other woman's chest and arms.

Clare fought back, trying to kick Anna's legs or force her arms from around her. Lack of food and care had made her so weak that Anna found it no harder than holding a small child. "Stop it," Anna growled.

Clare landed a heel on Anna's instep, and Anna bit off a shriek, then sank her teeth into the other woman's shoulder. The pain got Clare's attention.

"We don't know what's out there," Anna said insistently into the ear that was closest. "We don't know what the dog smells. We'll do it, but let's do it right."

Since they'd gotten off on the wrong high-heel-shod foot, there really was no right way, but there had to be something righter than charging headlong through doors that could open onto any damn thing.

"If this is the fancy house—"

"It is!" snapped Clare, but she didn't start struggling again.

"Then it's going to have security. Men with guns. Bouncers, thugs. If the chief of police is involved, you can bet there's a few off-duty cops doing his dirty work for a cut of the money." Clare felt a bit more compliant, so Anna let her loose.

Clare didn't turn around. In a voice as flat and heavy as a manhole cover she said, "Go if you want. I'm not leaving." There was no doubt in Anna's mind what she meant. Clare would find her children or she would die, and it would be done tonight. Through the door they faced the proverbial lady or the tiger, and it didn't sound as if Clare even knew anymore which she preferred.

"The door locked behind us, so it looks like I'm staying," Anna said. "I'd rather like to survive this next bit, so can we do it my way? Slow, careful, with great stealth and cunning? Ready to run away should the situation call for it?"

Clare, evidently beyond speech, managed to nod her head, once up, once down, like a poorly lubricated robot.

Leaving the detested high heels on the floor of the dressing room, Anna slipped around Clare and the dog, turned this second knob silently, opened the door a crack, and looked out into an unpeopled hallway, dimly lit with wall sconces reminiscent of those in the Chance, with doors opening to either side. The walls were papered in flocked maroon on red, classic cartoon whore house. Given that cartoons had to be derived from something, perhaps it was authentic to the Victorian era.

Anna stepped through. Mackie started to dart ahead of her, and she stepped on the end of the belt-leash, jerking him to a halt. "Maybe we should leave the little guy here, in the dressing room," she suggested.

Clare took the makeshift leash from her fingers. "No. He smells his girls."

Anna let it go. In operations as ill begotten as this, having a fluffy little dog in the mix probably wouldn't alter the outcome.

Moving quickly, knowing Clare couldn't bear any

undue delay, Anna padded quietly to the first door, listened, opened a crack, and then looked inside. Clare did the same on the opposite side of the hall, only with less stealth. Fortunately the floor they were on was apparently deserted.

The first two rooms were dormitories, with small wooden bunk beds, eight to one room and six to the other. Each bed was neatly made. The bedspreads were all the same, but on the bunks were the things children loved: stuffed animals and dolls. A couple had picture books.

"Boys' dorm on the other side," said Clare. Clearly, little boys were of no interest to her at this juncture.

"Girls' here, I think," Anna said as she stepped into the room. The charm of the scatter of childhood paraphernalia lulled her. For a moment she dared hope there'd been a mix-up and the children Daoud Suliman transported illegally into the country were being adopted into good homes by a caring institution. Then she caught sight of one of the "children's" books on the nearest bed. It was hardcore child pornography.

A gift from an admirer.

A short, sharp intake of breath brought Anna's attention back to Clare. The woman's face was screwed up as if she might cry, but her mouth was held in a hard oval, lips pulled back freakishly from the teeth. It put Anna in mind of Edvard Munch's *The Scream*. It wasn't the crude picture that had undone her—Anna had seen photos as horrific on the walls of Clare's apartment—but that Clare now saw her daughters in the pose, in the beds, on the laps of the men who put on anachronistic suits for an age-old perversion.

Mack pulled loose from his mistress's nerveless fingers and trotted from bed to bed, finally stopping at one, reaching up the short ladder to the top bunk, and whining.

The Munch scream looked about to become audible.

Anna laid a hand on Clare's arm. "Let's go. The bunk is empty. It doesn't matter whether Mackie smells Dana or Vee or a Hostess Twinkie." Anna pulled Clare out of the dorm room, leaving Mack to come or not as his black button nose told him to. After another whine, he followed.

The next room looked to be the governess's quarters. There was a queen-sized bed, a television, an armoire, a full bath, and a walk-in closet. A pair of jeans, two tops, and a handful of scarves were scattered across the bed, shoes littered the floor, and the closet door stood open. Inside were the clothes one would expect to find in a thirtysomething's closet and two pegs with the dreary ankle-length gray gowns of the stereotypical nineteenth-century governess.

"Watch the door," Anna said and whipped the gossamer confection Star had kindly lent her over her head. The governess's dress fit well enough; the skirt was a bit long, but it would serve to hide Anna's bare feet. In the bathroom, she found the hairpins she knew would have to be there, given the no-nonsense bun the woman had worn. In less than a minute, she'd coiled her hair tight at the nape of her neck and secured it there.

Stepping out of the bathroom, she said, "I can't say that I feel less obvious, but I probably am. Go back and put on a costume jacket," she ordered Clare. "Maybe we'll get out of this in one piece after all." She said it to try to make the white around Clare's pupils shrink, to calm her enough that she wouldn't get them caught or killed. What she believed was that the protective coloration would probably only serve to get them deeper into the hornets' nest before they were found out.

Clare jogged back to the men's dressing room. Anna opened the next door. A large-bellied man, wearing vest, shirt, and cravat, a half-smoked cigar in his sausage-like fingers, was reclining on a fainting couch upholstered in green velvet. The walls picked up the green of the fabric and chased it through with turquoise and gold that complemented an ornate mirror above a cold fireplace and heavy drapes pulled over what Anna suspected was a blank wall.

The man wore no pants. A small African American boy, dressed in loincloth and turban, complete with jewel and feather at the brow, knelt between the barrel-sized thighs. Both looked up, startled, when Anna opened the door. The man blinked with slight annoyance. The child kowtowed, forehead to floor, rump in the air, as he had no doubt been taught to do when he was made a slave. The half-naked man put his foot to the boy's rump and pushed hard enough to knock him over. "Mind your master, boy," he said and winked at Anna as if she were in on the joke.

"Pardon me," Anna managed and closed the door

with difficulty. The hinges were oiled to the gliding point of silence, and the door moved easily. The difficulty was in turning her back on a child being abused when every instinct demanded she rush in swinging. If she and Clare were to find Clare's daughters, now was not the time to start the war.

"Fuck it," she said and jerked the door open again.

"What the hell?" the fat man growled, not amused to be caught with his pants down a second time.

"No smoking," Anna said. "Fire codes." She marched purposefully across the room and picked up the heavy glass ashtray he'd been using. Before he had time to think, she brought it down on his skull hard enough to kill him.

THIRTY-SEVEN

Clare could not control her brain as her body went through the familiar motions of donning yet another character. *Disassociation,* she thought as she watched her hands sort rapidly through the clothing racks, pull out jacket, shirt, and trousers, and then, like creatures from a horror movie, strip her of her garments and put on the others.

Not only did she feel her hands were alien, but she no longer inhabited her body. It was as if she watched it being dressed from a corner near the ceiling. Jordan had gone, and she stared down on Clare Sullivan, poor broken, hopeless, useless Clare. The bunks where Mackie thought Dana or Vee or Aisha might have slept should have given her strength, but they had destroyed the last of it. Her children had been tortured; that thought burned through mind and body in an acid tide. It was all she could do to focus on the body following the pigeon ranger's orders.

As she watched, Jordan's rich pervert was converted

to an Edwardian dandy, the illusion completed with the
speed of someone used to quick changes in the dark
backstage. The dandy moved through the door of the
dressing room, and Clare followed, floating, ghostly, as
the body that had once housed both her and Jordan
walked quickly down the hall. The clothes had changed
the stance, and the Edwardian gentleman moved with
grace, spine straight, shoulders back, a slight swing as
if he were accustomed to carrying a walking stick or
umbrella.

He stopped before an open door and looked in. With
nauseating familiarity Clare felt herself slamming back
into her corporeal form at the sight of a little boy, forehead to floor, hands outstretched before him, in front of
a half-naked man murdered on the sofa.

"Up you come," Ranger Pigeon said not unkindly
and lifted the boy by the arm. "What's your name?" she
asked.

Clare's mind scrabbled over mountains of emotion in
search of coherent thought. Part of her wanted to gather
up this child, protect him against all evil, hold him and
love him and, in him, all children. An equal part was
thinking coldly, *Not Dana, not Vee; dump the little bastard and get a move on.*

"Simba, milady," the boy told Anna Pigeon, not dar-
ing to raise his eyes from where they were fixed on the
carpet two inches from his toes.

"No. Your real name," Anna said. "Your before-here
name."

"We're wasting time," somebody said, and Clare

realized the words had come from her mouth. Anna shot her a look that should have shamed her, but she was beyond such paltry agonies.

For a moment the child looked dazed; then he said tentatively, "Tyrone?"

"You're working for me now, Tyrone," Anna said briskly. "Ten dollars an hour. Slavery is illegal in America."

"Yes, milady."

Clare knew the ranger liked to think the kid understood the dignity she afforded, but, more likely, he was accustomed to doing whatever any adult told him to, regardless of how perverse or painful.

Tyrone was so small Clare felt a distant ache from wherever her heart had gone. She looked away from him to the man on the fainting couch. A thin trickle of blood at the hairline above his right eye was the only sign of life in his ashen face.

"Did you kill him?" she heard her voice ask, not caring one way or another.

"We can always hope," Anna replied and, leading Tyrone by the hand, stepped into the hallway beside Clare, then closed the door on the unconscious pedophile.

The little boy began to look frightened, to realize this was not business as usual. Like the children wallpapering Clare's apartment, Tyrone was sufficiently well versed in the seamier side of life to be constantly looking for which way to jump to survive another day or two.

Clare turned and walked down the hall with the outward confidence of a man of means, at home in his own club. At least her body did. She had again vacated the premises and floated near the ceiling watching herself, the ranger, and the boy in the slave costume. *Disassociation;* the defense abused children learned, the ability to escape from the bodies where the abuse was taking place, to go elsewhere till the torture stopped.

Clare was running from the pain her children suffered. It was the basest form of cowardice. The shame the ranger had failed to engender when Clare wanted to abandon Tyrone flared hot in her throat. With an effort she pushed herself back into her body. As a young woman she'd played Peter Pan; she pictured herself stitching herself together as Peter had sewn on his truant shadow.

Stopping at the top of the stairs, she waited for Anna and Tyrone. Mackie sat at her heels, seeming to sense she had come back, and waited with her.

"How do you want to proceed?" Clare asked and was pleased at the sane voice she managed.

The pigeon looked surprised at the question. No doubt she had simply been planning to try to pick up the pieces of whatever Jordan smashed.

"Lay of the land," the pigeon said. Squatting till she was on eye level with the boy, she put her hands on his shoulders. The little fellow flinched, and the ranger dropped her hands to her sides. "Tyrone, what is at the bottom of the stairs? Can you describe what's down there?"

He looked ready to cry, or bolt, as if she had asked a

trick question and he would be punished if he came up with the wrong answer. Then he said, "Like rooms and stuff?"

"Smart boy," Anna said. "Exactly. Tell me about the rooms and stuff."

He squinched his eyes shut and screwed his mouth up with the effort of thinking. He couldn't be more than five or six. Clare wondered how many of those years he had spent servicing clients in the insane confines of Candy's "fancy house."

"There's a big room with a piano and places to sit and have beverages brought by the boys and sometimes the girls but they sing and do other stuff mostly."

"Beverages." The word struck an odd chord. Perhaps the children were taught to speak in a pseudo-antique language to heighten the illusion of a time and place where being a monster could be passed off as a genteel pastime.

"What else?" Anna asked. Her voice was gentler than Clare would have given her credit for being able to make it.

"Um . . ." Again the screwed-up face. "There's an outside. The courtyard. And there's a fountain and benches and the guests like to sit there and we do things for them. Or they talk to each other and smoke cigars and us boys fan them sometimes. Sometimes we do dances with the girls there."

"Is there a little girl named Vee or Dana?" Clare demanded.

Tyrone froze. The urgency in her tone had come

across as dangerous to his precarious safety. "I want to take them home," she said as reassuringly as she could over the thrum of desperation in her throat. "They're my daughters." As she spoke of her children a wave of dizziness hit her. Had she not caught hold of the banister she would have fallen. To speak of them here was to put them here.

Tyrone straightened his turban and petted the feather as if it were his friend. "I don't know," he said finally. He wanted to say yes, to say whatever it was she wanted him to say, but there was no Vee and no Dana. The dizziness turned into a wild spinning; tears came up in a flood, choking her.

"Hey!" the ranger snapped and, still crouching, punched Clare in the thigh. "The kids get new names. Tyrone-Simba, remember?"

The jab of pain slowed the merry-go-round. Clare nodded, not trusting herself to speak.

"Tyrone," Anna said, her full attention back on the child. "Are there any police down there? You know, men with guns who make sure everybody does what they're supposed to?"

"There's the gatekeepers?" He ended his sentence with a question so, should he be wrong, he would not cause offense. Clare's need to feel her teeth sinking into the throats of the people who dressed this baby in a slave costume and used him was sudden and narcotic. Guns, knives, clubs—none of that was personal enough; she lusted to tear them apart with her nails, hands, and teeth. Jordan's rage boiled up from her stomach. She didn't know if she could hold out against it; didn't know if she wanted to.

"How many gatekeepers?" Anna was asking, but Tyrone had done as much as he could. Eyes wide, mouth shut tight, he was—disassociating.

The pigeon reached over and unbuckled Mackie's collar. "Dog off leash will probably be the least of the laws we break tonight," she said. "Follow your nose, Mack," she said to the dog. "Find Dana. Find Vee."

Mackie stared at her, tongue lolling, tail whisking across the carpet. Then he turned and trotted down the staircase.

"Do you think he knows what I asked of him?" the ranger asked, oddly more herself in the governess's costume than in the cocktail dress of her own era.

"Does it matter?" Clare followed the dog. With a mad patter of bare feet, Tyrone zipped by, taking the next landing at a run and down out of their line of sight.

"Probably running to tell," the ranger said from closer behind Clare than she'd expected. "He guesses we'll do less damage to him for tattling than the powers here will for not tattling. If he's gone to tell his governess—kids are probably more connected to her than to security— she'll spot me as soon as she sees me. We need to split up. That way you might have a bit longer."

Another time, Clare might have felt the need to stay with, and try to protect, the woman helping her. Not now. She descended quickly to the main floor, leaving Anna to follow as she would.

The ground level was the lobby and had been outfit-

ted like a fine old hotel. The several rooms, separated by
wide gracious arches, were carpeted in green with a cab-
bage rose motif in pinks and burgundies. The walls were
decorated with mirrors in gilt frames. Potted palms created private nooks for overstuffed chairs. A fountain
sang gently, and beyond that, in front of French doors
opening onto the courtyard, was a baby grand piano.

Men and children were the only people to be seen.

Two men in flared top hats stood, one foot on a brass
rail, at a bar of dark wood. Behind it was a painting of
a reclining nude, the model no more than ten years old.
The bartender, obviously working on a raised platform,
was a little girl.

Clare's heart jerked like a landed fish, but the child
was several years older than Dana. Panic sickened her
as she wondered if she would know her own children.
These wore high complicated wigs or hairdos; their
faces were powdered till they were the color of pearls.
Pink lips were painted on in cupid bows, beauty marks
pasted on chins or cheeks, their fragile bodies deformed
by costumes. They were Hispanic, African American,
Mideastern, Indian, and Caucasian.

On a divan close to the stairs where Clare had frozen, a Latina child sat on the lap of a man in his forties,
playing with the paste jewel in his stickpin as he chatted
with another man of like age seated next to them. The
child wore the Victorian dress, full skirt and neckline
frothed with lace, but the neckline was cut to the level
of her sternum so her smooth chest and tiny nipples
peeked over the ruffle. The man holding her had one

hand up under her skirts. Another child, with soft brown curls piled on her head, clad in a velvet dress of midnight blue with white trim, walked by, concentrating hard to keep from spilling a drink she carried on a tray. The back of her gown and petticoats had been cut away so, as she passed, the naked little bottom and thighs above her black cotton stockings were exposed.

Clare managed the last two steps down. In front of the ornate curving staircase, she stood in a daze, turning. On a low, richly upholstered bench, two little girls in costume played quietly together with dolls dressed as they were. Waiting for customers.

Clare kept turning. Through the archway in the room behind the stairs another slave boy, this one Asian, tried to wield a peacock-feather fan. A trickle of blood ran down the back of his thigh, and tears ran silently down his face.

Clare turned. A girl in Bo Peep pink, a monkey doll held tight to her shoulder, was sitting on a table with her dress rucked up around her hips, being fed sips of champagne by a laughing man in shirtsleeves and vest.

And turned: Four girls sang and danced, *ring around the rosy, pocket full of posies, ashes, ashes, they all fall down,* the nursery rhyme from the plague years, when children died and their bodies were thrown onto burning piles because there were too many to bury.

And turning: A man carried a beautiful black child in his arms, nuzzling her soft face with his bearded chin, ascending the stairs.

Turning: Clare felt herself falling.

The boy, Tyrone, was pointing up the stairs, where Anna Pigeon was coming down. The governess was at his shoulder.

Clare staggered to the bench where the girls played with their dollies and slumped down as blackness closed around her.

From somewhere she heard Mackie crying.

THIRTY-EIGHT

Having counted one-Mississippi, two-Mississippi, all the way to twenty-Mississippi, Anna started down the stairway. Heroes in books and movies never counted one-Mississippi—at least not out loud—but Anna had learned that twenty seconds of waiting to do something stupid and dangerous was entirely different than twenty seconds to catch a bus. At a rough guess, about seventeen thousand times longer. More like holding one's breath underwater. She descended carefully, the long gray skirt held tightly in her fists so she wouldn't trip.

As she moved delicately down the carpeted steps, trying to look as if she belonged in a nineteenth-century gown in a nest of pedophiles, she brought to mind the photographs of Dana and Vee that Clare had shown her. Both had dark eyes and heart-shaped faces. The younger one—Vee—had lighter hair, cut shorter and with a touch of natural curl.

The faces would not come into focus. Young children—lucky young children—had yet to have identifying marks carved into their flesh in the form of scars, droops, and broken noses, lines carved by care, capillaries broken by sun and smoke, eyes dulled by disappointment. Other than to those who loved them dearly, one child could look pretty much like another of like age and coloring.

Anna resolved simply to whisper their names in the ears of any likely candidates. If they were here, they hadn't been prisoners long enough to have forgotten their birth names.

Unless they were so traumatized they'd forgotten everything.

Anna chose not to think about that.

Reaching the halfway point, where the stairs curved in a graceful sweep so that one might make an entrance in style, she stopped. The real governess, a grim look on her face, was staring up at her, following Tyrone's pointing finger.

Snatching her dress tail into a great wad, Anna fled back upstairs. The governess didn't cry out or otherwise disturb the clients but ran after her. Anna could hear her feet striking the carpet. The woman ran lightly and without effort—Anna was only a woman, after all, and the governess could see she was younger than her quarry and taller and outweighed her by fifteen pounds.

But I am old and mean and on the side of the angels, Anna thought as she turned the corner at the top of the stairs and grabbed up a waist-high porcelain vase filled with yellow silk gladiolas. Pressing her back against the wall, she held the narrow mouth of the vase so she could swing it like a baseball bat. She'd scarcely planted her feet when the governess, skirts whirling, rounded the corner into the second-floor hall. Anna swung hard.

The governess threw up an arm. The vase struck in a shower of silk blossoms. The governess grunted with the impact, but the power of the blow was deflected upward. Before Anna could pull it back to try for a more vulnerable area, the woman closed on her with the speed and confidence of an individual accustomed to physical violence. She didn't try to punch or pry the vase from Anna's hands; she just plowed in, her shoulder ramming Anna's chest. Air exploded from Anna's lungs, and for a terrifying moment she couldn't breathe. Whipping a forearm over Anna's windpipe, the governess leaned in with all her weight, her heels braced on the carpet, her face so close Anna could see the tiny hole in the woman's nostril where she wore a ring and smell the Juicy Fruit gum she'd been chewing.

Anna had done the very thing she'd scorned the governess for; she had underestimated her adversary. Without enough air to fill her burning lungs or fuel her scattering thoughts, Anna could black out. Once down, she would probably never get up again. She would be murdered in a reeking children's brothel by a twit half her age with a goddamn nose ring.

"Enough," Anna growled through clenched jaws and

narrowing windpipe. Walking her fingers, spiderlike, along the underside of the arm crushing her throat, she found the woman's hand. Then she found the web between thumb and forefinger.

Too busy killing her to bother noticing these tickles, the governess didn't even twitch her fingers out of Anna's way. Feeling for the soft spot where she'd learned the pain would be most intense, Anna pinched as hard as her failing consciousness allowed.

The woman grunted. The arm moved. Not much, but enough that Anna could suck in a lungful of air, the literal second wind. Using this newfound strength, she focused every erg of it on the tiny patch between her finger and her thumb. Pain compliance; when negotiations failed there was nothing like it.

Finally, screaming as much in anger as in pain, the governess backed off, her need to stop the pain overcoming logic. Anna squeezed harder, and she went down on one knee.

"Shut up," Anna said. She stepped behind the woman, dropped her hand, and locked her forearm across the governess's throat, pulling it tight with her opposite hand on the wrist. Twisting, the governess managed to get her chin into the crook of Anna's arm, but she'd stopped making noise.

All at once, she went limp, deadweight slumped forward. Anna hoped it was the sleeper hold and not a ruse. Her hopes were dashed in a swift hard shove. Staggering back, Anna caught her bare foot in the bottom of the dress, and the two of them fell to the carpet. The sleeper hold broke, and the governess shoved her fists between Anna's arm and her own throat.

Anna abandoned the hold for the tried and true fighting style of women and cats. Catfights were mocked in a man's world, but Anna had had too many cats not to give them the respect they were due. More than once she'd seen a six-pound tabby turn into a storm of claws and teeth that made grown men quail and large dogs flee the room.

With a low guttural cry, she sank her teeth into the first bare bit of flesh she found, an ear. She raked her nails where she could, pulled hair, slapped, and all the while growled low and fierce.

Under the insane onslaught, coming as it did from behind, the governess lost her will to stay in the clinch. Throwing herself forward, hampered by the yards of fabric that wadded up around them, she tried to crawl free.

A small bit of her ear remained between Anna's teeth. She spit it out. It was not something she would think about now. Or ever, for that matter. Struggling up from her knees, she hurled herself after the crawling woman. Now that the governess knew it wasn't a prank or a game, but in deadly earnest, she would run for security. Probably the only thing that kept her from shouting the house down was the ingrained need to keep things on a seemingly even keel for what had to be a skittish clientele. Politicians, moguls, movie directors, doctors, lawyers—all the bigwigs could recover from an affair made public. Many could recover from being indicted for fraud, tax evasion, drunk driving, and wife beating. Nobody recovered if the public got even a whiff of the kind of perversion Anna'd seen tonight.

The taste of blood in her mouth, Anna threw herself on the governess's back and grabbed the bun at the nape of her neck. Using it as a handle she smashed the other woman's head against the hardwood floor beside the carpet runner. And again. And again. Blood gushed from the governess's nose and lips. Anna banged her head down once more, and she went limp. This time she wasn't playing possum.

Exhausted, Anna let her weight fall on the inert form beneath her. The battle had lasted no more than sixty seconds, but she had not held back; there were no reserves, and her breath was coming in great gasps. It was probably that which saved the governess from being killed. Customarily, Anna didn't like killing, maiming, or even causing psychological pain to others. She much preferred life flow along in a peaceful vein with time for listening to the birds sing and watching cocoons open to butterflies, and butterflies as their newborn wings dried. Here in the "fancy house" she wanted to kill or, rather, was indifferent to whether she killed or not. The crimes were too heinous, the hope of rehabilitation too slim, the damage to the victims too great. Some evils deserved no second chances; they merely needed expunging.

Recovering, she rolled off the unconscious governess.

The woman smelled of sweat and expensive perfume. Now Anna smelled of it as well. Under other circumstances she might have liked the scent. From now on she would associate it with vile odiousness. With difficulty she found her feet in the morass of skirts and got up. Breathing returning to normal, she could hear again and listened to see if their tussle had set off any alarms. There was no yelling, no sound of running feet. From below came raucous laughter, the kind she associated with viciousness, but that might have just been her state of mind.

One floor up was a fat man with a headache or dead. At her feet was a bloody woman. If they lived, either of them, they would be recovering consciousness, hollering for help. She could kill them both and drag the bodies out of sight. That would give her and Clare more time to look for Dana and Vee, but Anna'd lost her killing rage. Necessary as it might be, she couldn't bring herself to put anyone to death at the moment.

Since she wasn't going to turn butcher any time soon, it behooved her to move. The time she and Clare had before they were found out was short. Given the secrecy, moneyed backing, and security of the operation—and that its managers had no qualms about murdering children when they were of no more use—Anna doubted house security would have any qualms about killing her and Clare. Nor would any of the patrons raise a finger to stop it or, once it was done, report it to law enforcement. Anna would simply go missing. Clare was already missing.

Paul would never know what happened to her.

Anna had never lost anyone close to her—some had died, but never had anyone gone missing. Reading the ordeals of parents with missing children or brothers and sisters who simply disappeared one day, she always thought that would be infinitely harder to cope with than death. The dreams alone would be devastating: the good dreams of finding the beloved, only to wake up to the truth and the nightmares of where they might be that one would never wake from.

She could call Paul. Then Paul would call in the cavalry. And what was the problem with that? The more the merrier, the bigger the guns the better; Clare had found what she was looking for, if not whom. The police would look at her differently because of it.

For a long and miserable second, Anna couldn't remember where she'd left her cell phone. Then it came back to her: She'd given it to Jordan to carry because there were no pockets in the dress Star lent her. Moving quickly, she frisked the governess. No cell, but a radio. Anna doubted it called out—or if it did it wouldn't be to anyone she could consider a friend. It would be for internal use.

Taking it with her, she ran to the next door and threw it open. A man was sitting splayfooted on the edge of a pouf. A tiny girl was stroking his cock and singing the alphabet song. Holding firmly to the doorjamb so she'd not strike the man down with the heaviest object she could find, Anna said, "Girl, come with me. Now!" The child turned at the sound of her voice, the dark brown eyes as lifeless as two buttons sewn onto a Raggedy Ann's face.

"What the hell are you thinking, coming in here like this?" Pants around his knees, abusing a little girl, the man had the gall to be affronted. Anna held more tightly to the jamb.

"Herpes," she said succinctly. "She's got it. Come." With those words, she stepped into the room, grabbed the child by the hand, and led her out. "I'll send you a clean one," she said over her shoulder. "Don't lose your place."

The door to the Chance had locked behind them. The only way out was through the courtyard Tyrone had mentioned, either through the parking garage or the port door. Between here and there would be whatever thugs the Chance paid for and a bunch of "good decent family men" who didn't need publicity.

Bridges burned, the only way was forward. Towing the child, Anna walked purposefully to the next room and snatched open the door. A naked boy about eight was bent over a bed. "Goddamn it!" Anna roared at a partially dressed man who shared the room. Then, "AIDS, that boy's infected." Before the man could react, Anna grabbed the dazed boy and left the room; two children now.

Their only chance was to create as much confusion as possible. In the next room she yelled, "Fire, evacuate!" The man snuggling with a tiny Hispanic girl dumped her from his lap and ran without a backward glance.

"Buddy system," Anna said to the three children,

wondering if they had ever heard of it, wondering if they spoke English. The naked boy evidently had. He took the little girl's hand. The four of them went on.

The next door Anna thrust open, she cried, "Police raid. Run!" The pedophile ran downstairs without pants or shoes, the white costume shirt flapping over his flabby buttocks. Two more children joined Anna's forces, twins, African American and no older than seven. The radio she'd shoved down the front of the gray dress began to bleat. "Paula, what the hell is going on?" came a man's voice from somewhere around her sternum. The bouncers or guards were beginning to notice that all was not right. Clients were streaming down with conflicting stories.

"Come on, kids. Let's run." Anna scooped up the nearest child and ran down the hall, her bare feet making no sound on the carpet. Every door they came to she threw open. The men she sent running. One of the children panicked and followed her abuser. One man, perhaps one rung higher on the evolutionary ladder than his cowardly fellows, carried the child he was molesting with him when Anna yelled, "Fire!"

After that she stuck to "Police raid."

The last door she pulled open was where she'd first begun. The fat man had come around and managed to pull on his trousers. Forgoing the fun of bashing him on the head again, she yelled, "Police raid! Run!"

He didn't run. He didn't even look particularly alarmed. "Who the fuck are you?" he demanded. He reached toward the hat stand where he'd draped his jacket and shirt. Behind the coat was a shoulder holster with the butt of an old-fashioned wheel gun sticking out of it.

It was then that Anna recognized him. He was the man in Candy's picture, the man who had gone on to become New Orleans's chief of police. He knew the police raid was a farce because he didn't call it. For a fat man he moved faster than a striking snake. The gun was in his hand before Anna could divest herself of the child she carried and pull shut the door.

"You," the chief snarled at one of the twins, "come over here. Now." Scared not to, the child ran to him. He grabbed her slender arm and moved the gun from Anna to the child's temple.

"Now," he said to Anna, "who the fuck are you?"

THIRTY NINE

Dropping her head between her knees, Clare forced the darkness to recede. Futilely she wished she'd smoked less and eaten and slept more. When she felt she could stand without passing out, she rose. The girls who were playing with their dolls on the bench when she collapsed had stopped their game and were staring at her. Here in the fancy house falling-down men were surely a greater danger than those who remained sober. The children hadn't run away. Probably because they would be punished if they did. So they waited for whatever horror might come to them and their dollies.

"It's okay," she managed with a shaky smile. "I won't hurt you."

The eyes got wider, the dollies clutched tighter. They'd heard that before, and it was never true. The only kindness Clare could offer was her absence. Before she left she asked, "Do you know any little girls named Dana or Vee?" and, as an afterthought, "Or Aisha?"

They shook their heads.

"Thank you," Clare said mechanically. Thinking was so hard. She wondered where Jordan was and cursed him for going AWOL. Progressing on legs growing shakier with every move, she stumbled from room to room.

Jordan had abandoned her. The pigeon ranger was missing. Maybe she'd seen the governess and gone back upstairs. Or she'd been taken or killed. Mackie was gone, maybe to sleep in a corner, maybe thrown out to be run over in the street. Clare couldn't care. All that mattered now—all that had ever mattered—was Dana and Vee.

In corners behind potted plants, in niches with half-drawn curtains, in front of a small audience gathered around a divan, two of the three smoking cigars and sipping booze with the show, she found children being used.

After several more children and their captors, she wanted to go blind, to gouge out her eyes like a character in a Greek tragedy, but the need to see the faces of her daughters forced her to take in each miserable picture, knowing it would be burned on the back of her eyes until she closed them for the last time on earth. Probably longer.

The men perpetrating this basest of evil faded and blurred until they were as shadows; she could scarcely believe that they were real, that they existed. The period costumes, the low hum of conversation, the palms, and the strains of piano music—it all made them seem like something from an old black-and-white movie.

All her adult life she had worn costumes, played roles. Clare loved acting, loved bringing a character to life with her skill. Was that what these men were doing? Cloaking their sickness in a kind of glamour? Creating a world of wealth and grace where their criminal perversions were as acceptable as having a glass of wine on a summer afternoon?

Skirting the baby grand, averting her eyes so she would not see who played the piano in hell, she entered the courtyard. The fancy house and grounds took up half a city block. Even with the house there remained space for a courtyard large enough to hide a myriad of sins. Bricks formed the walls up to about twenty feet. Gas lanterns, low enough for privacy but bright enough for enjoying the scene, were affixed at shoulder height every few yards. From the top of the brick up, the gray of more prosaic building material took over. Climbing fig greened the walls. Bougainvillea in hot pink, lavender, gold, and red showered through the lamplight in waterfalls of color. Night-blooming jasmine and gardenia filled the still air with perfume. The garden had grown up over the years until many of the trees and shrubs were taller than the walls, leaving winding paths and darkened nooks throughout. The sound of water came from many directions as fountains joined together to make soothing music in a place where children found no solace.

Because she knew what happened in the garden, the beauty came to Clare stinking with debasement: Shadows were too dark, colors too opulent, foliage threatening and laden with ugly memories. The scent of flowers was fetid in her nostrils as she remembered Candy's description of the fancy house, the singing and the thumping and the smell of flowers. Insupportable weight pressed on her eyes and the back of her neck. Piano music clogged her ears. The odor of gardenias was filling her lungs till air could not penetrate.

Unless Anna had found the girls upstairs, but for this small maze there was no place else to look for her children. Her steps slowed. Thoughts ran from her skull like the pattering of fountains. Finally she stopped, still as death, in a darkened turn and was nothing: not awake or asleep, afraid or hopeful, alive or dead.

Into this trance came a hushed voice counting, "One, two, three. Like pin the tail on the donkey." This was followed by men laughing and then a child's cry, short and sharp, and more laughter.

One more.

Here in the garden was one more child being taunted, raped, molested, made drunk, or beaten. Clare could not let herself sink into the void until she had witnessed one last horrific act, taken on the pain of one last lost child. She owed her daughters that.

The six or seven feet she had to force a body that was shutting down from starvation, exhaustion, and stress to reach the laughter seemed an endless push through a darkling jungle. Then she was at the end of the brick path. Ahead, tucked into a corner of the wall, was a lion head fountain, water trickling from the beast's mouth into a triangular basin. Benches angled out from it in an ell. On each bench sat a man, both startling in their complete unremarkableness, one nearly bald, the other with hair thinning in two runs up from his eyebrows. They could have been a middle-aged grocer gossiping with the driver of the bread truck or a stockbroker trading stories with his Realtor. The bald man wore a wedding ring. Both wore glasses.

Between them on the minute stage floored in brick and lighted by the gas lamps was a dark-haired child wearing a blindfold. One of the men was turning her gently around and around as one might in a child's game of hide-and-seek to render the one designated as "it" dizzy.

The child was naked but for the blindfold and button-up boots. Her dress was crumpled on the bench near the man who spun her. The powdered wig she'd been wearing lay like a dead cat half under the other man's foot. The spinner lifted his hands from the child's shoulders, and she staggered several steps, and then righted herself, hands outstretched in a macabre game of blindman's bluff.

The man who'd watched the proceedings thus far reached out a fine, long-fingered hand and tweaked the child's nipple hard enough that she cried out. Both laughed. The other man, not to be outdone, goosed the child in the bottom with the toe of his shoe.

The child was Dana.

"Stop," Clare whispered as her mind screamed incoherently. Intent on their game, the men hadn't noticed her silent arrival, hadn't seen her standing in the shadows. Now they did. "Stop," she said again, and again it came out as a mere breath of sound.

"Why don't you mind your own business, buddy?" said the man who'd spun Dana.

"She is my business," Clare said, and she fell to her knees, hitting the brick so hard that the pain flapped black wings in her mind. When had she gotten so weak? So sick.

Dana tentatively raised a hand, lifted one corner of the blindfold, and shot a quick glance at her captors to see if they'd noticed she was breaking their rules.

"Honey," Clare croaked and held out her arms.

Dana pulled the blindfold down again. She didn't recognize her mother. "Have I changed so much?" Clare murmured, but she knew she had. This brittle, black-haired man of bones and cigarette smoke was just another client come to join the game to Dana, and one she didn't want to see.

"Look, pal, why don't you bug off?" the bald man said and stood. Clare flashed on the annual Halloween show Seattle Rep toured to the grade schools; Ichabod Crane, his hideous skeletal length unfolding to the horror of the children.

Clare tried to stand and managed to get one foot on the ground so she knelt like a suitor about to propose marriage. Her head swam. She couldn't see the man for looking at her daughter, afraid that if she looked away for even a second Dana would vanish.

"This is my child," she managed.

"No, asshole, this is our kid for the evening. We paid triple for a virgin, so fuck off," the second man said, and he, too, stood. Ichabod turned to his cohort. "You think we should call security? One of those rent-a-cops?"

Instead of answering, the shorter man lifted his foot and kicked Clare in the face. She didn't even have time to raise her hands to deflect the blow. The heel of his boot struck her forehead, opening a cut near the hairline. Blood poured into her eyes. Ichabod reached down with one long mechanical arm and lifted Dana into the air.

Clare grabbed his leg, clawing up his body to get to her child. "Dana, it's Mommy."

"Doggone it," Ichabod said, shaking his leg as if to free it from an aggressive Chihuahua.

"Going long," the man who had kicked Clare said and jogged backward a few steps. Ichabod threw him the blindfolded child. Dana screamed. Freed from his burden, Ichabod backhanded Clare, and she fell the few feet she'd gained. Crawling, blinded with weakness and her own blood, she crossed the bricks to the man holding Dana.

"Please," she said. "She's my little girl."

"And a pass down the field," Ichabod cried, getting into the spirit. The kicker held Dana above his head and danced away from where Clare begged at his feet. Dana was old enough it took two hands to hold her, and he threw hard. Her arms and legs windmilled in terror.

"Punt," he said and kicked Clare again. The boot struck her shoulder, and she fell hard, the side of her head cracking against the brick. Midnight flowed from the edges of the world until all she could see was a narrow bit of brick, red and close, in front of her.

"Jordan!" she screamed.

"What the hell?" someone said.

White-hot rage, the anger of failure and cruelty and life on the run, the fury of the gutter punk, poured into Clare, and, as her consciousness receded, Jordan came to his hands and knees. A booted foot flashed toward his face. He raised one hand and shoved it aside. Clenching his fist in the trouser cuff, he roared to his feet, snarling. The man he'd caught stumbled backward and sat down hard on the rim of the fountain. Jordan let go of the cuff, grabbed him by the ears, and smashed his own forehead into the man's face. Blood splattered: Jordan's, the pervert's. Jordan reveled in it.

Sputtering, the pervert fell back, butt sinking into the shallow catch basin.

"You hurt me!" he cried out in shock and outrage. "You broke my nose! I'll sue you for everything you've got!"

"Sue this," Jordan growled. He jerked the man out of the water by his shirtfront, head-butted him again, and let him fall back.

Snarling like a rabid dog, Jordan spun around to catch Ichabod watching the scene in dumb shock. "You bastards can deal it out but can't fucking take it." Jordan spit out the words. With a feral growl, he sprang at the tall, bony frame, striking the man in the chest with knees and elbows. Hands around the skinny throat, he bore the second man to the ground. A brick had come loose where the edge of the walk met with the soil of the planter, and Jordan prized it up.

"Don't kill me!" Ichabod cried.

"Why not?" Jordan said and brought the brick down hard.

FORTY

Instinctively, Anna started forward. The chief rapped the barrel of his revolver sharply against the little girl's skull, causing her to cry out. Anna stopped. The child's twin sister moaned as if the blow had hurt her as well. The children pressed closer, clinging to Anna's hands and skirts, hobbling her as effectively as the pistol pointing at the girl's temple.

Several men rousted by Anna's intrusions paused in their exodus to stare at the odd gathering.

"We've an intruder," the chief said calmly. "It's being taken care of. I suggest you gentlemen take your leave."

Two of them raised their hands to shield their faces in the way of politicians being walked to jail before banks of avid photographers and sidled by. Anna heard one murmur, "Excuse me."

When they'd gone, the chief jerked the girl up against his chest and nestled the gun under her full skirts, where it was obscenely concealed. "Who sent you?" he demanded.

"Paula's mother died," Anna said. "I'm going to be the new governess until she can get her father settled in an extended care facility. This is on-the-job training."

For a moment the man's face wavered the way Jell-O will if set down too hard. It firmed up quickly.

"Right. And your first lesson was bashing visitors over the head with ashtrays."

"No," Anna snapped. "I learned that at my previous job."

"And what, pray tell, was that?"

He seemed to be enjoying the conversation in a creepy sort of way. There was no tension in his shoulders, and his feet were planted with the confidence of a big man used to being in control.

"The security here, your boys?"

"Can't live on a beat patrolman's pay," he said affably. "Who is here with you?"

"I'm alone," Anna said. "I paid Paula a couple hundred to let me in through the service door from the Bonne Chance."

He thought about that. Anna could tell he liked the lie; it exonerated his security people of any failing. "Paula lent me the dress so I wouldn't upset the guests," she continued. "I'm from the *Picayune*. I'd hoped to get a story on the sex slave trade here in the Crescent City. I got lucky. This is Pulitzer Prize stuff. Would you mind giving me a quote for the piece? My photographer is downstairs, but we'll be sure and set something up with you before we go."

The chief liked this even better. Anna could tell he

loathed the local paper. The paper probably felt the same about him if he was as crooked and venal in his other dealings as he was in the area of vice. He would enjoy dealing with a reporter on his own turf.

Just then the front of Anna's dress cackled and the words "Hey, Paula, what the fuck's going on?" came out from her bosom.

It didn't take the chief long to react. "Fish it out," he demanded. "Two fingers, just like it was a gun and I might shoot you if it looked like you wanted to use it."

Anna fished Paula's radio out of her bodice.

The cop set the little girl at his feet. "Lay down," he told her. She did, her face on the floor, her tiny hands over her ears, the absurd period dress bunched up, her feet in their Mary Janes poking out from the petticoats. Never taking his eyes off Anna, he lifted one booted foot and, like a circus elephant, lowered the mighty hoof onto the back of the child's neck.

"Now hand me the radio nicely," he said.

Anna did.

The chief thumbed the mike. "Gershwin, this is Ziegfeld. Come back."

"Yeah, boss."

"We got a spot of bother. Maybe a newspaper photographer down there. Look around, will you? Find Paula; looks like she let 'em in. Call the Magician. Evacuate the clientele. Tell them everything's under control. You got all that?"

Anna noticed he didn't bother to tell the other cop that he had a gun on one of the "newspaper people."

She tried to look deserving of such an oversight, harmless and small and one who actually believed the pen was mightier than the sword. Just as she was thinking she was glad that Jordan had changed into costume to blend in, the chief asked, "What's your photographer wearing?"

"I lied," Anna said, "I came here by myself. I'm not really with the *Picayune*. I work for Chase Bank out in Metairie, but I thought if I could get this story it would be my big break." Rounding her shoulders, she offered him a sheepish smile.

He narrowed his eyes. He'd swallowed the newspaper bit as far as it went, but this was too much even for his big gut. Leaning forward, he ground his foot into the back of the little girl's head. She squealed; her twin echoed the cry.

"He's wearing black Levi's, a black long-sleeved T-shirt, and black running shoes," Anna said quickly. "I don't know where he is. He could be anywhere in the house."

"Has he got one of those goddamned iPod things that can send his pictures to the Internet as soon as he takes them?" the chief asked and pressed harder on the little neck beneath his foot. This time the child did not scream. Anna hoped her neck hadn't snapped under the pressure.

Would it be better for her if her photographer could send the images instantly or better if he could not? She didn't have a lot of time to ponder the issue, but guessed the instant another intruder became priority one the chief would gun her down and go for the next target.

"No," Anna said. "He's only got a small thirty-five millimeter. The phones don't take high enough quality photographs." She had no idea if that was true or not, but then, neither did the man with the gun and the hostage.

Clicking the mike button again, the chief relayed Anna's description of the imaginary photographer to a "Gershwin" and a "Busby."

"Find the photographer. I'm bringing down Miss Marple." Anna winced; her days of being called Nancy Drew were at an end. "Get Blackie here. We've got some disposal to take care of."

"Blackie quit," came back.

"Get Dougie, then," the chief snapped. He tucked the radio into the side pocket of his pants, then crooked his finger at the free twin. Thumb stuck in her mouth, she stumbled over in her stiff skirts. Grabbing her wrist, he jerked her up as he had her sister, then removed his foot from the other child's neck. The girl on the floor didn't move, but Anna was fairly sure she could see her breathing.

"Give me your cell phone," he ordered Anna.

"I don't have one."

The chief thought that was the biggest lie of all, right up there with "I don't watch television."

"I mean, I *have* one," Anna said quickly. "But not on me. It was in my pants, and I left them in Paula's room when I changed."

To this he just grunted. "You kids get out of here," he said to the group huddled around Anna. None of them moved. Whether they knew Anna had come to save them or were just paralyzed with fear was hard to tell. Anna could feel small hands clutching and plucking at her skirts.

Disturbed by this show of noncompliance, the chief cocked the pistol with his thumb and pointed the barrel at a child, the white powder of her makeup streaked with mascara from crying, her elaborate wig askew. "Get out of here," he said.

"For Christ's sake!" Anna exploded. Those would very possibly have been the last words she ever uttered had not a man come rushing up, taking the stairs two at a time.

It was Dougie.

He skidded into the crowd of frightened children like Kramer into Jerry's apartment on the old *Seinfeld* show. The gunman's attention flicked to the newcomer. If ever she was to act, this was the time. Once she and the children were taken downstairs there would be too many guns.

Dougie wasn't a big man, not more than a few inches taller than Anna and no more than twenty pounds heavier. As he stopped amid the confusion, he turned toward the chief. Seeing the gun, he threw his hands in the air like a cowboy in an old Western.

Scattering children, Anna slipped behind him, wrapped her arms around him, and slid her hands up his chest and around his neck, trapping him in a full nelson. Locking her fingers together on the base of his skull, she yelled at the children, "Run!"

For a second they stood immobile, the girls in their miniature gowns, the boys in short pants or loincloths and turbans. Then a boy broke and ran. The others followed, pattering past Anna and Dougie and down the long carpeted stairs. Only the twins remained, one in the chief's arms and one on the floor, no longer prone but up now on her knees.

Dougie began to squirm. Anna put pressure on his neck until he yelled with the pain and grew still.

"Let the children go," she told the chief of police. "Or I snap your man's neck."

"Are you my man, Dougie?" the chief asked, making no move to set the child down.

"Yeah, boss," Dougie managed through his crimped throat.

The chief lazily raised the gun and pulled the trigger.

Dougie slammed back against Anna with the force of the bullet. The chief pulled the trigger a second time. Dougie went limp, and Anna felt a blow as if a fastball had been hurled into her as the bullet passed through the dead man and smashed into her side.

Then she was falling backward, Dougie with her. There was the odd sight of the chief disappearing, then the ceiling unfurling, then the banister heaving up, then nothing.

FORTY-ONE

From a long ways away, she heard a cry.

Feebly, Clare struggled through fogs of drifting layers, skittering shadows of movement and sensation until she came into her eyes. Below her, glasses broken and askew, tears streaming, was the face of Ichabod Crane. He looked at her with abject terror, and she didn't know why. Then she felt the brick in her hand, saw the blood on his bald head, and knew she was murdering him.

"Mommy!"

Clare dropped the brick and scrambled off Ichabod, leaving him sniveling in the monkey grass. Dana, making herself as small as she could, her naked body curled into a ball and squished beneath the low bench, was crying for her mother.

"I'm here, honey, it's Mommy," Clare crooned as she crawled across the bricks. "It's me, baby, I'm all dressed up for a play, but it's me. It's Mommy." She reached beneath the bench and laid a hand on her daughter's back.

"Come on, honey. It's over. You're safe now, Mommy's here."

Water was dripping from somewhere, splashing the brick, and Clare realized she was weeping.

Dana took her hands away from her face and looked up.

"Mommy's in costume," Clare said. There was still no response. "Oh!" Clare had forgotten all but her daughter. "I've got on makeup, so I'll look all beat up and bloody like that time when we did the scary play."

With sudden recognition, the little girl exploded from beneath the bench and wrapped her arms so tightly around Clare's neck and her legs so tightly around her middle that Clare couldn't breathe and wouldn't have traded the embrace for all the oxygen in the world.

"Do you know where your sister is?" Clare asked, forcing calm into her voice. "Do you know where Vee is?"

Dana shook her head against her mother's shoulder and cried harder.

"Shh, shh," Clare murmured. "It's okay. We'll find her. Don't you worry. We'll find Vee." Dana's crying seemed to lessen a little, and she burrowed her face into the hollow of Clare's shoulder as if she would hide forever near her mother's heart.

Had there been the luxury of time, Clare might have sat just that way for hours. Instead, never loosing her hold on her child, she levered herself up from the bricks, using the edge of the bench.

Ichabod had found the courage to sit up. The blow he'd taken to the head was bleeding copiously, and the sight of his own blood seemed to be terrifying him. A good bit of it had splashed on his hands, and he held them before his face, staring at them as if they belonged to someone else.

A mother again, sane again, Clare reached for Anna's cell phone to dial 911. The pocket was empty. She'd left it in the trousers she'd shucked off when she donned the costume. "Doggone it," she whispered, careful as always not to swear around her children. To the pathetic bastard bleeding at her feet, she said, "Give me your cell phone or I will kill you." She meant every word and knew that she and Jordan had integrated, become one.

Ichabod fished his phone out and handed it to her. Clare flipped it open and punched in 911.

Ichabod scuttled crablike to the edge of the clearing, got to his feet, and ran down the path on long shaking legs, hollering for help.

The emergency operator answered. Clare began pouring out her story. It sounded unreal, like the story of a prankster or psychopath. She took a breath to mentally reframe what she'd seen and heard this night.

Into the silence the operator said warily, "Where are you?"

Clare started to snap, "I told you that!" but remembered she hadn't shared the address. She didn't know it. "It's behind the sex club on the north edge of the Quarter, the Bonne Chance."

For a beat or two the operator said nothing, then, "There's nothing behind that club but city warehouses filled with old pumping station machinery, obsolete computers, broken crime cameras, things like that. It's called the Bone Yard."

City warehouse, chief of police. Possibly others from the upper echelons of Louisiana politics were involved. Clare changed tack. "My name is Clare Sullivan," she announced. "I'm wanted for four murders in Seattle, Washington. I'm ready to give myself up."

"Are you still . . . behind the Bonne Chance?" the operator asked.

"Yes," Clare said firmly.

"In the warehouse?"

"Yes," Clare said again.

"If you'll go out to the street, I'll have an officer come by to arrest you if you'd like," the dispatcher said with only a hint of sarcasm.

"I can't," Clare said. "I can't get out of the warehouse."

There was a distinct sigh from the other end. "Stay on the line, please." A list of helpful hints of what to do in case of emergency began playing over the phone.

Clamping the slippery device between ear and shoulder, Clare lowered Dana to the bench. The child wouldn't let go of her neck but, with coaxing, was willing to set her feet on the stone seat. Having wriggled out of the Edwardian jacket, Clare wrapped it around her daughter's naked body and gathered her up again. The night wasn't cold, but she couldn't bear the thought of Dana feeling any man's eyes on her.

Through the foliage came the sound of raised voices. Ichabod had reported her. Holding Dana tightly, Clare pushed into the dense elephant ears and Australian ferns between the brick paths. They would not hide her long, but it was the best she could do. Not quite the best; stepping back into the clearing, she picked up the bloody brick she'd used in her aborted attempt to bash a pervert's brains out and slipped it into the folds of the coat wrapped around Dana.

Radios crackled, and the men hushed. The operator had called out the police, and the police were receiving the call on their radios, in the garden, in the fancy house. Edging through the dense greenery, Clare moved the half-dozen yards to where the paths left the patio. Three guys in black suits were standing close to the piano, listening to their radios.

After the dispatcher made her report, another voice came over the air. "Amy, this is the chief. That's a crank call. Officers Barrett and Downs are with the caller now. We'll get back to you."

"Night of the full moon," the dispatcher said.

"Always brings 'em out," replied the chief.

Without waiting for the operator to come back on the line, Clare closed the cell phone. The way out through the house and sex club was locked. Vee was either dead or shipped overseas or in this house somewhere. Anna was probably dead or dying. The rats were abandoning ship, stripping off period costume jackets, vests, hats, spats, and ascots as they rushed a door in the garden wall that led to a garage or other screened exit.

Carrying Dana, Clare would be stopped if she tried to blend in with the men making their escape. If she walked back into the house, bloodied and filthy and carrying a child, the three off-duty policemen would stop her in a heartbeat.

Hugging her daughter tightly, she sank down into the ferns.

FORTY-TWO

A nna opened her eyes. She was looking at a black shag carpet. No, she was under a greasy shag carpet. Shit. She was staring at the back of Dougie's head. Carefully, lest her spine be snapped, she rolled her head to the side. The two of them lay on the stairs, her head smashed awkwardly into the angle between stair and wall. Her right arm was trapped beneath her and her left flung out as if she'd tried to break her fall. Dougie lay partially over her chest, his head resting on her cheek.

Oddly calm, she wondered if he was dead. Not that she cared, but if he wasn't, maybe he'd get the hell off her lungs so she could breathe. Dougie had been shot.

Anna had been shot by the same bullet—or bullets. She only remembered feeling one hit. What should a gunshot person do on awakening?

Stop the bleeding.

Check airways.

Treat for shock.

Set up a saline IV.

That was for when other people got shot, *victims,* she remembered. Nobody ever taught rangers what to do if they got shot. Don't die, she thought and started to laugh. With x number of pounds of Dougie on her chest, it didn't work out. As long as she stayed still, the wound didn't hurt too badly. Was it too bad? Only a crease, she told herself, don't be scared. Fear was deadly. There'd been a story going around the parks one year about a man who was bitten by a corn snake and died of shock because he believed he'd been bitten by a rattler. It might not have been true, but it was a good teaching point at campfire talks.

"Corn snake," Anna whispered and was pleased to find she could talk without making ominous gurgling sounds. Her lungs weren't punctured. Before she made the commitment to moving from under the man she'd shared a bullet—or bullets—with, she listened past the sound of her own heartbeat in her ears and the breath in her throat.

"Load up the jewels. We're shutting this place down. And find that goddamn photographer," she heard the chief shouting.

He was downstairs, where the children had run. Why hadn't he shot her again for insurance when he passed her and Dougie on the stairs? Maybe with her head jammed against the wall and the copious amounts of blood—Dougie's, she hoped—drenching her, she'd looked too dead to waste a bullet on.

Without moving overmuch, she frisked the body that

lay across hers. Last time she'd been this close to Dougie, he'd been carrying a knife, a long blade that folded into the haft. With luck, in the intervening days, he'd augmented his arsenal with a gun or two. Her quota of luck had evidently been used up when the chief decided not to finish her off; there was only the knife. Holding the open blade across Dougie's throat in case he wasn't dead enough, she pressed two fingers on his carotid. No pulse.

The weapon hard in her fist, she wriggled from beneath the dead man. Pain roared up through her side, making her breath catch, and the wretched skirts tangled around her lower legs. What should have been a relatively simple operation was a slow misery.

Panting and sweating and swearing nonstop under her breath, she got free of Dougie and could see down the stairs.

Her escape maneuvers had gone unnoticed. The chief was just in sight, his back to her, standing by the baby grand, clad in period trousers and anachronistic leather bedroom slippers, shouting orders to Barrett and Downs—presumably his men in the courtyard. The .357 was shoved in the waistband of his trousers. Despite his considerable girth, the antiquated cut of the trousers left them roomy. They were meant to be held up by braces, not a belt. Most of the gun had slipped down his ass. Only the tip of the wooden grip remained visible.

Except for the chief, the pedophiles were leaving, scuttling down the stairs to their limos, no doubt, to prey on other children at other times. They stepped over and around her and Dougie, indifferent to the fact that she lived or that he did not. She watched them pass, but with the costuming, the confusion, getting shot and whatnot, Anna doubted she would be able to identify any one of them in a court of law.

Beyond the chief, on the patio in the courtyard, two men in black suits were trying to herd the children streaming from the building into a group. There was no sign of the whorehouse staff or of Clare. Anna hoped she had managed to escape and wasn't lying dead somewhere. The hope was feeble; Clare would not leave without her children.

Anna supposed she could creep upstairs and hide. Maybe the chief wouldn't notice the dead had walked, wouldn't look for her, wouldn't drag her out and kill her. It was a slim chance but better than nothing. Had they not been taking the children away to torture at their later convienience, she would have done just that.

Seven steps to the bottom of the stairs.

By the time she'd reached the last one, she'd have a plan, she promised herself.

Gathering her skirts up in her free hand, she began to pull herself to her feet, using the banister. Each movement felt as if it tore the hole in her side wider and deeper. Because Dougie had been cad enough to bleed all over her, she had no idea how much blood she was losing, whether the wound was grave or just a scratch. Pain was no indicator. Often the worst wounds damaged the nerves and hurt less than non-life-threatening wounds.

"Barrett!" the chief barked. The shorter man in black

turned. Anna froze. Indoors, uncertain light, panicked men and children: If he wasn't looking for her he might not see her.

"Yeah?"

"We got any gas?"

"A five-gallon can in the garage. Why?

"We're going to burn this place down. There's been too much radio traffic. Some nosy parker's bound to have been scanning."

"Where's Paula?"

"I don't know and I don't care. Get the gas."

"Gas is easy to detect, boss."

"You got a better idea?"

Barrett turned and trotted in the direction Downs had led the children.

With Barrett out of line of sight, Anna got to a standing position, congratulating herself on the decision not to hide. Burning was way down on her list of favorite ways to go. The Chance would burn as well, and she wished she could warn them. With sunrise only a few minutes away, surely most of the revelers would have gone home. The two dominatrices must have to take the kids to soccer practice or something.

Dropping her skirts and holding on to the banister, she took her first step. Six more to the Plan. Toddling barefoot into three handguns was a plan of sorts. Five steps to a Better Plan.

Damn. Somehow she'd slid down the railing till her butt was on the tread. Putting her head between her knees, she tried to bring her drifting consciousness back into focus. Perhaps the bulk of the blood on her dress wasn't Dougie's. Maybe it wasn't a corn snake. Maybe she'd been bitten by a rattler. The knife was still in her hand, but she wasn't sure what she'd intended to do with it.

Soon the chief would turn around or Barrett or Downs or whoever else was still on-site would come back. Either they'd see her and kill her or they'd burn her up sight unseen. Paul would never know what had become of her.

One day he had talked to his wife on the phone. She'd told him she was fine and having a nice rest with her girlfriend in New Orleans. Then she was never seen or heard from again.

Jesus, Anna thought. How can people survive not knowing, looking in every face on the street, craning to hear voices in the dark, thinking against all reason that maybe, maybe this time, it will be the lost love. Suddenly, over all the horror she'd seen and all the horror yet to come, washed a wave of grief so dark it eclipsed them. She realized what she had done to Paul, how she had lied to him by omission, and how she had lied to herself in pretending that she did it to shield him. She had wanted to feel in control, meaningful; she'd wanted distraction and a sense of importance. Well, she had gotten all that in spades. The cost was yet to be totaled up.

"Barrett," the chief yelled as the other officer trotted back lugging a heavy red gas can. "Start on the third floor. Go light. Save a couple gallons for the second and ground floors."

Anna could hear Barrett's boots loud on the tiles that fronted the house proper. The arsonist was heading for the stairs.

Anna's mind snapped back to the business of survival. She couldn't make it down unseen, nor had she a chance of getting to the top unseen. Unseen and unshot were synonymous.

No more perverts were passing by. They were clearing from the lobby as well, funneling through the garden. Bumping back up the single stair she'd traversed, she lay down in a pose as close as she could manage to the one the chief had last seen, arranging her skirts so they covered but did not entangle her legs. The knife she opened and held in her right hand, the skirt covering it. Weak and in a hurry, she found Dougie too heavy for her to shift more than a few inches. Grabbing a handful of hair, she dragged his head up and let it drop on her chest and neck, partly obscuring her face.

Boots hit carpet. Barrett was coming fast. Grunting under the weight of the gas can, he ran up the stairs. Anna resisted the temptation to hold her breath. Then he was over her, his boot mashing the little finger of her left hand, the other kicking her calf as he passed.

Lying as one dead, she listened for him to reach the second flight of stairs. There he would turn and would no longer be able to see her. Where the chief had gone, she had no idea; the garage, she hoped. If she could get to the greenery in the courtyard, they might not be able to find her before they had to abandon the place. They wouldn't dare be here when the fire department showed up, not dressed—or half dressed—as they were. In the green, she might even be able to survive the fire.

In that instant she heard the chief's soft-soled shoes hushing across the marble of the foyer between the piano and the stairs. The bastard was coming back. To get his shoes? Check on Barrett? Put on street clothes? Fire that insurance bullet into her skull? Closing her eyes, she became as dead as she possibly could with a heart that was hammering a hundred beats a minute.

The slippered footfalls became muffled. He'd started up the stairs moving fast. Fast was good. His mind was on the floors above, not the carnage on the steps. As he reached Anna and Dougie, he slowed. She tightened her grip on the knife. She didn't think of death, of what it would feel like to have a shard of metal shatter her skull and take out the life when it slammed through her gray matter. She didn't picture Molly or Paul or Piedmont or Taco. The only image in her mind was that of the chief of police's bare heels.

Her left arm lay along the tread, the hand open where it might easily be trod upon. She felt the brush of leather against her fingers. He was directly above her. Opening her eyes, she grabbed his ankle hard in her left hand and with her right slashed deep across his Achilles tendon.

Screaming in pain and shock, he tried to raise his other foot from the step below, but the ruined tendon wouldn't take the weight. Grasping the banister rail, roaring in fury, he reached back for the gun in the waistband of his pants. Anna took hold of the seat and yanked.

The butt of the Colt vanished into his trousers, landing in the roomy seat like an unsightly load.

This would be funny in the telling, she thought absurdly.

No good moves left to her, she began hacking at anything that moved. A blow to the side of her face stunned her. Rather than fighting it, she went with the force and rolled down the stairs. The crashing woke up the nerves in her injured side. Blood began to flow that she knew was hers alone. The tumble was only a few yards, but it seemed to pass slowly. She saw her right hand fly up and noticed she had lost the knife. She watched her bare feet flash by and wondered at the childishness of being without shoes. She saw snippets of ceiling, fronds, and flocked wallpaper.

Then she rolled to a stop on the landing, where the ornate newel post curved into the drawing room in gracious invitation. Other than the loss of the knife and the blood, she didn't think she was any worse for wear.

Screaming curses and demands for his men, the chief was hanging on to the banister with one hand while trying to fish the gun out of his pants with the other. Again funny; again Anna had no urge to laugh. She turned tail and crawled down the last of the stairs on her belly like a reptile.

FORTY-THREE

The rats were deserting what Clare hoped was a rapidly sinking ship. She watched with cold eyes as sick men, with money and evil in equal proportions, streamed from the three-story mansion. Close in the ferns and the leaves of the subtropical garden, Clare held on to her daughter and wondered what had caused this exodus. Had the pigeon survived? Or had her death scared the whoremongers?

Two gunshots, close together, snapped her from her thoughts, and she ducked, wrapping herself over her daughter. The shots probably marked the end of the ranger. A law enforcement pigeon, but she hadn't found Vee, and now she'd gone and gotten herself killed before Dana was out of danger, Clare thought sourly. A faint pang of guilt left over from when she was civilized nudged her.

If she and Dana survived, she'd put flowers on the woman's grave. If they didn't, no flowers for Anna Pigeon.

When Clare again found the nerve to peek out of their tiny woods, little girls and boys in the hateful trappings of their slavery, some fully dressed, others with bits or pieces of the costumes still on, some dragging a ripped skirt or a wig fallen half off, were pouring out through the French doors. Most were not crying or running but moved with a stoicism that should never be seen on such baby faces.

Clare didn't move. She searched for the one face she needed to see. If Vee was not here, then she'd been shipped overseas or secreted away in some man's basement. Or she had died. Clare prayed for the last.

In a remarkably short time, the garden was free of perverted clientele. The only sound was the soft rustling of the children on the brick patio. This momentary hush was broken by the chief of police. In Edwardian trousers and bedroom slippers, he roared from the house, "Load up the jewels. And find that goddamn photographer."

The black suits began herding the children to the door where the perverts had swarmed out of the courtyard. The children, the jewels, diamonds beyond price, and they were being prodded ahead like cattle to be taken to another "fancy house" and another set of "clients."

The one the chief called Barrett had run by carrying gasoline to burn the place down, with its evidence. There would be traces left, but, without Anna or the children or Clare, the arson investigators might not know what they were finding evidence of. They might think it was done to cover the theft of the presumed city property that was supposedly stored in this imaginary warehouse. The police would push that theory, for sure.

Moving slowly so she wouldn't trip and cause Dana to cry out or the chief to decide the goddamn photographer—it had to be her—was hiding in the bushes, she began folding herself through the wide fronds toward the door where the children had been taken. If it led to the outside, there was a possibility that in either confusion or darkness she could carry Dana to safety.

A howl of rage and pain from the direction of the house stopped her. Had it not, she would have stepped out onto the brick and run right into the man rushing back from wherever the black maw of the door in the brick led to.

Downs, the chief had called this man. Downs was compact and fast, probably in his early forties. His head was shaped like a bullet from working out his neck muscles and covered with close-cropped dark hair. As another roar of pain and rage came from the house, Downs faltered. He stopped several steps from where Clare stood in the shadows and, hands shaking, began fumbling for his pistol.

Downs was only used to facing down frightened children, Clare thought. The chief's shriek was from a larger predator. Coolness coalesced around her like the still, cold air of a walk-in freezer. The smell of gardenias was gone. The sorrow of her lost baby girl was muted. The rush of blood in her ears was silenced. Lifting the brick from where it was cradled in the crook of the arm that held Dana, she stepped lightly into the chill and the silence behind Downs and brought it down hard on the back of his skull.

With an "oomph" that sounded like the noise a bear might make, he fell to hands and knees. In one graceful movement Clare brought the brick down a second time. He didn't move again.

Dana, the coat pulled up over her head, pushed her face deeper in the hollow of her mother's shoulder. Clare was glad her daughter hadn't witnessed the violence. Like good dry wine, revenge was an acquired taste, and one too bitter for the palate of a child.

Dana clinging tightly to her neck, Clare leaned down and took the pistol the officer had managed to get out of his holster just as she struck him. It was a sleek semiautomatic. What make, Clare didn't know, but she recognized the feel from the gun she'd been given by props for the small part of an CIA agent she'd gotten in a movie shooting in Vancouver. That gun had been rendered harmless, but it had been a real weapon at one time in its life. So the character she played could handle it with confidence, Clare had taken lessons at a shooting range in Seattle.

Downs's gun felt good in her hand. She thumbed off the safety and dropped her hand to her side, the barrel pointed down the line of her leg to the ground. Torn between walking into the darkness where the children had been taken or going back toward the house, she remained motionless. Minutes before, she'd written the ranger off, but there was no doubt in her mind that Anna had been the cause of the chief's anguish. The icy calm did not abate. She turned toward the house, following the winding brick walk with sure and silent steps.

As she crossed from the patio onto the marble of the entryway, she saw blood on the tiles. The tail of the governess's dress was peeking from beneath a bench between the potted palms in the crook of the curving banister; the bench Clare had shared with the girls and their dollies.

Above, leaning over the banister, .357 pointed at the plush velvet cushion, the chief stood on one leg. His skin was pasty. Sweat beaded on his forehead and dripped from his jaw. The hand that held the gun was trembling, but at that distance he would have no trouble shooting through the bench and hitting Anna.

Clare raised Downs's gun and fired two shots into the chief's center mass. Watching him crumple, his hands groping like blind things trying to find the holes where she'd let his life out, she felt nothing but a mild sense of relief at a dirty chore completed satisfactorily.

Barrett, gas can in hand, appeared behind the fallen chief, shouting, "It's burning good—" When he saw Clare he snapped his mouth shut. Clare did not move or blink or breathe. Barrett dropped the gasoline can and pulled his gun. Clare shot him twice.

"The last scene of *Hamlet*," she said softly. "Hamlet is dead, Ophelia is dead, the king is dead, the queen is dead, Laertes is dead—"

"But everybody else lived happily ever after," came

the ranger's voice. Clare switched her gaze to the pile of gray muslin boiling from beneath the bench.

"Wendy Darling's bedtime story. *Peter Pan*," Clare said. "Mr. Nye said I learned to fly faster than Mary Martin."

"Bully for you," Anna said. With growls and curses, she got herself right way around and out from under the bench. Using the nearest palm tree, she pulled herself to a standing position. "Jesus!" she said as she took in the carnage. "Holy smoke. Good job."

"They've set fire to the place," Clare said.

"So I heard," Anna replied. One hand was clamped tightly over her side. What color remained in her face was made by blood worn outside the skin, not inside.

"You're hurt," Clare said.

"Smart and pretty, too," Anna mocked her.

A crash sounded from above. A choking gout of smoke gushed down the stairs, burning their eyes and lungs.

"Let's get the hell out of here," Anna gasped. She stepped from the support of the little tree and would have fallen if Clare hadn't dropped the gun to steady her.

"I'm good," Anna said. She pulled her arm away, took two steps, and fell headlong onto the floor.

Clare squatted down as Anna pushed herself to her elbows. "Anna, I'm saving your life again, but if you don't stop making it so hard you can just die." Taking Anna's arm, she stood, pulling the ranger with her. Clare tried to walk her toward the courtyard, but Anna stayed rooted in the burning house.

"Listen," she said.

Clare listened. Faintly, through the increasing cracks and hisses of the fire devouring the building from the roof down, Clare heard it: a tiny sweet howl.

"Mackie," she whispered.

FORTY-FOUR

Anna sat on a bench holding Dana on her lap. Clare had gone back into the burning house to find Mackie. For a pathetic minute, Anna had tried to go with her but had trouble standing upright long enough to make her point. Dana shifted, and the pressure of childish knees against her side hurt. The comfort Anna derived from the feel of a live and wriggling child more than made up for it. As she rocked Dana gently, Anna's mind drifted like the smoke reaching out from the upstairs windows.

This time, she hadn't killed anyone. That had to count in her favor. There was a small matter of crippling the police chief, but since Clare had subsequently shot him to death, Anna's damage was a mere footnote. The scariest thought was of the sticky bit about why she didn't report Clare Sullivan to the FBI as soon as she realized the woman was on their wanted list for murder and escaping across state lines.

Telling them it was necessary to save the lives of

children wouldn't hold water. It was tantamount to telling a judge the perjury was necessary because the legal system was not to be trusted. She could lie. Then again, lying to the FBI was never a good idea. The punishment for the lie was often more severe than the punishment for the crime would have been.

When she'd first been drawn into Clare's search for the girls, she'd given it some thought, but not nearly enough. Aiding and abetting a fugitive wanted for a capital offense wasn't a casual crime. It was a stint-behind-bars kind of crime. Like the proverbial frog, Anna'd boiled herself to death one teensy illegal act at a time.

Jail terrified her. Falling into the machinery of the legal system terrified her. Being at the mercy of lawyers terrified her. The thought of being incarcerated poured panic into her until her bones felt soft with it.

Maybe she could tell the truth, the whole truth, nothing but the truth, and damn little of that—as an old cowboy she'd known growing up had been fond of saying. She could tell them that she'd met a man named Jordan who shared a courtyard with her, that she had gone to Bonne Chance with him because she was curious about what went on inside, that he had led her down the stairs to the whorehouse and she'd decided she'd be safer if she dressed as a worker. Then mayhem ensued.

Sure, seasoned law enforcement officials would buy that without asking any embarrassing questions. Without realizing she did so, she buried her nose in Dana's soft hair and took some comfort from the sweet smell of a child.

Try as she might, she couldn't remember just how or why she thought she would be able to get away with it. There'd been some vague notion of, should she and Clare succeed, just drifting quietly away unnoticed while Clare pretended never to have known her. Three dead policemen, a dead thug, a governess burned to death, a major structural fire, and a herd of costumed children had a way of shining the spotlight of the law on a girl.

Would Paul come to see her on visiting days?

Could she keep from killing herself long enough to get to visiting days?

Hacking coughs and rattling voices brought Anna back into the courtyard, and she watched as Clare, carrying two children, Mackie at her heels, emerged from the gray fog of smoke like the Pied Piper, seven tiny children in pajamas and two teenagers, one with an infant in her arms, clustered around her.

"Vee," she said, her smile wide and white in the sooty face. "Vee was in the nursery. Mackie found her."

Anna didn't think she had a smile left in her but noticed she was grinning back.

"This is Aisha," Clare said, indicating the second little girl in her arms, a bird-boned child with huge dark eyes.

"Aisha, *alive,*" Clare said.

From inside the house came a roar, and smoke gusted through the French doors filling the courtyard.

"The place is coming down," Anna said and struggled to her feet, Dana heavy against her side. "Help me," she ordered, and one of the older girls took Dana from her. "Hold hands," she said to the children, and, leaning heavily on the girl carrying Dana, Anna led the way toward the back of the courtyard where the men had herded the "jewels."

Through the door in the brick was a sizable parking garage. The doors to the street were open, and whatever they'd intended to use to transport the children was gone. When the fire started, the driver must have panicked and gone, leaving the children to burn to death. In a confused clot the kids in their absurd costumes milled around; some sat on the concrete, some cried, some just stood mute and still.

Together, Anna and Clare brought them out onto the sidewalk and across the street where the flames would not reach them. Sirens sounded loud in the distance. Fire trucks were coming.

Anna started to sink down to sit on the curb. "Wait!" Clare cried. A single cab was meandering down Rampart. "Up," Clare said, grabbing Anna's arm and hauling her back to her feet. "You can't be found here." With the jacket she'd used to shield Dana, she covered Anna's bloody dress, then hailed the cab and helped her into it.

Anywhere else, the cabbie would have been full of questions. In New Orleans, crowds, even of children, in costume at daybreak caused little comment.

Logic, and the searing pain in Anna's side, would have had her ordering the cabbie to the nearest emergency room, but, by law, doctors had to report gunshot wounds. Anna returned to Geneva's, let herself into the garden, and made her painful way to the guest cottage. The governess's dress was stiff with blood and beginning to adhere to her body. She found scissors in a kitchen drawer and used them to cut it off. That done, she wet a dish towel and washed the blood from her hands, face, and side.

When the wound was exposed, she was surprised to find it wasn't the black round hole left by a bullet but a deep gash. Pressing the edges gently, she could feel a foreign body lodged beneath the skin, as if a shard of glass had been broken off inside of her. The wound was still bleeding, but not copiously.

Sacrificing another of Geneva's dish towels, she folded the cloth into a square and pressed it over the gash. The trek up the stairs to her bedroom took much of her remaining energy and started the blood flowing again. Leaning against the wall for support, she pulled on a pair of old khaki shorts and a shirt. By the time she got to Geneva's French doors, the edges of her vision had turned black and the world was beginning to swim sickeningly.

"It's too early and you stink," Geneva said in welcome.

"I've been hurt," Anna said. "Could you call me a cab?"

It was after four when she came out of the anesthesia and the strange and troubled sleep that followed it. Her side was bandaged, her mouth tasted of burning plastic and bile, and she had to go to the bathroom. Clare sat in the blue plastic visitor's chair next to the curtain dividing the room. There wasn't a patient in the other bed, and three little girls, dressed in real little-girl clothes, played quietly on the white cotton blanket, a game involving the worn stuffed dog she'd seen on Clare's pillow, a metal water pitcher, and an emesis basin.

Clare was showered and dressed in a flowing skirt and top she'd probably picked up at the French Market. The light fabric did little to cover the terrible thinness the past weeks had wrought on her form. The crown of thorns had been scrubbed from her forehead, and she wore lipstick.

"You look like a girl," Anna croaked.

Clare rose, poured water into a plastic cup, put a straw into it, and held it to Anna's lips.

Anna took the cup, pulled the straw out, and drank.

"You look like shit," Clare said kindly.

"It wasn't a bullet," Anna volunteered. "It was a chunk of Dougie's rib."

"God! I hope they loaded you up with antibiotics," Clare said. "Have you called your husband?"

Anna hadn't. She'd been awake between the anesthesia and the nap—the doctor had told her about the bone fragment. She'd told him she'd fallen while running along the river walk, tumbled down the rocky side toward the river, and felt something gouge into her. He didn't believe her, but he didn't seem to believe much of what his patients told him and had neither the interest nor the time to try to ferret out the truth. There'd been time to call Paul then, but she hadn't gotten up the nerve.

"You want to call him now?" Clare asked.

"In a bit," Anna said.

"Is he going to be pissed?" Clare asked.

"In a word," Anna said. "What's happening with everything?" she asked to change the subject. "I take it you aren't going to be arrested for murder."

Clare didn't laugh. "Believe it or not, it was a close thing. Cops—all cops—hate to be wrong. I was interrogated for over six hours. They stopped short of waterboarding, but just barely. You can't believe how bad they wanted to get me on something. I have to go back for another 'session' tomorrow."

"The death of the police chief and his minions?"

"It looks like I'll get a pass on that. I guess the brotherhood breaks down with corrupt locals and federal agents. They'll leave me alone if I keep my mouth shut. The statement given to the newspapers was that the girls had been kidnapped by a person or persons unknown and that I found them locked in the storage garage behind Bonne Chance. The 'unsub' "—Clare gave a wry smile at the jargon—"is suspected of setting fire to the warehouse to destroy evidence." Clare sat again. Her eyes never off the three children for long, she watched them dancing the dog around the pitcher. "The police came when the fire trucks did. They got a guy driving a van that they think was the van they were going to transport the kids in. The FBI grabbed him, and maybe he'll talk. Nobody wanted to tell me much. I know the other children were taken to a shelter. They'll try to find their parents but aren't hopeful. Most of them were probably sold rather than kidnapped, and most of them are from out of the country. The two older girls who were watching Vee and the littlest kids were graduates of the whorehouse and shouldn't face any kind of prosecution."

"The policemen and Dougie's bodies burned?"

Clare nodded. "Yes, but they'll still probably be able to identify them. The fire department got the fire out fairly fast, from what I hear. I don't know what will be said of police participation. The agents who talked with me don't want to make too much of it yet. They want the man called the Magician. Evidently he's the core of the operation, him and two others they know of. David—" At the sound of their father's name, both Vee and Dana looked up hopefully, and Anna guessed Clare hadn't told them he was dead yet.

"David was working with the FBI to find this Magician. He was doing everything he could to get Dana and Vee—and Aisha—back." This comment was for the three little girls, Anna guessed, so they would feel better about their father. After what they had suffered, it would be a comfort to know their daddy had never abandoned them.

"Was that why your house—" Anna began, but Clare shook her head fractionally and looked at the girls. She gave them a smile. They went back to their game.

Clare pulled her chair up close to the bedside and

partially pulled the curtain between her and the children. Leaning her elbows on Anna's bed she said, in a voice scarcely louder than a sigh, "Yes. That's why the house was bombed. The FBI said David had told them a container holding illegal aliens was arriving in the harbor. He gave them the wrong dock number, and by the time they got there it was empty. They thought it was an honest mistake."

"You don't?" Anna asked and was shushed though she hadn't said anything alarming.

Clare went on in a faint whisper. "I think Aisha was arriving in that container. That's why David and Jalila rushed out to meet it. I think he wanted time to get her away before the FBI arrived. He lied so well the Feds didn't get there till after Dougie and Blackie had come and gone—there to harvest children. I think there were dead children in the container and Blackie and Dougie took them."

"Why?" Anna asked, genuinely confused. The obvious and odious answer clicked in her brain, and she wished she hadn't asked.

"Not that—God, at least I hope not that," Clare said, reading Anna's look of revulsion. "It's possible they switched Dana and Vee with the corpses. If the children weren't dead, I don't think they would have killed them."

"Unless they were too 'broken' to be of any value," Anna said.

"God," Clare said again. Shaking the idea from her as she might shake a spider from her hair, she went on. "The agent who talked with me did say they thought some men had followed David and Jalila to his apartment. Probably because they figured out David was exposing them. They killed Jalila and left her corpse in David's apartment so it would look like a domestic thing—David, me, and the lover. Then put David back in bed and fired the house. That's when I think they put the dead children in the house and took Dana and Vee to cover their losses."

"Why—" Anna began, but Clare held up a hand, stopping her.

"We're never going to know why they did what to whom, why they carted bodies all over hell and gone, unless Blackie tells us. My guess is Blackie and Dougie were trying to cover their tracks at the behest of their boss, who knew the Feds were closing in."

For a while Anna digested the information. She hoped Blackie would cooperate with the FBI, hoped he would finger the rest of the ring, but had a feeling he might not live long enough to do it. Even if he lived and talked, Anna doubted he knew who the Magician was. That this creature was still out in the world sickened her. After a while she nodded toward the curtain. "Are the girls . . . okay?"

Clare nodded. "So far as it goes," she said tersely. "Vee and Aisha were in the nursery. It had been on Bourbon Street, but when an agent got too close, they moved to the fancy house. The littlest were saved for special occasions."

Anna waited.

"Medicinal uses," Clare said.

It took a second or two, but Anna got it. It was still believed in many parts of the world that sex with very young virgins cured AIDS and other STDs. This time it was she who called upon the Almighty: "God."

"Or not," Clare said.

Clare was but inches from Anna's face, breathing on her. Something was wrong, different. "You don't smell like an ashtray!" Anna exclaimed.

"Clare Sullivan, mother of two—now three—doesn't smoke," Clare said evenly.

"And Jordan?"

Clare winked solemnly. "He may sneak a fag now and then." With that she stood and shook out her skirts. "We should go. Give you some privacy to call your husband. Besides, the four of us need some serious nap time." To Anna's surprise, Clare leaned down and kissed her on the cheek before she left.

For a while, Anna stared at the phone beside the bed as if it were a snake about to bite her. It crossed her mind just not to tell Paul anything, but, as a good and attentive husband, he was bound to notice a new vicious scar on her middle. Then she thought of lying to him, feeding him the same line she did the doctor.

She was more afraid of losing him than of anything she'd ever been afraid of in her life. He would forgive her. Not only was he a good man, but he was, after all, in the business of forgiveness. Technically, the only promise she'd broken was to tell him beforehand if she planned on doing anything risky, but love wasn't about the technicalities. It was about the totality of who one was and the respect for the totality of the beloved. Anna had not been open or forthright. She'd let in the creeping darkness of half-truths, evasions, and secrets. She'd broken trust. That sort of break was long in the mending.

She picked up the phone and set it on her lap. Steeling herself, she dialed his number. When he picked up she told him everything, every law broken, every lie by omission, every move she'd made. Then she shut up.

And listened to the silence.